## DATE DUE

| | |
|---|---|
| APR 28 '98 | |
| | |
| | |
| | |
| | |
| | |
| | |
| | |
| | |
| | |
| | |
| | |
| | |
| | |
| | |

BRODART, CO.                    Cat. No. 23-221-003

GAYLORD S

# PRIMAL SCENE

# PRIMAL
# S·C·E·N·E

## Yale Kramer

**ARBOR HOUSE**
**WILLIAM MORROW**
*New York*

Grateful acknowledgment is made to the following
for permission to reprint previously published material:

Charles Scribner's Sons, an imprint of Macmillan Publishing
Company: Excerpt from "Percy Shelley" in *Collected Poems* by
John Peale Bishop, edited by Allen Tate. Copyright © 1948,
and renewed 1976, by Charles Scribner's Sons.

Warner/Chappell Music Inc.: Excerpt from "Night and Day" by
Cole Porter. Copyright © 1932 Warner Bros. Inc. (Renewed),
All Rights Reserved.

Library of Congress Cataloging-in-Publication Data

Kramer, Yale.
  Primal scene.

  I. Title.
PS3561.R254P7  1989        813'.54        88-13472
ISBN 1-55710-025-X

Printed in the United States of America

First Edition

1  2  3  4  5  6  7  8  9  10

BOOK DESIGN BY LINEY LI

*For RK,*
*my dearest friend and most faithful critic*

*It* was a record year for murders in New York City. There were eighteen hundred. During one week that summer there were fifty-seven, an all-time high: twenty-four shootings, twenty-six stabbings, five assaults, one murder by fire, and one victim thrown out of a window. Unusually hot weather always increases the number of crimes of violence. The temperature that week was in the nineties.

Love is merely a madness, and, I tell you, deserves as well a dark house and a whip as madmen do: and the reason why they are not so punished and cured is, that the lunacy is so ordinary that the whippers are in love too.

—WILLIAM SHAKESPEARE, *As You Like It*

The action of the play consists in nothing other than the process of revealing, with cunning delays and ever-mounting excitement—a process that can be likened to the work of a psychoanalysis—that Oedipus himself is the murderer of Laius . . . .

—SIGMUND FREUD, *The Interpretation of Dreams*

*Part One*

# MANIFEST CONTENT

# Chapter

# 1

"*F*reud was wrong," he heard himself think.

He was drowning again, struggling to reach the surface of consciousness. Heart pounding, he was fighting for breath. He felt the light now, through the lids. Strong, painful light.

The pounding in his chest became the pounding on a distant door and the imperative ringing of a telephone somewhere.

". . . Conrad! Dr. Conrad!" Miles away he heard his name being called. Then the phone stopped, and its sudden silence jogged him.

Lifting himself from the sticky sheets, he saw that he was still wearing last night's hospital whites. The thumping on the heavy oaken door increased in tempo.

"Shit! What the fuck's going on?" he croaked, and cleared his throat; it was tense and hurt. "Hold on. Christ! I'm coming. Who the fuck is it?" The phone at the foot of the bed began again, urgently, and he groped for it to stop the jangling.

"Yeah?" he said, and let his eyes close against the glaring summer sunlight.

"Dr. Conrad?" It was a woman's voice, but deep and authoritative.

"Yeah."

"Dr. Lemmon would like to see you right away."

He opened his eyes and squinted. "Who's this?"

"Mrs. Rowan." Now he placed the voice. He knew her. Lemmon's secretary. "He wants to see you right away."

"Listen, I've been on duty all night." He cleared his throat again. "Christ, what time is it?" He glanced at his watch; it was four minutes past nine. "I'd like to get cleaned up first."

"I know you were on duty last night, Dr. Conrad; that's why he wants you. And he wants you now." She meant business.

"Christ! Okay, give me five minutes." She clicked off.

He sat there stupidly for a few moments, as though he couldn't figure out what to do with the receiver in his hand. Finally a shower of blows at the door roused him.

Rising quickly, he moved to quiet the pounding. Suddenly he felt dizzy, and his heart raced again. Grabbing at an old white dresser with cigarette burns all over its top, he stood for a moment waiting for his pulse to settle, then lurched for the door and yanked it open.

"Jesus!" He blinked through steel-rimmed glasses. The doorway was filled with an oversize man in a police uniform. Hat tipped back on his head, he was sweating and smelled of stale tobacco.

"You Conrad?" the policeman asked.

"Yeah. What the hell's going on?"

The cop looked at him impassively. "They want ya downstairs. Director wants to see ya."

"I know, I know." He clawed at his damp collar as though he needed air. "What's it all about?"

"I guess he'll tell ya."

For a moment or two the brawny cop surveyed the slovenly white trousers and rumpled necktie, then, in a leaden voice, "Let's go."

"Listen, do you mind?" Conrad cocked his head toward the open bathroom. "Only take a minute," he heard himself pleading.

"I suppose it's okay, but make it snappy."

Like any man who becomes addicted to thinking at an early age, Seth Conrad was not at home with surprises. Now, closing the bathroom door, he stared vacantly at the white shower curtain drawn carelessly across the bathtub. The fugitive images of his unfinished dream had already faded in the sun streaming through the window. He wanted to hold on to them a moment longer, dream them again, and make them come out better.

Standing over the toilet bowl, he was aware of the cop's presence outside and realized that he'd been urinating noiselessly, demurely.

> The question, lords and ladies, is
> With what did Percy Shelley piss?

He gave the flush lever a savage tug. Nothing happened. "Shit!" He yanked the lever again. Slowly, as though the machine had a life of its own, water began to bubble listlessly into the bowl. He gave it a final jolt with his foot and slammed the cover down.

The sunlight hurt his eyes, and he squinted at himself in the mirror through sweat-smeared glasses.

> We ask and ask, till silence palls,
> Did Percy Bysshe have any balls?

He saw a faint smile cross his lips. Harvey. "That son of a bitch," he said softly to his image. The wisp of a memory flitted across his mind. A room, dark, except for a green-shaded desk light, and Harvey, disconsolate and hairy, slumped in a chair, reading, his huge bulk wrapped in a dark cape.

> And Percy's love, as he has said,
> Resembled roses when they're dead.

"You're not listening! Is this stuff too deep for your flat prairie mind?" He slammed the book shut. "The gods of ribaldry and oaths will weep for you, boychik."

Where the hell was he? Fucking satyr. Conrad stared at himself. Disheveled, a granular taste in his mouth, a day's growth of beard. What the hell was going on? What did Lemmon want? His pulse was racing again.

He ran his fingers through dark hair, unkempt and wet at the temples and forehead. His white cotton trousers, wrinkled and soiled around the cuffs and pockets, hung loosely from his slender frame.

Shaking his head, he tried to think. He'd come on duty in the admitting office at midnight, the end of the long, hot Labor Day weekend, when flaky people begin to fall apart.

There was pounding on the bathroom door. "Hey, Doc! Hurry it up!"

He gave the cold-water tap a vigorous turn. A thin stream of tepid water appeared. Waiting for the water to cool, he became aware of a dull pain on the bridge of his nose and realized that he'd fallen asleep with his glasses on. He focused on his gray-green eyes. Weak, he thought. Definitely weak. He had thought so from the beginning when they presented him with the first pair of glasses on his sixth birthday. He removed them, and his image receded into a tolerable blur.

Splashing his face with the still-tepid water, he searched in vain for a towel. "Shit." In desperation he dried himself with the grimy shower curtain.

"Hey, Doc, let's go." More pounding, this time more urgent.

Straightening his tie, he hitched up his pants and appraised the net effect. Skeptical, he reentered the room where the policeman stood. With an unnatural smile he held both his hands out in front of him. "Okay, get the cuffs ready." The joke sounded tinny even to his ears, and he regretted it.

"Relax, Doc. I'm only here to get you downstairs fast. Just a traffic cop. Come on, let's go."

Parading down the corridor toward the elevator, Conrad leading the way, they passed an aide in a blue uniform polishing a floor that had been polished every day since 1933, when Bellevue Psychiatric Hospital was built. It didn't need polishing, but that didn't matter. In a mental hospital the therapeutic power of routine is well understood.

Waiting for the elevator in awkward silence, they heard the sound of a ball bouncing in the recreational therapy room. A moment later a tall, good-looking black man appeared in the doorway, holding a basketball.

"How ya doin', Doc?"

Grateful for the intrusion of everyday life into the melodrama of his sudden captivity, he smiled too brightly. "Too early to tell, Jonesie." Jonesie disappeared with a wave, and as the elevator slammed shut, he heard the sound of the basketball again.

Taking the initiative, Conrad pushed the worn button, and with a whine the car began its slow institutional descent. For no reason his heart began to pound again. He dug his hands into the pockets of his white jacket, and feeling the familiar contour of his stethoscope, he gripped it tightly. A trickle of sweat slid down his forehead, and he wondered whether his breathing was audible.

"Christ, it's hot," he muttered.

Flicking the sweat away, he glanced at the cop out of the corner of his eye. The brawny policeman, who had stationed himself behind Conrad, was staring at him.

He pushed the glasses back up onto the bridge of his nose, and to conceal his heavy breathing, he embraced himself as if he were cold.

His thoughts pursued again the disturbing dream that had begun his day. An image forced its way into his consciousness: a woman, darkly beautiful and laughing. A face he had seen before, thrown back in contemptuous laughter. A sound, harsh and brassy, he had heard somewhere, long ago.

"Okay, Doc. Let's go." The elevator was standing open. The policeman touched his arm.

The corridor to the director's office led through the main lobby of the hospital. High-ceilinged, faced in once-elegant marble, it was now dingy and poorly lit, devoid of any life or function. The counters at one side, meant to serve as information centers, had fallen into disuse over the years and now stood empty, convenient places to deposit empty coffee containers or their morning tabloids when the aides left for the day.

As he walked through the lobby, trailed by the policeman and beset by dreams and elusive doubts, a voice boomed across the gloomy space from the direction of the coffee concession.

"Boychik! boychik! What have you done?" Harvey Bloch, a great bear of a young man with longish hair and a bushy black beard, came toward him, balancing a volume of Freud and a coffee container in one hand and a sweet roll in the other. "I warned you not to touch yourself in public."

There was something comic about his bulky body wrapped in its baggy seersucker suit.

"Christ! You son of a bitch! Where the fuck have you been? This your idea of 'a little late.'" He tapped his watch. "Nine hours?"

"Love"—Bloch took a large bite of sweet roll—"or at least sex does strange things to people, as you will learn when you reach puberty." He raised the volume of Freud with the coffee container precariously perched on it. "And read a little more of this stuff." He swallowed and gasped for air. Arms aloft, hands full, he looked like an insane juggler.

A little of Harvey Bloch went a long way. When he was in one of his hypomanic moods, no room seemed quite big enough for him.

"You took your goddamn sweet time. When did you get here?"

"Now, boychik, just now. A hundred and ten miles in two hours and"—he checked his watch with pride—"eight minutes. With panache, Seth, baby. Panache and brilliance." He gulped some coffee, and with a sigh his bearlike body seemed to relax.

At that moment the cop coolly insinuated himself between the two men—the one lanky and bespectacled, the other hairy and voluminous. "Let's go, Doc," he said quietly, and moved Seth off.

"Repent, boychik! Repent!" Harvey proclaimed, flourishing his sweet roll. "I'm sending you a copy of *Crime and Punishment*. And with another mouthful he shouted a final muffled reminder: "Lunch. Twelve-thirty."

*M*ore alert now, Conrad pushed open the heavy oak door marked "Medical Director."

Phyl Rowan dominated the anteroom. A big-boned, rangy woman, raised on the outskirts of Dallas, she could type faster than most people could talk and fancied herself tough.

She glanced at him matter-of-factly over her half glasses and the telephone she was holding. "Dr. Lemmon, Dr. Ettinger is on the

line, and Dr. Conrad just walked in. . . . Right," she said as she
punched the lit-up button on her phone. "Dr. Ettinger, he'll be right
with you." She put him on hold and, without looking at Seth,
rasped, "He's waiting for you."

Despite the look of pain on his florid face, George Lemmon spoke
to the phone in his most confident baritone.

"Morning, Bob. How are you?" He paced restlessly behind the
huge Grand Rapids desk, turning this way and that, with tiny
steps—a plump, agitated pigeon.

"Well, look, Bob, I only heard about it ten minutes ago."

With a soggy handkerchief he waved Seth to a chair in front
of the desk and then used it to mop the sweat from the strands of
his dark, thinning hair.

Taking the seat Lemmon had indicated, Seth became aware of
the unsmiling presence of two men across the room who were
studying him. They sat bent forward on the brown leather sofa.
The younger of the two held a manila file folder open between
them, occasionally pointing to something of interest in it.

Seth looked away and focused on a small burn in the carpet.
Cops, he knew instantly. There was something about all of them.
He covered the burn with the toe of his shoe. They all got solemnity
and authority mixed up.

"Naturally nobody called me," Lemmon said, now in retreat.
Folds of fat overflowed the back of his collar, and he patted them
with the handkerchief.

"Identified?" Lemmon looked down at a slip of paper on his
desk. "Yes. She's been identified. She works—worked for Graver.
Just a second." He fumbled for his glasses and with a pudgy hand
picked up the paper. "Jennifer Light," he read. "Research assistant
or something. I said Light. Jennifer Light." He articulated slowly
as though Ettinger were hard-of-hearing.

The unsmiling men across the room watched as Lemmon replaced
the paper and mopped his head again.

"Now, hold on there, Bob! You have no right to say that to
me." Lemmon flushed. "This hospital has never been in better shape,
and you know it. This could have happened anywhere."

The new acting chairman of the department was obviously pressing his political advantage.

"No, I didn't know. When did he find out about it?" Pause. "Oh, Christ! Look, Bob, there's no point in talking about this in a vacuum. Let me find out what's going on, and I'll get back to you later." Pause. He glanced at Seth, then, turning away, said in a subdued voice, "Conrad. Seth Conrad. Yes, I'll tell him."

Putting the phone down, he turned to the two men on the sofa like a chubby child in distress. "Jesus, the dean of the medical school heard it on the morning news and wants a full report by noon."

Dark stains had appeared across the back of Lemmon's tan silk suit. "Dr. Conrad." He turned to Seth as though he were asking a favor. "You were on duty last night. Is that right?"

Seth nodded. His pulse jumped to 110.

"This is Detective Coyle." He turned to the older of the two men. "And Detective, uh?"

"Fontana," the younger man interjected, and nodded slightly.

"They'd like to ask you a few questions, if you don't mind."

Coyle looked to be in his early fifties. He was thin but flabby. His light blue eyes were watery, disinterested, and overcast. A man beyond surprise or revulsion.

The younger cop, Fontana, started the questioning. "Doc"—he reached into his shirt pocket and pulled out a stick of gum—"tell us what you did yesterday. You know, how ya spent the day."

"The whole day?" Seth asked irritably.

Fontana studied him. "Yeah."

"Okay, let's see." He began slowly as though he were talking to a child. "It was Labor Day, and I was off duty, so I got up about ten o'clock. As a matter of fact, my friend Harvey called and woke me—Harvey Bloch. We share an apartment a couple of blocks from here. On Thirtieth." Seth leaned forward in his chair and pushed the glasses back up onto the bridge of his nose as though to sharpen the focus of his memory.

"He was away. For the weekend, I mean. East Hampton. He called to ask if I'd cover for him—midnight shift last night." He shrugged. "I didn't have any heavy plans for the evening, so I said okay." He glanced at the notebook in which Fontana was writing. "Am I going too fast?"

"Okay, so that's why Bloch's name was down on the roster and you were the one on duty. That kosher, Doc?" Fontana asked, looking at Lemmon.

"Sure, sure," Lemmon said with a wave from behind his fortress desk. "The on call roster is pretty flexible. We make it up every month"—he tilted backward in his chair with accustomed grace; his voice had regained some of its administrative resonance—"but the residents can work out trades and changes. Nothing unusual about that."

"Okay." Fontana turned back to Seth. "Then what? And you can cut the bullshit, Doc." He was a big man with coiled energy contained inside his open-necked sport shirt. "Just talk natural and be nice, and we won't have any problems."

Surprised, Seth turned to Lemmon, but Lemmon looked away and began to examine with interest some papers on his desk.

"I guess I had breakfast and read the paper," he said, trying to look amused. "Then I called a friend and asked her if she'd like to go to a movie and have dinner with me."

Coyle broke in and asked dully, "Who's your friend? What's her name?"

"What difference does it make? I really don't see the point of all this."

Coyle's expression didn't change. His posture remained toneless inside his polyester cord suit. "Look, son, this isn't your ball game, and it doesn't matter whether you see the point or not."

Seth had grown unaccustomed to obedience. The princely jurisdiction which came with his medical degree had made him at home in every part of the huge city hospital, and he felt entitled to examine and command almost at will. Now, as he sat back, arms folded across his chest, he realized that, at least for the moment, he had lost this jurisdiction.

"Dr. Conrad," Lemmon said with an apologetic shrug, "these gentlemen are only trying to do their job." He glanced at his watch. "It's getting late. I think it would be better if you tried to answer these questions."

Seth didn't care about the time or their goddamn questions, and above all, he didn't want to be reasonable.

"Martin," he said finally, barely audible, "Connie Martin."

"Yeah? Who is she? Where does she live?"

"A friend." He stared back at Fontana. "East Thirty-sixth Street. I don't remember her address," he lied. "I'd have to check it." He hoped Fontana knew he was lying.

"How long have you known her?"

"Couple of months. Since I got here in July."

"Okay, now what else did you do after you made a date with her?" Fontana asked.

He thought a moment. "I had some reading to do. A monograph on schizophrenia." He smiled tightly. " 'Chance favors only the prepared mind.' "

"Huh?" Fontana looked confused.

"Pasteur. Pasteur said that—to suggest that discovery isn't accidental. You have to think"—he tapped his head—"once in a while and read."

Fontana's eyes narrowed.

"Dr. Conrad, please . . ." Lemmon looked as though he were in severe pain.

"Then what?" Fontana asked coolly.

"Then I picked up Hal Garland, another resident, and we drove up to the park to play tennis. Lost both sets," he added with a poker face, "five-seven, six-seven."

Fontana gave him a fishy look. "What time was that?"

"We had a court at three." He shrugged. "I don't know, I guess I got back home about five. Showered. Dressed. Listened to some music while I waited for Connie. She got there about six. We had a drink and talked."

"Then?"

Seth leaned forward, pushed the glasses up on his nose, and spoke to the burn on the carpet. "We went to a restaurant in the Village, Rocco's, then walked to the movie on Bleecker Street, an old movie called *Breaking the Sound Barrier.* We got out about eleven. I took her home and went to the hospital. It was about eleven-forty when I got there."

"How do you know?"

"I checked the time," he said, glowering at Fontana. "I didn't want to start working in the PAO until I had to."

"PAO?"

"Psychiatric Admitting Office," Lemmon chimed in.

Fontana turned back to Seth. "So?"

"So I went down to the hospital cafeteria for a cup of coffee."

"Where's that? The cafeteria?"

"Basement of the main building."

"How did you get there? Through the main building?"

"No, through the psychiatric building. There's an underground tunnel that runs the whole length of Bellevue."

"What about the tunnel?" Coyle snapped. He had come alive for the first time.

"Nothing. Only that's how I got to the cafeteria."

"Did you see anything unusual on your way?"

"Now, how the hell should I know what you think is unusual?" he burst out. "I see unusual things every day. For Christ's sake, I work in a mental hospital. Every day I see unusual people who see unusual things that aren't even there. Why don't you guys tell me what this is all about? If you told me what you were looking for, then maybe I could answer your questions."

"Come on, Doc. Quit crapping around," Fontana said, leaning toward him. "You know why we're here."

"Jesus! I don't know what the fuck you're talking about." He took a deep breath and began again, with exaggerated calm. "I've been on duty since midnight. I didn't get to sleep until five o'clock this morning. Then your goddamn storm trooper marched me down here, and nobody has told me one goddamn thing since I walked in."

"Well, son, you must be the only one in the hospital that's still in the dark." Coyle remained expressionless. "A woman was beaten to death last night while you were on duty."

"But . . . it's . . . not possible," he said at last without conviction. He'd been staring vacantly at an unshaved patch at the corner of Coyle's drooping mouth.

"We've got a body to prove it, son. What d'ya mean?"

"Christ, I mean it must have just happened. After rounds, I mean."

"When was that?"

"I made rounds at four. What's her name? The nursing supervisor? Walters—with Dorie Walters."

"What do you do, Doc, making rounds?" Fontana sat down on the edge of Lemmon's desk, brazenly interposing himself between Lemmon and the young resident. "I mean, exactly."

"We check every ward. For problems, complications." Seth was sweating again now. "I had to change some orders, increase medication—"

Lemmon broke in. "You see, from twelve to eight A.M. the hospital is very lightly staffed." He leaned forward across the desk, trying to get Fontana's attention. "The house officer on duty in the PAO is technically the chief medical officer of the entire psychiatric hospital, and the nursing supervisor is the acting administrator. So both of them have to make sure that everything in the hospital is okay." Satisfied with himself, he leaned back and smiled at Coyle. Coyle, unmoved, looked down again at the folder.

"How many patients in the hospital, Doc?" Fontana asked, half twisting in Lemmon's direction without looking at him.

"I don't know what the census was last night, but it runs about seven hundred. Just about a hundred percent over capacity," Lemmon added with a touch of pride. "Full house. Sold out every night. I guess it's the longest-running hit in the city." He winked at Seth.

"Seven fourteen," Seth said, ignoring Lemmon. "I admitted eleven last night, and when I went to bed, the census was seven hundred and fourteen."

Fontana, who hadn't taken his eyes off Seth since he'd entered the room, asked, "What time was that?"

"Let's see." He touched his glasses. "We finished rounds around five. So I must have gone up to my room about five-fifteen."

"You share a room with anyone?"

"Yeah, Hal Garland and Avi—Avi Schwartzman use that room."

"So they heard you come in then?" Fontana said.

"No, of course not. They weren't there last night." He felt a drop of sweat trickle down his forehead. "They weren't on duty, so they slept home. We use the room only when we're on."

"Right," Fontana said mechanically, as though he hadn't been listening. He was silent for a moment, staring at Seth as though they were lovers. Then: "What about those rounds, Doc? Any problems?"

"Not too bad." The trickle of sweat, it seemed to him, had become a river, and he saw now that Fontana was staring at it. "Couple of old alkies in DTs on N-5. The ward," he explained, answering Fontana's questioning look. "Fifth floor of the N wing. A big guy on psycho-medicine with a cortisone psychosis. Agitated, grandiose, giving the nurses there trouble." The droplet ran down the bridge of his nose.

"You check every patient?"

"Of course not. I wouldn't have time to do anything else if I did that," Seth said.

"Are all these wards locked?"

"All the wards are locked except N-1," Lemmon explained. "That's a special ward for, uh, not very disturbed patients."

"Who has keys?" Coyle asked him.

"One basic key opens all the wards except the prison ward, and you fellas run that one. The roaches can't even get out of there without a court order." He grinned at Coyle.

"Doc"—Fontana turned back to Seth—"did you know this woman—ah, Jennifer Light?"

Seth touched his glasses again. "Look, I've only been here for two months. There must be a couple of hundred people on the staff." He shrugged. "Maybe I've met her. I don't know. Maybe I'd know her if I saw her."

"Why don't we go down and see if you know who we're talking about, Doc?" He started toward the door. "Who knows?" He cocked his head at Seth. "Maybe that prepared brain of yours'll come up with some bright ideas."

"I'll stay here and finish up," Coyle said. "Check in with me when the lab crew gets here."

Seth got up to go, and Lemmon pulled him aside. "Ah, Dr. Conrad, don't give them any trouble. Just cooperate and tell them whatever they want. We've got to clear this up as quickly as possible." He pulled the soggy handkerchief out of his inside pocket and wiped his head again. "Oh, by the way"—he made a sour face—"Ettinger wants to see you. He wants to keep on top of this thing." He gave Seth's arm an avuncular squeeze. "Call his secretary for an appointment, will you?"

"Where—where'd it happen?" Seth asked as they strode toward the elevator.

"Basement, just off that service tunnel you were talking about," Fontana said.

They stood in uncomfortable silence, waiting for the elevator. "Little guy from the hospital laundry found her this morning. Around seven. While you were snoozing." He punched the elevator button. "How many wards you got here?"

"Thirteen, fourteen," Seth answered stiffly.

"What about security? Who's got keys?"

"Just about everybody on the staff has a key." He showed his, a large, cast-iron, medieval-looking skeleton key that weighed almost half a pound.

They got off the elevator and entered the service tunnel under the building. The tunnel, used to transport laundry, food carts, and even patients, was the only thoroughfare that connected all of Bellevue's many sections, grown up over the last hundred years. It was steamy and full of musty plumbing smells and often distant scuttling noises or solitary footfalls.

Led by Fontana, they turned off the tunnel into a cul-de-sac with a low ceiling and tanklike apparatus sprouting a crop of valves and gauges. The alcove was now lit by auxiliary police lights which had turned the scene into a movie set. Standing just outside the area, two uniformed cops chatted quietly. Fontana called to them as he approached.

"Lab crew here?"

"Yeah," the little fat one answered, "they just got here. They're driving the van around so they don't have to lug all that stuff from Twenty-sixth Street."

Behind them on the floor of the alcove was an inert mound covered with a heavy white canvas. Fontana knelt at one end of the mound and carefully folded down the soiled covering, as though he were a maid turning down a bed.

As he watched the canvas shroud drawn back, Seth's pulse began to race, and his mind flashed back to the first autopsy he had ever seen. The smell in the autopsy room, he remembered, was warm, alive, and disgusting. A bouquet of abdominal contents, body fluids, and heavy-duty detergent.

The corpse on the prosector's table had been a fat, bald man who had died of unknown causes the night before. He lay naked on the stainless steel table as the pathologist began his description of the body.

"The subject is a white, obese male in late middle age. . . ." He had gone on to describe the postmortem changes that were observable from the body's color and muscular tone. Then, quite suddenly, with the grace and virtuosity that come from long practice, he had cut through the abdomen in a straight line from the sternum to the pubic bone. The suddenness of his movement had taken Seth by surprise, and he heard the sound of his own revulsion as he watched the abdominal contents rise through the incision that had just been made.

Now, as he watched Fontana furl the last few inches of canvas, those old sensations of fascination and revulsion stirred in him. He saw below him the body of a young woman with jet black hair and suntanned skin. She lay on her side, her face turned to the concrete floor, as though she were studying a speck of dust.

Her arms were flung out on either side of her, like a windmill, and the muscles in her hands were beginning to contract like claws. Her legs, too, were caught in a grotesque caricature of living movement. They were flexed at the hip and knee and spread, scissorslike, as though she were running.

Seth could see her tanned, well-shaped legs and thighs. He couldn't see her face from where he stood, but he could see that there was matted blood in her black hair and the back of her head was flattened and misshapen. "Nice-lookin' kid," Fontana said.

He forced himself to look at her crushed skull as he had forced himself to stay at the autopsy that day and at every other autopsy, thirty-two in all, that year.

He didn't know what that had proved—except maybe the power of the Conrad Curse. "What you don't know can hurt you. Knowledge is safety, Seth," his father would say as they walked across campus to the lab. "It's your friend." Then once he added sadly, "Sometimes your only friend, Sethy." He had to run, in those days, to keep up with his father, and in those days he believed him; later he wasn't sure. "You can't escape, Seth. Reality finds you when you least expect it. Direct, astonishing, implacable reality."

The girl had been wearing an attractive, bright print summer dress. It was sleeveless and revealed her shoulders and soft arms. The neckline was deep and showed that she had been full-breasted and hadn't been wearing a bra.

"Doc . . . Doc . . ." Fontana had been talking to him. He flushed and finally tore his eyes away from the body of Jennifer Light. "You can't see her face from where you're standing. Come on over here." As Seth came around, Fontana gently raised her head and turned it toward him.

He saw that she had been an unusually beautiful woman. Her eyes were wide open, staring, with a look of incredulity. The muscles of her face were beginning to contract—the classic risus sardonicus.

"Christ," he murmured. "She was the one . . . I know her . . ." He stood up slowly. "The one in the dream . . ." he said, barely audible.

"What the hell's that supposed to mean?" Fontana snapped. "Is this some more bullshit? For chrissake, we don't have time to crap around anymore."

"Look, Fontana, I don't remember. Only the face. I had a dream last night"—he flushed—"this morning, and it was this girl."

"Did you know her?" Fontana demanded.

"I've seen her around the hospital, I guess."

"You never talked to her? Come on!"

"No. I never even knew her name." But he did know that she was stunning and unforgettable. She had a way of floating in and out of rooms and corridors.

"How come you dream about her but you don't know her name?" Fontana leaned toward him.

"How the hell should I know?"

"I thought dreams are supposed to be such a big deal with you guys," Fontana said with a mocking smile.

Seth shrugged. "Maybe they're not." He paused and added without conviction, "There was nothing special about her."

The sound of voices behind them in the tunnel made them turn, Fontana wheeling suddenly like a cat. The uniformed cop had stopped a young woman coming toward them.

"You in charge on this one, Fontana?" she called from where she stood.

"Shit," Fontana muttered, "that's all I need now, a smartass reporter to go with my smartass doctor."

Shielding her eyes from the floodlights, she peered past them at the body.

"Lindsay Cooper. Remember? From the *News*."

Crisp, very crisp, Seth thought. Reminded him of Katie, his grandmother. The flash in her blue eyes, maybe.

"How could I forget ya?" Fontana said sourly as he signaled to let her pass. "That was a lousy story you guys wrote about the bar stickup."

"I thought it was pretty good," she said, with a smile. She fished a steno pad and pen out of her canvas musette bag. "You boys better get your act together. Now, how would you like to tell me what's going on?"

Army brat, Seth thought, like Katie. He liked the way she stood up to Fontana. Also, he liked the shape of her breasts under the blue Lacoste shirt. He edged closer.

"Even if I knew what was going on, I wouldn't tell ya." Fontana crumpled a gum wrapper and chucked it vigorously to the side. "But I don't know any more than this kid was found down here at seventen this morning with her head bashed in. That's it. The whole story in a nutshell." The reporter began scribbling in her pad. "How the hell did you get down here anyway?"

"Every aide in the hospital knows about it," she said without looking up. "They told me where to find the *policia*." She stopped writing and looked at Fontana. "And if you ask them, they'll probably tell you who killed her."

Fontana scowled and let her ease by him and move toward the exposed body. She stared down in silence.

Seth watched her as she gazed at the head wound and then at every detail of the body. He thought he could see the pulse in her neck quicken. He liked her guts—and her neck.

"God," she said at last. "Who is she?" she asked without looking up.

"Her name is Light, Jennifer Light. She worked here," Fontana said.

She jotted this down and turned to Seth for the first time. "What did she do—I mean, here in the hospital?"

"Research assistant for one of the people on the faculty. Guy named Graver." Seth gave her a modest smile.

Ignoring him, she bent over her pad and made some more quick notes.

"You know you don't have to answer any questions you don't want to." Fontana glared at him.

Seth shrugged and turned again to watch the young woman operate. She was writing rapidly now, with intense concentration, glancing down at the body occasionally to check some detail.

"She looks like a kid. How old?" she asked Fontana.

"Twenty-four," he said grudgingly.

She stopped writing and stared again at the girl as though she were studying a work of art. Then she turned to Seth again. "Was she sexually assaulted?"

"I—I'm—I don't know." He shrugged. "Sorry."

"Who are you?" she asked dubiously. Then, reading his identification badge, she made a note of it and turned back to Fontana for a response to her unanswered question.

"We don't know yet," he said with irritation, and looked away.

"Why does she have only one shoe on?"

"Come on, Miss Cooper. Why don't you guys leave us alone and give us a chance?"

Three men wearing blue shirts and police badges came down the tunnel, making a racket with photographic equipment.

Seth turned to Fontana. "Listen, I've got a lot to do. You still need me?"

Fontana studied him. "Yeah, I wanna talk some more," he said slowly, chewing between thoughts. "How about later? I got a few things on my mind now"—he looked around—"if you know what I mean." He reached into his shirt pocket. "I'll be on duty till midnight." He shoved a card with his name and the precinct address in Seth's direction.

"Believe it or not, Fontana, you're not the only one around here with responsibilities." He wondered whether the reporter was listening.

Fontana went on chewing and held the card out to Seth. "Go ahead, Doc, take it. Now or later. Now means long. Later is short. You decide, Doc." He decided "later"—that evening at the address on the card.

Walking through the gloomy tunnel toward the stairwell, he tried to get the images of the dead girl's thighs, the contour of her breast, and the bloody, misshapen skull out of his mind. He glanced at his watch. Ten twenty-eight. He had to get to the ward now. What "implacable reality," he wondered, awaited him there? He wanted to anticipate, prepare. "Chance favors only the mind that is prepared." He smiled. The sign had hung in his father's laboratory—over the tissue culture equipment—like a mute conscience, nagging and inspiring doubt in those who passed beneath it. It seemed to him that he was forever preparing—another Conrad Curse. He wondered when chance would at last favor him.

His father, hands thrust into his long white coat, was always prepared—day or night. The lecture of your choice: the Geology of the Midi; Tovey's Theory of the Late Quartets; the Best Years for Claret Since 1900. Push the button and get a generous little treatise. Generous. Like his call yesterday.

"Do you need any cash, Seth?"

"No, thanks, Dad, doing fine. How's the weather there?"

"One of those miracle days, son. Brilliant blue. Cloudless. The Canada geese have started coming down. Sethy, you won't believe this. I saw a lesser golden plover. Yesterday. A real beauty. Golden spots all over the back with a white stripe over the eye. Looks like a sandpiper, but the black axilla—"

"How's Mom today?"

"A little down, naturally, but we're managing. We're going to the Barnetts' for dinner. That'll cheer us up. . . ."

Without warning, images from his morning nightmare crowded into his thoughts. He is in a sailboat, flying downwind. Birds— gulls—careening all over the sky. Heading for jagged rocks, the boat out of control. Suddenly he's underwater, plummeting down, down, like a stone, unable to move arms or legs. Then with a tremendous effort he reaches toward the light, but it's too late, his lungs are bursting, and he knows he's going to drown—

"Hey! Hey, there! Wait up!"

Awakened abruptly for the second time that morning, he whirled around in momentary confusion. This time Lindsay Cooper was striding toward him, her sunglasses perched on top of her head.

"The army brat," he mumbled, and pushed his glasses up on his nose.

"Creepy down here, isn't it?"

"Not when you get used to it," he lied.

"Listen, would you mind if I asked you a few questions?"

"As long as we keep moving." He tapped his watch. "I've got a conference at eleven—and plenty to do before that."

They clattered up the iron staircase and reached the elevator just in time to see it begin its glacially slow ascent.

"He's a real type, isn't he?" Seth slouched against the elevator door, trying to look casual.

"Who?"

"Fontana. They really like to push people around, don't they?"

"He's not so bad. Actually he's better than most. At least he cares. The burned-out ones are the worst."

"You've got a funny way of showing your admiration." He looked up at the elevator indicator. The car had finally reached the second floor.

"Who said I admired him? I hardly even know him. He's just a cop."

In the sultry atmosphere outside the Psychiatric Admitting Office, with its battered door covered with witless graffiti, Seth watched her out of the corner of his eye. Standing there in the swirl of human wreckage—hallucinating patients escorted by overheated policemen; unshaved, unbathed derelict men—she was an island of freshness. He could make out a faint trace of cologne.

"Did you know her?" Her eyes cornered him.

"Not too well," he said, watching the pulse in her neck.

"But you did know her?"

He seemed not to hear the question. Instead, he glanced at his watch and looked up at the elevator indicator again. It had reached the fourth floor.

The reporter looked at him. "What do you do here?"

"Resident. Psychiatry." Suddenly, with a clumsy jerk, he pulled the stethoscope out of his pocket as though she were a cardiac emergency.

"A psychiatrist?" she said with a quirky smile. "First one since I came to New York."

"You must not have been here for more than ten minutes."

"Believe it or not, I've been here a year, and you're the first. God knows I've met plenty of patients. I probably have a larger case load than you do." Seth decided not to smile and busied himself with the whereabouts of the elevator. It had reached the eighth floor and was now slowly descending.

She was studying him now, measuring his responses. "You say you knew her?"

"Not well, really," he said, trying to smooth his tie.

"Look, I know you're busy, and you've probably got dozens of things to take care of; but there's something about this case."

Standing next to her, fixed by her clear blue eyes, he was having trouble keeping his mind off that lovely pulse in her neck.

"If you could give me just an hour and tell me what you know about her." She folded her steno pad and found it a place in her bag. "There's something special about this girl, and I'd like to—

you know—get a handle on it. I have a good instinct for these things."

"Sure, there's something special about her," he said with unaccountable irritation. "Somebody killed her. That made her special." He turned away and jabbed the elevator button for no reason.

"No, that's not it. I've covered dozens of stories about people who get killed. Most of them are not special or interesting. I don't know why this one gets to me, but she does. Just an hour. No more, I promise." She was asking, not pleading, and he liked her for that. "Just to get some background about this place."

The elevator doors opened and disgorged a handful of plump, motherly women in blue uniforms. One of them pushed a wheelchair with a grizzled old man tied loosely into it, babbling to himself.

"Look," he said, trying not to sound eager, "I'll be finished here about six-thirty." He pulled a soiled envelope out of his pocket and scrawled a number on it. "Here, give me a ring." He stepped aboard the elevator, nodded coolly to her, and punched six.

*Chapter*

# 2

*E*veryone around the conference table was sweating when Burden
arrived. Boiling with speculation about the murder, they quieted as
soon as he closed the door and walked to the head of the table.

" 'Life is short, the art long, the opportunity fleeting, experience
treacherous, judgment difficult.' " Burden turned away from them
as if they all were invisible and walked up to the blackboard.

Joe Burden was quirky. No doubt about that. Quirky and more
moody than ever, the senior residents had warned him. Seth glanced
across the conference table at Lisa Stone's cleavage. He pushed the
glasses back up on his nose as much to disguise his interest as to
sharpen his vision.

Burden tossed the chalk he'd been holding absentmindedly. He
was a string bean of a man, and somehow his sad eyes made him
seem leaner. He took off a rumpled linen jacket, threw it onto a
nearby chair, and turned back to them. He had written on the board
"Principles of Psychodynamics" in large, careless letters.

"We'll be meeting once a week for the next year—by the way,
we'll start promptly at eleven with or without you—and by the
end of that time you'll know a lot more than you know now about
psychopathology: why people fall ill with obsessions, or the symptoms
of schizophrenia."

With his shirt sleeves rolled, his solid arms gave unexpected confirmation to the rumor that had surfaced years before—because of his misshapen nose—that he had been a middleweight boxer in college.

"But don't be disappointed if at the end of that time you don't quite have it all together." He replaced the chalk on the ledge of the blackboard. "There's as much art as there is science in all of this." He walked back to the table and took his seat. "It'll take awhile to learn, so we'd better get started."

He looked around the table, pausing at each face as though to memorize it. Suddenly there was a tiny metallic clatter at the end of the table. Lisa had dropped her earring. Scooping it up quickly, she smiled at Burden.

"Since I don't know any of you, I wonder if each of you would mind saying a few words about your interests and perhaps a word or two about your background."

He turned to a chunky, red-headed man on his left with thick glasses, who seemed older than the rest. "Avi Schwartzman." The red-headed man beamed at Burden as though he had just told a hilarious joke. "Yeshiva Medical School. It's a little difficult to explain. Well"—he shrugged and adjusted the skullcap on top of his head—"you see, I studied Talmud before I studied medicine. I was—I am a rabbi."

"Every Jewish mother's dream, I suppose—a rabbi and a doctor," Burden mused. "How come?"

"Well, I decided there was a need for somebody who understood the problems of Orthodox Jews." He chuckled again, his jowls quivering. "I'm going to lead my people into the land of mental health."

Burden smiled and turned to the person sitting to the rabbi's left.

"Drummond, Fiona Drummond." The young woman nodded to Burden, her blond ponytail snapping smartly. "Well, actually, I did my medicine at St. Bart's, London." She pronounced it "med-sin," as though it were a form of malpractice.

"Bart's?" Burden looked impressed. "Why psychiatry?"

"Sir?" She leaned forward, squinting at Burden. She had the

unattractive habit of thrusting her jaw forward when she was puzzled, which was often. At those moments she resembled nothing so much as a female impersonator of Winston Churchill.

"Bulldog," Seth wrote in tiny letters in his notebook and then quickly worked them into a grinning masklike face. It wasn't so much her appearance as that irritating habit of missing the point and hanging on to it tirelessly.

"Well, actually, I rather like managing people's problems. In the UK people want bucking up when they're down, you know." She nodded her head as though agreeing with herself and thrust her jaw forward again.

"Thank you, Dr. Drummond. I'll make a note of that."

He turned to the next resident, a sallow-skinned, bony young woman. She pushed several strands of dark, kinky hair out of her face. "Pam Price. Yale Medical School"—she pulled a Kleenex out of her white jacket pocket and dabbed at her nose—"interested in"—she sniffed and let her gaze slide away from Burden's—"the psychology of women."

She had every reason to be, Seth thought. For the last two months she had dragged herself around the hospital. She often called in sick. When she did appear, she was red-eyed or sleepy or shrouded in worried silence. What she had just said was, for her, a lively performance.

Pam had retreated again, and mercifully Burden nodded to the young man sitting across the table from him, who blinked and flashed a luminous smile. "Whit Shields." He blinked again and with unconscious tenderness touched the initials of his Dunhill lighter on the table in front of him. "I've been working with Ruiz-Capalbos at NIMH for the past year. Cerebral hemispheric specialization." Whitney Shields III, son of an old New Hampshire family, came, it seemed to Seth, equipped with special top-of-the-line skin and hair, all golden and silky.

"Before that, at Harvard—"

There was another tiny clatter as Lisa Stone dropped her earring again. She mouthed the word "sorry" to Burden and gave an apologetic little shrug. Burden, susceptible, absolved her with a smile.

"I worked for one brief glorious moment with Gabe Shine, than which there is nothing closer to divine revelation." Again he flashed a brilliant smile.

"Yes, I know Gabe." Burden nodded and turned to the dark-eyed beauty with the uncontrollable earring. "Dr. . .?"

"Stone." She paused and then added with a smile, "Lisa. After P and S, I went to Paris for a year to study structuralism—with Lacan." She bent forward. "I'm *very* interested in analysis." As though to emphasize her interest, a soft curtain of lustrous chestnut hair fell forward over one cheek. She pushed it aside and smiled with alien modesty. Next to Whit, Lisa was the most attractive member of the group. Every organ of her body, every movement invited trespass.

Slumped in his chair, fidgeting aimlessly in his notebook, Seth, of course, missed his cue. When he finally glanced up, they were staring at him, Burden looking more amused than the rest.

"Chicago," he blurted out, and snapped upright. "Sorry." He adjusted his glasses. "University of Chicago." He fell silent and closed his notebook.

"Dr. . .?"

"Oh, sorry. Seth Conrad." He felt the tops of his ears redden.

"And why psychiatry, Dr. Conrad?"

"I—I'm not sure." He tried to smooth the creases out of his rumpled tie. "I mean, I know I'm more interested in causes than cures, but I don't know exactly how to pursue that." He paused and put down his pen after a moment, as though he were making a final offer. "Some kind of developmental research maybe. I don't know."

"Well, Dr. Conrad, some say that the capacity to tolerate ambiguity—keeping an open mind—is a sign of mental health. But I wouldn't count on that if I were you." Burden turned back to the group.

"By the time we finish this seminar, I hope you will have learned the theory and technique of diagnosing the intrapsychic conflicts that cause psychopathology." He opened a metal box and withdrew a dark, longish cigar. As he puffed it into life, he glanced around the table, making contact with each of them. "But in order to do that, you've got to learn how to collect the evidence you'll need."

He paused and exhaled a cloud of blue smoke. "What is the best method for generating such evidence? Dr. Drummond, you had your hand up."

"Well, what about the good-old-fashioned mental status examination?" She thrust her jaw forward, making it seem more like a challenge than a question. "We used it quite a bit at Bart's. Worked quite well actually."

"Do I see signs of mental life stirring, Dr. Shields?"

Shields blinked. "Are we making a distinction between the mental status examination and the psychiatric interview?"

"That question"—Burden pointed at Whit Shields with his cigar, as though he were making an accusation—"involves historical and conceptual issues which have an important bearing on what you do with patients. As some of you may know, Freud was not a psychiatrist. He never studied psychiatry. . . ."

Slumped again in his chair, Seth watched the ribbon of blue smoke unravel at the end of Burden's cigar. It rose, without end, like the ribbon of Burden's words, into a haze that hung over the table, making the air heavy. He wanted to pull his collar open but felt tired, terribly tired. He thought of the lifeless body sprawled below him in the harsh light of the tunnel. He glanced at the others around the table: Whit, relaxed, cynical; Lisa, eager, hungry; even Pam, listening, attentive. What was wrong with him? The words hovering in the air seemed elusive, like the images of his dream that morning. He remembered waking, reaching for light, for breath. His tiredness was like a body sadness. In a distant part of the hospital he heard the whine of machinery in pain, or was it a patient in some agony?

He straightened himself in his chair all of a sudden and reopened his notebook.

"In the 1880's there wasn't even a profession of psychiatry. Freud was trained as a neurologist. He would never have thought of treating 'crazy people,' patients we call psychotic today. The patients he treated with psychoanalytic techniques were more or less normal in their outward behavior—"

"But Freud did write about psychosis." Lisa Stone objected in velvet tones. "What about the Schreber case?"

"That's perfectly true, Dr. Stone, but it was only after fifteen years that he addressed himself to the question of psychosis, and even then he didn't undertake to treat Schreber; he never even met him." Burden stood up suddenly and began to pace in front of the blackboard. He seemed to draw energy from those remote events, as though they held some latent power that nourished his analytic soul. "Freud's brilliant clinical hunches about the meaning of Schreber's 'soul murder' delusion were based completely on his study of Schreber's memoirs. . . ."

There was a commotion somewhere in the corridor outside, and Seth glanced over his shoulder toward the door. Agitated whispers, a flurry of bodies, giggling. What was Burden talking about? Soul murder? Schreber case? But he had already raced beyond. Christ, why was he so stupid this morning? He stared dully at his open notebook. The masklike face he had scrawled grinned up at him derisively. Jennifer Light—he saw her bloodless face again, with its look of wide-eyed surprise, the flattened, bloody skull, the white breast he had glimpsed. As he looked about, Burden and the others around the table seemed remote.

Familiar images flooded in on him from his morning dream. And too tired now to resist, he let the leash of his attention slip quietly away. . . .

Again she had returned, the laughing woman, the one from his dream, vivid, familiar, like an old enemy. He knew that long dark hair, but now, as though to mock and confuse him, she bore senseless stigmata over her cheeks and forehead, a swirling tattoo of dots and circles. . . .

"The trouble with the mental status examination, Dr. Drummond"—Burden accused her with his cigar—"is that it homogenizes patients." His voice was louder now, more intense. He paced back and forth, confined by the limits of the blackboard. "If I were to read to you the mental status examinations of two individual schizophrenic patients, they would sound almost exactly alike."

He grabbed a chart from the table and read: "The patient is a slightly obese, disheveled white female who appeared suspicious and withdrawn. She is oriented to time, place, and person, with recent and remote memory intact. She has loose associations and believes that she will save people from World War Three. Affect blunted. Proverbs are concrete, calculations fair, judgment poor, no insight."

He took the page from which he had read, crumpled it into a ball, and threw it on the floor beside him. "I won't say which one of you wrote that." Seth sat himself up and looked around the room.

"It's worse than useless," Burden said passionately, "because it corrupts your capacity to observe, to see. Routine observations are non-observations, death to science and death to good clinical work." He pointed to the crumpled paper at his feet.

"You've got to be sharp, vivid. Catch every detail about a person, his clothing, his posture, his expression"—he passed his hand in front of his face as though he were a conjurer—"the way he combs his hair, whether his fingernails are clean or dirty, how many cigarettes he smokes, whether he blushes or sweats or smells. . . .

"If you describe a person so that he comes alive in an individual and unique way, you can't help but create a clinically meaningful mental status examination. But you'll be doing much, much more. You'll be developing the necessary data to understand your patients psychodynamically. You don't start with that id and superego crap. You start with the clinical facts, the observable evidence, the unique, individual, specific, particular facts about a person.

"Only through the accumulation of subtle and minute observations can we begin to learn about the character of an individual. The great novelists understood intuitively that the inner life of a man is expressed at least in part in the symbols of his appearance. When you present a patient to me, I want to be able to see that patient when I close my eyes like the character in a novel—a Miss Havisham or a Raskolnikov. When the patient is alive in your mind, you'll be able to make him alive in mine. If patients don't come alive for you, your work will be boring, and you will make my work boring, and I won't let you do that. If you want to work with me, you'll have to make it interesting for both of us.

"Next time I'd like one of you to bring a patient for me to interview—how about you, Shields? You look as if you've been paying attention—so I can demonstrate some of the things I've been talking about."

Then, with a cool nod to the group, he picked up the hospital chart, threw his jacket over his shoulder, and left.

Passing the spot where Burden had been sitting, Seth saw the crumpled ball of paper on the floor, the mental status examination Burden had discredited. He tapped it with his toe, hesitated a moment, then picked it up.

Melodramatic bastard, he thought. The page was blank.

"Suspect? Who?"

"Me!" Whit blinked twice. Somehow he made even this nervous affectation attractive. It had become an expression of his boyish modesty, a part of his princely aura. "As much as poor old Seth over there. I insist." He smiled ruefully.

"You? Don't be ridiculous, *bubele.*" Myra Karp, the social worker on the adolescent unit, loved playing Jewish earth mother to Whit's golden young aristocrat.

The staff dining room had been humming with rumors about the murder throughout lunch. Now, the meal half over, the level of conversation in the large, sunlit room turned sluggish as the heat increased. Some in the room were fanning themselves with whatever was handy, and most of the men had already removed their coats.

"He was in the hospital at the time." Whit nodded in Seth's direction. "I was in the hospital. He came to the PAO a few minutes late. I left a few minutes early. He slept in his bed"—he glanced at Seth coyly—"he claims, and I slept in mine." Whit inserted a cigarette into an ivory holder with the precision of a surgeon. "But neither of us can really prove it"—he turned to Seth—"can we, old man?" He raised the gold lighter he had been fondling, flicked it, and inhaled deeply.

Only half listening to the desultory talk across the lunch table, Seth didn't respond.

"What could they suspect you of?" Myra whined, her voice rising for emphasis. "You're adorable!"

"Thank you, my dear, for your vote of confidence." Whit toasted her with a nod and the gift of one of his smiles.

"She didn't say she had confidence in you," Harvey Bloch rejoined sourly. "She said you were adorable. I don't find you adorable, and furthermore, I find your narrow ties and your finely chiseled features suspicious. And, I might add, annoying."

"What's the matter with everybody?" Pam Price blurted out. "I don't understand why you're all clowning this way." As though she had gone too far, she pulled out a wad of Kleenex, buried her face in it, and quietly blew her nose.

"Maybe it's because we're nervous," Harvey said irritably.

"What you got to be nervous about?" Mark Jones asked, looking down at the tablecloth. As a rule the young black recreational therapist remained watchful and silent during outbreaks of mealtime skirmishing. Today, though, was different. Special, as though the rules had changed. As though something, the heat or the murder, had bent them out of shape, melted them like the asphalt out on First Avenue.

"Well, Jonesie, it may come as a shock to you, but being nervous is part of being intelligent."

A look of surprise flickered across Mark's face, and he seemed to shrivel like a touched oyster.

"Relax, Harvey! What's eating you?" Seth said quietly.

"Take it easy, man." Mark held up a hand. "No offense."

There was a slight movement of air from the open French doors leading out to the red-brick terrace. Pam Price, seated close to the doors, shivered despite the oppressive heat in the room. "God, it's freezing in here." Mark got up and closed the door nearest Pam. The tension eased, and Harvey loosened the collar under his beard.

"Nobody's hardly touched anything today," their waitress grumbled, clearing away the heavy china plates, each holding a few lifeless ravioli floating in a sea of orange sauce.

The dining room on the seventh floor of the psychiatric building was an anachronism. In an age of self-service, plastic knives and forks, and disposable plates, the staff dining room seemed to exist in a time warp, untouched by the realities of modern accounting methods. It held twenty or so round tables, each one covered with a crisp snow-white cloth and set for eight. The tables were served by sweet menopausal Irish ladies, some of whom had been there since the hospital opened. All wore hairnets and yellow uniforms and seemed distantly related to one another.

"She was a nice person," Pam said to no one in particular.

"What . . . I mean . . ." Whit blinked. Not often at a loss for the right word, now he searched the steamy air for inspiration. ". . . in fact, happened, old man?"

The details had been skirted since lunch began.

"Seth?" White repeated.

"Hey, boychik, wake up!"

Seth looked up from the half-empty coffee cup and seemed surprised to see all of them.

"Sorry. Guess I was off somewhere."

"How—what was the cause of death?"

"Cause of death?" He looked at Whit stupidly, as though Whit had been speaking in a foreign language, then shrugged. "I don't know. Head injuries, I suppose. It looked like the back of her head was smashed in."

"Ugh!" Pam shuddered, and the table fell silent.

The silence was broken by Mark. He spoke softly to the crumpled napkin that lay before him. "When I was a kid, I saw a guy beat a dog's head in. Dog didn't do much—ate a chicken, maybe, summer I was on the farm. He just took an ax handle and beat at the dog's head until there was hardly any head left—"

"This some new parlor game?" Harvey snarled. "We all tell our worst experience now?" He turned away with a look of disgust. "What do you call it—Dostoyevsky?"

Mark smiled tightly. "You ain't heard my worst experience, man."

A silent shadow fell across the table. Silhouetted against the strong, hot sunlight, the figure of Jonathan Graver appeared suddenly.

"How about it, Shields? Have you decided . . . what we talked about last week?" Towering and solitary as usual, Graver waited for some reply.

"Hello, Jonathan," Myra said pointedly, refusing to be ignored, even by someone she didn't like. "Have a nice summer?"

Hands in the pockets of his white lab coat, he stared down at her through half-closed eyes. "Hello, Myra. I didn't notice you there," he said. He was not unaware of her point, only untouched by it. He had developed a reputation in the department for a singlemindedness that obliterated anything he considered irrelevant.

"I'm flattered. I didn't think I'd lost that much weight this summer."

Graver's sleepy lids flickered once, and he continued as though uninterrupted. "We were at the house in Amagansett all summer. I didn't take any time off to speak of. Just the weekends."

"Sorry about Jennifer Light."

"So am I. It couldn't have happened at a worse time." He touched his breast pocket, checking its contents for no reason. "I warned her a dozen times not to walk around the hospital at night alone. Stupid," he muttered, shaking a massive head of dark ringlets, some beginning to silver.

"It's a goddamn shame. It's this crazy place— What happened to your hand?" Myra asked, waving her plump fingers in his direction.

Graver looked down at his hand, still touching his pen and glasses. It was bandaged. He turned it over as he seemed to turn the question over in his mind. A smile flickered between life and death.

"Nothing much, just an infection." He slipped the bandaged hand back into his pocket and turned to Whit. "Why don't you drop by my office after lunch, Shields, and we can talk some more? We need somebody badly now."

His heavy eyes slid back to Myra as he nodded and turned away.

"Bastard," Myra muttered.

"There goes one of the finest minds of the fifteenth century." Harvey scowled after him.

"He didn't use that girl well," Myra added, shaking her Shirley Temple curls.

"That asshole really thinks he can find the cause of schizophrenia by analyzing snot. Would you believe that?" Harvey looked around the table for allies.

Whit Shields flicked his cigarette. "I like your intellectual taxonomy, Harvey old man. Assholes and"—he looked down at himself—"narrow ties—"

"They're not mutually exclusive."

"—have a kind of simple but primitive beauty. Your animadversions notwithstanding, don't you think you're being a little unfair to Graver?"

Harvey didn't bother answering, except to scowl.

"He's analyzing all body fluids, not merely nasal secretions. Really, old man, you may not agree with his point of view, but his methodology is impeccable."

"So I'm unfair. He's still an asshole," Harvey grumbled.

"Ah, nothing like reasoned discourse." Whit flicked his cigarette again.

Seth, who had been staring vacantly at the currents of tropical air shimmering in the cityscape below, turned back to the table. "What was she doing there?" he said suddenly. "What the fuck was she doing there on a holiday weekend? Graver obviously hadn't expected her to be in the hospital." He focused on Whit. "What then?"

Whit was silent, his ivory holder clenched between his teeth, his gaze escaping quietly up the ribbon of smoke from his cigarette. "Look," he said finally, with a shrug, "maybe she was with someone down there or meeting someone."

"Who? Who knew her?" Seth asked listlessly, not expecting an answer.

Myra tilted her head so that her Mexican earrings tinkled. "What about you, adorable?" She squinted at Whit through glasses with rims that matched her lipstick.

Whit raised his eyebrows for an instant, then undertook, with unusual care, the extraction of his cigarette from its holder.

"Yes, you." Myra persisted. "Don't look so surprised, lover. Mother Karp knows what goes on in this place."

"Well, Mother Karp, I thought she was one smashing-looking woman." He smiled a golden smile.

"You knew her?" Seth sat up straight for the first time and leaned forward.

Whit shrugged. "About as well as you can know a person after spending an evening with her. I first noticed her a couple of weeks after I arrived, and"—he paused and looked with mock innocence

straight into Myra's warm brown eyes—"we had dinner, and that's
all there was to it, really."

"But what was she like? Did you see her again?" Myra was
in hot pursuit. She wanted to know more, much more than she was
asking.

Whit blinked and fidgeted with his cigarette holder. As he labored
to respond to Myra's probing, Paul Silk appeared like a deus ex
machina and flounced into the seat between Whit and Myra.

"God, what a night! I've been up every goddamn minute."

"That's funny, you don't look it, darling."

Silk was a big man, bigger than he seemed. The illusion of
slightness was due in part to his bone-and-wire frame and in part
to a gracile tenor voice compromised even further by a faint lisp,
which remained almost subliminal except in moments of excitement.
The net effect was a tendency on the part of his colleagues to
underestimate him.

"I don't look it, sweetie"—his dark eyes flashed at Myra—
"because I wushed home at seven-thirty this morning, showered,
and changed into fwesh clothes. This place needs somebody around
with a little self-respect. It's certainly rare enough at this table."
He scowled as he looked around and asked the waitress to bring
him his cup of tea.

Seth smoothed his wrinkled necktie, and as he looked at Paul
Silk in his fresh Cardin suit and crisp blue shirt, he felt like a
schoolboy again. Silk was always impeccable—fussiness, some called
it. He had a well-designed and finely trimmed black beard and,
though balding, wore his hair fiercely short. His skin was smooth,
tanned, and drum-tight over the bones of his cheeks, and it was
said he watched his weight to the ounce.

Silk was a man given to discipline, discipline of himself and of
others. It was a passion, however, that seemed to work on his
behalf, as the chief psychiatrist of the adolescent unit, a service that
needed discipline if it needed anything. Over the last ten years the
ward had become a smoothly functioning, trouble-free service, and
Silk had earned the respect and gratitude of the hospital administration. All this despite a personal crisis which had given rise to
unsavory rumors and a messy divorce.

"Surpwise, surpwise! God's gift to physical culture!" He made a flourish in Mark's direction, as though he were a toastmaster introducing the young man. Mark smiled shyly. Suddenly Silk put the fingers of both hands to his temples like a man with a brain tumor. "My poor memory must be playing twicks on me. I could've sworn that I left instructions that a certain very tall, very dark, very handsome wecreational therapist wemain on the ward until one o'clock." He glanced at his watch, an elegant platinum rectangle without numerals. "Twelve-thirty. Who"—he paused and raised his right eyebrow dramatically—"is watching the speed fweak?"

"Come on, Paul, cut it out. He was sound asleep when I left the ward—"

"Speed fweaks don't sleep! They wait! And don't call me Paul. I'm not your bwother! I like to delude myself into thinking I still have some authority around here," he said, appealing to Seth with a look of staged exasperation. He leaned forward in Mark's direction. "I want that kid under stwict observation"—he jammed the table with a long, tanned forefinger—"wepeat, stwict. Especially during visiting hours. I was up half the night with him—"

"I told Carmen to call me as soon as he got up," Mark said, half pleading.

"You know damn well Carmen is out to lunch most of the time. Don't give me an argument. Just get down there, and make sure nobody else slips him anything."

Mark reached under his chair, where he had stowed his textbook on recreational therapy, and rose slowly without looking at Silk. "See you later," he said to Whit, and ambled toward the elevator.

"And for God's sake, don't sulk," Silk called after him. "That boy better watch it," he muttered to no one in particular.

Silk courted no one's favor and was, therefore, a natural target for departmental gossip, which he never bothered to refute, which in fact he seemed to cherish. One of these rumors was that Mark Jones had become something more than a protégé and less than a son to him. Myra said Silk was too critical of the young man: "Always correcting him, grooming him, prompting him. Too much. Really." To casual observers it was simpler: "That's Paul—a catcher in the rye." To Harvey it was: "Catcher in the raw, you mean."

"No one to blame but yourself, Paul," Myra said, looking at the bangles on her thick wrist. Then: "You've heard about Jennie Light?"

"Oh, God, don't remind me. I heard as soon as I got back this morning. I still can't believe it. And I was here the whole time it was happening. Why? Why?" He shook his head, dramatically. "It's so senseless. She was a harmless kid."

" 'Harmless' maybe, but 'kid' I doubt it. You know as well as I do that she was having an affair with—"

"Listen, Myra"—Silk's eyes flashed—"I've had a very long, hard night, and I could do without your burrowing. I don't gossip about my ex-wife or my dead friends, so let's drop the matter right there— Joe Burden!" Silk suddenly twisted around and put up his hand as though he were a traffic cop. "Don't move!"

"Ah, Paul. How are you?" Surprised, Burden looked like a man awakened out of sleep. As he stood there, jacket slung over his shoulder, waiting to be released, he nodded to the others at the table.

"Been trying to reach you. Fascinating kid came in yesterday. Male anorexia."

"Oh?" Burden remained noncommittal as Silk described the highlights of the case with his usual theatrical flair.

"How about it, Joe? Come on over and discuss the case with the staff."

Burden pulled a thin black leather date book out of his shirt pocket, and as he flipped through its pages, he asked, "How's the house coming?"

Silk rolled his eyes upward. "Oh, thank God, thank God, it's finished. Never again. A Paul Silk Extravaganza, two years in the making, with a cast of hundreds of thousands of you know what. Did you see the article in the *Times*? God, that's a story in itself."

The article had appeared early in August in the Sunday magazine section, "Austere Elegance on Fire Island," and the color photos showed a stark whitewashed stucco-and-glass house cantilevered over a ribbon of golden sand and blue ocean.

"You must come and see the place." He kissed his fingertips Italian style. "It's gorgeous."

"I'd like to, very much. How about next week—for the conference, I mean, Wednesday?" Burden stood with a slender silver pen poised over a date in the book. "Would you like me to interview the boy?"

"Are you kidding? Did Oedipus love his mother?" Burden shot Silk a doubtful glance. "That's the best part, Joe, watching you spin a patient's history into the gossamer web of personal myth." Silk's fingers undulated like an Indian dancer's. "Wednesday's perfect."

Despite the irony in Silk's performance, obvious to all, Seth noted a tiny smile of self-satisfaction on Burden's lips. Burden was a man, he thought, like many academics, not entirely unsusceptible to flattery.

"Well, we'll see," Burden said with a touch of false modesty. "We'd better make it ten-thirty then." And he jotted the time down. He tucked his book and pen back into his pocket and began to move off with a wave.

"End of September, Joe," Silk called after him. "Gorgeous then. I'll do bouillabaisse for you."

"Now there's a man," Myra Karp mumbled, staring after Burden with a dreamy look in her eyes.

"Do you think it would have been diffewent, sweetie, if Burden had been your analyst?" Silk asked with a smirk.

"Are you kidding?" She laughed, stood up, and, taking her bulky bag from the back of the chair where she had slung it, said, "I would've been a star." She hefted the bag onto her shoulder, and as she walked slowly toward the exit, her heavy hips and buttocks seemed to mock them in unfettered defiance.

" 'There's a divinity that shapes our ends/ Rough-hew them how we will,' " Whit murmured as they looked after her.

*H*e didn't have to look at his watch to know that he had to get off the ward and out of the hospital. Soon. All afternoon Dr. Coles had been studying him, making silent notes. All afternoon Mrs. Scola had given shuffling pursuit, wordless, miserable, asking nothing but to be near him, like a bereft child. All afternoon Mrs. Lipsky, disheveled and worried, her bony fingers clinging to the pocket of his jacket, had begged him to listen once again to her somatic delusion. "You don't understand, Dr. Conrad. They're rotting—my bowels. I smell them." Repeating every detail of the story, "just to make sure I didn't leave out anything," she pulled on his coat. "Please, Doctor, you've got to give me something to move. I haven't moved in two weeks." And once again he told her that he would order something for her as he pried her fingers loose. And there were the others, touching him, pleading, staring reproachfully, and nibbling, always nibbling away.

As usual, Benson Coles seemed to materialize out of nowhere. One would have thought it difficult for a man of his size. It wasn't that he was tall; it was the barrel chest and powerful shoulders that made him seem formidable. He liked to catch people off guard, silently watching them until he was ready to signal his presence with a nervous little cough.

"Ahem."

Surprised, for the moment Seth didn't know which of Coles's eyes to acknowledge—one was false. He'd been bent over the nursing station counter, writing hurried orders on a patient who'd spiked a fever that afternoon.

"Hi . . ." He searched desperately one eye and then the other for a clue. "Just finishing up." He smiled and held up the metal chart as though it proved his point.

Coles coughed once again, this time touching his lips affectionately with well-manicured, polished fingertips. "We missed you at rounds this morning." Coles spoke with a faint drawl.

"Sorry about that. I had to see Dr. Lemmon."

"Right." Coles looked down at a metal can of movie film he was holding. "Ahem. This is the fourth time you've missed morning rounds. Is there . . . some problem about that, Dr. Conrad?"

Seth shrugged. "I guess there were things I had to take care of."

"Right, Dr. Conrad. Ah'm well aware of the conflicting nature of a resident's duties. You see, Ah've had a resident or two on the service before."

Coles had what Harvey Bloch had described as an "obscenely

babyish face . . . ridiculous with that dyed red hair." His baby-smooth cheeks now showed some color.

"Four times in the last month is a little, ahem, excessive. Wouldn't you say, Dr. Conrad?"

"I suppose it looks that way. But today was a little special."

"Oh? In what way?"

"It was about the murder. The police—they wanted some information."

Coles looked down again at the can of film and ran his finger around its perimeter. "Why you, Dr. Conrad? Did you know her?"

"I was on last night. That's when it happened—after midnight, they think. Pretty gruesome down there."

The color rose in Coles's cheeks and suffused down his neck. "Yes, so Ah hear." He coughed gently again. "Ah know you're in a hurry, Dr. Conrad." Seth stopped tapping his pen on the counter. "Other pressing matters, no doubt." He smiled primly. "But would you mind telling me why Mrs. Scola hasn't been started on her shock treatments yet? Miss McVey told me Friday that she's been here almost two weeks." It was a well-known fiction that Coles ran the ward. In fact, most of the orders were written by Milly McVey, the head nurse, and put in front of him every morning to be signed.

"I guess it's taken longer than I expected. I was waiting for the last reports to come in from her other hospitalizations." Seth tapped the chart he was holding impatiently. "I thought it would be helpful in establishing a diagnosis." A note of self-righteousness found its way into his voice.

"Ah don't think there's any need for that, Dr. Conrad. We can make our own diagnosis, can't we?" Coles smiled. "Please put Mrs. Scola on the ECT roster. E-lec-tro-con-vuls-ive ther-a-py," he repeated slowly, enunciating each syllable separately, as though Seth might not have heard of it. "ECT. As Ah suggested. Right? Milly's on vacation this week, havin' a little fun, Ah guess, so we'll have to do our own housekeepin'. Right?

"You'll do that before you leave for the day. While Milly's away, we'll have to keep some discipline around here. Right?" Starting to turn away, he caught himself. "There's an interview on this film you might be interested in, Dr. Conrad." He held up the film canister. "You might learn a little somethin' from it." Coles was interested in only two things: cameras and making film recordings of psychiatric interviews. These, he often said vaguely, were to be used for research someday.

"Yes, sir, I'd like to see it sometime." Asshole. Gratefully Seth fixed his gaze on the metal cylinder.

"Right." Coles wheeled, started to march off, then turned back once more.

"Oh, just one more thing. It would help morale a great deal if you tried to"—he patted his own cheek—"spruce yourself up a bit. Right?"


*U*nbuttoning his collar, Seth stared at the elevator indicator, motionless at three. "Come on. Move," he muttered, focusing all of his mental power on the bronze pointer. No response. Nothing. He worked on it, his eyes narrowing with strain. "Shit!" he burst out finally, and barged through the door into the stairwell, to take the steps two at a time.

"No . . . wait . . ."

He'd already passed the fourth floor when he heard their voices, and before he could stop, he was almost at the mid-landing.

There were sounds of scuffling. "Please. I promise. Listen to me, Jonathan."

The voice, at once strained and familiar, like the image in a bent mirror, he recognized as Milly McVey's. "I drove all the way back just to see you, talk to you. Talk to me, please. I won't make a scene." She suppressed a sob. "I promise."

"There's nothing to talk about."

Seth stood motionless. He could see nothing but sensed that Graver was still turned away from Milly, facing up the stairway.

"Nothing to talk about? Seven years? Here, take it back. Don't you care anything about me?"

"Of course, I care about you, Milly." Graver, icy and remote, had turned back toward her now. "But I don't want it. It's no use. Let it go, Milly. Let it *go.* There's nothing more there."

Transfixed, as though the powerful emotions rising from below had turned him to stone, Seth wanted to retreat up the stairway, but he knew the slightest sound would interrupt the scene below. He thought, as he listened, that it was for their sake that he waited, unseen, unheard, and unknown.

"You didn't say that last week. You promised you'd come this weekend. Why not? Why didn't you call? Where were you?"

"I couldn't come. And I didn't want to call. I didn't want another tantrum. I can get all the tantrums I need at home."

"You were with her this weekend, weren't you?"

"Milly! You're crazy!" The sounds of scuffling. "Let me by!"

"You were with her. I know. Why don't you leave her alone? For God's sake, she's a child. She doesn't know what she wants."

"Damn it, Milly, shut up. You're doing it again."

"She doesn't love you. She doesn't even know you. She doesn't know what a bastard you are."

"Look, Milly, I'm tired of this. I'm tired of your paranoia, tired of the impossible promises I have to keep making, tired of the rages. Here, Milly, take it, I'm through." There was the sound of a metal object on the stairs.

"Jonathan, wait—"

"Milly, stop it! Let go . . . Milly . . ." There was scuffling again and finally a thud and a cry of pain. A flurry of footsteps, and Seth was suddenly face to face with Graver.

Stunned, Graver stood like an animal caught in a searchlight, the color rising in his face. Then, with a guttural sound of rage and disgust, he rushed past.

Listening to the quiet sobbing below, Seth realized that he would live to regret that moment of unbidden intimacy. He knew, the way old men know they are going to die, that there are certain things a man like Graver could never forget and would never forgive.

He slipped past the mid-landing and saw Milly McVey crumpled on the stairway. She was massaging her temple as she rocked slowly back and forth, whimpering, "Bastard . . . bastard . . . bastard . . ."

He eased his way down to her. "You all right?"

She looked up, not surprised, still holding her head, her gray eyes brimming.

"Are you okay?" he repeated gently. "Let me take a look at that." He turned her head and tugged her hand away so that he could see her temple and cheek.

Milly was not easy to like. Impatient and demanding, she was often contemptuous of the residents. And despite the first-name basis of their ward relationship, Seth was still unsure of how close he wanted to be.

"Stay away, boychik. She's a lightning rod," Harvey had told him. "Even on a sunny day a thunderbolt will find her. Someday I'll tell you her story. . . ."

He marshaled his best professional manner. "Must've ruptured a little vein . . . there's a hematoma—"

"It's not the first."

"Well, let's hope it's the last." As soon as it was out of his mouth, he regretted the banality, and her look told him of the impassable distance between them.

She had stopped crying now and was beginning to compose herself. She rarely smiled—she had already lived half her life and had found little reason for smiling. But for that fact and her implacable devotion to plainness she might have been pretty. She had the features for it: an Irish pug nose, wistful, intelligent eyes, and silky red hair she wore in a severe style pulled straight back.

"Coles said you were on vacation this week."

"I was. I am. I had some business I had to take care of, so I drove back from the beach this afternoon."

"Him?"

"You heard?"

"A little."

She turned her head away. "I should've stayed out there. It was useless." Slowly, like a starving person, she pulled herself to her feet. "I better get started; it's a long drive."

"Is he worth it?"

"Oh, Christ, what do you know—" She glared at him. Then, recovering, she turned away again. "I'm sorry."

"Here, I think this is yours." Seth had picked up a latchkey and handed it to her.

She looked at him. "Do me a favor, will you? Forget this."

"Sure," he lied.

## Chapter

$$3$$

*H*e was oblivious, even of the green Jaguar tooting at him as he crossed First Avenue, oblivious of the greetings called from its cockpit—Paul Silk at the wheel, Mark beside him, already in cozy reunion.

Like a sleepwalker, Seth headed west toward the apartment he shared with Harvey, unmindful of the darkening sky and sheets of lightning flickering over the Hudson. All day the temperature had hovered in the mid-nineties, tormenting the city. Now, white jacket slung over his shoulder, collar open, he tried for the first time since he'd come on duty to sort out what had happened to him in the last eighteen hours. It was automatic now, like a knee jerk. You don't simply gobble up experience like a pig; you savor it, ruminate over it, analyze it, integrate it. "The unexamined experience isn't worth having." Another Conrad Curse.

"Remember, boychik, the unexamined crap isn't worth taking," Harvey would needle.

The air in the darkened apartment was dead—unexpectedly cool and dead. "Christ, this place stinks!" he said aloud. He wondered who had turned the air conditioning on. There was the sour odor of undone laundry and the faint acrid smell of Harvey's Monte

Cristos. He flicked the light switch. "Fuck," he muttered, and remembered that the overhead bulb had needed changing since Friday.

This discovery seemed somehow to demoralize him, and he sank onto a chair in the entrance hall, which doubled as an eating area.

The apartment he and Harvey shared was in a modern high rise, one of many undistinguished red-brick structures built along Third Avenue with boxlike rooms and thin walls. They all had grand names like Empire House or The Biltmore and were occupied by squash-playing account executives and smart-looking airline personnel who browsed in uniform among the convenience foods late at night at Joe Hug's delicatessen.

The apartment was shabby, an incoherent accumulation of cheap Scandinavian furniture, most of it Formica and Leatherette. They had bought the sublease from two surgical residents, and Harvey had negotiated the furniture into the deal for an extra $150. The only things they brought with them were Harvey's harpsichord and his pornography collection. "The largest collection in the city outside the Morgan Library. Look, boychik, reading pornography is disgusting, infantile, but studying it, that's scholarship, high culture."

Seth sat there, his jacket in his lap, like a stroke victim, staring mindlessly at a faded print of two flamingos in flight. There was a sound from Harvey's room. He looked apathetically at the closed door. The soft, steady hum of the air conditioner called to him, promising repose and dreamless sleep.

"Harv?" he called dully. There was silence except for a distant roll of thunder and the yapping of the Lhasa apso upstairs. He heard the sound again, metal scraping on metal.

"Harv?" This time he heaved himself to his feet and shuffled across to the closed door. For no reason he knocked and waited. He knew that Harvey wasn't home yet, and wouldn't be for another hour. Upstairs the excited Lhasa yapped again, and again he heard the sound from within the room. Tactfully he opened the door.

The room, he could see in the half-light, was empty. The bed had been neatly made, and as he watched, the powerful current from the air conditioner blew the drawn blinds against the window frame, scraping metal on metal.

Standing in the doorway, he felt a dissonant tug at the back of

his consciousness; but his brain was tired, and his eyes burned, and
he didn't want to think. He shrugged and moved automatically into
the tiny kitchen. He knew he wanted something as he stared into
the bare refrigerator. The bed was made. Why? He realized, finally,
that he was thirsty and reached for a container with a picture of
a girl in a grass skirt and a basket of oranges on her head. He
stood holding the container as though he didn't know what to do
with it. Harvey never made his bed. A made bed, he had said often
enough, made it difficult for him to regress in the service of his
sexual life. Without thinking, Seth worked the container open with
his fingers, and suddenly shrugging, he raised it to his lips. Nothing
came out, and as though trying to prove to some disinterested god
the injustice of it, he held the container upside down over his
upturned face and shook it. A single drop of juice fell on his cheek.
"Shit!" he muttered, slamming the container into the already over-
loaded sink.

The tie came loose, and he sank back onto his cool pillow. He
took secret pleasure in his weariness, as though it were a form of
moral affirmation.

As he lay there, his body submitting to its state of insensible
exhaustion, he found himself thinking, for the first time since he'd
left George Lemmon's office that morning, of the rounds he'd made
of the hospital in the middle of the night. He tried to recapture the
look of each stop on his rounds, to retrace his steps, rewind his
memory, peer into the dark corners and shadowy alcoves. Had there
been some solitary figure awake somewhere, a dangerous paranoid
who should have been safely locked on O-7? His responsibility?

Despite the tiredness of his body, his thoughts continued a restless
life of their own. He felt another, familiar, ancient tug, one he
didn't want, but couldn't refuse. A memory forced its way into his
consciousness, of the chilly, fog-ridden night he lay awake on the
island—and all the nights after that—trying to retrace his steps, to
understand what had happened that night. He took off his glasses
as if to blur his memory. The crack in the ceiling magically
disappeared, repaired by his myopia. The shapes and colors of the

room became soft, soothing, analgesic. There was no myopia, however, to soften the images from within. He saw again the body of
Jennifer Light lying on the damp floor of the musty tunnel, with
unforgiving clarity and definition. He thought of her in the last
moments of her agony alone, in the dark, unable to move.

He heard thunder again, this time closer. The Lhasa upstairs
replied with its usual lapdog bravado. Now there was no stopping
the reflux of small insults he'd suffered in the past twenty-four hours,
ugly, unexamined experiences that pushed their way forward for
further attention: Fontana's bullying, Ettinger's war, Coles's carping,
Graver's rage, Milly's humiliation, and subtler claims and dissonances.

When at last, eyelids hot and heavy, he fell into a troubled
sleep, it was not before a final, tiny discrepancy demanded recognition:
the irrelevant and unexamined memory of Harvey's unmade bed,
glimpsed as he'd left the apartment the previous evening.


Again he was the dreamer and the dream, and again the ringing
of the phone shattered the fragile scenes like a winter wind on
water. For an instant he thought it was morning again and that
he was back in the hospital, that nothing had happened, and that
Elly was alive again.

He reached across the bed and groped for the phone. After several
rings he raised himself on one elbow and made fingertip contact.
Depleted, he fell back onto the pillow and grunted something into
the mouthpiece.

"Dr. Conrad, please. Seth Conrad," the voice said crisply into
his ear.

"Uh . . . right," he mumbled just as the phone slipped from
his tenuous hold. He opened his eyes and picked it up, this time
with more commitment, cradling it against his ear with his shoulder.
"Who—who's this?"

"Lindsay Cooper." There was a silence. "You suggested I call."

"Oh, yeah, I remember. Last Saturday." He closed his eyes
again. "At the museum. The Temple of Dendur." His words slurred.

"Wrong time, wrong place, wrong girl." Seth opened his eyes.
"Look, we met this morning over a dead body—"

"Oh, the reporter . . ."

"—and I've got a story to write and I don't have time to play."

Army brat, definitely, he thought. He raised himself on one elbow again and reached for his glasses. "You're pretty starchy, you know that?" He remembered the pulse in her neck and her fresh smell.

"Look, maybe this isn't one of your good days. I didn't call to be analyzed."

"Hey, hold on. Let's talk. How about dinner?"

There was a silence. "I don't know." More silence. "I've still got some things to do tonight." He could see her studying her watch. Probably digital. "Look, okay—but on two conditions. No analysis, and I pay—well, let's say the paper pays."

He maneuvered his glasses into place with one hand, and the room came into focus. "It's a deal."


The hot water pulsed over his back and shoulders. The sound of its beating on the plastic shower curtain was familiar, friendly. It held no surprises, no challenges, and for the moment there was nothing to prepare for, nothing to examine. He let the sensations wash over him as he rocked back and forth, vacantly watching the course of a drop of water as it slid down the pink tile.

As he stood swaying, lost to the sound and feeling of the steady thrumming on his skin, without his willing it and without warning, he knew that he had encountered Jennifer Light that night. Somehow on the night of her murder their lives had touched. He knew it. He knew it with a certainty he couldn't explain. An explanation his father would have searched for and found. But at the moment, the water beating against the back of his neck, flooding down his chest and arms, he felt released from explanations. Later, he told himself. He'd explain it to himself later.


Wearing only a towel and some lather on his face, Seth rummaged through the medicine chest. Through the half-open bathroom door he heard the sounds of Harvey's heavy, shambling gait in the apartment.

"Harv?" There was no answer except for a clap of thunder and heavy drops beating against the window.

"Harv? Got a blade?" More rummaging. "I need a blade," he shouted.

"I haven't shaved anything but my legs in three years, and I use your razor for that." He heard Harvey open the harpsichord that occupied much of the living room and a moment later the sound of a Handel suite.

*S*adie Bloch, a large-breasted operatic woman with a cupid's bow mouth, had given up what in the afterglow of middle age she had come to believe was a promising career in the Yiddish Art Theater to deliver and nurture her first and only son. Harvey, designated at birth as his mother's gift to the arts, was adored, adorable, precocious, and eventually both a blessing and a curse to his mother.

The harpsichord had saved Harvey's life, he claimed. He built it—with Sadie's blessing and her curse. "You want to build a what? What for? Papa will buy you one . . . they drive you crazy, kids . . . you shouldn't know what I went through for you . . . all right, all right. Build it, don't build it. . . . If you build it, how will you play it? . . . You'll be an old man. You'll have arthritis in the fingers by the time it's finished. . . ." In the end she gave in, of course, and they bought him the kit, and he built it, every stick and string of it, during the worst years of his adolescence. "It saved my life, boychik. I would've OD'd on masturbation. Know what that means, *bubele*? I would've been in *Guinness*. The first valedictorian from Bronx Science who ever jerked himself to death."

But that was nothing. "You should've been there when I told her the bad news. It was her greatest scene." And Harvey's, too. He loved reenacting it, playing all the parts, Sadie's especially, and no version was ever the same. "Her greatest role since she played Tykel in *The Rabbi's Shame*. Scarlet O'Hara, Medea, and King Kong rolled into one. She was magnificent, boychik."

" 'Herman, get me an aspirin. Your son's playing games with me again. What do you mean, medical school? You're a music major. You write music. You're a composer . . . you're gonna look at people's tonsils all day? In the ears? Are you crazy?'

" 'No, Ma,' " He imitated himself as a beardless undergraduate. " 'I'm gonna be an analyst.'

" 'An analyst?' She sinks down into an armchair and clutches her heart, or where she thinks her heart is, which is up around the splenic flexure of the colon. You see, boychik, it's hard to tell affection from gas in my family. Anyway, she has this agonized look on her face, and she says, 'You mean you're gonna lie on a couch in an office and hum?'

" 'I don't lie; the patient lies. I sit. What do you mean, hum?'

" 'You're gonna spend your whole life alone in a room with another person and say mm-mmm? That's what I sweated blood for? Herman, where's the aspirin? Your son is a real card, a real sweetheart, this one. Come here, you want to hear something? Your son, your little boychik, is gonna throw his whole life away on some *meshugge* idea. It's that crazy doctor he's going to.'

"Then the finale. The water show. 'Harvele, sonny'—out comes the pathetic shred of Kleenex, a simple but powerful prop—'you're a brilliant composer. Don't give it up. Your grandfather, my father— may he rest in peace; it's a blessing he's not here today—was not only a cantor in Vilna but a great musician, a violinist, an artist. It's in our family. Harvele, your songs make people happy. Don't throw it away! For what? A swanky office? A couch? Sonny, you can make people happy. You can make them smile. You can make your mother smile.' The curtain falls slowly as Sadie smiles with adoration at Harvele—her blessing and her curse."


Now, slowing the tempo and modulating the key, he began to bellow, " 'Like the beat, beat, beat of the tom-tom/When the jungle shadows fall . . .' "

"Put your pants on, genius," Seth called over the noise. Harvey, a disciple of personal comfort since early childhood, in the hot months lived in his underwear.

" 'Like the drip, drip, drip of the raindrops/When the summer shower is through . . .' "

"There's an attractive woman on her way over"—Seth had found a rusty blade in the wastebasket and was inserting it into his razor—"and I don't want her frightened by the abnormal appearance of your genitalia."

There was a crashing chord. "That's a lie!" Another chord followed by a passionate arpeggio. "About the woman, I mean. You don't know anyone who fits that description."

"Harv, you knew that girl, didn't you?" Seth called. "Jennifer Light?"

There was a sudden burst of rain at the windows followed by the sound of the Lhasa upstairs doing a nervous little dance, then a progression of dissonant arpeggios and aimless chords.

"Harv, did you hear me?" Seth appeared in bare feet and a pair of suntans. A piece of toilet tissue clung to his chin by a drop of coagulating blood.

"Yeah, I heard you," Harvey said sourly. "I knew her." He stopped playing. "I met her at Silk's place on Fire Island."

Seth pushed his head through a navy blue knit shirt. "What about her?"

Slowly Harvey unwrapped a long Monte Cristo cigar, lit it, stuck it into his mouth, and began a Mozart sonata.

"Hey, what's with you?" Seth said.

"You heard what they said at lunch today. She was a strange girl, a flake." Harvey's eyes closed as he came to a poignant passage, and the huge body began to writhe in a romantic agony as he puffed away on the cigar stuck in the corner of his mouth.

For a moment Seth listened to the Mozart and the rain beating against the windows, then with a shrug padded off in the direction of the tiny kitchen.

"Listen, Harv," he called. The refrigerator door slammed. "I had a dream—"

"You had a dream? Who do you think you are, Martin Luther King? Just because you dream, you think you're so special—"

"No, listen . . . last night . . ."

"Probably ten or fifteen people have dreams every night."

Seth returned carrying two beer cans. "Beer?"

Harvey opened one eye.

"Last night, after I finished working, I had a dream about this girl—Jennifer Light—*before* I knew about the murder."

Harvey opened both eyes. "A premonitory dream, you mean?"

"Well, no. There was no murder in it. Just the girl's face . . . with"—he made a circle with the beer can in front of his face—"with some design . . . marks over it."

Harvey stopped playing and gulped some beer. "You saw her last night." He made a sour face. "Don't we have any Jap beer left?"

"No, I don't think so. Saw her, I mean. I would've remembered."

Harvey reinserted his cigar and began the Mozart again.

"Now, listen to this. When I got home a little while ago, I fell asleep. And when I woke up, I had the feeling that I'd had some kind of encounter with this girl last night in the hospital cafeteria. In some way I sensed her presence." Seth sat back, pleased with himself, as though expecting some reward. "What do you think?"

"Sure. That's Otto Pötzl, prince of subliminal perception."

"I'm not talking about perception alone. I'm asking whether it can find its way into dreams."

"Sure. Fisher proved that conclusively." Harvey turned away from the keyboard and leaned in Seth's direction. "He did a study based on Pötzl's original work. He took subjects, exposed them to subliminal stimulation, and then studied their dreams. And there it was." He pointed his cigar dramatically at some invisible datum. "What they didn't see, what they couldn't have seen appeared clearly in their dreams. This stuff is shit." He slammed his beer can down on the table. "Any wine around?" Without waiting for an answer, he got up and shuffled into the kitchen.

"Harv," Seth called, "were you in the apartment this morning?"

Even before the doorbell rang, sitting alone in the darkening room, half listening to the rain against the window and Harvey's puttering in the kitchen, Seth knew what the answer would be.

"You got Alzheimer's?" Harvey roared back. "What's the matter with you?" Seth heard the squeak of a cork. "I told you I drove straight from the Island to the hospital."

The buzzer sounded then, and as he opened the door, he was unaware that he had forgotten to smile at her. She stood there, the army brat, hair and face drenched, trench coat soaked through.

Harvey, shuffling into the room with his trousers on and several glasses of wine, poked one at her. "Here, you look like you could use this. Good evening. I'm Harvey Bloch, Seth's wealthy uncle."

He raised his glass in celebration of himself and smiled.

"You never answered my question."

He studied her crisp features against the background of the restaurant's red-brick wall.

"Whether you'd help me—introduce me to the people who knew her?"

"I know," he said, snapping a breadstick in two and offering her half across the table. She had sensible eyes, clear and bright blue and in the candlelight even brilliant.

"Well, will you?"

"Why are you so interested in her? I mean, why her in particular?"

"I don't know. I haven't really thought about it. What difference does it make?"

"What difference does it make? Jesus, you've never heard of the Conrad Curse. It makes a difference because"—he made quotation marks with his fingers—" 'The unexamined life is not worth living.' "

"Well, Dr. Conrad, in the land of Lincoln and Four-H where I come from, we have a saying, too. 'The unlived life isn't worth examining.' That's the Cooper Blessing, and it's all yours. Now stop trying to analyze me. Remember our deal."

"Look, you're not on the prairie now." He looked past her and thought of Milly McVey holding her head and sobbing. "Maybe things aren't so clear and simple." He looked at her, and her sensible eyes came back into focus. "They're kinkier."

"That may apply to you and your life, but it doesn't fit mine. I write about what I can see and touch and hear."

"I'm not so sure. You don't mind digging for her motivations—Jennifer Light's. You don't mind analyzing her life."

"That's different. It's bread and butter with me. It's my job to write about crime." She bent forward and asked abruptly, "Do you know how many murders are committed every year in New York?"

She didn't wait for an answer. "Last year there were almost seventeen hundred. And do you know how many of them ever get solved?" She frowned.

He smiled. "How many?" He liked her indignation.

"Half. And the ones that get solved are not the ones that need solving."

"Meaning . . ."

"Meaning they're crimes committed in front of dozens of witnesses. There's nothing to solve; all they have to do is catch the guy. The others are the hard cases, cases without witnesses, like this one. 'Mysteries.' Those don't get solved. And if they do, it's because of some fluke."

Her eyes were brighter now, larger. Not sensible. He wasn't really listening anymore. There was a slight flush in her cheeks from the wine, and he sensed her excitement. He wanted to heighten it and share it and watch it all at once.

"They'll never find out who did it," she said quietly. "And maybe that's why it's an interesting story. She was beautiful, young, innocent, and now she's dead. And we'll never know who did it or why."

He poured her some more wine. "What makes you so sure?"

"I've seen it over and over again. You have to be very stupid or very crazy to be caught, but even in the crazy cases it's not easy. Remember the Son of Sam case?" She leaned forward again, her hand brushed his. "His behavior was bizarre, and he left dozens of clues around; but the only reason he was finally caught was because some ordinary people got together and showed the police who he was. The cops kept refusing to pay any attention to them until they just couldn't ignore them anymore."

She sat back, silent, staring down at her plate. "Maybe that's why. I want to celebrate her a little. Give her a little justice after all."

The silence was filled by the burnished sounds of a Brahms quintet on the hi-fi. She glanced up, "Why are you smiling at me that way?"

"I didn't realize I was smiling." He took another sip of wine. "You don't have very much confidence in the cops."

"Look, most of them haven't gotten beyond high school. Some of them are bright, but believe me, no geniuses. If they were brilliant, they wouldn't be cops, they'd be molecular biologists." She smiled. "Or psychiatrists."

In the candlelight the pale green of her summer dress highlighted the contours of her arms and shoulders, and for the moment everything else seemed to recede. He watched, as though it were an old friend, the pulse in her neck, now beating more rapidly than before. Suddenly the music and mood were pierced by a police siren speeding down Second Avenue.

"Christ! What time is it?" He fished out of his pocket the card Fontana had given him with the address of the precinct on it.

"Almost ten."

"Will you walk with me to the precinct?"

"Will you help me?"

He was silent, thoughtful. He held out his hand. "If I don't, who will?"

*T*hey strolled southward in the direction of the police station, neither of them much inclined to talk. The air was cooler now, after the rain. A few women in faded housedresses still sat on the steps of their tenements, talking quietly together.

They walked closer than before, and their bare arms occasionally touched, but only by accident.

They stopped for a minute to watch Hang Loy through the lighted window of his hand laundry as he ironed and smoked and listened to music on the radio. As they turned away, Lindsay touched Seth's arm and stopped. She looked up as though she were trying to see something on another planet. "I just remembered something about my mother I'd forgotten." They began walking again, more slowly now. Lindsay looked down as though reading the past in the debris of the present. "It must have been the winter just before she died. She used to get up in the middle of the night and iron my dad's shirts and listen to music on the radio." She half turned back in the direction of the hand laundry. "She didn't have to; the maid would have done it. I suppose she was in a lot of pain by then, and she didn't like to drug herself. And I guess it made her feel better."

An ambulance careered past them on its way to the hospital, and it reminded Seth of the emergency room and its remorseless triage of life and death.

"I was ten or eleven, I guess. Sometimes I'd wake up, too, and I'd come down and read to her, until I fell back asleep right there in the kitchen. I read her all of *Jane Eyre* that winter. She just kept getting weaker and sadder.

"One day she told me she wanted me to know whatever she knew that was important so that someone would know what she had discovered and it wouldn't just die with her." She paused. "The funny thing is that all I remember were the tricks she taught me about cooking that winter. You know—like what you do if you put too much salt in the stew. I know she told me other things, too, but I can't remember. Sometimes I lie awake trying."

They had reached the precinct station. In the half-light of the streetlamp Seth saw that the muscles of her face had softened. As he looked at her, a breath of wind from the river blew a wisp of hair over her cheek. He brushed it back. He touched her face and then the lustrous highlight of her hair.

"Shall I walk you over to Third?"

"No, I'll be all right."

"I'll call you tomorrow."

She nodded and turned west toward Third Avenue. She walked more slowly than she had that morning, and Seth knew that she was trying to remember.

He looked after her for a few seconds and then went up the stairs into the Thirteenth Precinct and the First Homicide Squad.

He walked up to the tubby, bald desk sergeant and asked for Fontana.

"Squad room. Up those stairs, to the right."

Following the directions, he found himself in front of a locked steel door with a small rectangular window in it. He knocked loudly, and a moment or two later it was opened a crack by a chunky Hispanic man with a shoulder holster under his left arm. He squinted suspiciously until Seth asked for Fontana; then, half turning, he called out, "Hey, Vince, for you." The man continued to block the doorway until Fontana arrived.

"Oh, it's you. Come on in." The swarthy man with the shoulder holster went back to looking through a file, and Fontana led him to the other end of a large tiled room, scattered with five or six abused desks and an assortment of filing cabinets. Fontana sat down at the farthest desk in front of an old typewriter with a sheet of blue paper in it. He pointed to a battered chair beside the desk. "I'll be finished with this bullshit in a couple minutes, Doc. Coke?" He nodded in the direction of a dispenser in the corner.

"No, thanks."

The room had the smell of places inhabited by men without women, a blend of male sweat, stale tobacco, and coffee, a smell that Seth had never learned to like.

The walls were bare except for a cork bulletin board with the words "Duty Roster" written in block letters along its top margin. Two of the papers tacked onto it looked as if they'd been there for several years. He noticed that the two windows in the room were covered with a steel grating and wondered about the kind of mind that would burglarproof a police station filled with armed men twenty-four hours a day.

"Say, Doc, how do you spell 'brassiere'? One *s* or two?"

"Two." Christ!

"Just a couple more sentences."

Seth watched Fontana as he laboriously searched for and jabbed each key as though it were an enemy. He seemed less formidable now than he had that morning, sitting there, head bent forward, frowning with concentration, beset by the letters of the alphabet.

Seth studied the snub-nosed revolver Fontana wore over his right hip. It was blue steel, and he wore it with the handle raked forward for easy access. Seth thought, as he sat there waiting for Fontana, of pulling it out of its burnished leather holster and feeling the weight of it. Suddenly he turned away. Kids, he thought. Five-year-olds playing games.

Fontana finished pecking away with a staccato flourish and

turned forcefully to Seth. "There. I hate this paper crap. Docs have a lot of this bullshit, too, huh?" He got up and stretched.

"Yeah," Seth said.

Fontana rubbed his eyes. "Long day." He looked at his watch. "Only an hour to go. How about a cuppa coffee, Doc? We got the worst coffee in the department. But we been drinking it so long, everything else tastes lousy." He smiled. The fluorescent lights made his lips look dead.

"Look, Fontana, I've had a long day, too. Do you think we could get on with this, whatever it is, without all the niceties?"

Fontana's smile faded. "Niceties. That's good. Gotta remember that." He sat down on the edge of the desk and folded his muscular arms across his chest. "Well, to tell you the truth, Doc, when I asked you to come by this morning, I had something else in mind. I thought you were going to have to answer a lot more questions about what you were up to last night." His smile returned. "But I've got some good news for you."

"That's nice. I could use a little good news," Seth said, staring vacantly at the snub-nosed revolver, heavy with the power to kill.

"Well, the ME was able to pretty much pinpoint when the kid died. She was attacked around one A.M. and died around four—"

"She didn't die right away?" He looked up at Fontana, surprised.

"No. ME says she didn't die until four, and since you're accounted for during that time in the admitting office, you're in the clear."

Seth took off his glasses and rubbed the bridge of his nose. He had stopped listening to Fontana. He remembered Elly again. Well, it was the anniversary. Fourteen years.

"In fact, you're about the only one who is. At least until we finish checking out everybody's story."

"Brain laceration?" he asked, staring past Fontana.

"Yeah, how'd you know?"

"Fractured skull. Laceration of right occipital and parietal cerebral cortex. Extensive hemorrhage. Probably subarachnoid."

"Not bad, Doc, not bad." Fontana reached across the desk for a sheet of paper with several single-spaced paragraphs on it. " 'There is an extensive irregular defect of the scalp and skull involving chiefly the occipital bone but extending somewhat into the right parietal

region.' " As he read, he moved his finger across the page from line
to line. " 'Multiple fracture lines are seen to radiate from the defect
at the occiput. The complexity of these fractures is best appreciated
in photographs and roentgenograms.' " He stumbled on words like
"roentgenograms," but like some rash, bullnecked Gulliver plowing
through an army of unfriendly Lilliputians, he was undeterred.

" 'Right occipital region of the cortex is markedly disrupted with
extensive laceration and loss of the cortical substance. There is
marked engorgement of the right parietal and occipital regions with
considerable subarachnoid hemorrhage—' "

"Okay, Fontana, enough. I get the idea."

"Occipital—back here, huh?" he asked as though he already
knew the answer. He tapped the back of his skull.

"Yeah," Seth said without looking at Fontana. He was back in
the autopsy room at the medical school, watching again the countless
brain dissections. It was as though he couldn't get enough of
neuroanatomy and neurosurgery that year. As though he were searching for the answer to some question that had never been asked.

"You're pretty good at this stuff, Doc." Fontana put the report
back on the desk and touched the dark mole on his cheek absentmindedly.

"How do you know she didn't die right away?" Seth heard
himself demanding.

"We found the exact spot where it happened, where she was
hit. Right outside the cafeteria. The stains on the wall match her
blood." He studied Seth for a moment or two and touched his mole
again.

"The cafeteria?" He'd seen her there, he wanted to tell Fontana.
But he hadn't. Maybe he'd heard her laugh, that was all. But maybe
he hadn't. All he really knew was that he'd dreamed about her.

"Yeah, the cafeteria. Then whoever it was hit her. Real hard
on the left side of the face. Inside of her left cheek and her lip are
lacerated. Then he snapped her head backward against the wall,
crushed her skull. According to the ME, somebody big and pretty
strong and probably right-handed." Fontana looked up to the fluorescent fixture as though for divine guidance. "She falls down,
probably unconscious, and lies there bleeding." He glanced at Seth,

"Her sunglasses must've got knocked off. We found them there this afternoon."

"How did her body—how did she get to where we found her?"

"Good question, Doc." Fontana put his foot on a nearby chair and leaned toward Seth. "We figure that sometime later—maybe three, three-thirty—she must've got conscious again and crawled up the tunnel—about a hundred yards—northward in the direction of the psychiatry building—"

"How do you figure that?" Seth blurted out, and instantly regretted it. Fontana was in his element. Savoring every detail. Bastard.

"Well, first of all, her hands and knees were dirty. Second of all, her other shoe was found about halfway between the two places this morning by a nurse's aide. He turned it in to the cafeteria lost and found. She must've lost it while she was getting from one place to the other. Anyway, she walked or crawled until she came to the alcove where we found her. She must've been confused and thought it led to the stairway."

"She was probably half blind," Seth said more to himself than Fontana.

"She crawled in, collapsed, and probably died within an hour after that." He stood up, and flexed his shoulders. "Well, we know how and when." Without thinking, he felt his biceps. "All we gotta do now is find out why and who. Right, Doc?" He grinned.

Seth studied the big detective. The green sport shirt, the bull neck, the powerful arms. Probably a weight lifter. He smiled to himself.

"Robbery, it'll turn out," Fontana said with assurance. He reached into his shirt pocket. "Gum, Doc?" He proffered a stick of Juicy Fruit, which Seth didn't bother refusing. "Rape is out. ME says so. No sign at all." He slid the gum into his mouth. "Assault was probably incidental."

"Incidental?" Seth said with quiet scorn.

"I mean incidental to robbery, it'll turn out."

"In the end it's all the same to her." But Fontana wasn't listening.

"Yeah. We found her bag. Cop on the beat found it sticking

out of a garbage can this afternoon, about a block away from the hospital. Whatever money she had in it was gone." Fontana tossed the gum wrapper into the wastebasket artfully. "That's the most likely, Doc. Robbery." He turned away from Seth and gathered up some papers on the desk.

"Unless it had nothing to do with her murder," Seth said quietly to Fontana's back, "and she lost it like her shoe." The detective turned around. "Except whoever found it didn't turn it in."

Fontana looked smug. "You know, Doc, that's a nice idea, but it's a long shot." He felt his biceps again. "In this business, we don't have the time or the men to play long shots."

"Believe me, no geniuses . . ." Lindsay had said. Seth smiled coolly. "You mean you guys don't put yourselves out much." He stood up. "Anything that doesn't fall into your laps is a long shot."

Fontana reddened. "Hey, look, Doc! We got a total of twelve guys in this zone, working 'round the clock." The chunky Hispanic with the shoulder holster looked up from his desk. "That means on any shift we got about four. Maybe we got fifty, sixty homicides a year to investigate down here. That's one, maybe two a week. That little girl you saw this morning"—he jabbed his finger at the papers on his desk—"is our forty-seventh homicide this year. If we cleared maybe twenty, twenty-two, that means we got twenty-five still on the books. I personally have got five cases I'm working on right now. Coyle's already reassigned; he'll be off the case after tomorrow. I don't have time to screw around with long shots, Doc. I work the odds." He stomped around behind the desk and flung himself into his chair.

"It's not like in the books. We don't do anything fancy here. I'm just an Italian cop, and I live in Queens, and my name ain't Sam Spade." He tipped his chair back and put one foot on the desktop. "You know why Spade always wore shiny suits, Doc? Because he didn't have volume. He only had one case at a time." He held up his index finger and shook it at Seth as though he were an angry parent. "So he could afford to play long shots. We have plenty of volume here. We do a wholesale business. That's why I got a closet full of suits, and I live in a nice house with grass in my yard.

"Maybe you're right." Fontana put his other foot on the desk and tipped the chair back, balancing on two legs. Seth could see him lifting weights in some sweaty gym. "Maybe she did lose her purse in the tunnel and some little spick messenger picked it up, took the change, and threw the purse away. Then where are we? Then there has to be another motive for why she got hit so hard, Doc. You have it? I don't."

"You mean you just can't bother with anything that's not simpleminded." Seth punched the spectacles back up on his nose.

"Doc, you really know how to hurt a guy," Fontana said, untouched. "The thing is that most homicides are simpleminded. Simpleminded guys killing other simpleminded guys. If they weren't simpleminded, they'd be talkin', discussin', like you and me." He fanned the air between them. "Sometimes innocents get hurt; sometimes they're not so innocent.

"Look, we both work for the city." He took his feet off the desk and let himself fall forward with a thump. "We don't have to bullshit each other. We're not running for office. What I'm saying is that most crimes are committed by dummies. Jerkoffs. We clear a lot of those cases. But anybody with a lot of smart, a lot of tough, and a little luck—chances are he'll get away with it. Every once in a while their dumb luck runs out and we get 'em. Those are the facts, Doc; those are the facts. I don't like 'em, but I gotta eat 'em and spit 'em out every day." As though to illustrate his point he wrapped the wad of gum he'd been chewing and flung it into the wastebasket.

"Don't worry, we'll follow up every lead until our time runs out, and maybe we'll get the dumb bastard before that happens. And maybe we won't. Who knows? Don't look so disillusioned, Doc." He added with a crooked smile, "After all, what's your clearance rate? How many patients do you send home cured?"

The detective reached down and opened the file drawer in the desk. He took out a large white canvas purse that looked like a sailing bag. "I was just going to put this away in the vault."

"Hers?"

"Yeah, this is it." He cleared an area on the desktop and pulled out an antique silver cigarette case with an intricate Persian design engraved on it. He opened it and held it out to Seth. Inside there were a score of pills. Seth picked up one of five or six yellow capsules and examined it. "Had trouble sleeping," he said softly, as though he were addressing the capsule itself. "Nembutal." He looked up at Fontana. "Hundred-milligram capsules. A barbiturate." He dropped the pill back into the case.

Fontana shoved the case forward again. "What else?" Seth took the case from him. There were about ten or fifteen small yellow tablets with the letters *MSD* and the number 25 inscribed on them.

"Amitriptyline, twenty-five milligrams. It's an antidepressant. Not very effective." As he closed the delicate silver case and placed it back on the desk, Fontana fished out, one by one, a pair of expensive sunglasses with tortoise shell rims and rose-tinted lenses; a wooden hairbrush; a small rectangular mirror; a two-ounce plastic tube of suntan oil made from coconuts; a beige nylon bra; a checkbook issued by a bank in Roslyn, Long Island, with checks imprinted "Jennifer Light, 532 West 79th Street, New York, N.Y. 10023." Seth bent over the desk and opened the check register. There were no entries. The last check she had written in her life was number 074.

He touched the nylon bra and suddenly felt himself flush with embarrassment. He glanced up at Fontana, who was staring at him with a half-smile. He handed Seth a small pink plastic box with a dreamy picture of a flower and a butterfly on it. Inside he could see places for twenty-eight tiny tablets. Half of them were empty. There were seven white ones and seven pink ones left. She had been in the middle of her menstrual cycle when she died.

Without warning, his pulse began to race. He sat down and picked up a worn paperback novel which Fontana had just dropped onto the heap. On the cover was a modern house dramatically overlooking a rocky coast. Superimposed on this was a beautiful woman, with her eyes closed and an agonized look on her face. Seth turned the book over and read in bold letters at the top of the back cover, "Twenty Weeks on the Best Seller List," and below that, "Melissa Gordon emerged from the rubble of her parents' divorce into a young womanhood she had known only in her most secret daydreams. Finally, at long last, she must come to terms with the emotional and sexual part of her self that she had forgotten. A worldwide best seller, soon to be a major motion picture."

Last, Fontana handed Seth a brown suede wallet. The change purse built into it was completely empty. The various compartments inside yielded a plastic card which enabled Jennifer Light to cash her checks at the Manhattan branches of her bank, a Master Charge with her signature on it that would not expire for a few months, and a driver's license with a speeding violation entered on it. The address imprinted on the front of it was 16 Willow Path Lane, Roslyn, New York 11576. There was a color snapshot of a slender young man in an academic cap and gown; a stub of a ferry ticket to Fire Island, dated the day of her murder; and finally, a receipt from the Prompt Dry Cleaners, its address about two blocks from the hospital.

Fontana leaned forward. He'd been watching Seth, touching the dark mole on his cheek as he watched. "Well, Doc, what do you think?"

"I think I'm being conned, Fontana. That's what I think."

"What do you mean, Doc?" Fontana asked innocently.

"I mean, since when do the cops invite their suspects in for all this kissy-talky stuff? You feed me all these goodies"—Seth nodded to the contents of the purse spread over the desk—"the medical examiner's report, all your hottest hunches. Do you do that with all your suspects?" He paused. "You're setting me up for something. Look, I'm too tired to play games. I don't know about you, but I'm going to be in bed in fifteen minutes." He stood up.

"You're right, Doc. Absolutely. I should've been up-front with you. But you know how it is," Fontana said without conviction. Then, resolutely: "Look, it's like this." He got up suddenly, almost knocking his chair over, and came around the desk face-to-face with Seth. "I think whoever killed this kid didn't intend to. He only wanted the money, and then maybe she struggled or tried to scream and he let her have it." He paused with his mouth half open, hunting for the words as he'd hunted for the letters on the typewriter. "And I figure there's some skel who used to work there, somebody who was maybe fired recently and needed cash—"

"Skel?"

"A skel. A lowlife, the lowest form of life you can think of. Somebody who'd sell his mother for a quarter. Maybe an addict. You know, a lot of addicts try to get jobs in hospitals." He was talking faster now, urgently, leaning toward Seth. "It puts 'em in touch with all kinds of drugs. Maybe this creep was on his way to the cafeteria to freeload, saw the kid as she was leaving, and decided to make a try. That's how I figure it. We're checking the records to find all males who worked at the hospital and who left within the last two years. We're also checking out everyone on the staff who was on duty that night—"

Seth, arms folded across his chest, looked doubtful. "So? Where do I come in?"

"I'm coming to that, Doc. Like I said before, we have to play the odds, and the odds are this is the way it happened. Nothing fancy, nothing mysterious. And if we get the guy, we'll get him by outwalking him, not by outsmarting him. See that sign over there?" He jerked his head in the direction of a small sign on the wall over his desk with the letters TED on it. They were printed in simple, primitive block capitals. "You know what that stands for, Doc? 'Try every door.' " He paused and smiled as though he'd just coined *Cogito ergo sum.* "That's how we'll get the son of a bitch."

Seth looked at his watch. "Okay, you've got seven minutes. Because at eleven I turn into a tired doctor. Now, get to the point."

"Right, Doc. We can't afford to play the long shots, but look, there are couple of funny things about this case. One, if the skel who hit her wanted cash, why didn't he take her credit cards and checks? They're worth fifty, a hundred bucks on the street. Any skel knows that.

"Two, we can't find where she lives. There's something a little funny about this kid. We checked out the address on her checks, and she's not there. It was a studio apartment, and she moved out about a month ago. We checked out that Roslyn address on her driver's license. That's where her parents live." He shook his head and looked unhappy. "Mother says she had a fight with them about six weeks ago, and she's been out of touch since. They thought she was still living on Seventy-ninth Street. So we got no idea where she was living. And"—he raised his hands like an Italian tenor—

"what the hell was she doing in that goddamn tunnel anyway? If we knew more about her, I'd feel a lot better. And that's"—he touched Seth's chest with delicacy—"where you come in, Doc. For the time being you're the only safe contact we have into the place. We know you're okay, see?" He smiled and flicked a tiny speck of dust off Seth's shirt. "But we don't know about anybody else yet." He paused and shrugged his shoulders. "Look, there are a hell of a lot of people on that staff, and it'll take a few days. You see, Doc." He paused again, mouth open. Again he was at the typewriter of his mind, hunting and pecking for the right word. Suddenly Seth felt a wave of sympathy for the weight-lifting detective.

"You can find your way around better than us right now," Fontana said carefully. "Maybe you can find out a little about her. You know, just keep your ears open. Who she knew, what she did, where she hung out."

Seth stared down at the empty purse on the desk, its contents spread out before him. Each item, like the knot in a net, tied to the others by some invisible, secret strand of her life. He picked up the wallet and looked at the picture of the slender young man in the graduation costume. There was an incurable defeat in his forlorn posture.

"Kid brother," he guessed quietly.

He opened the silver pillbox and stared into it. He picked up one of the yellow capsules, the Nembutal, and rolled it in his palm as he looked over the network of her life. Already he knew something about her sorrow, her troubled nights, the ebb and flow of her body. He had touched the soft nylon that had touched her soft breasts. He glanced at the cover of the paperback best seller. The rocky coastline and the agony of the girl reminded him of Elly.

He stared at the yellow capsule for a moment longer, then replaced it and tactfully closed the case. "Look, Fontana—"

"Call me Vince. We ain't so formal around here. Gum?" He held out another stick of gum. Seth ignored it.

"I've got my job, too. I don't have time to start playing detective." Suddenly the conviction in his voice sounded tinny. He understood what Fontana wanted, and he knew that he would do it, that it was too late to say no.

"I understand, Doc," Fontana said, knowing that the contract had already been signed, sealed, and delivered. "You don't have to do anything special. I know you're busy." He gave Seth an easy smile. "Just give me a ring if you hear anything."

"I'm not promising anything, Fontana—"

"Vince."

"Okay, Vince . . . but if I hear something, I'll let you know."

"Fair enough, Doc."

As they approached the heavy metal door, Fontana pointed to the brown spot on his cheek, "Say, Doc, take a look. Think it might be a cancer?"

# Chapter

# 4

The eighth floor of Bellevue Hospital had no patients or wards. It housed the central services offered by a great city psychiatric hospital: a small but authentic wood-paneled courtroom where a justice of the State Supreme Court adjudicated the impossible—patients divided and at war with themselves. Commit the sick part for care and the healthy part is punished; let the healthy part go free and the sick part destroys them both.

In the classroom next door devoted teachers wrestled with the wild demons of children in a grotesque caricature of education.

Down the hall occupational therapists wheeled patients out of their autistic fantasies into the real world of number painting and soap modeling.

Across the corridor a fully equipped gymnasium invited highly wired young men to discharge their pent-up feelings in the endless offensive and counteroffensive of basketball.

Finally, a beauty parlor equipped with hair dryers and cosmetic supplies allowed uptown volunteer ladies with silver-blue hair to bring a touch of self-respect to disheveled women who shuffled about in paper slippers.

Seth glanced at his watch in the dim light of the corridor. He was early. There was no response to his knock. Just a dreary institutional silence and distant sounds of activity coming from the gymnasium. He turned the knob and looked in.

The strong afternoon sun poured in, illuminating the room with a golden light. With his forefinger Seth pushed the door open and stepped inside. The room was restrained, well organized, and luxe like Whit Shields himself. The bed, crisply made, was covered with a blue spread with an insignia—an anchor and the initials NYYC. There were golden oak tables and leather armchairs. Son of a bitch. He thought of his own cramped, shabby, and chaotic room down the corridor. He was always surprised at Whit's easy resourcefulness when it came to his personal comfort and convenience.

Despite its solid and agreeable effect, the room said little about Whit. It could have been a room in a smart university club or a spare room in an Oyster Bay mansion. Only the large glossy black-and-white photograph which hung over the library table spoke to Seth. It was a picture of a trim sixty-foot yawl, sails set, close-hauled, and heeling over in the snapping breeze. Seth could make Whit out at the helm and the figure of a young woman in a slicker standing precariously on the lee side of the boat. So that was the *Robber Baron.* Not bad for a graduation gift.

From the first day of his arrival Whitney Shields III had been something of a mystery. First of all, he was unexpected. As far as the faculty knew, the first-year class of residents was "five of the very best we've had in years." Then, out of the blue, after orientation week was over, almost a full week after—according to "sources" in Ettinger's office—two calls came in that made the old man's week. One was from the chairman of the board of overseers of the university, and the other from the assistant to the senior senator from New Hampshire.

Whit had appeared the following Monday.

At the lunch table that first day Whit shrugged when someone asked what had kept him. How come he was a week late? He gave the group one of what Harvey afterward called his "shameless rich boy smiles. . . . Goddamn Commies are right! Did you see the tawny color on that bastard? Man is free, boychik, yet everywhere he is pale and flabby." Whit inhaled deeply from his ivory cigarette holder. "Hubris. Pure hubris. Chastened by the gods for trying to outrun my fate."

He told them about the *Robber Baron*—his grandfather's and, now that the old boy was dead, his. Sailing the boat up from Bermuda for the summer, "We caught an impudent little hurricane two days out of St. George's Harbor. So we hove to and sat there for three days, eating hardtack, drinking vintage port, and listening to the *Ring* at full volume." He explained patiently, modestly, how with a perfectly tuned boat one could stymie the rage of wind. All one had to do was to set the storm jib to the windward, rig a storm trysail with the main sheet hauled tight, and secure the tiller to the leeward with a becket. "But it wasn't the seamanship; it was the Wagner. A magnificent, tragic struggle between the forces of chaos and art . . . Sometimes we'd hear only the sea roaring and closing in around us; then suddenly a crescendo of music or a great chorus of voices would hold the crashing waves at bay . . . a furious, desperate, majestic moment." He looked around the table. Stupefaction. "Has anyone here ever been in a storm at sea?" His cool gaze halted for a moment on Pam Price. He smiled at her and blinked. Her eyes glazed over, and she seemed to liquefy.

There were some, though, who were not only unconvinced but untouched by Whit's charm. "All that windward and leeward bullshit. Let's see how he heaves to in the admitting office."

Seth peered into the half-open closet. It was empty except for a limp old safari jacket with an Abercrombie and Fitch label and a pair of heavy white flannel trousers from another age. Seth wondered whether they had belonged to the Robber Baron himself. He smiled as he reached up to the shelf above and fingered the straw hat, a real Panama that also belonged to another generation. Whit was rare.

In front of the closet there was an open leather suitcase filled with clothes and one or two books. Whit must finally have found his "decent little apartment, perhaps with a view. Nothing jazzy. It's so hard to tell the difference in New York between jazz and style. Know what I mean, old man?"

"Sure," Seth had said.

Despite the troublesome rumors that drifted into port after his arrival, Whit continued to win hearts. Even Seth succumbed. Not to Whit's personal magnetism, he assured Harvey. "He's good. He's clinically sharp. He's a good observer, and he thinks, goddammit, which is more than I can say about the rest of them."

"Oh, yeah," Harvey had snarled, "we'll see what happens in September when Joe Burden and little Hansi Lucas get hold of him. Those guys don't charm so easy. They play hardball."

Seth squatted over the open suitcase and picked up one of the books, *Transoceanic Sailing,* signed by the author. The inscription, dated several years before, read, "New York—Gibraltar. An old Norse legend says that to be a great helmsman, you must have a heart of stone and water from the Skagerrak in your veins. Here's to the best helmsman I know! Next time around the world! Sven."

Seth shook his head and tossed the book back into the suitcase. There was something special about Whit. It wasn't just his generosity—he lent what he owned freely, books, reprints, records—or his unfailing, even irritating affability, but something fugitive and shy, something vaguely troubling and elusive.

Seth checked his watch again. Already after five. He picked up a folded newspaper from the desk and flung himself into an overstuffed chair. The paper, that morning's *Times,* was opened to the article about the murder. BELLEVUE HOSPITAL SCENE OF MURDER. It rated about half a column on page 36, next to a Lord & Taylor ad for back-to-college clothes—tartans and shetlands. "Goddamn maniac," he muttered as he thought again of Harvey's explosion at breakfast over the article. He put down the paper. Should've walked out, he thought.

Harvey had been laboring impatiently over the Chemex as Seth read aloud. " 'Police said that Miss Light's purse had been found in a garbage can within a block of the hospital. It had no money in it, and detectives indicated that robbery might have been the motive for the slaying.' "

"How about that for in-depth reporting?" Harvey said with a yawn. He began to feel for a lump in the angle of his jaw. "It's definitely bigger. Probably Hodgkin's. Oh, Christ!" He gawked at his reflection, misshapen, in the toaster. "It's huge!"

He flopped into a chair and fluttered his eyebrows Groucho Marx style. "Speaking of tumescence, *boychik,* how was the girl reporter last night?"

Seth looked up. "What do you mean, 'how' was she?"

"I mean sex-u-al-ly."

"You're disgusting. Is that all you can think about, even before brushing your teeth?"

"What does brushing my teeth have to do with it? That's all that matters between a man and a woman. Pasteur was right, boychik: 'Chance rewards only the prepared phallus.' "

Seth buried his head in the newspaper again.

"Another missed opportunity!" Harvey shuffled into the tiny kitchen. "Alas, the gods of love shall weep for you."

"I spent about an hour with the cops last night," Seth said without looking up, "if that's any consolation to the gods of love."

"Oh, yeah? What'd they want?" Harvey asked, tilting his head and again exploring the angle of his jaw.

As Seth described the details of his visit to the First Homicide zone, Harvey began to fidget. He dropped half the newspaper, picked it up, folded it and refolded it several times, burned himself with the coffee, and finally at the news of Fontana's proposal to Seth the explosion came.

"Do you mean to tell me that this glandular half-wit from Queens, whose arches probably function at a higher level than his Neanderthal brain, asked you to help him on this case? And you agreed?"

"Well, I didn't exactly agree. I said that if I came across anything, I'd let him know."

"Boychik, you don't have time to get involved in bullshit like this. You're up to your ass in work as it is. When are you going to do any reading? It would be nice"—he smiled sadly—"if you could keep a step or two ahead of your patients."

"I'm touched by your concern for my professional development." Seth stood up, glaring at Harvey across the table. "However, I do recall getting through medical school with some distinction and even managing to cure a few patients without your help. You know damn well that the time I take to play tennis or detective—or anything else I damn please—has nothing to do with how I take care of my patients."

"Wrong as usual, wrong, wrong, wrong! It has everything to do with your patients," Harvey bellowed at Seth's retreating back. "It's a little odd that just when you're about to start your first psychotherapy cases, you start distracting yourself with all this chicken shit. I think, Seth, baby"—he was shouting now as Seth banged around the living room, collecting books and papers—"you're a little scared of the prospect. Sitting in a room with a half-crazy patient, one to one, isn't as easy as you thought it would be, especially when the patient expects you to do something."

Seth whirled on Harvey. "When I want your pathetic formulations of my unconscious, I'll ask. Until then save them for your patients—poor bastards." He strode toward his room.

As Seth rummaged noisily through his closet for a tie, Harvey appeared in the doorway to his room. "Seth, Seth, boychik. What are we fighting about? I'm sorry I said what I did."

"I'm sorry you said what you did, too. Move," he said, brushing past Harvey. "I'm late for rounds."

Harvey pounded after him. "There must be some way of explaining this schmucky idea. For Seth Conrad, summa cum laude, M.D., round-the-worldnik with honors, to have gotten himself into this grotesque charade with a bunch of dull-normals who barely graduated from the Boy Scouts is unbelievable." Seth, busy checking the pockets of his white coat, was impervious to the tirade. "Do you realize that you'd be spying on your friends and colleagues?"

"Do you realize that maybe some of my friends and colleagues need spying on? That girl didn't die of dandruff, Harvey. Her head was bashed in. You can't talk that one away, old buddy. You can't joke it away or laugh it away." He jabbed his finger at Harvey. "Somebody *did* it. Can you swear that it wasn't one of my friends or colleagues?" He slammed the door to the apartment.

□ □ □

The newspaper was still in his lap as sounds from the gymnasium drifted through the open door and stirred him out of his reverie. He'd thought all day about what Harvey had said. It had rankled that he couldn't explain what he'd done. He saw again the forlorn kid brother, the desolation of that yellow capsule in the palm of his hand, the weight-lifting detective bravely groping for words, and her last lonely, half-blind agony. How did you explain the sad residue of her life spread out on Fontana's battered desk?

He threw the paper to the floor as though to rid himself of the whole matter, of her, the bone splinters and lacerations of Jennifer Light's life—and Harvey's stinging reproaches.

But what if he was being naive, stupid? What if that prick was right after all?

The sounds from the gymnasium down the hall increased.

"Third!"

"Uh!"

"Disengage!"

"Uh!"

There were shouts, grunts, and the sound of metal clashing on metal. They drew him to the open doorway and, like a magnet, down the hall.

"Beat!"

"Eighth!"

"Uh!"

"Too low!"

Seth hesitated a moment before the gymnasium door. Then furtively, quietly, like a thief, he pushed open the heavy door.


It was the bare feet, the powerful bare brown feet he noticed first. Like the roots of sturdy young trees, they clutched at the smooth gymnasium floor.

Dramatic, even outlandish, as it was, there was something in the scene he recognized, like an old dream suddenly remembered.

As he stood in the doorway of the huge, dimly lit gymnasium, it seemed to Seth that he had stepped from the gloomy world of schizophrenia and chronic alcoholism backward into his boyhood.

Mark Jones was barefoot, his tall, powerful figure clothed in a white Oriental pajama suit tied at the waist with a black belt. The karate uniform was out of keeping with the fencer's mask he wore and with the powerful saber thrusts he was making.

Slowly, almost reluctantly, Seth pushed the glasses back on his nose, as though unwilling to suspend the disbelief in what he was seeing. Vivid scenes suddenly flashed into consciousness, of combat and square-jawed heroes, of long winter Saturdays when Elly was still reading to him. The books were old with vast deserts of words to cross before they came to an oasis of color and movement. There he would linger like a thirsty child, taking in every detail of the picture. Bent over so that his new glasses almost touched the page, he studied the swords, the dress, the heroic postures, the powerful limbs until they were safely hung in the museum of his memory.

"Good . . . Marcus. Very . . . good." Whit Shields, square-jawed and princely, was beautiful in his classical fencing uniform—mask, padded tunic closed at the neck, and white knee breeches.

"Keep the . . . point up." He stood with his left hand on his hip, and holding the saber lightly and with grace, he parried Mark's thrusts and feints. Entranced, almost magnetically, Seth moved toward them. "Conrad, hello. Hold it! Marcus, hold it!" He gasped in pain as the point of Mark's blade tore through the shoulder of his tunic.

"Damn you."

Even as he was touched, he twisted away and with a lightning dance of parries and ripostes tore the weapon out of Mark's grasp and sent it rattling across the gymnasium floor. Now both men ripped off their masks as Seth rushed between them, increasing the tangle of tension and dissonance. Whit was pale and tight-lipped.

"Jesus, man, you okay?" Mark asked. "I didn't see what happened. You okay, Whit?"

"Christ . . ." Whit muttered through clenched teeth, and jammed the point of his saber with all his might into the hardwood floor; it didn't hold and clattered to rest in front of him. He grabbed at his left shoulder.

"Let me take a look!" Seth ordered.

Whit was silent, his right hand trembling as Seth unbuttoned his tunic and examined the underlying area.

Mark's usual quiet reserve had vanished. "You okay? You didn't parry. What happened?" Great beads of sweat appeared on his face.

"Take it easy, Marcus," Whit said with a grim smile. "What's a little mutilation between friends?"

"It's okay," Seth muttered. "Broke the skin, but just barely. Laceration, superficial . . . about two inches." He poked his finger through the padded jacket where the saber point had made a gash. Then he picked up the saber lying at Whit's feet, hefted it, looked at its point, and felt its edge. He looked at Whit, who had regained some of his color now. "You're a very lucky hero. A bit of a schmuck, if you ask me, but lucky."

Mark, still looking worried, was mopping his face.

"What are you two maniacs doing in those ridiculous clothes?" Seth shook his head. "For Christ's sake, how fucking reckless can you be? What is this charade?"

"Transcultural exchange, right, Marcus?" Whit said without looking at Mark. "Marcus and I"—he reached for the weapon Seth was holding—"trade martial arts." He sliced the air with it and smiled. "It's an heirloom. Belonged to the Robber Baron himself." He blinked. "Won it in a poker game at the Negresco." He caressed the pommel of the sword. "From a Hungarian captain. Right, Marcus?" he touched the black man's shoulder with the blade as though conferring knighthood. "And Marcus, here"—he let the point of the saber travel slowly down the front of Mark's body until it rested on his black belt—"knows a little about tae kwon do." Then, with a flick of the sword, the belt fell to the floor. "The art of unswerving aggression, isn't that so, Marcus?" he asked, turning away without waiting for a response.

"In fact, old man, I owe you an apology," he said to Seth, glancing at his watch. "Five o'clock, wasn't it? I'm sorry. I let the time get completely away." He looked about him and began collecting the odds and ends of equipment.

Mark picked up his black belt and saber and with no explanation handed the sword over to Seth with a shrug like a contrite child.

"Jesus, Whit!" Seth muttered, and touched the naked tip.

"Tiresome, old man, very tiresome." Whit smiled one of his Golden Boy smiles. "I'm about to reveal an ecumenical truth, a transcultural insight, and you want to read me the *Boy Scout Handbook.*"

"How about a couple of point guards?"

Whit shrugged. "Point guards then. I have some around somewhere. I didn't realize," he said, turning to Mark, "you're only a half-trial learner, Marcus."

"What's that supposed to mean?" Mark asked, glowering.

Walking between the two muscular athletes, Seth was aware of his own fragility. Even though he tried to cultivate a careless cynicism toward what Harvey sourly called "body-phallus hobbies for small-brained people," it always came up tangled, subverted by his secret admiration for physical courage and mastery. He pushed his spectacles up on his nose with the monograph he was carrying.

"It's supposed to mean, you black brute, that you're a fast learner and therefore a dangerous man with one of these." He waggled the heirloom saber.

Mark grinned. "Dangerous? More of that bullshit philosophy. Man, you don't know what dangerous is until you been where I been. There's guys who'd blow you away easy as look at you. Is that your economical truth?" he added scornfully.

"No, my economical truth, as you so charmingly put it, Marcus, is that what makes you dangerous as a karateka is your morality." He stopped and faced Mark as he massaged his bruised shoulder.

"The way you fight, the Taoist way, emphasizes virtue rather than force and defense rather than attack. I think that's what you said, wasn't it? Don't let me put any words in your mouth, Marcus."

"I guess so. Come on, Whit, what are you messin' around for?" Mark looked down at the black belt he was holding and began to busy himself retying it around his waist.

"Just trying to get it straight, Marcus, just trying to get it straight. You said—didn't you?—that a master karateka would try to disable an attacker without killing him but the attacker might die by impinging himself against the master's defense—in effect, killing himself."

His belt now in place, Mark looked up, thoughtful. "Buddha

said, 'Whoever deserves punishment must be punished.' You bring
it down on yourself. It ain't the judge or the executioner."

"Now you can see why a karate blow is so deadly, Seth," Whit
said. Mark's powerful shoulders were clearly outlined now by the
drenched white suit that clung to him. He mopped his face once
more with his sleeve. "Every blow is struck in the service of moral
perfection. When a master karateka hits you, his Ch'i is concentrated,
his heart sings, and his spirit soars. It's deadly because it's unam-
bivalent. Right, Marcus?"

"If you say so, Whit." Mark tried to smile.

Suddenly, then, as though he had overstepped some invisible
boundary, Whit turned and strode away. "Come on, Seth, old man,
don't dawdle. Ever do any fencing?"

Seth, shoulders hunched, adjusted his spectacles and acknowledged
halfheartedly that he had tried it during his freshman year without
much success.

"Pity. You've got the reach for it."

"I don't have the heart for it," Seth called after him as Whit
headed across the gym to stow the sabers and masks.

The humidity, gloom, and smell of stale sweat mixed and melded
and became a shadowy ocean through which he and Mark floated
silently until they reached the battered old desk at the gymnasium
entrance. Mark opened the file drawer and pulled out a towel and
an imposing ring of keys. He pushed one of them into the switch
mechanism that operated the lights of the gymnasium and let it
hang there as he mopped his head and neck.

"Hey, man, make sure that door's locked," Mark called out.
Whit, standing in front of the open equipment closet, was fussily
inserting the sabers into a dirty canvas bag. "Shit, half the time
they leave it open. Aides come in and steal stuff. Especially around
Christmastime," he added, indignation creeping into his voice.
"Christmas spirit, I guess." He grinned, then jerked the desk drawer
open and folded his towel into it.

"It's funny. You know, Doc, all my life, since I was a kid, I
wanted a desk. Now I've got a desk, and look what I keep in it—
dirty socks and a jock." He held them up as though Seth didn't
believe him. He paused and looked thoughtfully at Seth, smiling. "I

guess that's the way it is when you get your wish." He slammed
the drawer shut, sat down on the desktop, and looked around with
a mixture of pride and chagrin. "I never wished for this, but I guess
it's the place I know best now. Every inch of this place, every piece
of equipment, every loose screw, every squeaky floorboard." He
jiggled his key in the light switch. "Hey, man, your buddy Bloch
was really flyin' today. He was really wild. Maybe it's because of
that girl." He jiggled the key switch again. "Hey, Whit, move it.
I want to lock this place up."

Suddenly the windowless gymnasium became totally dark and
silent. Only a crepuscular slab of light squeezed under the door from
the hallway beyond.

"Marcus! Behave yourself or I'll have your keys removed." Whit's
voice rang through the void. No response. A moment later the door
to the equipment closet slammed shut, and they heard footsteps
squeaking toward them across the gymnasium floor. The light snapped
back on; Mark smiled impishly.

"Anytime you want to use the equipment, Doc, lemme know, and
I'll open the place up for you." Mark jangled his keys with authority.
"'We got good weights. Put a couple of inches on your chest and
shoulders. You could use it, Doc."

Seth dug his hands deeper into his pockets and squinted through
his spectacles at the polished floor tiles. In the dim light he thought
he saw a cockroach and made a halfhearted attempt to crush it as
it scuttled back into the shadows.

"Jonesie, this girl, the dead girl. You were talking about her
and Harvey. . . ."

Lounging in Whit's doorway, Mark tossed his keys rhythmically.
"Oh, yeah, the kid. They were always together last year."
He stopped tossing and looked thoughtful. "This year, too, I think.
He was always leaning over her, whispering." He leaned forward
in a hulking way and threw an arm over an invisible Jennifer
Light. "And she was always laughing. He's really crazy. He's manic,
ain't he?"

"I wouldn't say that," Seth lied.

"Well, he was sure all messed up with her last year. Then something happened—before the summer, I guess. She must've dumped him." He shrugged. "I don't know."

"How do you know he didn't dump *her,* Jonesie?" Seth asked with unnecessary sharpness.

A puzzled look spread across the young black man's face. He shrugged again. "Dunno, maybe he did. She probably wasn't so hot anyway." He began tossing his keys again. Now they heard the sound of Whit's baritone. German. Wagner, Seth thought.

"You know, Doc, my name ain't Jonesie," Mark said quietly. "That's what the kids call me. They don't know no better. You know what I mean?"

Seth felt a rush of blood to his ears. Since adolescence he had lived in quiet fear that someone might notice this weakness. He reset his glasses and without thinking groomed the hair around the earpieces.

"I thought everybody called you that."

"No, just the kids."

"Nothing personal," Seth said fatuously. "How long?" He nodded with a forced smile at the black belt around Mark's waist. "I mean, this tae kon . . ."

"Kwon do. Tae kwon do. It means the study of kicks and punches." Mark made a fist for emphasis and then let it relax as though he had said too much.

"Seth, do you know what the name Parsifal means?" Whit Shields slid into view, hair still dripping, his tanned, solid figure covered only by a towel around his waist. He fixed a cigarette in his ivory holder, lit it, and inhaled deeply.

"Doesn't everybody?" Seth slipped into the room and eased onto the edge of the desk nearest the door.

"I better check the ward before I leave," Mark said quietly from the corridor and turned to go.

"Marcus! Catch!" Mark plucked the key out of the air like an infielder. "I'll have my chattels out of here by tonight. It's all yours for the rest of the year, Marcus. I'll leave a few odds and ends around just in case anyone asks."

"Right on, man." Reinflated, Mark grinned and raised his hand with the key in it in a comradely salute. "See you cats around."

Whit had slipped onto the bed and was leaning comfortably against the headboard, staring at Seth through half-closed eyes and a veil of tobacco smoke.

"A little touchy, isn't he?" Seth asked.

"Marcus? No more than any authentic genius."

Whit's gaze slid away as he flicked the ashes from his cigarette into a pewter ashtray standing on his bedside table.

"Yeah?" Seth uncoiled into the armchair and prepared himself for a dose of perverse charm.

"He has more class in the wriggle of one of his toes than— forgive me, Seth, I say this only to make the point graphically"— he inhaled—"your entire body, prosthetic devices included."

"Leave my prosthetic devices out of this." Seth took off his glasses and, squinting at Whit, breathed on the lenses.

"Except for the accident of being born poor and the bad luck that goes with it, he'd be a world-class athlete today."

Seth finished smudging his glasses and replaced them. "You don't think this tae kon—whatever you call it—is a little stupid?" Trying not to be disdainful, he succeeded in being only irritable.

"Wouldn't you like to possess the secret of killing birds on the wing with a shout or be able to penetrate an adversary's body with your bare hand and withdraw his still-beating heart? He's an original." Whit smiled cynically. "A romantic, a teller of tales. And according to Paul Silk, at least half of them are true."

Whit slid off the bed and padded toward the bathroom. "Besides, I like him because he's deprived, like me. You'd be surprised how similar the burdens of wealth and poverty are." Seth heard the clinking of glasses from the other room. "Fino?"

"Huh?"

"Some dry sherry?"

"Oh, fine, sure," he called. "I thought you'd never ask."

Whit emerged with two short-stemmed glasses, holding them at the base. Seth took the glass the "wrong" way, by its stem, and raised it in a hybrid gesture of defiance and salutation.

"Looks are deceiving, old man," Whit said as he reensconced himself on the bed.

"Clichés are boring, Golden Boy."

Like some charmed being, Whit seemed totally impervious to sarcasm. "Innocence personified. Why is Coles gunning for you? You've been either very naughty or very foolish. I suspect the latter."

Whit paused and looked at Seth thoughtfully over the rim of his sherry glass. "He's been hunting you all day, old man."

"Shit! Mrs. Scola!" He sat up. "She doesn't have involutional melancholia any more than I do."

"Seth . . ."

"Christ, I *know* what's wrong with her." He was up now and pacing back and forth. "Coles is an asshole. All he knows is frying people's brains." He punched his glasses up on his nose. "All I need is a couple of days. Just a few more days, and I'll be able to stick it to him." He jabbed the air.

"Seth, it's not Mrs. Scola. It's Coles. He has some . . . thing about you, some preoccupation." He held his glass up to the light. "Seth, I know you and Bloch think he's an incompetent, and maybe he is, but . . ." He looked down at the track of red across his shoulder where the saber had scratched him and touched himself tenderly along its path. "God, I feel like old Amfortas. . . ." He looked up. "Well, you know what I mean. He's no fool, whatever your friend Bloch may tell you. Look here, it's not my place to interfere. . . ." He smiled and blinked his owlish blink as though he had gone too far.

Seth flopped back into his chair. "Listen," he said wearily, "I've been slandered and lectured all day, why should I draw the line at you? What's *your* sermon?"

"Naiveté. I don't know why he has it in for you, but he does. And he's vindictive. That comes straight from Milly McVey, and she should know; she's worked with him long enough. Tact. Go easy with him. He doesn't like heroes." He leaned over his bedside table and touched a lever as though to make a point. Instantly the strains of *Parsifal* floated across the room. Whit sipped his sherry and seemed to relax. "It means 'guileless fool,' " he said almost to himself. He stared vacantly out of the window at the sky of late summer.

"What does?"

Whit nodded toward the source of the music, a speaker on the bookshelf. "Parsifal. A pathological innocent and," he added dryly, "undoubtedly the least interesting character in the opera."

He listened for a few moments, only his fingers betraying his familiarity with the theme. "Know it?" Without waiting for a response, he extinguished the music with a finger as though it were an offensive insect. He stood up suddenly and walked toward the bathroom.

"Another sherry?" he called from inside.

He reappeared in a pair of pale blue boxer shorts with the sherry bottle in his hand. "Don't you find Bloch a little tiresome?"

"Yes, please."

"I thought so. He's like some kind of primeval force, isn't he?"

"No. I meant the sherry."

"Oh." He filled the glass Seth proffered, now held the "right way," at the base.

"Thanks. Whit, I'd like—"

"There's so much of him. Like Niagara Falls. How do you turn him off?"

"Well, you know, the divorce . . ." He found himself making the same dreary excuses, which even to him sounded suddenly mechanical and meaningless.

Whit reached for his slender gold lighter and, for a moment, studied his initials on its face. Then, looking up at the ceiling as though for divine guidance, he recited in sepulchral tones:

> The Jews, a headstrong, moody, murmuring race . . . ,
> God's pampered people, whom, debauched with ease,
> No king could govern nor no God could please.

He inhaled deeply and glanced at Seth, the lighter flame dancing in his eyes. With a blink he extinguished the lighter, exhaled, and

smiled. "Don't look so scandalized, old man." He shrugged innocently. "Dryden." He stretched his sun-bronzed body and flicked his
ashes into the pewter ashtray. "Besides, he really meant the English."

In the past Seth had been able, had wanted, to discount the
unpleasant rumors about Whit that began to trickle in after his
bravura arrival. They didn't amount to much, considering their
source. They seemed extravagant and, Seth thought, mischievous,
attempts to expose unknown areas of Whit's personal life and intrude
on his code of privacy.

Late one night in the PAO Lisa Stone had appeared in the
doorway of Seth's tiny office and leaned languidly against the open
door. She wore her stethoscope with an asymmetrical wantonness
so that both of its arms embraced her left breast under the pale
blue silk blouse she was wearing.

"How's it going?" Seth drawled. He put down the monograph
on twin studies he had borrowed from Whit.

*"Quel ennui. Pourquoi nous forcent-ils à passer la nuit ici?"*
She tapped furtively with her toe at the wooden wedge that held
the door open.

"If not us, who? If not this, what?"

*"Tu es un sage,* Seth."

"This is a citadel, an outpost—" The wedge came loose, and
the heavy door swung shut as Lisa eased her way around it and
slipped over to the desk. She sat down on top of it, undid her
stethoscope, and pointed her voluptuous body at Seth. It commanded
him to surrender.

He pushed his spectacles back up on his nose. "—of civilization
in a world gone mad. And we are its sentinels. . . ."

*"Très profond."*

"We must interpose our bodies, Lisa. . . ."

*"Ton corps,* Seth." She leaned toward him. "I don't do things
like that with my body. *Ôte tes lunettes, cher."* He was suddenly
aware of the bouquet of her scent and felt like a victim of nerve
gas.

"Jesus, Lisa, didn't you take the Hippocratic oath?"

She leaned closer and whispered. *"Non. J'ai seulement remué
les levres."* Her tongue flicked into his ear.

"Lisa! For Christ's sake. We're on duty!"

"Seth"—she sat upright and swung off the desk—"you disappoint me. I thought there was a light under that bushel. I see I was mistaken." She snatched at the monograph he'd been reading. "What's so interesting?" She glanced at the title page—"Whitney Shields the Third!"—and threw it back, catching him off guard. She wrapped her stethoscope around her neck again and brushed some invisible lint from her skirt.

"Oh, by the way, remember that little tropical storm Whit told us about when he came?" She didn't wait for an answer. "Well, it didn't happen on the high seas. It happened while he was safe and snug in Bethesda."

"Meaning?"

"Meaning, the big storm was that he was fired from NIMH!"

"What are you talking about? Whit?"

"Whit! He was asked to resign by the head of Mental Health."

"Bullshit! Whit could buy NIMH!"

"No, he couldn't. My daddy tried. It's not for sale. Very heavy weather there in Bethesda. *C'est une sale histoire.*"

"How do you know?"

Lisa leaned over the desk and put her finger on Seth's forehead. "The news escaped from Mental Health, drifted down the road past Neuromuscular Diseases." She etched a path with her finger down his neck and shoulder. "It turned the corner at Gastroenterology"— she tickled his abdomen—"and arrived at the Heart Institute." She jabbed him in the chest. "Where my ex-husband listens to fibrillating hearts all day and begs me to remarry him all night."

"What was the scandal?"

She turned briskly, stepped to the door, and flung it open. *"Désolée, cher, peut-être une autre fois. Le devoir. Tu comprends."*

The follow-up came a week or two later and was clearly so preposterous that Seth had no difficulty in discounting the rumor and discrediting the source.

"Defenestration?"

"Defenestration!" Harvey belched and blotted his lips daintily. "You want me to spell it?"

"I know what it means." Seth scowled. "I just can't understand why you're broadcasting this vicious crap."

"What's vicious about the truth, and what are you getting so excited about?" He took another sip of Chianti. "Someone fell, was pushed, or jumped out of a window owned by him—Golden Boy. 'Window' plus 'person' plus 'out of' equals defenestration."

"Where do you dig up this shit?"

"What difference does it make? The question is only, Seth, mine boy, *ja oder nein*." He was waxing more and more expansive with each sip of wine.

"Lisa! You got it from Lisa, *n'est-ce pas*? Bitch," he muttered. He sank back into a corner of the red plastic booth and eyed Harvey clinically. "Why do you dislike him so much?"

"Dislike him? Me? Dislike him?" He batted his eyelids. "Whatever gave you that idea?" He leaned toward Seth. "You want to hear savoir faire, boychik? You know what he said when I confronted him with this?" He leaned toward Seth conspiratorially. "Tactfully, of course. You know how tactful I can be. He blinked me one of his innocent, owlish blinks, gave me one of his buttery smiles, and said, 'Harvey, old man, even if the story were true, I wouldn't for a moment think of burdening you with my personal affairs.' How do you like that for WASP cool?" Harvey sat back in triumph and finished his wine. "Dislike him? Why should I dislike him? Merely because he's a pathological liar, a congenital hypocrite, a quintessential phony, a certified prick, and a registered Republican? For this I should dislike him?"

Now Seth studied the pale golden sherry as Whit's sly derision slid into the late-afternoon silence.

"What do you think of it?" Whit teased.

"Good color. Little young, though, isn't it?"

"He's really quite clever. Today he accused me of being a sangfroidian." He inhaled and blew the smoke gently upward. "He's good, entertaining, I mean. But then that's his trouble, isn't it? He's like a great pasta machine gone wild. Something always tumbling out of his mouth." He squinted through the thin blue haze at the ceiling. "He was going on this afternoon in his usual perfervid way about you. No stopping him." He smiled thinly. "It seems that you had taken leave not only of your senses but of his; that you had given up the life of the mind for the life of the fallen arch"—he turned away to flick his ashes—"and finally, that you were still— let's see now, what was it? I don't want to do him an injustice"— he knitted his brow in feigned concentration—"oh, yes, completely in the grip of your infantile phallic exhibitionism and therefore hopelessly in the thrall of muscle-bound policemen, but that he would pray to the god of reality testing for your early release and salvation." He turned to Seth with raised eyebrows and blinked.

Seth heaved himself wearily out of his chair. "Just another tempest in the teapot of Harvey's mind." He ambled over to the table, examining, absentmindedly, the contents of a journal. "Christ, you know he's brilliant half the time and crazy the other half. The problem is knowing which is which. Besides," he snapped, turning back to Whit, "what was I supposed to do, just tell this giant cop to fuck off?" He drained his glass. "This stuff isn't bad once you get used to it." He raised the glass. "May I?"

Whit gestured generously in the direction of the bathroom. "Help yourself. It's in the fridge."

"Golden Boy," Seth called out to the next room, "I have a favor to ask." In response he heard only the solemn strains of *Parsifal* again. "I have a friend . . . a reporter who's covering this story  . . you know . . . the murder."

Whit was reclining, staring at the ceiling as though his thoughts had been set adrift by the music.

"I promised I'd help her. You know, in whatever way I could, I mean." He shrugged apologetically, oblivious of Whit's detached state. "Since you knew this girl, would you mind, even if it's not much, would you talk to her? A few minutes, maybe . . ."

For several moments there was only the sound of the music. "There's not much I remember," he said absentmindedly to the ceiling. "It was all over so quickly." He touched his shoulder, then, as though recalling a distant pain.

Suddenly sitting up, he flashed one of his famous smiles. "Of

course, old man. Tomorrow. Why don't you and your friend come?
See the new apartment. It's quite decent. Come for dinner."

"Good view?"

"Yes," Whit said, surprised, "how did you know?"


*He*'d made another mistake. He knew that by the time the elevator
doors had closed again. Christ! But it was too late. Jonathan Graver
had appeared without warning—larger than life, like some icy god
or bad conscience—when the car stopped on six.

Alone, as the elevator droned pleasantly, almost hypnotically
downward, Seth had been smiling to himself, thinking about Whit's
dinner invitation.

When the elevator doors opened unexpectedly, they stood facing
each other: Seth, smiling foolishly at nothing; Graver, tall, impassive,
his hands thrust deeply into his laboratory coat. For a silent moment
or two Graver's cool gray eyes flickered with unforgiving recognition;
then, instead of boarding the car, he turned away.

The doors slammed shut—too quickly, it seemed to Seth—
heightening his momentary confusion. Christ! Why hadn't he at least
nodded to Graver? He felt his ears redden and without warning a
vision of his nightmare came tumbling back into consciousness as
though a locked door had burst open: the careening sailboat; the
contemptuous laugh, fragmented, splintered, already disconnected
from his life, from any sense. Now a new, absurd image flashed
onto the screen of his mind. Shoes. A pair of meaningless shoes.
Part of the dream? Suddenly he wasn't sure. Was this reality?
Something he'd seen? A memory? Where? He remembered, then,
the dying prisoner he'd seen on the night of the murder. Those
feet—filthy and cyanotic.

He had been called to the prison ward in the general hospital
shortly after he came on duty that night. When he had been passed
through the heavy steel doors by the sweating, garlic-ridden policeman
on duty, he was told that a prisoner sent over from the Tombs
that afternoon had become increasingly disturbed and disoriented and
finally had lapsed into a coma. By the time Seth arrived, the medical
resident and the nurses were busily at work on the prisoner. He

lay there inert, nude except for a sheet which covered his corpulent body from his knees to his abdomen. He was pale; his feet, in a comic Charlie Chaplin-like attitude, were blue; his breathing was labored, and his face flabby and grizzled, with dark, beetled brows. They worked on him for forty minutes before Seth was called back to the PAO.

And now he stared over the rims of his glasses past the elevator door, trying to focus on the new fragment, trying to fix it before it disappeared into darkness, like an untreated photograph. A senseless pair of feet, shod in a senseless pair of shoes, Charlie Chaplin-like, grotesquely comic like the prisoner of the night before.

He wondered whether the prisoner had lived out the night.

They were staring at him, the three aides in blue uniforms, smiling, waiting for him to step off the elevator. He looked at his watch briskly, officiously, and brushed past them in a hurry, pretending that he had just remembered some important business in the PAO.

As he bulldozed through the door to the PAO, he came face-to-face with Fontana, almost knocking him over.

"Doc! You got my message."

"What message?"

"Doesn't matter. Got a minute?"

"Oh, Christ," Seth groaned. "Not now, Fontana. I'm closed for the day."

It was six-fifteen, and he was due at Lindsay's at seven-thirty. But Fontana, like a giant bulldog, refused to let go. He tugged at Seth and insisted on walking with him to the hospital lobby.

"Okay, Fontana . . ."

"Vince."

"Okay, Vince," Seth said with a dramatic sigh. "What is it?"

"Jesus, it's nice and cool here." They had reached the deserted lobby, and its dingy marble walls afforded a small measure of relief from the heat. "We can't seem to get a line on this Light girl. Nobody knows where she's been living for the past month." His gum chewing slowed, and he looked sharply at Seth. "Graver claims he didn't know she'd moved. Her parents don't know. The other people in Graver's lab say she was, you know, a loner. They think she was living with someone around the hospital somewhere." He paused and fished around inside his trousers pocket. "Any ideas? Coke?" He didn't wait for Seth to answer but slammed a couple of coins into the red Coke machine. He stared at the foaming liquid being disgorged into the paper cup. "The ME says she wasn't raped, but she was . . . sexually active within twelve hours before she died. So she must have had *some* friends. You know what I mean? Who were they, Doc? Who knew her?"

Seth pushed his glasses back up and lied with a shrug. He thought of Silk, Whit, and Harvey. All of them knew her.

"Coke, Doc?" The muscular detective pushed the cup at him. "No, thanks."

"You docs are pretty tight. Like a bunch of Sicilians." He set his drink down on a nearby counter and removed his gum.

"You know, out there on the street it's different. Everyone's scoring. You know what I mean? Got scores to settle. So they *wanna* talk. . . ." Pausing, he glanced at Seth, then placed the gum delicately in the wrapper he had saved for this purpose.

"Gum and Coke don't go—like Chianti and peanut butter." He grinned as though he'd been clever.

Seth stared at the moisture forming on the outside of Fontana's cup.

Fontana took a gulp and said with a shrug that it didn't much matter anyway. He put his drink down again and cracked his knuckles. As far as he was concerned, he told Seth, he was still betting that whoever did it was an outsider—some creep, an addict, because in the dozen years he'd been in the department, he'd never seen a smart homicide.

"If it's homicide, it ain't smart, and if it's smart, it ain't homicide, it's fraud, embezzling, you know—white-collar stuff."


As he moved slowly through the heavy air of late afternoon, Seth thought about Fontana. There was a foxiness about him that was irritating. Did he really believe that Jennifer Light's life had ended as stupidly as that? As though she'd been hit by a flowerpot falling from an anonymous windowsill? Too bad, that's the way it goes.

Business as usual. Probabilities. Put ten million people together in a city, and like molecules in a test tube, a couple of them will come together with a bang every now and then. Thermodynamics, statistics, part of the implacable and remorseless design of nature. Sometimes a skel has your number, and you end up with a crushed head in a dirty basement looking surprised.

But to Seth it didn't seem so. There was something unique about Jennifer Light. He saw the symbols of her life spread out again on Fontana's battered desk. She wasn't just another particle bumping around randomly in the laboratory of life. She was unusual, mysterious, unnaturally beautiful. When she died, she wasn't just a victim of the rush-hour traffic. She had been haunting the subterranean tunnels of Bellevue Hospital in the small hours of the morning with . . .

He felt his scalp tingle, and he shuddered. It came over him with an uncanny certainty that Jennifer Light had been with someone in the staff cafeteria that night. Those shoes. Those senseless shoes in his dream. He'd glimpsed them there in the cafeteria that midnight. He strained to remember them, but the door to his subliminal experience had slipped shut again and left him only with the phantom knowledge of a pair of disembodied, evanescent feet.

He knew it wasn't just a matter of probability, thermodynamics, accidents, and outsiders, as Fontana thought, but of people interacting—people who knew one another, people who had reasons for being together that night, people who had reasons for doing what they did. Oddly enough, he felt comforted by the idea that Jennifer Light had not died at the hands of some faceless stranger just for the sake of a few dollars.

## Part Two

# FREE ASSOCIATIONS

# Chapter

# 5

Lindsay Cooper lived on the north side of West Eighty-first Street, in an airy apartment overlooking the sedate old buildings of the Museum of Natural History. One of the city's decorous bastions of civilization, the museum was surrounded by a dilapidated park where every night quietly desperate men searched for their unremembered past in the seductive glances of passing boys.

Lindsay told Seth she often visited the museum just before closing time. At that hour she found it quiet, almost deserted, cool, and unexpectedly calming. Somehow, she told him, the musty exhibits, smelling as though each had been there for generations, comforted her. The paradox and promise of taxidermic-life-everlasting charmed her. And the constant reminders of the vastness of time and space made her think about transience and death in her own life.

Standing at the window, Seth looked down over the low, scattered buildings of the museum. South, beyond them, he could see the exciting vertical masses, dark now, of midtown office buildings. Lights were beginning to appear in the windows as maintenance crews worked their nightly way from top to bottom. The MONY sign blinked its pulselike message of temperature and time: 85 . . . 10:42 . . .

Suddenly he called out querulously, "Graver? Attractive?"

"I said *darkly* attractive." Lindsay was clearing the table in the dining alcove. "There's a difference. Coffee soon. At least that's the way he came across." She disappeared into the kitchen.

"He's the most hated man in the department," he called out. "At least by me," he added as he sprawled onto a beige rough-textured couch. At dinner Seth had retold the mythology of the department as he'd begun to piece it together for himself: the long-hoped-for death of the "old man," dictator-chairman for twenty-three years; the shock when it came; the scramble for power between Lemmon and Ettinger; the long-standing hatred and shadowy feuding between Graver and Silk.

Now he stretched his legs and looked around the softly lighted room. He noted with approval the wall opposite, with four or five shelves packed with books. Very well organized. Maybe a little too well organized. He wondered whether they were grouped by platoon or battalion. There were several posters announcing recent museum exhibits, one from the Bargello showing a Della Robbia angel—mother's influence, for sure. Another from the British Museum, announcing an exhibition of Mycenean armor, pictured a fierce but gorgeous headpiece wrought of gold. It figured, he thought. The old man—that would please him.

Though the room seemed uncluttered, it contained many carefully chosen things: a silver teapot; a rolltop desk in one corner; an antique hobbyhorse in another—cavalry background? A charming wooden toy soldier—naturally—on an upright piano against the wall.

There was a sense of person in the place, a feeling of color and warmth. He contrasted it with the apartment he and Harvey shared, with its foam rubber and stale air, like a motor lodge on Interstate 66. The clatter of dishes roused him, and suddenly he wanted to be near her, the author of this room.

"What's the difference? 'Darkly attractive,' I mean?" Seth noted the systematic way in which Lindsay was scrubbing and stacking the dinner plates in the sink. Regulation, obviously.

She smiled. "Well, he's detached, arrogant—and those cold, piercing eyes."

"I knew it! It makes all the difference to have cold, piercing eyes."

PRIMAL · SCENE · 109

She looked at him quizzically, then added, "I suppose some women like that."

"Bastard!" He told her how Graver had hit Milly McVey the day of the murder.

Since then Graver had treated him with icy disregard at best and, during his seminar on psychopharmacology, with a sly, contemptuous teasing. Even poor, naive Fiona Drummond, whose ideas of human psychology came from reading about dogs and horses in the pages of *Country Life,* noticed. "Bit raggy, wasn't he? Seemed to like pricking your sides today."

"Maybe I was wrong about him," Lindsay said as she absently sponged a dinner plate. "If this woman—Milly what's her name— is his mistress . . ." Without looking up, she handed him a white porcelain soufflé dish. "Dry this, will you? What was it he said?"

He saluted her smartly. "Yes, sir!" he added with a smile and a knowing wink.

Lindsay half smiled, as though she were humoring a child.

"He certainly didn't put himself out." She handed him a dish towel. "Everything he said was evasion and generality. Worse than a politician."

She was barefoot and had tucked a towel carefully into the waistband of her skirt as an apron. The rolled sleeves of her button-down shirt gave her, Seth thought, a lovable, no-nonsense look.

"Up there." She pointed with her yellow sponge. Everything had its place in her world. Like a good soldier, he placed the soufflé dish on top of the refrigerator.

"Did you know the Light family and the Gravers used to be neighbors?" She asked without looking up. "And that Jennifer used to baby-sit for Graver?"

Seth lounged against the refrigerator, watching her brisk, efficient movements.

"In fact, she was their au pair girl for a whole summer when she was sixteen or seventeen. Families weren't really close, but close enough. You know, same tennis club. That's how she got the job with Graver."

Her hair, soft, lustrous, the color of honey, had fallen over her right eye as she rinsed the salad bowl. She pushed it into place with the back of her hand.

"He did say one thing, though, that was interesting."

"What was he?" Seth asked.

"A real bastard, I'd say. How many affairs can one man have—"

"His rank, I mean."

"His rank?" She looked surprised. "I don't know." She shrugged. "Professor, I suppose."

"Professor? Oh, you mean he taught at West Point. Like a professor-general. I see."

"West Point! What are you talking about? What does it have to do with West Point?"

"Your father, the professor-general."

"My father! Is this another one of your disgusting Freudian insinuations?"

"I thought you said your father was, you know, a professor-general at West Point. You're an army brat!" He saluted her smartly again and smiled approvingly. "I could tell right away. When I first saw you. Courageous, never-retreat, no-nonsense Cooper."

Lindsay had stopped rinsing. The water still running in the sink, she stared at him, mouth open, dripping hands at her sides.

"Top sergeants for nursemaids, right? Cut your first tooth on a shell casing. Mess halls. Battalion mascot. Bed to the sound of taps. I knew it. Everything about you says Army."

Suddenly there was silence. Seth, delighted with himself, stood there smiling. He snapped his dish towel at her just to break the silence.

Coming to life suddenly, she turned the tap off and began to fuss with the coffeemaker.

"That's amazing! Incredible! How were you able to figure all that out? It's like something out of Sherlock Holmes."

Seth, slouching again, arms folded across his chest, shrugged. "It is a little like that," he said, modestly. Then, warming to the idea, he went on. "It's all a matter of making careful observations of subtle details about people and then putting them together in a meaningful pattern. It's really quite simple, Watson, once you know how. Would you like me to teach you the method?"

"Would you?" Lindsay said over her shoulder as she reached for two coffee mugs.

"Sure. Might help in your work. You know, give it some depth?"

"Depth? You think?" She stood for a few moments looking at the linoleum, giving serious consideration to the invitation. "I'd be foolish to pass up an offer like that, wouldn't I? A girl doesn't get a chance like this every day."

"Well, it's not all that special. Really." Seth smiled graciously.

"Oh, you mean you do this with all the women you know. Make careful observations of our subtle details until it all comes together in a meaningful pattern."

"Oh, no. You're the first—"

"I'm flattered."

"I'm just beginning to learn the technique. It's amazing when you know how to use it. Burden is brilliant."

"Well, you're no slouch either. You got me to a T."

"Can I help with the coffee?"

"No. It'll be ready in a couple of minutes. Cream?"

"No, black, please."

"There are one or two minor points that you were slightly off on. But I don't think they're really worth mentioning." She opened a cupboard and brought out an attractive silver tray.

"No, tell me, please. Trial and error—that's how you learn, right?"

"Right. Right." Pause. "Sure?"

"Absolutely. I insist. To be perfectly honest, there are some points that I'm puzzled about also. Like where does the journalism fit in. Just some sugar, thanks."

"Well, to begin with, it wasn't the sound of taps that I went to sleep by. It was to the sound of braying."

"Ah, of course, army mules."

"No. Asses. The braying of asses and the bleating of sheep. Asses and sheep—of which there may be one or two too many in the world. But those were the creatures, harmless and friendly, on our farm outside Springfield, Illinois, where I grew up. The farm

has been in my father's family since the Lincoln-Douglas debates."
Pausing, she looked at him with interest, her head tilted, as though
she were judging a picture.

"I see," Seth said with knitted brows as though he'd been
listening to someone speaking another language.

"Oh, and the other tiny detail is that my father is a huge,
myopic, witty man who knows more about words and how to use
them than anyone I know. He is the editor and part owner of the
Springfield *Republican*—one of the few Democratic newspapers in
downstate Illinois—and has been for the past twenty-five years. He
has never been a general; he has never even been a private. The
Army wouldn't have him. They rejected him in the Second World
War because of his eyesight—to his everlasting chagrin. Not because
he loves war but because he loves experience. He's that kind of
man.

"The closest he's ever been to an army or a war is Act Four
of *Henry the Fifth*. Most of which he can quote to you by heart.
You'd laugh if you saw him, he's so unmilitary. He has a snow-
white beard. He's like a giant nearsighted Santa Claus who walks
around all day in carpet slippers and a checked flannel shirt at the
paper. Other than that, you were right on the mark."

Sweeping past him in quiet triumph, she placed the tray of coffee
things on the dinner table. Seth watched her dumbly as she poured
the boiling water through the conical filter.

"Now, Dr. Conrad, let's talk about you and this keen appreciation
of character you've developed." Her smile faded suddenly. "Are you
all right? What's wrong with your ears? They're all red."

Seth readjusted his glasses. "I guess I have weak ears, too."

"You're blushing!" She moved back to where she'd left him in
the tiny kitchen.

He shrugged. "I suppose I deserved that. Hubris."

She touched his cheek. "My father, the old general, says that
thank God most people don't get what they deserve. And just to
show you how right he is—" She reached up and kissed him on
the mouth. Not a serious kiss, he knew, but it lasted for an instant
longer than necessary. He caught her arms and held her. He felt
the softness of her breasts against him. He saw the pulse in her

neck again, an old friend, and kissed it. She twisted away and shoved a cheerful yellow potholder into his hand, "Pour!" she commanded, pointing to the unfinished coffee.

He gave her a sloppy salute with the potholder and carefully poured the simmering water over the coffee grounds. He watched the brown froth form on the surface and heard the trickle of coffee liquor as it poured out of the filter below. It took him back to the biochemistry laboratory. He'd been at home there. It was a predictable, controllable world. He liked the feel of the equipment. He liked fussing with the instruments. They were dependable old friends. He understood how they worked the way he understood how his own fingers worked. Suddenly he longed for the clarity and definition and certainty of the laboratory. When he had it, he'd misprized it, he remembered. Tame, he had thought then. Now, as he measured out another portion of steaming water, he thought of the pleasure of small surprises.

"Psychiatry. Why?"

"Who? Me?" Seth straightened up. Lindsay had been studying him for several minutes from the doorway. She nodded quietly. "You."

"Oh, I don't know. Challenging, I suppose. It's exciting. Every day is . . . chock-full of surprises." He smiled to himself. It was a question that had haunted him since the previous winter in Chicago, when he had told his father. It nagged at him around the edges of his consciousness like a bad tooth.

"Why?" his father had asked, too, with a look of civilized disappointment. Just what you'd expect from someone with an endowed chair. Restrained, accepting, like someone who'd just been told he had a fatal illness. It was Christmas Eve. He'd escaped from the surgical ward, finally, by late afternoon. His father was still in his white coat when Seth arrived at the lab.

It was quite dark, and a freezing rain was falling outside. The laboratory staff had had its Christmas party early in the afternoon, and everyone had drifted off to other parties at home.

The two bespectacled men, tall, slender, slightly stooped, talked quietly as they stood in a circle of light in one corner of the large, darkened laboratory.

It seemed to him, in retrospect, that he had given all the wrong answers to the question that night, the usual clichés that he'd heard and repeated so often that he didn't know, didn't want to know whether he believed them or not. It was more human and humane than other branches of medicine. People, not pancreas. Jesus, blood and urine values—they just weren't *intellectually* stimulating. The mind—that was where it all came together: biology, sociology, and the humanities. He leaned on a workbench and fidgeted with the knobs of an oscilloscope as he gave his sophomoric little lecture, occasionally glancing up at his father. When he finished, he continued to stare at the dead screen of the instrument. At that moment his father seemed to him a platonic ideal of himself, and what he'd just said sounded as dull and false as a cracked bell.

Nicholas Conrad stood leaning against the workbench, his arms folded, studying his youngest son in medical whites. His head was cocked in Seth's direction, and as Seth turned to face him, the light that glanced off his steel-rimmed glasses created the illusion of softness in his father's features.

"Well, Cal and Margot will be coming in on the seven-thirty flight," he said flatly. Then he smiled quickly and added almost as an afterthought, "Let's break open some champagne, and we'll all drink to it."

In the middle of putting on his galoshes, he stopped suddenly and looked up at Seth. "You know, only one psychiatrist ever won the Nobel Prize. Wagner-Jauregg in 1927. It was stupid work and a stupid choice. Freud certainly should have won it. He was the only really brilliant one in the field. And, you know"—he stood up and took his coat off the peg—"he never really wanted to do anything but research when he was your age."

They were quiet in the car driving to the big house on South Kimbark, both lost in their own worlds—one the future, one the past.

Then, only half audibly, as though he were addressing the drops of rain on the windshield: "You kind of got lost in the shuffle, Seth, didn't you?" He smiled at Seth and looked puzzled, as though he was surprised by what he'd said.

That night they toasted his new career with Veuve Clicquot, 1966.

*H*e swirled the brew around in the flask and held it up to the light, scrutinizing it with knitted brows.

"I think we've got it this time, Troobnik. Bring the sick child."

"Stop joking. Why?"

He shrugged. "I don't know. It's probably buried somewhere deep in my unconscious, a little to the left of my warped ego ideal." He paused. "Harvey started feeding me little tidbits of Freud in college. We were at the U of C together. Then he came to Bellevue, and I followed him here. For more of the same, I guess." He gave a wry smile. "It started with a paper called 'The Poet and Day-dreaming.' Easy stuff, you know. I guess he corrupted me."

"And you were easily corruptible," she said with an edge of self-righteousness.

"I was. Compelling stuff. There was one paper—'A Disturbance of Memory on the Acropolis.' I defy anyone to read it without shedding a tear or two." He shook his head. "Well, anyway, I don't know why. Harvey knows why." He looked into his coffee and swirled it. "Once on a very long train ride from Luxembourg to Rome he laid it all out for me: deep, unconscious motives, the works. We'd finished off our third bottle of cheap Italian wine by then, and I was half asleep and sick to my stomach. So fortunately I didn't hear much of what he said. What I heard I didn't understand, what I understood I didn't believe, and what I believed I forgot." He smiled into his cup. "Probably ten thousand bucks' worth of insight down the toilet that night."

*A*s they sat over coffee and the last of the wine, Seth stared across the park at the solitary lights in the buildings on Fifth Avenue. Lindsay studied him in the soft yellow candlelight. The wine had made his neck muscles ease, and his eyelids drooped a little as though he were far away again. The light gave the curls on the back of his head and neck a reddish tint.

"Are you supposed to act as though nothing had happened?"

she said, breaking her studied silence. "It's like trying to ignore an elephant that's wandered into your living room."

"Well, it's hard to understand, but I suppose he meant well." He'd mentioned his argument with Harvey that morning.

"Besides, why shouldn't you be interested? Don't you think you'd learn something, about life, I mean—real life?" The general's daughter was back, leading the charge.

"Christ, that's just what Eve said to Adam. Here, take a bite and see what life is all about. You women never learn."

"Start where it happened, in the basement."

He threw her a two-fingered salute. "Aye, aye, General."

She poured the last of the wine into his glass and sat back as he described how the basement cafeteria was laid out and how it was possible for him to see without looking, hear without listening.

The all-night staff cafeteria was a large, poorly lit room, with white tiled walls and a dark red linoleum floor. As one entered it from the tunnel passageway, there was a long steam table on the right. Behind it a couple of elderly Irish spinsters served up the leftovers of that day's lunch and dinner. Most of the time they spent gossiping in the kitchen beyond, occasionally peeping out like mice when someone called for service. One could always count on a steaming bowl of soup, even on the hottest days. American cheese sandwiches on bread beginning to curl were also a staple item.

On that particular night Seth told the white-haired lady that if the soup was as thick as the coffee and the coffee was as hot as the butter, perhaps they'd have more customers for the cafeteria. She laughed and shot back, "And if the air in this place was as fresh as your mouth, we'd all be a lot healthier."

The cafeteria held eight or ten tables and on the side opposite the steam table half a dozen booths with blue vinyl bench seats and red Formica tabletops.

After Seth picked up his coffee at the steam table, he chose the booth at the far end of the room, the last one in the row. He remembered sitting down with his back to the door of the cafeteria. He opened his copy of Bleuler and began to read, making notes as he read. Although two or three tables had been occupied when he entered the dining room, there had been no one in any of the booths.

Eventually he became aware of a conversation in low voices behind him: a man and a women, perhaps some quiet laughter. Then, suddenly, a loud, brassy, unpleasant laugh. It broke his concentration, and he stopped reading. After a moment he tried to go back to the book.

"But"—he paused and began to act out his recollection—"not right away. I must've turned around to see who it was, who'd laughed."

"And . . ."

He hesitated. "Feet—the shoes! They were sticking out beyond the booth."

Had he heard anything? What were they talking about? Lindsay wanted to know. No, of course not; he was trying *not* to listen, he was trying to read.

Then what?

He had continued to read until suddenly he remembered the time. It was already a few minutes past midnight. He grabbed his book and jacket and hurried out of the cafeteria, past the disembodied voices two or three booths away, distracted and not caring at the moment who they were.

That was all he could remember of the fringes of his experience that night. Ask him what he had read in the monograph on schizophrenia, and he could tell you.

"How much are you really sure of?"

"Not much." He shrugged. "I wasn't paying attention. My mind was anywhere but there. I was thinking about the movie, Connie Martin, schizophrenia—I don't know, a dozen different things."

Without warning the energy seemed to drain out of her, and she said in a depleted voice, "It's late. I've got to get some sleep." She hoisted him to his feet and dragged him unwillingly to the door. Suddenly he stopped resisting her pull, unbalancing her. She fell against the door, and Seth, following quickly, corralled her.

He stood looking down at her. "Sorry about that. Has anyone ever told you that you have a beautiful carotid pulse?"

"Many men," she whispered, "but never with such authority."

"I thought so."

She closed her eyes as their lips and bodies touched. He felt her heart pounding in her chest.

Suddenly she pushed them apart. "You know, Seth, I'm not easy." She was breathing hard. "I don't love you. I'm not even sure I like you."

"You're a tough lady. I see I'm not going to do this on looks alone. It's character all the way with you."

"Joke if you want to, but I take my loving seriously."

"I take your loving seriously, too."

Her hand had found the doorknob behind her back, and she swung the door wide. "Now, go home."

He allowed himself to be pushed into the corridor and stood swaying after the door had closed, staring at it. Then, slowly, stupidly, he smiled at the door, threw it a sloppy salute, and lurched toward the elevator.

The ugly red-brick psychiatric hospital was like a military field hospital. Its main function was triage, a way station where the casualties of life were sorted, some to be sent back behind the lines to remote places and treated intensively with the cool tranquilizing rays of daytime television and some to be pushed out the door with a prescription and a cheery smile and told to return to the struggle. "Diagnosis and Disposition" it was called, sorting out the overwhelmed from the merely bruised. You go this way; you, that.

The flood of human wreckage never stopped. It swirled down through the hospital from ward to ward—disturbed, semidisturbed, quiet—and out again. At the front door baffled relatives with scuffed shoes and shopping bags stuffed with clothes waited for the walking wounded. At the back door yellow out-of-date buses from places like Valhalla or Grassyknoll State Hospital collected the basket cases.

Seth wondered on the late nights in the PAO what would happen if a blockage developed in the system. Would the hospital overflow, like a bathtub? Would the city drown in its own mental illness?

In exchange for its help in this interminable reshuffling, the house staff was given the opportunity to learn psychiatry at one of the world's great medical centers and, in Seth's case, under the mixed tutelary blessing of Joe Burden.

"*S*atanic?" Seth asked with a doubtful look, as though he hadn't heard correctly. He felt warm and restless and began to roll up his sleeves.

"Yes, of course, your interest in this young woman's murder is satanic." Burden now swung slowly around to face him. He'd been staring out over the grim warehouses and factories that lined the Brooklyn shore of the East River. Through his window high above the river, he'd gazed eastward into the leaden, overcast morning as Seth talked on about his clinical experiences. It seemed to Seth at times that the older man was barely listening.

"Don't look so hurt, Dr. Conrad. It's just a telegraphic way of making a psychological point. Nothing more, really. Know any Latin?"

Oh, Christ! "A little."

"How about the word *tectum?* Any ideas?"

Christ, would he ever be free of pendantry and pendants? *"Tectum?"* He rifled through some of the unused files of his mind and jarred loose some rusty vocabulary. "Means 'roof,' doesn't it?" Then, trying to muster some interest, "Why?" he asked mechanically.

Burden glanced at him, shrewd eyes lost in mournful features. "Well, the word 'de-tect' means literally 'uncovering'—'taking off the roof,' so to speak. That's what being a detective is all about— taking off the roof, dis-covering secret and hidden things." He swiveled away from Seth and looked off into the distance again. After a few moments of silence Seth protested by recrossing his legs.

"But I think I'm telling you more than you want to know, Dr. Conrad." Burden turned away and moved to a table with a hot plate and flask of coffee on it. "Like some?" he asked without turning. As he fussed with the two cups, Seth looked around impatiently. No surprises, really. Standard Scandinavian-analytic. Simple, anonymous, solid. He had expected more books and journals. Like his father's office, he supposed.

"Now what exactly did Dr. King say about your psychotherapy

patient?" He handed Seth a cup of black coffee. Seth took as proof of Burden's aloofness toward the rest of the faculty that he always referred to his colleagues as Dr. So-and-so rather than John King or Jack as others did.

"He said another two or three weeks at least. Good cases are a little scarce at the moment, apparently." He smiled and then regretted it.

Joe Burden was a difficult man, unresponsive to blandishments. A lonely man, lonelier, according to Myra Karp, since the death of his wife five years before. Her death had somehow released him from patterns of life that no longer pleased or surprised him. Within a year he had become an important member of the full-time faculty of the medical school. His only real constituency, though, since this appointment, remained the medical students and residents to whom he devoted increasing amounts of time. The rest of the faculty, for good reason, kept a respectful distance. Burden, contemptuous of clinicians who led their professional lives like sheep, grazing contentedly in doctrinaire pastures, was equally scornful of researchers who thought they could capture the song of the nightingale by cutting it into bits.

Burden knew he was remote and perhaps even that he was lonely, but he would have denied what some proclaimed behind his back: that he was a snob. He would have explained wearily that he didn't have enough time left. He would have told them that he had been profligate and had let time slip through his fingers. And now he could find time only for important things, unexpected things. One sensed that he had been intimate with death, and death had made him a connoisseur of time.

There was nothing, he thought, that was more important than passing on to the next generation the art and experience that he had collected, sifted, and shaped for thirty years and that could never be acquired by reading but only by encountering the direct and terrifying experience with someone who had been there before.

"Three weeks," he said quietly. "That would be about the beginning of October." And with the trace of a weary smile he added, "We have three meetings before October. How do you propose to keep my interest until then?"

"I . . . don't know." Seth looked to the chuffing tugboats below for help. "How about the new diagnostic nomenclature?"

"Ah, you have a burning interest in the new nomenclature," Burden said into his coffee cup.

"No . . . not particularly. I was just . . . trying to—"

"Forgive me for interfering, Dr. Conrad." Burden held up a hand in graceful protest. "A few minutes ago when you were talking about Jennifer Light's murder, you were obviously fascinated by it."

"Not really." Seth recrossed his legs. "Well, yes, a little, I suppose."

"That's what I mean. Why are you so diffident about this?"

"Diffident?" Seth adjusted his glasses and smoothed the hair over his ears.

"Yes, almost apologetic . . ." Burden looked down into his cup again. "Most of our lives are lived from one coffee break to the next. . . ." His voice trailed off as he turned again to gaze out of his window.

"Why shouldn't you be interested in it?" he said quietly almost to himself. "How often does it happen in a man's life that a murder falls into it?" He paused as though studying the refuse of the river. "What were those two people like, the one who could kill a beautiful and defenseless woman, the other someone who could find herself in that unlikely place, at that unlikely hour. . . ." His voice, his attention had drifted eastward, away from Seth, beyond the river, beyond Brooklyn to land's end. "We read about these things, we dream about them. . . ."

After several minutes the sound of Seth's fidgeting roused Burden. Without turning he said flatly, "Yes, the new diagnostic nomenclature. What was there about it you wanted to discuss?"

"Well . . . actually, I *was* interested in what you were talking about before. The business about detecting." He made an opening movement with his hand as though it were the lid of a box.

Burden gave him a fishy look and remained silent.

"You never finished. What does it have to do with Satan?"

Burden swirled the coffee in his mug and stared at it thoughtfully. "Well"—he began almost grudgingly—"according to Barzun, this usage of 'detection' comes from a Spanish legend which says that disciples of the devil were allowed to accompany him as he flew over the houses of a village and took off the roofs so that they could watch the intimate activities in each house.

"Do you see how the legend brings together ideas"—the fingers of his hand began to contract slowly, powerfully—"that we don't usually connect, condensing them all into one word"—he made a fist—"detection? It's all there: evil, knowledge, guilt, and the primal scene. I suggest that if you go on with this business, Dr. Conrad, you read some of the literature on the subject. You'll find that murder and the primal scene are inseparable. What's the joke, Dr. Conrad? You're smiling."

"No, not really," he said comfortably. "It's just that for a moment you reminded me of someone."

"Well, in any case I hope you'll have a patient to tell me about by the beginning of October. Until then we can talk about anything you'd like as long as it's something you have an authentic interest in. For God's sake, don't just make up things to talk about. I have better things to do at my age." He turned back to his desk and picked up some papers as a signal of dismissal. "See you next week," he added quietly without looking at Seth. As Seth reached the door, he heard Burden's voice once more.

"Oh, and by the way, Dr. Conrad, there are no 'good' patients. There are only difficult patients and very difficult patients. I suggest that you try to find a difficult one."

Whit's building on Mitchell Place had a quiet, understated, thickly carpeted lobby. They were challenged by a suspicious broad-shouldered man in a gray uniform. His muscular neck and large, capable hands were obvious impostors disguised in wing collar and tidy white gloves. Under his impassive scrutiny Seth became suddenly aware of the frayed pockets of his suntans and his rolled-up sleeves and was grateful for Lindsay's fresh, respectable presence in blue linen. He found himself making insipid conversation with her to emphasize their connection as wing collar called upstairs for permission to pass them on. At the east elevator another gray uniform with white gloves examined them, less conspicuously, as he whisked them to the twenty-eighth-floor penthouse.

Getting off the elevator, Seth tripped and almost lost his glasses.

"Ah, grace under pressure. Welcome, Seth." Framed in the doorway, holding a glass of white wine, Whit smiled his two-hundred-watt smile. "And you must be my inquisitor. Hello, I'm Whitney Shields." He had on white trousers and, over bare feet, a pair of well-worn leather boat shoes.

Seth, still adjusting his glasses, missed his opportunity. Lindsay stepped forward and extended her hand. "Lindsay Cooper. Just a reporter. The other is out of my line."

"Ah, yes. Well, we'll see. Please forgive the disorganization. I've been here only a few days."

Seth, excluded, shrugged and allowed himself to fall behind the other two as Whit showed them about the new apartment in his easy, low-keyed way.

With gloomy precision Seth studied his host. Apologizing for the unfinished look of the walnut-paneled living room, Whit called their attention with gracious chagrin to the neatly stacked book crates standing in one corner. From invisible speakers which seemed to be everywhere Wagner played softly.

How did he manage to make everything seem effortless and right? Was it in the genes or some kind of divine power that turns old money into grace? Seth watched from a distance the way Whit courted Lindsay and thought suddenly that he'd been stupid to bring her.

Out of nowhere a young woman floated into the room, barefoot and dangerously slender, her jet black hair hanging down to bony shoulders. Her white chiffon dress was cut low, revealing, occasionally, understated but perfect breasts. She seemed rather a presence than a person, and except for an acknowledging nod when Whit introduced her simply as Patrick, she looked off into internal empty places. Lindsay recognized her as a face she had seen on covers of *Vogue* and *Bazaar*.

As Whit led them through the French doors to the terrace, Patrick drifted onto the living-room couch and in an almost liquid way assumed its soft leathery contour. Accepting their exclamations over the view with godlike modesty, Whit nodded to a dour middle-aged woman in a white uniform. She set a tray with glasses and a wine cooler down on a glass-topped table and retreated.

"Your mum?" Seth asked wryly, nodding at the woman.

"Better." Whit smiled and poured the wine. "At least she can cook. Mrs. Petersen is an old family retainer on loan for the night from Aunt Gretchen, who is, happily, still croqueting and tennising in Connecticut."

"Ah, the life of a poor psychiatric resident."

"My grandfather always said that someday we'd be glad he was a robber baron. He was right." He raised his glass to the spirit of the old man.

"Whit, why the hell are you running your tail off at the hospital—with all this . . . ?" Seth made a wide sweep with his arm, splashing wine onto the terrace floor. He shook the wine from his hand and flushed.

"Well, when you stop and think that I'm the youngest and possibly the dullest of five outrageously successful brothers, then it becomes very easy to understand." As he spoke, and without missing a beat, he reached over and handed Seth a napkin.

"Six. I thought you were six brothers," Seth said.

Whit stared at him and blinked like a captive frog. "Is that a question or an assertion, old man?"

"Lisa," Seth explained with an apologetic shrug. "The goddess of truth."

"So much for the goddess of truth." Whit sipped the wine. "Chilled enough? A still champagne. Brisk, isn't it?"

Mrs. Petersen had set a table for four on the terrace under a yellow awning. There were candles in hurricane lamps, a pink linen tablecloth, two crystal decanters of red wine, and three glasses of different shape at each place.

Oysters, their first course, provided an opportunity for Whit to give the final word on the matter as he lifted a bottle of white wine from a cooler beside the table—Chablis with American oysters, Muscadet with French. Never, never the reverse. Hemingway to the contrary notwithstanding.

"What do you think?" he asked, turning to Lindsay as he held

up the glass of golden liquid. She swirled the wine as she had seen
Whit do and took a small, careful sip. She was silent, thinking very
hard for several minutes. Even Patrick, roused by the silence, turned
toward her.

"I like it," she said finally with a note of reservation. "I see
what you mean about the briskness. But I find it a little young."

"Ah, I see you share Seth's happy prejudice for ripeness."

"Yes, I find maturity . . . very exciting."

Whit gave her a little toast and began to restudy the color of
the Chablis in the candlelight. And in the same light Seth studied
his host.

He looked about him at the view, the highly polished pieces
that any museum would have been pleased to own, Patrick, the
sublime, invisible, omnipresent music. Whit had everything. He was
surely the golden boy—a work of art, filled with perfect detail but
somehow without thrust or feeling.


". . . well, if they didn't hate each other before, they do now.
That's when he said that some psychiatrists are alchemists, who
can turn phenothiazines into gold. A rather nice conceit considering
what passes for wit at departmental conferences. Graver turned as
red as this." Whit held up the decanter of claret. "Here"—he poured
the silky red wine—"I think you'll find this mature enough even
for your tastes." He stopped to swirl and sniff again and looked
pleased. " 'He can see thirty or forty patients a day, and with a
smart nurse, twice that many.' " He was imitating Paul Silk's nervous
tenor now with Silk's adorable lisp at the very edge of his *r*'s. ' "He
has many diffewent families of pharmaceuticals. He has pills, capsules,
tablets, ampules, suppositories. He has the choice of the patient's
mouth, skin, muscles, veins, or wectum. The combinations and
permutations are, of course, infinite. They can keep the doctor busy
and the patient blunted for years.' I thought Graver would get up
and kill him. He loved it. God, he loved every moment of it."

"He's right," Seth said, thinking of Mrs. Scola.

"Of course, he's right, old man, but Graver had just finished presenting his work on drug therapy. The fact is that Paul is bitchy, brilliantly bitchy."

Mrs. Petersen appeared silently, a Scandinavian wraith, to serve the simple roasted chicken, selected carefully to set off the claret. She waited like an obedient child with her hands folded in front of her until Whit had tasted the bird.

"Perfect, Inger. Roti, the god of dry heat, will love you for this."

She gave him a tiny, grudging smile and a reproach for his blasphemy.

"Then why are you turning down Graver's offer? I thought you admired his work."

"Exactly, that's the point. Graver cares. Silk doesn't. I'd end up being Graver's bottle washer, his scut boy. If I do the project with Silk, I'll run the show *because* he's not interested. I know the method, and I can run twenty or thirty patients with no trouble. Look," he said with a shrewd smile, "Paul is interested in three things: pursuing—yes, that's the right word—his quietly decadent life down in Soho"—he blinked—"his painting; and last and, indeed, least as a source of personal satisfaction, but vital for his professional credibility, getting his full professorship." He sat back and smiled at his wine. "For that he needs to publish. And he knows that this project can generate four or five papers, maybe even a monograph."

"What do you mean 'decadent life'?" Lindsay asked, like a hound on the scent, almost quivering.

"How do you like it? Wonderful finish, don't you think? "Sixty-one Figeac." Whit swirled his glass and plunged his nose into it as though he were taking refuge. "Superb!" he said with a trace of excitement. He looked at Lindsay and said with a blink, "You're a very determined person. I admire your determination. It's rare— purity of heart." He looked into his glass again. "We were talking about it yesterday, Seth and I, unambivalence." He smiled. "Perhaps it's the secret of life. Look, Lindsay, I'm only repeating what I've been told."

"Lisa?" asked Seth.

Whit only smiled at Seth. "And I'm not telling you the bad part."

Lindsay leaned forward. "Is he gay?"

"Determination." Whit toasted Lindsay.

"I found Silk a thoroughly repulsive little man. He's prissy and sadistic. I interviewed him this afternoon, or at least tried to, and while I was there, he took a call. Someone had made some kind of mistake, I suppose; he was brutal. Gratuitously brutal. And what was worse, I think he was doing it for my benefit, as though I'd be impressed."

"Was he any help to you in your search for the real Jennifer Light?" Whit asked, looking more benign than usual.

"You're patronizing me."

"Forgive me, a family affliction—sardonic humor. It runs through our family like hemophilia through the Romanovs, recessive in the females, dominant in the males. Please don't take it personally."

Mrs. Petersen had reappeared and was removing the coffee cups. "Inger, please. bring the *Auslese.*" Patrick, who had said little and eaten less, had drifted off without a word and had never returned.

"In fact, he wasn't helpful at all." Lindsay's eyes flashed in the candlelight. "You know, I've never run into this! I've interviewed hundreds of people, friends and relatives of victims, injured and dead, and I've never run into this. Maybe they're shocked, or guilty, or mad, but they *talk.* They *want* to talk; they have to talk. But *this* is different. Nobody wants to talk." She looked at Whit defiantly. "All I get from everybody is evasion or silence. He told me at first he hardly knew her. Then it became perfectly clear she'd been to his place on Fire Island dozens of times in the last year or two."

Whit filled their glasses with the pale, flower-scented wine without taking his eyes off Lindsay.

"He managed to say one thing about her that was interesting"— she faltered for a moment, searching more for correctness than for truth—"that she was fragile, abused by people." She paused and studied Whit carefully, then turned away and scowled. "He didn't say Graver directly; but he did mention his name, and the implication was loud and clear."

"Fragile?" Whit savored the word as though he were tasting a new wine. From the terrace they looked south over the city, the river to the east, and the UN in the foreground.

"Perhaps I'm not a very good judge of women," he said, sounding false, "and God knows I haven't made a study of them"—again, a false note—"but she was about as fragile as a diamond. A magnificent diamond, certainly. She was an incredibly beautiful woman." He said the words slowly, with emphasis. "I make the point not only because she was so beautiful but because she knew the effect she had on men. But she was . . . shy. No, that wasn't it." He reached for his gold lighter absentmindedly. "Secretive. There's a difference. She refused to let me pick her up at home. Insisted on meeting me at the restaurant. She hardly talked about herself. Got me to talk about my interests." He smiled a charming smile. "Not hard." He shrugged. "Obviously bright—in a quiet way.

"She told me a little about a year she had spent in Paris. She lived with a student at the Sorbonne. His family owned, she said, a couple of hundred miles of oil fields in the Persian Gulf. He was part of the jet set, and he took her wherever he went, London, Monte Carlo, Rome, Gstaad." He listened for a moment to the music that rose in anguish and then receded. "Of course, she was trying to impress me. And she did—but not the way she thought. I think she was also trying to tell me something else."

"That she wanted you to make a play for her," Lindsay offered.

"Yes, of course," he said with a condescending smile, "in a dozen different ways. But there was a double message there. It was as if she were saying . . ." For once he seemed to have trouble finding the right words. He was no longer looking at Lindsay but through her. "'*Noli me tangere* for Caesar's I am,/ And wild for to hold, though I seem tame.' Maybe she was teasing me. I don't know exactly. . . ." He looked off again and inhaled deeply from the ivory cigarette holder. He cocked his head toward the tormented music which swirled softly over the terrace.

"The woman in *Parsifal.* The central figure, really. She reminded me of her, Kundry. She stood by at the crucifixion and laughed at Christ's agony, and from that moment she was doomed to wander the earth, seeking redemption. Her beauty and allure compel men to offer their love and help, but whenever she's within reach of salvation, she's caught again by her need to mock them and doomed again to torment." He paused for a moment and looked at Seth. "Sounds strange coming from a brain physiologist—doesn't it?—but Jennifer Light was like that. Maybe not cursed, but"—Whit smiled— "I suppose your friend Bloch would call it a repetition compulsion." He shrugged. "I don't see that there's much difference." There was a sudden eruption of music that seemed at the moment like some magical affirmation about Jennifer Light.

Whit inhaled again, satisfied with himself, then added suddenly, "The one thing she did mention about herself was that she was adopted. Made a little joke about it, romanticized it a bit. Said for all she knew, she and I might be related, half brother and sister. She obviously never knew my parents; they never do things by halves."

"Whit, do you mind if I ask you a personal question?"

"Be gentle with me, Lindsay. Remember, like the Romanovs, I bruise easily."

"Whit, with you it's sardonic humor. The Cooper affliction is directness. Recessive in the males and dominant in the females. Did you spend the night with her?"

The delicate color that rose in Whit's face made him a boy again. "Should Parsifal have slept with Kundry?" He lifted his glass in salute and gave her a tight, handsome smile.

# Chapter

## 6

The Roslyn Funeral Chapel was a modern four-story structure of limestone and glass, built to provide comfortable and trouble-free grief for the well-to-do families of the north shore of Long Island. Although its advertisements spoke of it as nondenominational, Reformed Jewish bereavement was its specialty.

They arrived a few minutes early, the four of them: Seth and Lindsay, Lisa Stone, goddess of truth, and Avi Schwartzman, the Moses of mental health. Jenny Light's funeral was scheduled for 10:00 A.M.

Seth knew as soon as they entered the chapel that it was like some advanced clinic for the sterilization of grief. The deep-pile carpet told him so; the quiet, gloom-free ambient lighting told him so; the powerful, silent air conditioning, poised at the perfect temperature-humidity index, told him so; the handsome, sober-faced young ushers in their Ivy League suits told him so. Oh, death, he wondered, what have they done with thy sting?

Because the chapel was almost full, they took places in the last row, Lindsay next to a fat woman with hungry eyes imprisoned behind thick lenses. Avi and the others followed and let themselves sink into seats designed for both pleasure and forgetting.

"Hey," Seth whispered, leaning across Avi. He reached out to touch Lindsay's hand. Withdrawing it, she gave him another icy smile. Christ, what was with her? She'd been this way most of the morning.

The drive from the city in Seth's ancient gray Mercedes had been pleasant enough. His "iron mistress," Harvey called it—"an expression, no doubt, of your repressed anti-Semitism. Probably the only real relationship you will ever know, boychik—that Nazi car." Pleasant enough, he reflected, except for Lindsay's ominous silence. Anyway, how could he help it? He couldn't very well have refused Lisa. Whatever he might think of her, they were colleagues, fellow residents. He supposed, though, that she'd gone too far—as usual— right from the start.

"Be a sweetheart," she'd said to Lindsay as they stood awkwardly in front of the open car. "I wrecked my knee last week. You know . . . tennis." She gave a halfhearted imitation of a backhand and gasped a tiny gasp akin to sexual pain. "I can hardly bend it. Would you mind if I sat up front?" With a shrug Lindsay clambered into the back with Avi and turned to ice.

Sliding into the dark leather seat next to Seth, Lisa ran her finger around the walnut dashboard sensuously. *"Very* classy, *cher."*

"Hm." Seth inhaled as Lisa leaned toward him.

"Nice, isn't it?" She flashed a smile to Lindsay. "Vent Vert. Every time I'm in Paris, I bring some back. Unbelievably cheap there." Turning, she curled her injured leg under, revealing the delicate and uninjured inner aspect of her thigh. Like an animal in heat, Lisa dispatched tiny sights and smells of her body like messengers of welcome.

Seth inhaled again and smiled gratefully, as though he were at the seashore.

For the rest of the drive Lindsay stared out the window at the passing Queens landscape as Lisa orchestrated the conversation with subtle precision, selecting its themes, setting its tempo, and assigning its voices.

Lisa poked him awake suddenly and called attention to the tall white-haired presence of Robert Ettinger. *"Pourquoi?* What's he doing here?" Seth shrugged. He was there, of course, out of courtesy, representing the department.

In fact, he saw a number of people from the department as he looked about. Graver was there, with a scrawny, depressed woman who Seth guessed must be his wife from the way he ignored her. He recalled that they were friends of the family. The other members of Graver's laboratory staff were also there, and several nurses from the hospital who must have known Jennifer Light.

Off to the right Seth met the gaze of Benson Coles and suddenly had the sense that Coles had been staring at him. His one good eye blinked a slow, reptilian blink and slid off in another direction. Coles. Jennifer Light. Any association between the two seemed remote and somehow obscene. There was a trace, some wisp of aberration about Coles, and as Seth struggled to define it for himself, he was distracted by a flurry of movement.

Paul Silk, his raincoat flung over his shoulders, flew up the aisle. Lisa smiled as he fluttered about like a sparrow in a birdbath, finally settling into his place.

*"Il est adorable, n'est-ce pas, le joli petit Silk."*

"What was the scandal?" Seth whispered, nodding in Silk's direction.

"Silk?"

He nodded conspiratorially.

"Oh, how the righteous have fallen," she said, her tongue darting playfully along her upper lip. *"C'était absolument délicieux,"* she said, carefully removing an invisible speck of lint from his thigh.

"Really?" Seth leaned toward her. "That perfume. What was the name?"

She let herself list in his direction, until their shoulders touched. "Perhaps there's hope for you, *cher,*" she said, smiling. She glanced at Silk again. "It was high Jewish grand opera. Everything. Love. Betrayal. Revenge, maybe." She looked at Seth knowingly. "Ever notice the back of Silk's right hand?"

The congregation suddenly quieted. The door at the front of the chapel had swung open as though by divine intervention. A tall, lugubrious man entered, wearing half spectacles, a black gown, and a prayer shawl. He mounted the platform and took his place stiffly behind the lectern. He was followed by two of the dark-suited pious young men, wheeling Jennifer Light's casket. It was large, twice the size of the girl herself as Seth remembered her, lying there in the dusty cul-de-sac under the naked police lights. The casket was made of some dark important wood and was fitted with brass finials, rails, and handles. On top of it were white lilies and gladioli.

The casket had remained closed at the request of the family. The young men disappeared, and through the doorway came three women dressed in black. All eyes were on the center one, who was staggering and being supported on either side by the two younger women. The features of her face seemed fragmented and recombined into a silent Picasso-like scream of pain and rage. Despite her stature—she was short and thickset—a restless, unbridled energy flowed from her as though she were some dark, radioactive mass. Well behind her, almost as an afterthought, came a pale, flabby, dispirited man with thinning gray hair. He was followed by a sad-eyed youth with a mangy beard who moved stiffly in a navy blue suit that was too large for him.

The members of the family took the seats reserved for them in the front row. The rabbi began with a benediction in Hebrew, which he then repeated in English. He spoke slowly, each word articulated with millimetric precision, each word uttered with rabbinical confidence, as though each were God's chosen word. "I . . . have . . . been . . . asked . . ."

Seth thought of Jennifer Light, beautiful, now probably looking doll-like and inanimate, lying there, in the casket lined with white satin. He remembered the white satin of another coffin.

". . . by Mel and Ruth Light to officiate at this service not only because I have been the rabbi of their temple for the last twenty-five years but because Mollie and I have been close personal friends of theirs all that time. When Mel and Ruth came to me twenty-five years ago and said, 'We want to adopt a baby, tell us how,' it brought joy to my heart because I saw how much love they had to give and how disappointed they had been for so many years. And as I shed tears of joy with Mel and Ruth for her coming, now I must shed tears of sorrow with them at her leaving. . . ."

Seth remembered all the trouble it had been. His mother shattered, his father a walking dead man. The coroner's inquest, mercifully brief; the arrangements for a charter flight to carry the body from the island to Boston; more arrangements to transfer the body from

Boston to Chicago. He supposed death was always inconvenient. He remembered that night, the night it happened. He had lain tossing and turning, thinking terrible thoughts, thoughts he could never speak and never forget in a thousand nights. . . .

". . . nights and weekends Mel wasn't home. Things were not so easy then. I remember, they lived in a tiny apartment where the crib took up half the living room. Mel had two jobs in those days. But that's how you build an empire. . . ."

The service was quiet, in tiny Bond Chapel on the campus. There were some simple flowers chosen by his mother, and Dean Parker of the theological school conducted the service. There weren't many people there, only a few of his parents' closest friends. Elly's friends were all away, and by the time they came straggling back after Labor Day, she had already been buried two weeks. When they asked about it, he didn't know the answers to their questions and couldn't tell them that somehow he had known that it would happen. . . .

". . . and when Mel came home from Korea, what rejoicing there was in that little family. And what a wonderful surprise it was for little Jennie to get a daddy all of a sudden and, mirabile dictu, a little brother. All the doctors had told them it couldn't happen, but God knows that one child is not enough for a Jewish family. . . .

" 'Five fingers on one hand, yet no two are alike,' the saying goes. Neil and Jennie were as unlike each other as two children could possibly be; as sunny and good-natured as Neil was, I remember little Jennie, beautiful, shy, and wistful. . . ."

There was a guttural, uncanny sound from the front row. Mel, sitting gray and bowed during the commemoration, suddenly broke into great, heaving sobs.

Had he and Elly been so different? Elly had changed that year, from someone who was as familiar as the furniture in his own room to someone he hardly knew at all, heartless and cruel, totally uninterested in the rest of the family, in what they thought or did. The year before she died, before the "accident," she was not the sister he had idolized all his life, but some desperate and . . .

". . . unhappy little girl. Yes, it's true that she had fears, God knows. A plague of fears, she had. But with all her fears, there wasn't a mean or disobedient bone in her little body.

"I remember," the rabbi said, removing his glasses and studying the chapel ceiling. He smiled sadly. "She must have been six, maybe seven. She would say to me, 'Uncle Sidney, does God know what's in everybody's mind?' That's the kind of child she was. . . ."

Until the change he had envied and loved her. She always seemed to him marvelous, able to do things he could never hope to do. She was a constant source of excitement and intrigue, with her diaries and hidden books, and he had always wanted to be her friend, but somehow . . .

. . . "Little children, little troubles; big children, big troubles." The rabbi sighed a deep religious sigh. "They did everything they could. . . ."

Christ, what's this joker talking about? Only half listening to the rabbi's drone, Seth was suddenly aware of a narrative that had become ambiguous and climactic. What's he talking about?

"Was there ever a time when Jennie was happy? I don't know. I do know that Ruth and Mel did everything that loving parents could possibly do for her. . . . And then this terrible thing . . ."

Finally, during the last six months before the accident, late at night when they were home alone, Elly had begun talking to him, talking wistfully about her plans for the future: to get away, to get a job, to go to school, in California or Oregon or Washington, anywhere so long as it was far away. . . .

The rabbi, having read the service rapidly in droning Hebrew, announced, with somewhat more animation, that the Light family would be receiving friends at home after the burial service.

At the graveside it was as though the two girls, Jennifer and Ellen, their histories, their miseries, their mysteries, had fused in his brain. Half listening, half watching the storm clouds building up in the west, he drifted back to memories he hadn't known he'd kept. A cold morning in December, shortly before his sixth birthday. She was taking him to school but walking too fast for him and refusing to hold his hand. Suddenly he stopped dead in his tracks and looked at her through hot tears, "Why is it, Elly, I've always loved you, and you've always hated me?" She'd grabbed his hand then in one of her classic huffs and almost pulled his arm out of its socket the whole rest of the way.

They were lowering the heavy casket into the grave, as the rabbi read the Hebrew words. A faint sob from Ruth Light as the casket reached the bottom. Neil, the brother, had remained expressionless throughout the service at the graveside. Another survivor. Would he feel relief, as Seth had that autumn after the torment and drama were over? Would he feel the emptiness, as Seth had when the snows came? The excitement and struggle over, only the gloomy silence was left. It had taken him a long time to get used to that silence. He wasn't sure whether he was used to it yet. Even now when the family got together, her presence and absence were there.

Had he helped her enough that summer? That day he had had a premonition, and later that night, tossing and turning, sleepless, he thought he knew where they might have found her. He shook his head like a dazed fighter trying to focus, trying to find his enemy.

They had rolled a grass carpet over the opening of the grave, to soften the final separation, to spare the family forever the sound of earth as it landed on the dead. And now, drifting to where the cars had been parked, the mourners began to depart. Ruth Light was again being supported on either side like a smoldering, rudderless hulk.

Two figures remained standing at the graveside. One, an obese young woman with a bad complexion, now turned and walked slowly toward the waiting cars, leaving only Jenny's father. A moment later Ruth Light, face contorted and tear-swollen, commanded from a waiting limousine, "Mel, I want you here, where you belong!"

Mel Light, gray and drooping, leaned forward to touch the grass carpet that covered the grave. "I can't leave her . . . I can't."

□ □ □

The Lights' house was too big, even for an unhappy family.

A solidly built imitation Tudor of stone and stucco, it was on a full acre in the best part of Roslyn. House and lawns were surrounded by a shoulder-high fieldstone wall which terminated in posterns on either side of the semicircular driveway. It was a house, Lisa announced immediately, perfect for June weddings and October bar mitzvahs.

They filed into the library, where heavy drapes darkened the room and kept out the summer heat. Eight or nine people stood about, some drinking tea, one or two, old uncles, smoking cigars and chatting in subdued tones. On the couch near the fireplace sat Ruth Light, one puffy leg resting on a hassock, her feet in slippers, her coal black eyes burning intensely. She had once been a beautiful woman, but fifty extra pounds now made her formidable. The way she moved, heaving herself from side to side, the way she sighed, the way she breathed suggested passions unappeased, scarcely contained by the insulating layers of fat on her body. She allowed her hand to be held by one of the women in black, who resembled her and to whom she turned fitfully to utter a phrase or two. Neil was sitting, silent, on the other side of his aunt. Suddenly turning to him, she said, "Neilly, be a good boy, go to the kitchen and ask Ethel to bring your mama a cup of tea. She needs something." Obediently he drifted off in the direction of the kitchen. Mel Light sat opposite them, staring vacantly into the dark fireplace.

"She never called me," Ruth said. "For six weeks, I never knew where she was. What was I supposed to do, Rose, be a detective? Do you think I wasn't interested? Every day I waited to hear from her, and every day my heart would break a little more. . . ." Rose squeezed her hand.

"What good is my pride now, Rose? What should I do with it? I swallowed it so many times before, I'll swallow it this time, too . . . only now I'll choke on it. Already it's burning a hole here," she said, pushing in deeply under her sternum.

Avi, good at this sort of thing by nature and vocation, spoke to Ruth Light for them all. She thanked them for coming, asked whether they knew Jennie well, and, not waiting for a reply, told them to have some refreshments in the dining room.

Leaving the library, Lisa hurried them off to find some coffee, and suddenly alone, Seth found himself in the living room, fingering toby mugs and pieces of Wedgwood. Over the fireplace a portrait of Mel Light in his prime looked shrewd and robust. Beneath it, on the mantel, Seth was caught by a photograph in a gold frame. He picked it up and studied it as he had the illustrations in the books of his childhood. It was a picture of a beautiful girl in the very earliest stage of sensual flowering, in a white summer dress, her dark hair cascading down her back and splashing over her shoulders. Next to her, a head shorter, a slender boy stood stiffly in a dark suit that even then looked too big for him. And although the photograph had captured her presence, her eyes said no—"noli me tangere"; even then she had been in some wild, fantastic place. Seth held the picture closer and absently outlined the figure with his finger as though he were trying to memorize it.

Drifting out of the living room, he saw, at the top of the wide-sweeping staircase, the slender, forlorn figure of Neil and wondered whether he was going to her old room now, whether he would move about in it like a sleepwalker touching her things, as he had touched Elly's things years ago. Slowly Seth mounted the stairs, not knowing exactly why, half listening to two heavily corseted women ahead of him as they talked of the grandeur of Ruth's suffering.

At the second-floor landing he heard the scratchy sound of an old phonograph record coming from a half-open door at the end of the hall. One of the corseted women from the stairway looked down the hall and clucked sadly. "Dorothy," she said simply to the other, and shook her head.

Drawn by the music, he pushed the half-closed door with one finger and peered in. On the floor was a battered old child's phonograph spinning a worn record. Lying curled up in a fetal position on a white canopied bed was the obese young woman with the bad complexion he'd noticed at the cemetery. Her eyes were brimming with tears as she listened to a sentimental ballad from a musical show of another generation. He heard the voices of the chorus swell to a tinny crescendo of courage and hope, ". . . and you'll ne-ver feeeel aaa-lone."

"Sorry, didn't mean to—" Seth said, retreating.

"That's all right. You can come in." She dabbed at her eyes. "We used to listen to this. She'd play it over and over again. This song especially—it's about an orphaned girl." She heaved herself up into a sitting position and let her legs dangle over the bed. They were heavy and hairy.

"Corny, isn't it? I don't think we ever listened to it when we didn't cry. I just dug it up out of the bottom of the closet." She made a halfhearted gesture to soothe her kinky, angry hair but succeeded only in making it more agitated. "Who are you?" she asked abruptly. "I saw you at the cemetery."

"Seth Conrad. I'm from the hospital where Jennifer worked." He looked around the room. "Hers?"

She nodded and stared at him. "Did she break your heart?"

"No, I didn't know her well enough." He wiped the trickle of sweat from his temple. The room was hot and airless; the windows were closed and probably had been for months.

"If you had, she would have. She broke everybody's heart." The two frown lines etched between her thick eyebrows deepened.

"You were . . . close?"

"Close?" She looked past Seth. "Yeah, a little." She pushed herself off the bed. "Fortunately, though, people could tell us apart. I wonder how." She bent over and took the phonograph needle off the record. The rhythmic whooshing stopped. "But I wouldn't take what I say too seriously if I were you. I'm Cousin Dorothy. Little Dotty. Only I'm not so little. Just dotty."

"That sounds self-hating."

"You must be a psychiatrist. I could tell one anywhere. They flock to me like moths to a flame. Here I am, minding my own sorrow, and, poof, like magic, the door opens and a psychiatrist-prince appears."

"Now it sounds like you hate psychiatrists."

"Not psychiatrists. Princes. You see, I'm a princess, disguised as a hippo. Kiss me and see what happens!" She sat down on the floor. Next to the child's phonograph she was a small mountain. Her dark eyes, dry now, burned with a fierce energy.

Seth watched her in silence. He remembered something Burden had said: "You don't have to respond every time a patient says something to you. Wait and see what happens. If you say something, there should be a dynamic reason for saying it. Ever watch a good surgeon's hands in an operating field? It's like watching a ballet dancer: Every movement is there for a reason—no wasted motion. He doesn't go in and hack around; he knows what he's doing, what he's looking for, and so should you."

"Ah, that thoughtful look. That wise demeanor. You're *not* a psychiatrist-prince. You're a philosopher-king. God, this *is* my lucky day."

Seth was observing now, not responding; the spirit of Joe Burden was on him.

"Actually I've liked all my psychiatrists. All but two. One was a stupid incompetent and I fired him after a week, and the other understood what it was all about and he fired me."

"Doesn't sound very understanding."

"He was, though." Now she was serious. "He tried to get me to stop kidding around for a year, then told me to come back when I was ready to stop playing and start working with him." Then wistfully, she added, "Maybe someday I will."

He wondered whether it was Burden. Sounded like his style.

"But the others were very sweet, really. And some of them were even helpful," she said, giving and taking away more than she had given at the same time.

"You're right. I am a psychiatrist, and I'm sorry if I've said anything intrusive."

"I didn't really mind the intrusion, but next time, if you're going to intrude, please don't make it a cliché. 'Self-hating!' That's daytime TV doctor talk. I know, I watch it every day."

Observe her, he said to himself. Don't slug her. Besides, she's right. He remembered Burden saying, "If you tell a patient something about himself, it should be something he doesn't know. That's what they're paying you for—to tell them things they *don't* know. It should be news to them. But it should be tomorrow's news, not next year's news. Otherwise they'll never believe you."

"I'm glad I wasn't one of your psychiatrists. You must have used them up like Kleenex."

"Now that's the first honest remark I've heard all day. Actually I've only had eight psychiatrists altogether, and since I'm twenty-four, that gives each one a half-life of eighteen months. That's not bad. Better than a male praying mantis or a worker bee. I'm in between now. Position's open. Like to try?"

Don't answer. It's a trap; you can't win. Just listen.

"Or do you only treat beautiful women like Jennifer?"

He grabbed at her words for dear life. "She was in treatment?"

"Are you serious? Do birds fly?" She laughed bitterly. "Between the two of us we've brought the mental health establishment to its knees. Only she had worse luck than I did—with her doctors, I mean. Instead of looking for good ones, Aunt Ruth looked for expensive ones." She reeled off a list of four or five distinguished names.

"The last one," she added, picking at her face, "she wouldn't tell me about. Not even his name." She dug her nail into the side of her face. "But there was something wrong. All I know is she was very excited about it until May or June, and then, all of a sudden, she told me she'd quit. Wouldn't give me any reason."

She talked with intensity now, almost nonstop. They had been closer than sisters, more like twins. Dot was the older by a few months and the leader. They were shy together, sad together, dreamy together, and as they got older, they felt like freaks together. "She felt the way I look. That's why we were twins."

They were different also. They complemented each other. As "little Dot" became larger and larger and more and more housebound, Jennifer began to supply her with the raw material of life—encounters with other girls and, later, boys—while Dot enriched and elaborated the fantasies that Jennie cherished.

"From the time they told her, you know, that she was adopted, she always loved stories like this." She knelt and took from the bottom shelf of a small bookcase several worn volumes. "I gave her these." She held them up: *The Secret Garden, A Little Princess.*

"She read them over and over. I don't think she ever stopped reading them. As she replaced the books on the shelf, she said, "I don't know what she'd been reading lately.""

Seth remembered the paperback she'd had in her purse on the last day of her life. Not too different, he thought, just sexier.

"She had the idea she was like the little boy in the fairy tale about the Snow Queen. Something had happened to her when she was young that made her different from everybody else. There would always be something wrong with her," she said, looking out of the window.

"And then it happened, just what she was always afraid of. Afterwards I guess it brought us even closer than before."

"It?" Seth asked. And even before she answered, he knew.

"It happened that September. She had the abortion at the end of October."

"The police found her wandering around on a deserted road in the next town." She turned back to Seth. "She told them a bunch of guys had grabbed her, put her in a van, and raped her."

"They caught the guys who did it, but nothing ever happened to them. Suspended sentences or something. She led them on, they said, said she was asking for it."

"She was just sixteen." She plumped herself down on the bed again and stared at the silent old phonograph as though it held some crucial secret. "And you know—I would never have said this then—I think maybe they were right."

She looked up at him, as though she were asking for guidance, clarification. She was digging at her face again.

"See . . . I was the only one besides Jennie who knew that by the time she came home from the beach that summer she was already pregnant. Everybody thought she got pregnant from the rape. But . . . now I'm sure that's why it happened."

Suddenly she changed the subject, launching into a desperate monologue about her mother and Ruth Light. She could have talked on for hours, he knew, but he needed to get away now. He glanced at his watch.

A look of hurt flickered in her clever eyes. "Time up?" She walked briskly to where the phonograph lay on the floor and put the needle back on the record. She turned away. "You can send me a bill in the morning if you like."

*I*t was the last thing in the world he needed at that hour: an abrasive chat with Jonathan Graver. He glanced irritably at his watch: ten thirty-five. An hour and a half, and he'd be free. Free from the airless, overheated admitting office and free of Pam Price. He'd been on duty with her since four that afternoon. Friday nights, for some reason, were always busy, and Pam had been worse than useless.

Standing in the basement cafeteria, he pretended to be deep in thought as he waited for Agnes to bring his coffee. Out of the corner of his eye he watched, hoping that Graver would rise suddenly and hurry out of the dining room. He drummed on the countertop and secretly blessed Aggie for her stupid, plodding inefficiency. But when a flock of surgical residents, garbed in green OR suits, jostled and shoved their way out of the cafeteria, they left only Graver hunched over his bowl of soup, reading a journal. There was no way out now.

The funeral that morning had released a swarm of painful memories which Seth could neither escape nor subdue. He'd been testy with the others and inattentive to Lindsay on the way back to the city and only halfheartedly agreed to have dinner and show her the cafeteria—the place where his life had touched the life of Jennifer Light before she died. He glanced over his shoulder at the booth that she'd occupied that night, half expecting to see her.

The phone rang in the kitchen, and he heard Agnes shuffling toward it. He hoped vainly that it was the PAO calling him back, but he knew that it was too soon. He'd been irritable and foolish with Lindsay, and now he'd have to live with it the whole weekend. He thought of the endless expanse of duty ahead of him. God! Two days in the PAO with Fiona Drummond and her horses. Horses and Labradors—the whole goddamn weekend. "Sure I'm sure," he heard Aggie say with her querulous brogue. "There ain't nobody here in green. By God, if there's one color I do know, it's green." She hung up, and her voice trailed off into a tatter of muttering.

"Dr. Conrad," she croaked from the kitchen, "it's comin' soon. I'm makin' it fresh for ya."

"It's okay, Aggie," he said quietly, and opened his copy of *The Interpretation of Dreams.* "Take your time."

For the tenth time that night he tried to marshal his powers of concentration and struggle with the condensed and obscure sense of the text. He heard Aggie opening a refrigerator in the kitchen beyond. "Will ya be takin' cream, Doctor?" Aggie loved the word "doctor" almost as much as she loved catering to them.

"No, thanks, Aggie," he said into the tiny print of the text, "black." He felt Graver's eyes staring at the back of his neck. He forced himself to follow the line of argument on the page in front of him. ". . . we must recognize that the psychical mechanism employed by neuroses is not created by the impact of a pathological disturbance upon the mind but is present already in the normal structure of the mental apparatus. . . ." For the tenth time the words became obdurate and slippery, like polished marble. His mind slid off the page and returned once again to the quarrel with Lindsay earlier that evening.

*"I didn't* forget about you! But I couldn't leave six crazy old people sitting around in nightgowns while I went off on a lark with my sweetie pie." It was almost eight o'clock by the time he led her downstairs through the underground tunnel to trace the last hours of Jennifer Light.

"That's ridiculous! You can't really believe I kept you waiting because you were quote just a lousy girl reporter unquote." Sure he had told her his dinner break was at six-thirty, but how was he to know that a vanload of patients would arrive from Bronx Hospital just then?

They had entered the cafeteria hissing at each other, and the green-clad OR people—eight or nine of them—turned toward them with interest.

"Why did you ignore me all day?"

He'd clammed up and marched stiffly down the room to the last booth on the left. "This is where I was sitting, trying to read!"

he said, raising his voice again. Again the OR people looked. "And over here," he said in a grudging whisper, walking three booths back, "is where they were sitting." Then he added, as though he were thinking it through for the first time, "She must have been sitting there facing my booth, and the guy must have been sitting on the bench like this with his legs stretched out." He waved his hand over the banquette as though he were a conjurer. The image of the shoes returned, but now he didn't know whether he was remembering reality or dream.

He turned back to her. It was she who had ignored him all day. Going off with Avi that way. Christ, and she'd barely said good-bye afterward.

"I thought you meant for me to be with Avi. You put me in the back seat with him, *n'est-ce pas?*" Her eyes flashed. "I was only taking my cues from you." Her nostrils flared, and tears brimmed, making her eyes more intensely blue. He wanted to hold her, calm her, console her. "God, why are men such incredible idiots! How do I get out of here?"

He pointed the way, and she pounded off down the tunnel toward the signs that said MAIN ENTRANCE. And he stalked back to the PAO, fuming and forgetting his dinner. Now he was back in the cafeteria, bone tired and beyond hunger.

*A*rmed only with his monograph and a grim smile, he approached the lone figure sitting halfway across the dining room. Graver, absorbed in what he was reading, sat with his spoon poised in midair as though he had forgotten it.

"May I join you?"

Graver looked up, unsurprised. "I thought you'd never ask, Conrad." He lowered the spoon into the bowl. The dressing on his hand was fresh and had shrunk in size. "I'm honored," he added, and his sensuous lips grinned.

Despite his size and the streaks of gray in his tousled hair, there was something smugly boyish about him; perhaps the way his eyes tried to escape in conversation, like an excited child straining to get away. Seth had noticed that the only time Graver seemed alive and engaged was in argument.

Seth put his coffee and book on the table and sat down opposite Graver, whose eyes slipped back to the place in the journal where he had left off reading and which had been held by a longish fingernail with a thin line of dirt under it.

"Kind of late for you, isn't it?"

"No," Graver said without thinking. "I'm here most nights." He glanced up from the journal. "Not every night," he added. "Let's say many nights." His eyes returned to the page. "I like it. Relaxing. No distractions." His finger ran down a column of figures. "I do my best work at night." He looked up at Seth. "The silence, the empty corridors. How about you? Like working nights?"

Surprised by Graver's uncharacteristic interest, he answered too hastily. "Well, this weekend's a little rough. I'm on tomorrow and Sunday and then again Tuesday night."

"Too much, eh?" Graver leaned back to wipe his mouth. "Well, it'll toughen your *tuchis* up. You guys could use a little toughening up. When I was a first-year resident, we were on every other night, *all* night."

Seth sipped his coffee. "I guess times have changed."

"Busy tonight?" Graver asked, looking again at the journal.

"Yeah. Pam's sick for a change, so she kind of fades in and out."

This night had been her vomiting night. There had been other nights with Pam, and other organs. There had been the splitting-sinus-headache nights and the incapacitating-menstrual-cramp nights. This night, though, was the worst. Every twenty minutes up to her room to retch and lie down, lie down and retch.

"The body is delicate and unpredictable, Seth. It's like a sports car. You can't expect it to go pumping away, like"—she had brushed a wisp of dark hair away from her pale, worried face as she searched desperately for the appropriate analogue—"like a pump." Pam was the overprotective owner of an Italian sports car whose inner organs were as delicate and unpredictable as hers. "It has its own reasons, you know, humidity, altitude, whatever." She belched demurely, turned all of a sudden, and walked toward the elevator. "See you later." That was just before Lindsay had arrived with *her* madness.

"What the hell's wrong with her anyway?" Graver asked without looking up. "She never comes to conference." Seth's shrug went unnoticed. Graver was again studying a column of figures.

"What's your assignment these days?" he asked without interest.

"Still N-6."

"Uh-huh. Like it?"

"Hanging in there. Things are a little out of control without Milly to keep us organized. She runs a tight ship."

Graver looked up. "Yeah, she's okay." His dark eyes searched Seth's face for signs of underlying mischief. "A little emotional, but okay." He turned back to his journal. "Ben still futzing around with his cameras?" he said with a little scoff, and mumbled something which sounded to Seth like "schmuck."

The phone rang in the distance, and Aggie went through her routine.

"Know anything about tracer elements?" Graver asked, flipping through the journal pages.

"A little." Graver looked up. "Spent about six months studying the transport of radioactive serine across cell membranes."

"Really?" Graver pushed the empty soup bowl a little to one side and leaned forward with interest. "Ever been upstairs? The lab, I mean." He smiled. "Why don't you come up sometime over the weekend and I'll show you what we're doing?" He leaned back and jangled some keys in the pocket of his white coat.

"Whit's been telling me."

"Shields?" he said, dismissing the name with a wave of his hand. "He's decided to study perversions."

"No, he's doing an EEG study with Paul Silk."

Graver smirked and stuck his tongue into his cheek. "He was cute today at the funeral, wasn't he? Flouncing in that way. Repulsive little pansy!" He paused. "Don't look so shocked. I'm only stating a well-known fact. What you're shocked about is that I say openly what I think. I'm not a hypocrite. And I don't believe in shielding children from the facts of life."

Seth sipped his coffee, proud that he had registered no emotion. "I think the residents appreciate that, Dr. Graver."

"What were you doing there this morning anyway? Did you know her? Jennie?"

"A little."

"What do you mean, 'a little'? Jennie didn't know people a little. Either you knew her or you didn't."

"Sounded like she'd been unhappy all her life."

"You mean the rabbi's pious drivel. 'Uncle Sidney' is a fool. Besides, he never spoke to her again after she had that abortion when she was sixteen." He paused and gave Seth a fishy look. "Why are you so interested in Jennifer?"

'I don't know." Seth shifted in his seat and put down his cup. "Just curiosity, I suppose."

Graver leaned forward over the table and pointed with his bandaged finger. "It's that reporter, what's her name . . ." He leaned back and smiled knowingly. "Good-looking. You want to *shtup* her—*that's* your curiosity. Can't blame you. Nice body." He leaned forward again. "I'll tell you one thing about Jennie Light if you want to know. Don't believe anything you hear about her. She was incapable of telling the truth or even knowing what the truth was anymore. She had it so screwed up."

"What do you mean?"

"Never mind." Graver sat back again. "Look, Conrad, why don't you do yourself a favor and forget about all this? Study what you came here to study, and *shtup* whoever you want, but forget about it. The Lights have had enough *tsuris* from this kid without the reporter or you adding to it." As though demonstrating to Seth that the subject was closed, he reached over and picked up the book that had been lying on the table. "What've we got here?" He opened to the title page. *"The Interpretation of Dreams,"* he read with exaggerated awe. "That'll keep you out of trouble." He began flipping through the pages.

Seth studied his features. There was a vitality there, a combination of crude energy and intelligence. He thought of Myra's lament at lunch and smiled to himself. "Listen, he went to high school with my kid brother. It was a special school for spoiled brothers. Very progressive. It was perfect for Graver—and my kid brother. The Henry David Thoreau School." She pronounced it soberly, in a deep voice. "Where everybody majored in civil disobedience. Well, he was a snotty, narcissistic bastard then. And he's a snotty, narcissistic bastard now." She'd shaken her head then, for emphasis, and made her earrings tinkle. "By the time he graduated he had screwed all of the social science teachers in the school, and what do you think he got for it? Kicked out? Gonorrhea? He got the soc sci prize and a bad case of contempt for social workers—in case you haven't noticed. But"—she had paused reflectively and sighed—"he was better-looking in those days."

Graver went on, an edge to his voice. "Joe Burden still teaching this garbage?"

"Yup, I guess people are still willing to pay money for it and read it."

"Well, Christ, Conrad, what does that prove? The number one best seller last week was a book on astrology. Why don't you try that on your patients?" He threw the book on the table with a bang. "There are millions of suckers born every day."

"I guess so." Seth recrossed his legs.

"You enjoy this stuff?"

"It's interesting."

Graver jangled the keys in his coat pocket again. "You know, in science ideas are like socks. You have to change them every once in a while or they begin to stink. These guys haven't changed their socks in—when was this written?"

"Nineteen hundred."

Graver smiled derisively.

Seth looked into the depths of his cup. "I guess some ideas stand the test of time."

"Some ideas aren't tested, by time or anything else." Graver took his bowl and slammed it down on a nearby table. "Some ideas are just worshiped." He wiped his mouth and looked at Seth. "Any friends in analysis, Conrad?"

"One or two."

Graver leaned back and smirked. "Ever hear of any who finished? I mean *finishing,* not just getting up and quitting or having their analysts drop dead from obesity or nervous tension right in the middle of the treatment—paragons of mental health, they are. I mean really finished, Conrad, ended, discharged, cured. How many?" Seth heard the phone ringing in the background. "How many times have you heard those fabled words 'I finished my analysis'? Fifty?" He paused. "Ten?" He paused again, dramatically. "Five? Surely you have five friends who've been in analysis. Two? One! You must be able to give me one example! Not one?"

"Not one." He wished Aggie would answer that phone.

"Well, I have a few who didn't finish. Wives, bleeding their husbands white while they chatter away on the couch five times a week. Lousy kids who spend your money on shrinks to get even. I can even give you the name of a grandmother who's been in treatment for thirty years with the same analyst. What was that about the test of time, Conrad?"

He paused and fell back in his chair like a lover, spent. The phone had stopped ringing. Thank God, Aggie had finally picked it up.

"Tell your friend Bloch. I'm sure he can make a very funny sketch out of it for one of his hilarious shows."

"Dr. Conrad, you're wanted in the admitting office."

"Okay, Aggie." Seth stood up. "Tell 'em I'll be right there," he shouted to the kitchen. "Sorry, Dr. Graver, another time, maybe." He picked up the book and took several steps toward the exit. Suddenly he turned back to Graver. "By the way, how do you know they chatter?"

Graver's mouth smiled, but not his eyes. "How come, Conrad, you're always curious about the wrong things?"

Seth shrugged. "Family curse, I guess." There was a suffusion of color in Graver's face, but whether it was anger or the effect of the heat emanating from the steam table, there was no way to tell.


"Take your hands off me, you fuckin' ape. I'm a fuckin' princess!"

Seth stood in the middle of the PAO, pushed his glasses back up on his nose, and took stock of the situation.

Two burly cops were trying to wrangle a mulishly resisting woman into the waiting room. Strands of lank dirty blond hair hung over her face. Her hands were handcuffed behind her, and her legs stiffly balked the officers' attempts to pull her in.

"Come on, Barbara, cut out the rough stuff. Be a good kid." The three of them were soaked with sweat from the struggle.

When they finally managed to seat her and unlocked one hand, she promptly swung the arm with the handcuffs, narrowly missing the head of one of the sweating cops. Subduing her again, they put the handcuffs back on, this time in front of her. They informed her that if she made any more trouble, they would take her straight to the lockup, princess or not.

The taller of the two cops approached Seth. "We picked this beauty up in Hell's Kitchen," he said in a low, confidential voice, and read her name and address from a small black leather notebook as Seth began to make out an admission sheet. He knew already that she would have to be admitted to N-7, the women's disturbed ward.

The policeman took off his cap, mopped his forehead with his sleeve, and leaned over the desk toward Seth. He told him Barbara's mother had called the police because she had not eaten or slept for five days and had barricaded herself in her room and threatened to set herself on fire.

The leather notebook the cop consulted seemed tiny in his quart-size hands. He read from it in an official tone as though he were describing a speeding violation. He was dark, Italian, Seth thought; he reminded Seth of Fontana.

". . . refuses to answer to her real name and says she's married to a"—he looked at Seth and shrugged—"prince . . . named"—he consulted his little book again—"Amahl Jalali. She says her family is trying to poison her. Her mother said she'd come tomorrow and give you all the details."

"Anything else?" Seth inquired.

"No, that's all I got except this." He touched a spot behind his left ear. "Jesus, I don't think I'll ever hear the same. We had to break into her room, and she hit me with a broom as I came through the door. She's strong as a bull." Seth could see an egg-size lump had formed.

"Why don't you go over to the ER and let one of the surgeons look at that?" Seth suggested. He asked the other patrolman to bring the patient into the office and remove her handcuffs. As he fumbled for his keys, the cop glanced doubtfully at Seth. As soon as she was free, she plunged her hand into the pocket of her grimy housedress and ripped out a package of foreign cigarettes.

"You see these? They're Turkish. You know why I smoke these?" she said to the cop, who was withdrawing into a wooden silence. "Because I live in Persia and if I'm not there soon, you'll be very sorry!" She spoke like an angry mother warning a disobedient child. Then, as though she had forgotten what role she was playing, she pleaded to no one in particular, "Come on, gimme a light."

Seth asked the wooden cop to wait in the outer office, lit the patient's cigarette, and offered her a seat beside the desk. She acted as though he were invisible and had said nothing; instead, she began pacing back and forth, looking at the floor, mumbling, and smoking in furious bursts.

He watched her carefully as he wrote his admission note on the pink sheet headed "Department of Hospitals, City of New York." He wrote with the idea that Joe Burden might someday read these notes and remark on how astute and detailed the observations were, a model to be used in the instruction of future generations of psychiatrists. A classic, to be placed alongside Bienville's description of nymphomania and Charcot on hysteria. And now the complete mental examination of Barbara W. by Dr. Seth Conrad, written on a September night in Bellevue Hospital after sixteen hours on duty.

"Mental Status: The patient disregarded my invitation to sit down and talk and, in fact, acted as though I were an inanimate object. She paced back and forth in the examining room, head bent forward, eyes cast down as though she were looking for something she had lost. Her eyes had that appearance of 'inward gaze' which suggested that she was lost in some autistic reverie. She smoked as she paced; her smoking movements were rapid, nervous, and automatic, and after five or six puffs she would pull out another cigarette, light it with the old one, and drop the latter on the floor, crushing it angrily with her foot.

"Occasionally she would interrupt her pacing and stand silently, her head cocked to the side as though she were listening to something going on somewhere else in the universe. Then she would smile knowingly and nod. Her gait and movements, although agitated, were well coordinated, especially in the finer motions involved in finding and relighting her cigarettes. This degree of neuromotor intactness would tend to rule out any acute organic psychosis.

"The patient is a woman in her thirties who appears dilapidated and unkempt. Her hair is disheveled and oily, apparently ungroomed for many days; one can see tobacco particles and an occasional hairpin hanging loosely. Her face with its high cheekbones, straight nose, and oval shape might have been quite attractive at another time, but it would take a great deal of imagination to see her that way at the moment. Her skin is oily and grimy, and from the dry and cracked condition of her lips she appears to be dehydrated. It is possible she hasn't eaten or drunk anything for days because of her fears of being poisoned. Her stained housedress with its torn pocket and hem and her worn-out house slippers are in keeping with her total uninterest in taking care of herself or in the unhappy effect that her appearance has on those around her."

She was a mess. He remembered the point Burden had made that some patients—psychotic patients especially—present themselves as garbage and often get themselves treated like garbage. It was eleven-fifteen, he was tired, and he wished Barbara W. had been brought in later, after he had gone.

Seth had found it required a powerful creative act on the part of those who took care of patients in city hospitals not to treat them like so many defective objects to be wheeled from one place to another, opened, closed, tapped, filled, drained, and hauled away. Bellevue was better than some and worse than many in its over-crowding, its lack of staff, its diffusions of responsibility, and—not the least—its patients, the wretched refuse of the wretched refuse. The men and women who came here were beyond sickness, beyond poverty. They were the ignorant, the ugly, the dirty, used to degradation, asking to be degraded. Soon after he had arrived at Bellevue, Seth had resolved to resist the temptation to give them what they asked for.

He had stopped writing and was working on overcoming his

revulsion for Barbara W. The thought of Joe Burden somehow helped.

"Miss Weber, sit down!" he said with an authority which surprised even himself. It was calm, but because he was tired and meant business, it had the effect of moving the patient to the chair Seth had indicated.

"Your job is not to love your patients; it's to understand their pathology," Burden had told them.

She sat opposite him quite still, with her head cocked and smiling as though she were listening to an amusing story being told by someone on another planet.

"Miss Weber!" Silence and disregard. Not even close. It was as if they were separated by a glass wall ten feet thick. "Miss Weber!" A little louder and more authoritative. "Where are you now, Miss Weber?"

"I'm here with you, beautiful Doctor-boy." She punctuated this by blowing a lungful of smoke into his face. When the smoke cleared, he saw her dirty fingernails and nicotine-stained fingers. As she leaned toward him, he felt her foul-smelling breath. "If I push this button," she said, touching her right nipple with her index finger, "I can vaporize you. So don't fuck my mind over; I've been mind-fucked enough."

She got up suddenly and walked away. The act was abrupt and unheralded, as if she had gone up in a puff of smoke—vaporized herself or him, he didn't know which. She had receded into her autistic reverie.

"Who's been mind-fucking you?"

"He has," she said, cocking her head toward one corner of the empty room.

"Is he doing it now?"

No answer; she had receded again.

"Miss Weber! Please sit down!" Seth said emphatically and loudly, as though she were on the other end of a long-distance telephone.

She turned vacantly toward him and, without regarding him, sat down again in the chair, this time facing away from him.

"Tell me what you're hearing, the voices."

"He wants me to come."

"Where?"

"To Baghdad."

"Who?"

"My psychiatrist."

"Who is he? What's his name?"

"Amahl . . . Jalali. We were married yesterday."

"Where is he?"

"He's in Persia. . . . He's the richest man in the mouton world. . . ." She looked at him for the first time with half-seeing eyes as she let the cigarette she was holding in her left hand fall to the floor still burning. He smelled the odor of stale sweat.

". . . he owns Gimbels and Macy's . . . owns this hospital." She looked away again and slipped her right hand inside her dress and began to fondle her breast.

The grandiose delusions, the fragmented thinking, the auditory hallucinations, her inappropriate behavior—all pointed to a schizophrenic syndrome. He had finished writing this provisional diagnosis on his admission note and looked up to find her looking at him through half-closed eyes, her face flushed with excitement as she continued to fondle her breast. Her red-rimmed eyes under her heavy lids saw in him some autistic lover; her cracked lips pursed gently as she directed a kiss to him. She murmured ecstatically, "Touch me, kiss me, fuck me."

If she had smashed his face, he couldn't have been more stunned. He stared as she caressed herself, eyes almost closed now, head lolling backward, thighs opening and closing rhythmically. Suddenly flushing, he looked away, glancing through the doorway to the outer office.

Like waves crashing on a storm-swept beach, feelings assailed him from all directions. Before one could recede, another flooded in. From those first weeks in the anatomy lab he had carefully educated his feelings to remain under control until he had come to rely on his calm, dispassionate responses. And now he was furious.

He ordered Mary Ryan to have the patient bathed prior to admission and told her he'd do a physical examination later. She was still masturbating when Mary came to collect her.

"There now, dear, we don't do that in public," she said as she took Barbara Weber's hand from inside her dress and helped her stand up. "It's not self-respectin', dear. Come along. You're not smelling too sweet. We'll give you a nice, cool bath. You'll feel much better. Come along now." She held one hand, put her other arm around the patient's back, and led her to the bathroom.

Self-respect, Jesus, how simple it was. "Shit!" he muttered, and threw his pen across the room at a cockroach on the wall.

# Chapter

| 7 |
|---|

"C-O-N-R-A-D, Conrad. No, wait, hold it! Shit!" He'd been shouting into the phone over the din and commotion of the PAO. "Shit!" he muttered again, and sat down with a bump on the desk. Put on hold again, he was immobilized, suspended in a silent electronic purgatory between desire and the promise of connection. It was his fourth attempt to contact Lindsay that day. The first time he'd been told that she hadn't yet arrived; the second, that there was no one at the *News* by that name; and the last time, at three o'clock, that she was still out to lunch. Now it was just past four. He yanked at his tie and then his collar so that the button popped and disappeared from sight under the desk. He cursed again and cast the fugitive button out of his life forever with an apathetic wave of his hand.

The place was a sweatbox. He tugged at his damp collar and fanned his neck with it. Avi Schwartzman steamed energetically past and gave him a cheery wave. Without smiling he winked back in response. Avi and Lisa Stone were manning the PAO on the four to midnight shift and were bustling about, organizing things for the emergencies that were sure to come.

Monday nights were usually slow after the busy weekend, but this was the seventh day of ninety-degree heat and humidity. The papers called it the hottest mid-September on record, and there seemed, at least to Seth, to be a sense of impending crisis in the air. It was as though the city were one great febrile patient, restless, slightly delirious, raveled, on the edge. Each day brought vague promises of relief, higher temperatures, and disappointing reports that a cool air mass was stalled somewhere while some "high" or "low" pumped warm air remorselessly northward from the Gulf of Mexico. At the moment he was fed up with the heat, fed up with the hospital, fed up especially with the PAO.

Suddenly there was a click in his ear, and an impersonal voice came on the line to tell him that it was sorry but that there was no Conrad in that department; perhaps he should try the Sunday edition. It had heard there was a Conrad there.

"I'm Conrad," he shouted desperately, pointing to himself as though the voice could see him. "Don't hang up! Please!" Then, with painstaking deliberateness and exaggerated calm, he said, "I am Dr. Conrad, Dr. Seth Conrad calling from Bellevue Hospital. I would like to speak to Miss Lindsay Cooper, a reporter on your staff."

"Hold on, please," the voice said, and then the impersonal finger that went with it punched him back into silent suspension.

Oh, Christ, he was fed up. He sat down again, defeated.

"Hullo there," Fiona called to him lustily as she trotted by, her ponytail bobbing behind her. Seth forced a grin.

"Tally-ho, Fiona."

And fed up with Fiona. Pam and her organ systems teetering on the brink of dissolution were bad enough, but two days of horses and hounds had pushed him too far.

At first she had been a welcome relief from Pam. He rather enjoyed her dependable, chunky body and her stolid Kentish manner. But by Sunday he'd begun desperately to yearn for his long-legged, slim-hipped army brat, his fresh-faced, quick-witted, lovely army brat. He rang her apartment at frequent intervals all of Sunday, each time wondering where she was and with whom. A quick trip home to Springfield to see her father and brothers? A quiet weekend at the beach with Roger? It was a name he had heard Lindsay mention only once, in passing, but unaccountably, to Seth, Roger that day had become alive and formidable. Roger had twenty-twenty vision and wore clothes that fit. When he wore a pinstripe, no one sniggered. His shirt had a neatly embroidered *R* over the pocket, and under it rippled muscles that Seth had forsaken years ago. Quietly articulate in private, he was brilliant at dinner tables up and down Park Avenue. *Yale Law Review,* but equally at home in a twin-engine cockpit and with the metaphysical poets.

In fact, it was of clear-eyed Roger and Lindsay he was thinking, of the two of them speeding west toward Manhattan late on Sunday night in Roger's gleaming black Porsche; it was of them he was thinking as he struggled to keep his mind on his monograph; it was of them—in the semidarkness, their faces illuminated only by the soft light of the instrument panel, Roger handling the wheel easily with one hand, the other resting tenderly on Lindsay's arm as she dozed next to him—he was thinking as he fell into a jealous and fitful sleep.

The sharp click in his ear jolted him back into the sweltering, noisy PAO. "I'm sorry," the voice said with frosty indifference, "but Mr. Cooper has left for the day."

"Mr. Cooper! *Lindsay* Cooper. I asked for *Lindsay* Cooper," he shouted.

"Yes, Mr. Lindsay Cooper has left for the day," the voice snapped back.

"Lindsay Cooper is a woman!" he screamed.

Everyone in the PAO was staring at him, and he felt his ears redden. He slammed the handset down on the cradle, but missing its mark, it bounced off and slid across the desk with a clatter and onto the floor.

"Shit! Shit!" he growled, and ducked down to retrieve the instrument.

When he surfaced a moment later, a voice behind said, "Take it easy, Doc, that's city property."

Seth turned and saw the muscular figure of Vince Fontana looming over him. The detective, cool and fresh in a mint green sport shirt, looked concerned. "You okay, Doc? Your ears are all red, and you're sweatin'."

Seth pulled off his jacket and glasses and began to wipe the lenses with his tie. He squinted at Fontana. "Look, when I want medical help, I'll ask for it."

Fontana shrugged. "No harm, Doc. I thought maybe you were sick or something."

Seth slipped his glasses back on, wiped his face on his shirt sleeve, and leaned toward Fontana as though he were about to kiss him. "I'm not sick or something," he said in a harsh whisper. "What I need is to get out of here for a while."

"Rough day?"

"Day? Weekend! Week! Where was the homicide squad all weekend, Fontana? We missed you." He finished wiping his face and began without much thought to roll up his sleeves. "What was that sign over your desk? 'Knock on doors.' I didn't see you knocking on any doors around here."

Fontana shrugged, deaf—or perhaps dumb, Seth thought—to innuendo. "No. I was off this weekend. My kid took her first communion. She was a real little sweetheart. You should've seen her."

"Well, look, Fontana, give your kid—"

"Marie—that's her name."

"—give Marie my regards or whatever you give kids on their first communion. I have to get out of here." He slung his jacket over his shoulder and began to brush past Fontana. Suddenly he felt a powerful grip tighten around his arm.

"Hold it a second, Doc." Fontana smiled smugly. "I'd like to ask you something."

Seth, stopped in his transit, was astonished not so much by the force of Fontana's grip as by the idea of it. No stranger, no man had ever touched him—uninvited—since he was a boy. His whole adolescence, his adulthood, indeed, his whole life had centered on the idea that the basis of civilization was discourse, talk between reasonable men, the idea that might *didn't* make right and that persuasion was better than force. He had learned early in the Conrad Universe that you won by wits and words, not by hitting and hurting. As he stood there staring at Fontana in his mint-fresh sport shirt, he did not feel fear or repugnance or outrage. He felt only astonishment—astonishment at the innocence of the action. It seemed as effortless and native to Fontana as speech was to him.

Grinning stupidly now, Fontana allowed him to wheedle his arm away.

"Look, Fontana, I still don't know where she was living, and nobody I know knows." It was half true. He had asked only Myra Karp, and Myra, who knew everything about nothing worth knowing, knew nothing about where or with whom Jennifer Light was last living. She doubted, she told him, whether anybody knew, but he might try to wrest what she knew from the tight lips of Phyl Rowan. Lemmon's secretary was to Bellevue what the Delphic oracle was to classical Greece. He had only to bring her a container of tea as a votive offering.

"I believe you, Doc, I believe you," Fontana said without conviction. "We ain't had much luck either. Funny how a little thing like that can be so tough."

"Listen, Fontana, I want to get out of here today. What do you want to talk about?"

"This," he said with a conspiratorial look, and tapped the manila folder he held in his left hand.

"Do we have to stand right here in the middle of the PAO?" Seth looked around uncomfortably.

"Sure, sure, Doc. I got ya. Come on." He led Seth to a dark corridor off the PAO and an unmarked door. Unlocking it, he entered and flicked the light on. "Step into my parlor, said the spider to the fly."

He waved Seth in. "Cozy, huh?" The room was a tiny, windowless cell, created decades ago, when space was short, out of two closets back to back. It was crowded even with just its rickety little table and two old chairs. The globe had disappeared from the lighting fixture, and there was only a dim naked bulb left.

"This is what what's his name—Lemmon—gave us while we're here. A place to keep our crap and use the phone," he said, pointing to several bulging manila envelopes and a telephone with a cracked mouthpiece on the table. "I seen worse. You should've seen the dump I worked in before I took the exam for the department. A furrier. They called me an expediter." He shrugged. "It meant I carried big bundles of furs—you know, pelts—to this little room and counted 'em. I smelled from skunk all the time." He sat down, straddling the chair back to front, and looked around. "At least it don't smell."

"Fontana, you're not very interested in this case, are you?" Seth had found the words to hurt with again.

"What do you mean, Doc?" Fontana looked puzzled.

"Never mind, what's in the folder?"

"Oh, I got ya. You think I should bleed more." He was scowling now. "I should care about her like I care about my kid. Well, I got news for ya, Doc. I don't. I care, but I can't bleed over every case I got. This morning they found a cute little hooker in Stuyvesant Park with seventeen stab wounds in her body. She's my case, too. If I bled over every case I have, I'd look like that hooker in the park. I put in my time, Doc, just like you, and I do my job, just like you. 'Not interested'?" The color had risen in Fontana's face, and a thick vein pulsed in his temple. "You don't know what 'not interested' is. You know, there's guys in the department who don't make a collar for months, years sometimes. You know why? Because then you spend a day, maybe two, cooped up in court, where they treat you like an animal same as the collar. To them it's all the same. Equal justice for all, right? Cops, crooks. And then they let the motherfucker off on some technicality, so he goes out and does it again. So they say, 'screw it, what for? What difference does it make?' *That's* 'not interested.' " He snapped open the folder he was holding as if it were to blame and sat staring at the page before him. Seth pulled at his tie again in search of some relief from the stagnant, stifling air. Suddenly Fontana closed the folder and squinted at Seth, as though he were far away and difficult to make out.

"You know, you college guys break my ass. You think life is all about one great important thing." He made an expansive balloonlike movement with his arms. "Bullshit! Life is about a lotta stupid, little, pain-in-the-ass things, and I take care of my share the best I can."

Opening the folder again, he reached into his shirt pocket for a stick of gum. He unwrapped it slowly, carefully, and then folded the wrapper and stuck it back in his pocket.

"Now, like I was sayin'," he said without looking up at Seth. "According to this"—he flicked the top page as though there were a flyspeck on it—"the kid came to work here two years ago. She was recommended for the job by Dr. Jonathan Graver." He glanced up at Seth, who had slumped against the wall, his arms folded across his chest.

"So?"

"So, that figures, right? He's a friend of the Light family, personal favor, fixes the kid up with a job. All that figures. So she goes to work on"—he turned the page and consulted one of the typed entries—"NO-6 for a . . . Dr. Benson Coles for a year as ward secretary. Right?" He glanced up again.

"Okay, so what?" Seth said dryly. He made a special effort to register no surprise or emotion at the news that Jennifer Light had worked closely for a whole year with Coles.

"Now we come to the part that don't figure. You see, Graver'd already done the favor by getting her a job. But now it says, according to this"—he flicked at the page again—"he takes her into his lab as a technical assistant. A technical assistant." He looked down again at the folder and felt his shirt pocket. "Want some gum, Doc?"

"No, thanks, not right now."

"Technical assistant. Doesn't that mean you know something about something, like chemistry and crap like that?"

Seth nodded. "Usually."

"Well, we checked, and hell, she never even finished college. She went to NYU for a couple of years and dropped out. Most of her courses were artsy-fartsy subjects like pottery—what do you call it?—ceramics and literature. She took one science course, botany, but never even finished that. Does it make sense, Doc? That Graver would put someone with that background in his lab? Christ, my old grandma could have been a lab technician then."

"Why don't you ask Graver?"

"I did."

"What did he say?"

"He hemmed and hawed and then said she was smart and learned fast and"—he leaned forward and read from notes in the folder—

" 'I like to train assistants myself, so they don't really need a science background.' " He paused and looked at Seth. "How does that sound? You buy that?"

"No," Seth said emphatically. He didn't know why he had answered at all. Perhaps the heat, or because he didn't like Graver's bullying or Fontana's strong-arm tactics.

"I didn't either. I checked the other people on his staff. There's a guy and two other women. Not so good-lookin'—you know what I mean. And they all have good science background and job experience. So I asked him about that, and you know what?"

"What?" Seth said, glancing at his watch.

"He blew up and told me he didn't have any more time to waste on this. You know," he said slowly, "I think this guy Graver doesn't think about science all the time."

"Who does?"

Fontana looked up at the dangling light bulb for a moment. "I know, Doc, I know, but I guess I thought professors were different."

The idea came to Seth quietly, but with such conviction that he knew it must be true. Fontana would never find the murderer of Jennifer Light. At the University of Chicago he had read Hannah Arendt on the "banality of evil": that the monstrous forces of evil were everyday people doing their everyday jobs. Now, he realized that the forces of good led by Vince Fontana were a bunch of simple, part-time, good-natured guys with typewriters that didn't work and files that couldn't be found. He knew that decent, over-extended Vince Fontana with his two-fingered typing and his kid's first communion and his gum would never catch up. He knew with a sense of incontrovertible truth that Jennifer Light and her murderer were beyond the banality of goodness.

Fontana took the wad of gum out of his mouth and looked at it for a moment. Then, tucking it carefully into the wrapper he had saved for it, he studied Seth. "You know, Doc, you're a tight-assed bastard. You ought to loosen up a little."

Suddenly there were shouts and the sounds of a commotion coming from the admitting office. Fontana swung the door open and leaped into the corridor. Automatically he reached for the revolver

over his right hip but instantly aborted the impulse when he saw
the tangled mass of bodies in the PAO.

Avi Schwartzman, looking stunned, lay on the threshold of the
interviewing room, groping stupidly for his thick-lensed glasses,
mumbling warnings to the blurred shapes careening around to watch
out for them.

Not far from Avi, in front of Mary Ryan's desk, a tangle of
bodies looking like the Laocoön struggled amid shouts of contradictory commands, grunts, and curses. At the center a wild-eyed
man, half kneeling, half standing, fought off eight people trying to
subdue him. Three huge cops trying to control his flailing arms
pushed him backward onto the floor, where his feet were pinned
fast by three male aides.

Staring at the scene, Seth sensed the enormous field of force that
emanated from the crazed little man and the counterforce that was
required to control him. Was this what Burden had been trying to
tell them: that the instinctual drives had an awe-inspiring, majestic
power akin to the forces of nature and that one could not tinker
with them for long without getting into trouble? Even now the
man, his shirt in shreds, was beginning to squirm free from the
waist down and renewed efforts were required to reestablish immobility.

Flung across the man's chest in her white skirt and jacket, her
long chestnut hair, even in this melee, looking lustrous, was Lisa
Stone, fierce, dedicated, determined to make the final conquest.

"The syringe, the syringe, damn it!" She had just torn the sleeve
from the patient's shirt and rubbed an area over his shoulder muscle
with an alcohol sponge and now she was ready to plunge the syringe
holding a hundred milligrams of Thorazine into him. Someone handed
it to her, and deftly she shot the syringe home, pushing hard and
steadily on the plunger until the entire 4 cc dose had entered the
man's deltoid muscle.

Avi had found his glasses and was getting to his feet shakily
when he spotted Seth.

"My God, I've never seen anything like it," he said, adjusting
his yarmulke. "He was catatonic when the cops brought him in.
Completely out of it. Like a statue. I started asking him some

questions, and suddenly he came at me." His hands shook as he spoke, and he rehearsed the events again, this time in more detail, as though he were searching for some clue to what had happened to him. As he listened, Seth watched the whopping dose of Thorazine take effect. The struggling became uncoordinated; the eyes began to glaze and blink; suddenly the patient stopped struggling completely and relaxed.

Lisa Stone, flushed, smiling, syringe still in hand, arose and, gorgeous in her triumph, stared down at her quarry.

"Okay," Mary Ryan called out like the field commander she was meant to be, "let's get this patient up to O-7." Helping the aides load the patient into an old high-backed wooden wheelchair, she yelled across to Lisa, " 'Seclusion Room'—be sure and write it in big letters! God knows they're not too bright up there. And don't forget fluids or he'll burn up. And for God's sake, make sure everybody up there knows he's dangerous!"


"The last of the egg roll, boychik." Harvey held up the butt end impaled on a fork and studied it as though it were a diseased organ. "Lousy, really lousy." He rotated the specimen. "Soggy and tasteless." His gaze turned thoughtful. "A metaphor for my life." He brightened. "That's what I'll call my memoirs: 'The Last of the Egg Roll.' Posterity, when it thinks of me, will reach for the duck sauce. Pass the moo shoo." Seth handed him a serving bowl with a metal cover.

"Well, boychik, how'd you like it?"

"Too much moo shoo and not enough pork."

"Not the food, the sketch."

"You know what I think. Besides, I wasn't listening." He looked at Harvey over his moo shoo pancake, "Believe it or not, Harv, I've got one or two troubles of my own."

"Troubles, boychik? What do you know about troubles? You dare to talk of your petty squabbles in the same breath as my titanic creative struggles." He hiccuped and brushed the napkin to his lips with princely decorum. "Take it from me, my friend, you don't know from trouble. To quote Sadie Bloch, professor of life emeritus:

'Cancer—that's trouble. You have to go to a Mexican medical school—that's trouble.' " Harvey punctuated each trouble with an accusatory jab of his chopsticks. " 'A son comes home from freshman year at Wesleyan and says, 'Ma, I'm gay, don't tell Papa—that's trouble.' " He leaned across the table, "Seth, we're buddies, mates! Your troubles, my troubles." He grasped Seth's wrist. "Our troubles." He waited for a sign that didn't come. "Sadie would understand. I need encouragement. I can't do this all alone," he said urgently. "I'm blocked!"

Seth reclaimed his hand and swirled the dregs of his tea. "Take a laxative."

Harvey sat back and gave him a reproachful look. "Boychik, you don't understand. The show is half written, and it goes on in three weeks. I need feedback."

The word was that Harvey had done brilliantly the year before, although some in the department had said he had gone too far, that he had turned the corner from the gentle lampooning of previous years to savage disrespect. Founders Day—celebrated annually on the first Friday of October—had been the occasion. The academic exercises commemorating the 136th anniversary of the medical school had been followed, as usual, by faculty cocktail parties and in the case of the psychiatry department by its annual house staff show and chairman's dinner. Harvey, naturally, had been the star performer as well as writer, composer, and director of the show.

"Listen." He waved his chopsticks impatiently at Seth. "I've already told you, you can forget about Coles, despite Golden Boy's advice. He's a lunatic. Coles, that is."

Harvey looked down with relish at the moo shoo pork roll, its pallid, limp form a Fay Wray cradled in the hands of King Kong. He took a large, lascivious bite and swallowed half of Fay Wray with a gulp and a swig of tea. He lurched forward again and grabbed Seth's hand in his greasy fingers. "Boychik, tell me, how did you like it—the sketch?"

Seth extricated his hand and stared at him across the table as though there were a thick pane of glass between them. "You weren't there, were you?" he said distantly.

"If I wasn't there, it probably wasn't worth being there, boychik. Where?" He poured himself some tea.

"The funeral. How come?"

Harvey tossed his jacket over the back of his chair. There were arcs of sweat under his arms.

"Maybe it's because I don't deal in bullshit," Harvey said slowly, without looking at Seth.

"Six seconds."

Harvey looked at him blankly.

"It took six seconds." Seth tapped his watch. "You usually get there in three. The feel-good defense. Anything you do is okay if it feels good. Courtesy, good manners—all bullshit to you."

"Hold on there, big shot, when did you get the Nobel Prize for good manners? You'd better ask yourself why you *went*. You never even knew her, and maybe Graver was right: Stop mucking around." He lapsed into silence and mopped his forehead with the napkin he had crumpled in his fist. Suddenly he turned away and hailed the waiter. "Dessert?"

Seth shook his head.

Harvey gave the waiter a big tourist smile. "One lichee," he said loudly, holding up his index finger like a righteous prophet, "and one kumquat." He held up the opposing finger. "Okay?" The waiter smiled warmly and nodded.

"Now give it to me straight, boychik." He smiled benignly. "I can take it." He leaned forward, bracing himself. "The sketch— what'd you think?"

"Rotten! Execrable!"

"You know, you're the only friend I have who knows the meaning of that word."

"That's because I'm the only friend you have."

"That bad, huh?"

"It was stupid. Christ, Harvey, why do you make me say these things to you?"

"You could have said it was clever and witty."

"But it wasn't."

"Okay, I accept the verdict, but give me one more shot. Just one more time, and I ring down the curtain of maturity on my past." Harvey leaned forward, his eyes bright. "Here, have a lichee; they're good for premature ejaculation."

"Harvey." Seth took the proffered lichee nut, impaled on a toothpick, and tossed it back among its sibs. "Listen to me." He grasped the large, beefy hand tightly as though he were taking Harvey into custody. "Drop it. Drop the whole show. Let someone else do it. Sandler. Let him do it. He's been dying to do it. It was great in college. Even in med school. You did two shows. They'd never seen anything like it. Harv, you were terrific." Seth paused and sighed. "But it's over now. You're too old for this crap now." He let go of his hand. "You've got to grow up."

"I'm trying, boychik." He reached for his box of cheroots. "You think it's easy? I had rheumatic fever when I was a kid. It left me scarred for life." He breathed life into a dark, evil-looking cigar. "I swear I'll go straight after this one."

"Harvey, you're a doctor, a psychiatrist! Doctors do their thing; they don't screw around." He heard desperation in his voice. "Don't you have any sense of professional identity?"

"Sure I do. I think you're being grossly unfair to your old buddy." He blew a thin blue smoke ring toward the ceiling. "Look at Schweitzer. He didn't just treat hookworm and pull thorns out of lion paws. He was a musician. He played the organ, I play the harpsichord. What's the difference? Both keyboard instruments. He did a little biography; I do a little musical comedy."

"Schweitzer! How can you compare yourself to Schweitzer?"

"Shush. Cool off. You want a lot of Chinks listening?"

"Schweitzer was supposed to have a reverence for life," Seth hissed. "What do you have?"

"How many guesses do I have? A lust for life? No. A yearning for life? No. Don't tell me, I know. A passion for life—"

"You have a hatred for life." Seth let that sink in. "What do you do when you see a cockroach in the apartment? Are you glad to see it? Do you play a little hymn to God on your harpsichord when you see one, like Schweitzer?" Harvey was silent, staring reproachfully at Seth. "Come on, what do you do? Let's settle this Schweitzer crap once and for all." No answer. "I'll tell you what you do. You go ape-shit. The last time you took off your shoe and raced around the kitchen after that cockroach like a maniac. You broke two plates and a cup." Seth threw his napkin down on the greasy Formica table for emphasis. "Why the hell did you go to medical school if you wanted to write musical comedy?"

"How should I know?" He shrugged. "Why do salmon swim upstream? I got up one morning and suddenly started writing to medical schools. I guess it's genetic. Do you think those buggers know why they're breaking their little hearts swimming up water-falls?" His big hand wriggled upstream in unconvincing imitation. "Do you think they'd do it if they knew they'd have one chance to get their rocks off and then"—he let his head fall to one side and his eyes roll up in his head—"curtains." He sat up and flashed an amiable smile.

"Boychik, come on, be a sport. I swear this is my last time. Scout's honor. I've got less than three weeks left. I'm desperate. Listen and tell me what you think."

Defeated, Seth slumped forward and stared off toward the distant kitchen.

"We'll really sock it to 'em with this one, boychik." There was something ancient and festering, Seth knew, in Harvey's passion for ridicule, his pleasure in savage attack. It was as though he had some personal score to settle with the stupid, the mediocre, and the pretentious of the earth.

Across the room Seth caught the flash of a bare neck and shoulders, tanned and smooth. Should he try her once more? It was already after ten. He hadn't seen her, talked to her, in three days.

". . . get the picture? The *Mittel-europäisch* consulting room, cluttered, stuffy, obligatory bust of Freud in the foreground. Two o'clock, the charity hour, a hard hour for analysts to fill with paying patients . . . boychik, you're not listening. Jesus, you're just like my Chicago analyst; he didn't listen either."

"It's no wonder," Seth said without bothering to look up, "considering what you try to pass off as human thought."

Harvey, untouched, popped a kumquat into his mouth. "And we'll do one on the show biz analysts. Two hundred—that's what they charge, I swear. They also treat long distance, if you happen to be on the Coast. You know, lots of theater people. Natty dressers. Houndstooth check with a Tripler label, side-vented . . ."

She must be home by now. He glanced across the room at the bare neck and shoulders. There would be no harm, he decided, in trying once more.

Seth watched the numbers as they marched into his life and disappeared: 11:43:19, 20, 21. The numbers themselves had become meaningless; only their remorseless, unforgiving succession held him, the brief life of each snuffed out by the next.

The accident, as it was called in the family, happened on Martha's Vineyard. Elly had become increasingly moody and irritable that summer. Seth remembered the Saturday, the last Saturday, when she had pushed them to the breaking point. The final words came just before dinner that evening between Elly and her father—over nothing. He had asked her to fetch a bottle of wine for the dinner table. It was something Seth could have done easily. He knew the bottles by heart. She did it halfheartedly and brought the wrong one. A critical comment was the spark she was looking for; there was a violent explosion, and Elly ran out of the house in a hysterical frenzy. That moment was the last time he had seen her alive.

The watch now read "MON 11:45:04." He stared at the parade of numbers, remote, pitiless, inhuman, reflecting a life without regrets or hopes, no past or future, only the solitary now. He'd been lying there on the bed, clothes still on, feeling solitary since . . . 11:14:01, the numbers had said. He had tried her earlier, and after twelve rings and no response he childishly called Connie Martin's number. When she answered in her warm, bosomy style, he quietly, almost stealthily hung up. He felt his ears redden as he remembered his foolishness. She must be home by now, 11:47:11. He had decided finally against calling. An act of desperation, he thought. He would leave word for her tomorrow at the paper, calmly, civilly—like Whit Shields—with easy grace.

He thought of Lisa Stone standing flushed and victorious that afternoon in the PAO. Should get to know her better. Less spiky than Lindsay and, certainly, better body. He glanced at his watch

. . . 11:48:02. He sat up, reached for the phone on the bedside table, and dialed.

"Hello." The voice on the other end was cobwebby with sleep. Seth was silent, deliberating.

"Hello, who is this?"

"Seth." He took his glasses off and rubbed the bridge of his nose.

"Oh, for a minute I thought it was one of those breathers."

"I breathe, but I don't do it professionally—only for my friends at parties." He paused for an interval that he thought would suggest nonchalance, even indifference. "What've you been up to?"

"Uh, sleep. Sleep, I think. But it hasn't worked out. What time is it?"

"Oh, I don't know, been reading Freud, I guess I lost track of the time. Heady stuff."

"It's almost midnight, Seth."

"Oh, is it? Didn't realize it was so late. They keeping you busy?"

"No, no I've been in the Hamptons. I didn't get back until this morning. God, I was sound asleep when you called. We've been on the go all weekend."

"Oh? Yeah, me, too . . . the hospital, I mean. We're busy these days. The heat, I think. Melts people's brains after a while. Little-known fact. Great weekend for the, uh, beach."

"Not bad. Hazy and hot." She yawned.

"Play a lot of tennis?"

"No, no tennis. Too hot."

"Ah, yes, of course. Perfect weather for metaphysical poetry over cold lobster and a bottle of Muscadet."

"Metaphysical poetry? What are you talking about?"

"I thought he was a real hotshot on metaphysical poetry, not to mention arbitrage and international law," he added with a grim smile.

"Who?" Her voice was wide-awake now.

"Roger."

"Roger? What does he have to do with it?"

"Isn't he a lawyer?"

"No, he's a social worker, and he reads science fiction, not poetry. What about him?"

"He was with you this weekend, wasn't he?"

"Of course not. I haven't talked to him in months. I don't even like him, and I don't need any social work, so why would I be going on a weekend with him?"

"Who was the 'we' then?"

"I really don't see that it matters."

"It matters to me. I . . . like you, damn it."

"That's very sweet, very tender. Who writes your flattery, the Ayatollah? To like is not to own. Did you call me at midnight and wake me out of a sound sleep to soothe your inflamed pride? Look, Seth, I've got to get some rest. If you like me, then call me when you like me and not to play jealousy games. And if you really want to know, it wasn't Roger, it was Leslie, and it wasn't Muscadet, it was Chablis."

"Lindsay . . ." It was too late; she had clicked off. He sat there staring dumbly at the receiver for a few moments, then placed it on its cradle. He leaned back against the propped pillows and wondered again whether it would have happened if he had fetched the wine that evening.

He stared at his watch: TUE 12:00:43, 44, 45, 46 . . . and fell into a restless sleep, clothes and all, at 12:18:03.


**B**urden looked hurt by the question, as though he were about to cry.

Removing his glasses slowly, Seth Conrad pulled out a soggy handkerchief. He mopped a trickle of perspiration at the temple and began to smear the lenses as he squinted up at the ceiling, trying to look thoughtful. Only Fiona could have asked it—with that mixture of equine innocence and British presumption. She was like some kind of female centaur, half horse, with her thin legs and heavy, blunt shoes, and half rider, with her straight back and head tilted bravely.

"That's a perfectly natural question," Burden said with a weary smile. He looked at her sidewise and began to roll up his shirt sleeves as though he wanted to thrash her.

Seth glanced at his watch through the smear of his glasses. Christ, ten minutes till the end of the conference. She could have waited until next time. He'd been restless and irritable all morning. Although the temperature had not reached its high point for the day, the humidity had become intolerable; he knew it was his imagination, but he felt crushed by it. He took a deep breath, but it didn't help and only made him take another one. He looked at his watch again. Burden raised his voice over the rhythmic groan of the air conditioner as it exhaled a feeble stream of lukewarm air.

"The trouble, Dr. Drummond, is that to answer your question, we would have to understand more about the nature of dreams— dream theory. Something I wasn't planning to discuss for a month or two." He paused and looked at them sadly, as though all of them suffered from some fatal illness. "You know, I wish I could put all of this into your heads instantly and painlessly." He stood up and walked to the blackboard. "Well, let's see if we can answer your question briefly, Dr. Drummond."

Oh, Christ, "briefly" meant twenty minutes, at least. Almost noon. Fiona, Fiona, why couldn't you keep your mouth shut? He smiled at her across the table. He wanted to get down to the PAO before Fontana left for lunch.

"Let me rephrase your question, Dr. Drummond, to get to the heart of it."

Seth, rousing himself, sat up straighter and tried to focus on what Burden was saying.

Burden turned and wrote two words on the blackboard, "DREAMS" on the left and "PSYCHOPATHOLOGY" on the right. He pointed to the word on the left. "Normal," he said, and under the word on the right he wrote "PSYCHOSIS, NEUROSIS, PERVERSION, ETC." He faced the group and pointed to the list. "Abnormal." Then he drew a line between "DREAMS" and "PSYCHOPATHOLOGY" and a question mark over it.

Seth reopened his notebook with brisk anticipation and wrote the isolated word "DREAMS." Then, as though the effort had exhausted him, he sank back in his chair, slouching in mindless contemplation over the single word he had written. Unaccountably the information that he had gotten from Phyl Rowan that morning had made him jumpy. Now he wanted to be free of it, pass it on, and forget it.

"Dr. Drummond, what you want to know is, What's the connection? This normal everyday, or should I say 'everynight' "— he interjected a tiny self-adulatory smile—"phenomenon and these unusual, abnormal phenomena. 'Why do we bother with a patient's dreams?' I think you said."

The humidity seemed to muffle Burden's words and soften the edges of their meaning. Seth tried another deep breath, again without relief. As he scratched at the page with his pen, half listening, the single word in the notebook became elaborated and transformed as though it had a life of its own.

"Dr. Drummond, have you ever gone to bed feeling well and woken out of a dream depressed and out of sorts?"

"No, to be honest, I don't think I have. Couldn't one just give one's head a good shake—you know," she added brightly, "sort of like a colt when the snaffle's too tight?"

Fiona, Fiona, incorrigible Fiona. Seth looked up from the restless labors in his notebook to give her another comradely smile.

"Exactly, Dr. Drummond!" Burden pointed at her accusingly. "I'm not sure about your horse, but you may have some Freudian blood in you. You see, that shake of your head is a behavioral component of what Freud would have called a defense, an automatic attempt to get rid of some mental unpleasure—in your case by a combination of suppression, distraction, and physical movement."

Burden slid back into his seat at the table. He was wiry, and Seth observed his easy, graceful movements enviously. "In a nutshell, the theory of dreams says that we dream at night because things bother us during the day. And by the time we go to bed, if what has upset us has not been resolved, it continues to disturb us as we sleep, an irritant, like a grain of sand in an oyster. . . ."

Seth looked down at the face that he had without effort or thought re-created out of his nightmare, a face covered with swirling dots and its cruel mouth made of DREAMS that seemed to mock him. Already Burden's words were receding and slipping out of focus.

"The dream, then, is the pearl. Its purpose is to get rid of the irritation and to substitute something more pleasurable or tolerable in its place. . . ."

*H*e had stopped only long enough to pick up a container of black coffee for himself and tea for her. She had called the ward at eight o'clock that morning and in her gravelly drawl had told him that she was glad to know that he was still with them and would he kindly come down to Dr. Lemmon's office. When he arrived, Phyl Rowan, who lived by her own clock, was sitting at her desk in the empty office, her bony fingers flying over the keys of a large electric typewriter. The office was still dark except for a circle of light that fell on the typewriter keyboard.

Ignoring him for another four or five lines, she came to the end of a paragraph, punched the machine into silence, and turned to him. "You took your time."

Seth set the containers down on a nearby desk and looked at his watch dramatically, like a field commander. "Three minutes— I came on foot."

"Three days. I left word last Friday. I told them urgent."

"You should know better than that, Phyl. If you really want to get a message to me, tell them you have a secret you don't want me to find out about. See?"

Seth caught a flicker of pleasure from the corners of her mouth. He handed her the container with the Lipton tag hanging out of it. "Thanks, I was just going to get some. Now, what can I do for you?"

"You called me."

"I'll get to that," she said imperturbably. "Now, I wasn't born yesterday—unfortunately—and when a nice young doctor brings a tough old bird like me a cup of tea, he wants something—either to change his duty schedule or to get some information. Which?"

"Information." He felt his ears redden. "Look, I have a friend, a girl, I . . . promised to help," he stammered.

*B*urden seemed a long way off now, as though Seth were looking at him through the wrong end of a telescope. He tried to concentrate on what Burden was saying, to pull himself back into earshot.

"The dream serves the biological purpose of helping us to stay asleep. Most of the time it works well; sometimes, when the feelings are too strong, it doesn't, and we wake up thinking it was the dream that woke us when actually it was only an unsuccessful dream, one that couldn't preserve our sleep from the strength of the feelings stirred up during the day. . . ."

*F*inally, he had just blurted the question out, like a guilty child. Jennifer Light had been living with someone from the hospital. Who was it? Did she know? He'd tried to ask it casually, smoothly, with a charmed smile, the way he thought Whit would have done it. Why? Phyl had asked simply. Oh, that. Yes. He'd grinned stiffly, painfully. He began explaining who Lindsay was and why she wanted the information and why it was important to her. Phyl sat there, listening, poker-faced, judging him. Suddenly he was seeing it through her cool eyes, hearing it with her leathery mind. He sank down onto the corner of the desk, in silent retreat.

"Birdie Smart, Ettinger's secretary, called me Friday." She hoisted the teabag out of the container and squeezed the remaining life out of it before tossing it into the wastebasket. "Whose toes have you been stepping on these days?" she said abruptly. "Birdie says he wants to see you. Today. Two o'clock." Still in a state of passive war with Coles, he wanted his insubordination to go unnoticed, at least until Milly McVey was back. Phyl Rowan sipped her tea and looked at him over the rim of the cup. "Why can't you boys behave? You know, in the old days, the house staff just did what they were told. They never got into trouble." Robbed of her dream of being a doctor's wife in the closing months of World War II, she took secret pleasure in being near young doctors and secret solace in playing godmother to them. Now she scrutinized his worry lines. "Well, maybe they were a little too quiet." She put her cup down. "I'd be there a few minutes early if I were you. He hates to be kept waiting." But already marshaling arguments in defense of Mrs. Scola and himself, he hadn't heard.

Now Burden raised his arm as though he were about to conduct an orchestra and seemed, for some reason, to be talking to Seth directly.

"You dream because something in the present has reminded you of something that never got resolved in the past. We are constantly reliving our past in the present in some subliminal automatic way, and our dreams keep having to lay to rest these ghosts that haunt us."

The face stared back at him from the page. What ghosts in him, he wondered, plucked that mocking laugh out of the cafeteria that night to create his nightmare? He tried to remember it, rehearse it once more, but nothing happened. It was gone now, passed into the unconscious, Burden would have said. The face now seemed empty to him, a silly, primitive, meaningless pattern of lines on the half-empty page of a fifty-cent notebook. Maybe Burden was wrong. Maybe Freud was wrong. Maybe Graver was right.

"Look here, Dr. Conrad, it wouldn't do you any good. Even if I told you who Jennie Light was living with. It wouldn't help your friend." She had finished the tea and was slowly, thoughtfully packing the bits of refuse that remained into the empty container. Then, almost against her will, bluntly, she said, "She was living with Milly McVey." She jettisoned the paper cup and looked up at him accusingly. "But I'm telling you it's a waste of time. She won't tell you anything about Jennie Light. Your friend, I mean. She liked Jennie." She shook her head. "Why, I don't know, but she did. She was a loser; maybe that's why." She looked away and turned the typewriter back on. It began to hum, and she began to fuss with it, as though she had forgotten about Seth. Then, almost as an afterthought, painfully, she turned back to him.

"Look, Dr. Conrad, you're a nice young man. I like you. And I don't want to see you get into any more trouble. Don't get involved. This is a rotten business. You don't know the half of it. I don't usually give people advice, and I don't know why I'm doing it now. People should stay out of other people's business. And maybe I should stay out of yours."

Abruptly she turned back to her typing; he had been dismissed. As he reached the door, the typing stopped. "Thanks for the tea," she said.

". . . the answer to your question, Dr. Drummond, is this." He stood up and energetically walked to the right side of the blackboard, the abnormal side, and pointed to the list of symptom complexes. "You will find that each symptom," he said slowly, "each pathological structure, has the same structure and the same function as a dream." He paused to let his words sink in. "And every symptom, every neurotic character trait, is like a pearl inside of which there's a living demon from our past. The same demons, Dr. Drummond"— he drew her attention back to the blackboard with a graceful pass of his hand, like a toreador—"the ones locked inside our 'abnormal' pearls and those that escape at night and instigate our 'normal' dreams.

"Learn the secrets of the one"—he pointed to the left side of the blackboard—"and you'll be able to exorcise the other." His hand moved subtly to the right. He stood silently, staring at the blackboard as though he had lost touch with them. Only the rhythmic groan of the air conditioner was audible.

"You know"—he turned slowly back to them—"from our point of view a pearl is a jewel—rare, lustrous, desirable. The bigger, the better. But from the oyster's point of view it's a lifelong burden that robs it of its life space and energy." A tiny, crooked smile flickered across his lips.

"The lucky oysters of us have only small pearls to carry around.

The others, well . . . we'll talk some more about them next week."
With a nod he released them all.

Without thinking, Seth tore the half-empty page out of his
notebook, crumpled it into a ball, and tossed it into the wastebasket
as he walked briskly in the direction of the PAO.

*T*he note he left for Fontana read: "JL lived with Milly McVey—
nurse on NO-6. She's on vacation until next Monday. Conrad."

He decided not to include the address and telephone number he
had gently pried out of Phyl Rowan. He didn't know why he felt
grudging toward Fontana, but at the moment he didn't care.

He fetched a piece of surgical tape from the PAO and folded
the note. Jennifer Light/Milly McVey. It seemed to him that he
had discovered a linkage which was until then both unknown and
unsuspected. He also knew he was exaggerating its importance.

He thought of the diagrams in his undergraduate logic course.
It was easy then. The truth was always in the area of darkness
where the circles intersected. He tried to think of all of the linkages—
all the circles—that seemed to intersect with Jennie Light's: Graver's
circle, Whit's circle, Silk's, Harvey's, and perhaps other darker circles
at which Phyl Rowan had hinted.

He rattled the door to Fontana's closet-office again to make
sure. No one had seen Fontana yet, and it was already a quarter
past twelve. He taped the folded note to the door of the office and
scribbled "Fontana" on the face of it, then stepped back like a
painter assessing his work. He stared at the paper with misgivings,
and pushed the glasses back up on his nose. Up to now the linkage
was his secret. Whatever its implications, he alone possessed it. He
would have denied it if anyone had told him at that moment that
he was both excited and frightened by this tiny fact.

# Chapter
## 8

*H*e was killing time. As soon as he felt the tepid air of the dining room wash over him, he knew it. It was haddock Tuesday, and the steamy gusts of stale fish from the kitchen did the trick. The humidity, the interminable heat, Seth thought, had made him jumpy and now queasy. Even the thought of coffee seemed sour and burdensome. His meeting—during the morning the meeting with Ettinger had taken on in his mind the character of a trial—wasn't until two, and he had time to kill. As he stood in the doorway, his eyes scanned the large room, not knowing what they wanted. He noticed Burden at one of the faculty tables. He was smiling his sad smile as he listened to Max Homburg, the forensic pathologist. Homburg, silver-haired and beefy, was overflowing, as usual, with noisy mirth and anecdote.

For anyone who wished to take the trouble to read subtle signs, it was obvious that the table at which Burden and his colleagues sat was the most important in the dining room. It was easily the largest, and its crisp linen, changed daily, seemed impervious to the mutilating power of the hospital laundry. Its silver, always gleaming, was guarded and polished weekly by Marge, the senior waitress in the dining room, whose sole duty by long-established custom was to serve the gods and demigods of the department.

"The Great Pantheonic Table," Jonathan Graver called it, with his usual smirk from his usual self-isolation.

Passing it now, Seth noticed that all five of its regular members were already occupied in Olympic discourse. Joe Burden had formed a conversational trio with Homburg and Morris Waxman. Waxman was a courtly old gentleman with twinkling blue eyes, famous for his bow ties and his expert testimony in cases of homicide in which insanity was the defense.

On the far side of the table the central figure was Tom Freeman, a giant of a man and the university's premier sociologist. He liked to boast dryly in his seminars that he was the illegitimate issue of a great-grandmother who was a slave and a great-grandfather who was a scalawag. The black man had removed his thick, rimless glasses and was polishing them with his napkin as he spoke in an endless ribbon of polysyllables. His target, Hans Lucas, was looking astonished as Freeman described his recent testimony before the Senate Subcommittee on Urban Violence.

Squeezing past the table, Seth caught Burden's eye in salutation. He wondered whether Burden had already heard about his clinical "insubordination" and the accounting that he would have to render to Ettinger that afternoon. He wished he could have explained it— justified it—all to Burden and wondered whether Coles would be there at two o'clock to lead the prosecution and distract him with his glassy stare.

Even from a distance Seth could make out the tanned, sculptured features and crisp tailoring of Paul Silk, and at the moment he realized that he welcomed the distraction of Silk's irritating presence. Silk, leaning toward the young man beside him like a solicitous mother, had flung his arm casually over the back of the other's chair.

"I don't care what Shields told you. You're not qualified, and stop acting like one of those adolescent cretins you play beefcake with—Ah, Conrad, the young philosopher. I was just trying to tell Master Mark here some of the facts of life. God, you look ghastly!

You're gween! Whenever I see you, you're either a mess or about to thwow up. For God's sake, man, what ails you?"

Seth gave him a sick smile and unfolded his napkin. Behind him the curtains hung limply at the open windows; outside, the sky was hazy and white. There had been rumors all morning of a coming break in the weather, and wishful thinking had transformed the stagnant air and cumbrous humidity into premonitory signs. Through the windows came the sounds of the city impersonally, inexorably minding its business: the buses steaming up First Avenue; the trailer trucks shifting into second gear as they climbed Murray Hill; the stop and go of the traffic; the occasional siren of an ambulance as it pulled up to the emergency room of the hospital.

Mark suddenly stood up. "I got stuff to do."

"Sit down!" Silk snapped. He grabbed Mark's wrist. "Sit down! I'm not finished."

There it was, just as Lisa had said, a slash of white just below Silk's wrist, half hidden by the heavy silver bracelet which hung down. It was about the size of a half-dollar and shaped like a ragged star.

It had taken him almost an hour after the funeral on Friday to wheedle the story out of her.

It had been blackmail. "Some gorgeous psychopathic kid. The bartender at a gay club." The whole thing had been hushed up. The acid had missed the boy's face, and he'd been bought off. "Shipped the kid off to the Coast and bought him a men's boutique. It left Paul with a scarred wrist and killed his marriage and his old man—at least that's what they say. *C'est vrai. Je te le jure.* Have I ever misled you, *cher*?"

He had smiled tolerantly. "Never."

Surrounded by platters of haddock and the desultory hum of midday conversation, and with the cool, urbane presence of Silk in front of him, Seth found the whole story even more farfetched, feverish, and operatic than when he had heard it on Friday.

Grim-faced, the young black man sank back into his chair and sat there erect and robotlike.

"You think you can just walk in and say you want a raise and a title—just like that?"

"No, it's because I'm good, as good as Frank was—better. And you know it, Paul."

"That's irrelevant," Silk said contemptuously. "I told you, you need the qualifications on paper." He looked away, at another table behind Seth, then nodded to someone and smiled tightly. "Besides"— he paused, still looking past Seth—"why doesn't your new fwiend help you?" He turned back to Mark with a mocking smile. "He's vewy fwee with his consciousness raising. He has connections. Isn't that right, Conrad?" He winked at Seth, who was beginning to feel his usual irritation with Silk. "I see that he's a good provider in other ways." He fingered the sleeve of Mark's jacket. "Left over from an old safari, no doubt. Ah, Abercwombie and Fitch—only the vewy rich can wear such threadbare raiment. Vewy pweppy, wouldn't you say, Conrad?" He turned back to Seth. "You're Ivy League; you should know."

"He said I could use whatever stuff was in the room."

"No wonder you haven't had time for your old fwiends these days. That's life. Easy come, easy go, eh, Master Mark?"

"Sorry, never made it to the Ivy League. Prairie boy." Seth's nausea had receded, and he welcomed the opportunity to defuse Silk's bullying. "Surprised you missed that, Paul. You're usually pretty good on—"

"Superficials, you were going to say."

"—appearances. But I'll accept 'superficials,' if you like," Seth added with a smile.

Silk picked up a knife from the table and pointed it accusingly at Seth. "Of course, Conrad! The prairie virgin. She's *your* friend, isn't she? The Immaculate Reporter! You put her on to me, didn't you?" He traced a design on the tablecloth with the knifepoint. "You know she's wasting her time, Conrad. No one really knew Jennie well. She was born to be a mystery. That was her charm." The scar on the back of his hand stood out white now. "Alas, I don't think your girlfriend appreciates that. Pity. She's vewy determined, isn't she?" He added with a mocking little smile, "And vewy clean." He threw the knife onto the table and put the tips of his long, graceful fingers together in front of him mandarin style. "I can understand what you see in her—a welcome relief from your chronically decrepit condition. But what"—he paused and smiled— "explains her interest in you? Your fwailty, no doubt. It has a certain charm for those of us with a maternal nature—one of my twagic flaws. Ah, the other players in this vewy low comedy have arrived."

Fiona Drummond, stately and long-necked, had appeared with Avi Schwartzman in tow. Avi, huffing and perspiring after a reluctant climb from the fifth floor, flopped into a chair across from Silk. "If God had wanted us to climb stairs," he intoned to Fiona, "he wouldn't have given us fingers to push elevator buttons."

"May we?" Fiona declared as she took a place next to Avi. "Have you all heard the good news?" she asked, looking about at each one as though it were an examination question.

"Severe thunderstorms. Coming this afternoon," Avi blurted out.

"This evening," Fiona corrected.

They never agreed about anything. Like bookends, they saw the world from opposing points of view, but like bookends, they had become inseparable. Each was fascinated by the other's essential strangeness: the one dashing through life astride her hunter in tune with the pastoral beauty of her land and the unambiguous sense of entitlement and virtue that was her special gift; the other, dark, curly-haired, soft, a born pedestrian, more in touch with the fox than the hounds, whose wife kept kosher and attended the ritual baths each month.

"For an hour or two you'd make a liar out of me?" Avi turned to the others for support. "You want the letter"—he wiggled his fingers contemptuously—"listen to her. You want the spirit"—he made a voluminous gesture with his arms—"listen to me. Big thunderstorms!"

Studying the scar on Silk's hand, Seth followed its jagged outline as though he were trying to memorize it; suddenly Silk's other hand covered it, and Silk's mouth smiled at him. He turned away quickly, just as he had turned away from Elly as she lay in the casket. She had looked beautiful, wearing one of her prettiest flowered dresses, her lips redder than usual. He had wanted to stare, to drink her in: her face, now strange in some way he couldn't understand; her body; the hands he knew so well from watching them as she read

to him very, very long ago. He wanted to touch her but was afraid
and at the last moment turned away. Now Silk was staring at him.
He felt hemmed in, and to escape, he checked the time again with
exaggerated precision. It was 1:30, and in fifteen minutes he would
be sitting in Ettinger's air-conditioned office. Ettinger didn't like to
be kept waiting, Phyl had said. And yes, it was Tuesday, and at
4:00 P.M. he would be in the PAO for another long night of
emergencies. Maybe the storm would keep things quiet. In the
distance he heard Silk ask mockingly, "Where did you get that ugly
bruise, Schwartzman? Drummond bwowbeating you?"

The contusion over Avi's right eye had become swollen and
blue, and he recited again with relish the story of his assault and
rescue the day before in the PAO.

Would Lindsay return the call he had just put in to her? Christ,
would she even get the call? Unfriendly, definitely unfriendly last
night. He sat up straighter and focused on what Avi was saying.

"Turn the other cheek?" Avi grabbed himself by the throat.
"He had me like this," he said, gasping. "God was on my side,
but the *meshuggener* definitely had the upper hand. Besides, I'm a
rabbi, not a martyr." He readjusted the yarmulke, which had begun
to cascade down over his ear during the violent outbreak of his self-
assault.

"Well, we bloody well need something," Fiona said emphatically.
"It happened again last night. Same patient. One of the aides went
in to check him; knocked him down, almost killed him. Took four
of us, actually, to restrain the bloody man." She speared a chunk
of haddock.

Seth watched Fiona as she held her knife and fork, in the
European manner, tines curving downward in her left hand, predatory,
poised over the haddock. Was there nothing this woman would not
eat? He smiled at her.

"Wasn't he in a camisole?" Silk asked sourly.

"Well, actually, someone had taken it off on the earlier shift
because of the heat. And of course, they were right—you can't keep
someone in restraints 'round the clock in this weather—but they
should have given us a bit of a warning. Only fair play, don't you

think? Gamy, this fish," she said, chewing thoughtfully. "What do they call it?"

"Haddock." Seth barely got the word out.

"Really? Rather good, actually," she said with relish.

"Another gweat moment in psychiatric nursing. It's a wonder that we have any staff left at all. Not the way we do things on our ward, eh, Master Mark?" He squeezed Mark's forearm.

Friction was Silk's one reliable mode of touching others. Sometimes it was a gentle chafing, yielding warmth, sometimes it was rough and abrasive, yielding pain; but in the end it was always wearing.

Now Mark extricated his arm from Silk's grasp, stood up, and announced coolly, "I got stuff to do."

He turned and had taken no more than a step or two when Silk, without turning, called him in a high-pitched, steely voice.

Mark stopped as though he had suddenly become trapped in a force field. He stood there, his back to Silk, impassive. The sunlight had become erratic, and there were changes in the air.

"Wait for me on the ward," Silk said, staring over the rim of his teacup. "I want to talk to you. And tell Carmen to find out how many aides are definitely coming in tonight. You heard Dr. Drummond say we're going to have severe thunderstorms. It's amazing," Silk said, turning to Seth, "how water-soluble the professional dedication of the staff is."

Sensing his release, Mark walked slowly, proudly, Seth thought, across the dining room.

Silk continued his little tirade against the nursing staff, but Seth was no longer listening. His thoughts and stomach had turned unfriendly again, and despite his best intentions, he realized that he was already late for his appointment with Ettinger.


*T*he rain beat at the window of the gloomy little office in startling bursts, making it difficult to read. As promised, it had come as a wall of water thundering in across the Delaware from Pennsylvania, pushing its way over the Kittatinny Mountains and the top of New Jersey. It left the silky chestnut horses of Bernardsville quivering and heaving in their stalls. It flooded the eternally mildewed cellars of the professors living along the Millstone River and swept down the Ramapo Mountains like God's fury onto the cities of the plain.

Seth could see it coming. That afternoon, as he sat facing Ettinger, he had watched the storm taking shape, the massive slate blue clouds marshaling themselves across the western horizon.

Ettinger's office was cool and sleek, like the chairman himself. It was on the twentieth floor of the University Hospital and faced west and north. The ominous blue clouds behind Ettinger seemed like part of a stage set for some colossal Wagnerian opera. And it seemed to Seth at the time that the drama that was unfolding between the chairman and himself was, if not titanic, at least larger than life.

Seth had known enough not to take the smile seriously or even the little joke about his lateness.

"Ben warned me that you'd transcended the petty constraints of time, that you were more interested in the whys of things than the whens." He'd grinned, revealing what to Seth seemed like an unusually large number of teeth, and very white, like the keys of a piano. Although Coles was not there, he seemed a presence in the room, as though he stood at Ettinger's shoulder, prompting him, politely clearing his throat at critical points, his dead eye somehow more perceptive than his living one.

"I understand your father is some sort of physiologist," he said, looking down at a folder on his desk. "Does he teach?" Ettinger asked cordially.

"Yes, sort of, I suppose," Seth said, cocking the trigger. He knew he shouldn't, but it was as irresistible as swatting a mosquito.

Ettinger eased back in his tan glove-leather chair. "Where?"

"Well, actually"—Seth paused for effect—"He's the John Eliot Norton professor and chairman of the Department of Molecular Biology at the University of Chicago School of Medicine."

He'd uttered the words quietly, almost humbly, knowing that it was the humility itself that was the cutting edge.

When it was finally delivered, the thrust of Ettinger's message caught Seth completely off guard. It wasn't at all about Mrs. Scola and his conspiracy. It was about Jennie Light.

Ettinger had come on to it by easy stages. Naturally it was shocking—to everyone. But not everybody realized how disorganizing such an event was to the administration of a department like this one. Calls from the trustees, from the president, the dean, other chairmen. "A lot of pressure, you'd be surprised, Dr. Conrad. But perhaps someday you'll find out when you're a chairman . . . like your father." Smile.

All very nice and friendly, Seth thought. Smiles and little jokes. No hardball. Then Ettinger got up from his desk and walked over to the window. He stood there looking over the city from twenty stories up. Like God, Seth had thought. He remembered that it was just before the storm hit. For a minute Seth thought that Ettinger had forgotten him. Then he said, "Dr. Conrad, you're going to drop whatever involvement you have with this matter." As though he *were* God, it seemed to Seth. "You're going to stick to your own business, which is learning psychiatry. That and only that. Repeat, only that. You're going to tell the police that you're too busy with your duties because, by God, you're going to have plenty of duties. Coles will see to that. And if he doesn't, I will.

"I've been with this department for thirty-eight years. I started here right out of my residency. Three times I should have been chairman of this department. Nothing is going to interfere this time. No accidents, no embarrassments, no scandals. Not even murder." Then he caught himself. He turned back to Seth and sat down at his desk. "You're going to cool it. You're going to cool it, or you're going to find yourself another residency. And I assure you, you'll never find one in this city." He smiled. "You're a smart fellow, Dr. Conrad. Think it over."

Just as Seth was leaving, the rain had begun.

When the storm finally hit, it stopped the city dead. The evening rush became an evening crawl and then an evening impasse. By six commuter rail lines were flooded, power lines were down in northern New Jersey, and the Long Island highways out of the city were under three feet of water at low points. By eight the men of Wall Street had given up and were booking hotel reservations; and by ten-thirty a record 1.9 inches of rain had fallen in Central Park.

Sprawling with his feet up on the old desk, Seth removed his glasses and massaged them on his shirtfront. The light was poor in the bare room, making the words on the page even more elusive. He let the journal fall into his lap. It was difficult to concentrate for very long in the PAO. Whit was right: This *was* frontline psychiatry; you never knew when the next assault would come. He glanced through the open door across the large outer office, to where Whit stooped like a patient mother over Mark Jones, who was seated at the desk, puzzling over a book.

Paradoxically the rain had not lessened the traffic through the PAO. Both of them, Whit and Seth, had been busy continuously until after 10:00 P.M. For the last fifteen or twenty minutes, though, there had been a suspicious lull. Only Mary Ryan, keeping watch in the outer office, could be heard chattering to one of her aides about her niece's bridal shower. "God, I turned red as a beet. And I mean I've seen nightgowns before. But nowadays you wouldn't believe it . . . I say a girl needs some comfort and warmth in the morning as well, so I got her a toaster oven—four slices."

The phone rang in the outer office, and Mary Ryan pounced on the call with all of her Irish robustness. "PAO. Yes, Dr. Silk . . ." Another phone began ringing. "Hold it, Dr. Silk, there's another call coming in. . . . I know it, but there's no one else here to answer it—" This was a lie. An innocent but well-known convention of Mary's. What she meant was that there was no one she could trust to answer the phones. She ran a tight ship, and nobody fought her on this point.

"—and contrary to what some people may think, I'm a human being, and I've only got one head." She slammed the phone down on the desk and leaned across to the other one and picked it up. It was a request for a consult, and Mary took the details. Then leisurely straightening the tiny nurse's cap over her orange hair, she picked up the phone with Silk on the line.

"I'm sorry, Dr. Silk, but your service isn't the only one in the hospital. All the wards are short-staffed tonight." Eyes rolled ceilingward, she held the phone away from her ear.

"You can state your case to Dorie Walters if you've a mind to. She's the boss. She makes the decisions. But I'll tell you right now, I'm gonna tell her that if my aide goes"—pause—"I go." She hung up. And to all within earshot—and when Mary Ryan was on the warpath, earshot was from river to river—she added, "God Almighty, he thinks he owns the damn hospital. Just because he has a problem, the whole bloody world has to stop turning.

"Consult, somebody," Mary shouted, her left hand cupped to her mouth as though she were hailing a passing ship, her right hand waving a slip of paper.

Groaning, Seth threw his journal onto the scarred desktop and lurched into the outer office.

"B building. Delirious patient," Mary called. "Keeps wandering around the ward. They want to transfer to Psycho Medicine. Will one of you handsome doctors straighten them out over there?"

Whit had also appeared, heading purposefully for the table on which the black "consult" bag was kept. The bag was a large, old-fashioned one, filled with instruments, psychotropic medication, and even a camisole and was as much a talismanic comfort as it was useful on dreary night calls to distant parts of the hospital.

"I'll take care of it, old man," Whit announced amiably through teeth that secured his ivory cigarette holder.

"No, it's my turn," Seth said, taking hold of the bag. "You've been out twice tonight."

"Not to worry. This is sailor's weather, and you're looking delicate tonight, if not actually peccant." He began to take charge of the bag. "I'll just set a storm jib and make for a windward shore." He smiled and gave the bag a little tug.

"I'm fine, Whit. I don't mind, really."

"I insist, old man. You're probably incubating some virulent new strain of plague." With a deft movement, hardly more than a firm twist, he snapped Seth's fingers away from the bag. "Besides, I'd *prefer* it." He blinked and made everything right with a friendly grin.

There was something between them, Seth knew, some strain, some secret dissension. It wasn't just fatigue or the late hour, but some negative force that seemed to grow as they got closer, like magnets with identical charges. Since dinner the previous week Seth had sensed it, some haunting, wispy envy.

They stood there, both of them surprised, looking at each other. Then, returning a tight little smile, Seth shrugged and thrust his hands into his pockets.

"Whichever goes," Mary called, adjusting the uniform over her lumpy figure, "no transfers tonight. There are no beds on Psycho Medicine. Tell them about chloral hydrate; they probably never heard of it."

"Perhaps you should take the consult, Mary, my dear," Whit called, offering her the bag.

"You could do worse, Dr. Shields, a lot worse from what I've seen around here."

"Hey, need some crew?" Mark Jones burst out of Whit's office, still holding the yellow book he'd been studying all evening. "I'll come with you."

"Not tonight, Marcus, I can do it faster alone. Keep my friend here company." He pulled the collar up on his white jacket and hunched his shoulders. "Tell him tales of derring-do; he likes those," he called as he made his run.

Passing Fontana's closet-office, Seth stopped and ran his finger over the tape that held his note to the door, securing it. He hesitated for a moment, then went on.

Back in his own little office he plopped into the chair behind the desk and gave an apathetic sigh.

"Hey, Doc, got a minute?" Mark stood on the threshold of the office, holding his book with a forefinger stuck in the middle of it.

Seth tossed his journal onto the desk so that it made a harsh slap. "Sure." His old chair squeaked as he tilted backward and flung his feet onto the desk. He nodded at the chair next to the desk. "What's up?"

"Nothin', just Whit left, and I ain't finished." He held up his yellow book so that Seth could make out the title if he squinted: *Word Power: The Key to Success.* "I got a couple more to do."

"What's it all about?" Seth asked with more interest than he meant to show.

"Paul . . . he wants me to take this test. Some bullshit test." He looked down at the book. "I mean, I'm too old for this jive. I shoulda done this stuff when I was a kid."

"Why do you take that crap from Silk—like lunch today?"

"He's okay. He's been good to me. I don't know. He's just touchy, that's all. You gotta handle him, you know?"

Seth shrugged. "What're the words?"

"Pers—I come on these two tonight." He opened the book and pulled out a scrap of paper with several words in clumsy, childlike script. ". . . picacious."

"Clever, perceptive," Seth said abruptly. Then, more slowly: "Sharp . . . able to see things quickly."

"Like you guys, you mean?" Mark folded the paper and settled back in his chair comfortably. "Whit was tellin' me how you guys are supposed to be, pers-picacious, pick things up about a person, like whether they got long fingernails and stuff like that."

"Yeah, I suppose so."

Mark plunged his right hand into the pocket of the safari jacket he was wearing. "Okay, what kinda ring am I wearing?"

Seth scowled. "It's too late for games tonight, Mark. What's the next word?"

"Come on, Doc. Just once. I just wanna see what you guys can do. Whit says you're the best. Come on."

Seth looked up at the ceiling in mild exasperation and decided humor was the best policy. "Okay. You're not wearing a ring. Now, what's the next word?"

"That's really sharp, man." Mark looked impressed. "I didn't think you could see anything through them glasses."

"I can't. I guessed. What's the word?"

"No shit! You jiving me?"

"Would I jive you?"

"You bet your ass you would."

"Well, maybe. What's the next word?"

Mark opened the paper again. "Succubus."

"Succubus? Where the hell did you get that?"

"Just some magazine I was lookin' at. Sounds dirty."

"It is, kind of. It's a demon, a female demon, or a witch that visits you at night and has sex with you."

"I know a lot of girls'll do that. I got other names for 'em."

"No, they do it while you're asleep. Look, the idea is, they get into you, under your skin, inside your head, and you can't get rid of them."

"Ain't that just like a woman?" Mark said with a smirk, and tilted back in his chair. "My grandfather was an expert on women. Wrote a book about 'em."

"Yeah?" Seth said skeptically.

"I don't mean a real book. He was kind of a philosopher of women and wrote like a little pamphlet. Printed it himself and gave it out to his friends, anybody who'd take it."

"What'd it say? I could use some advice," Seth said, instantly regretting the familiarity.

"Things like 'They leave you when you need them the most.' 'They're deceitful and coy.' Let's see what else." He searched the ceiling for more wisdom. "Oh, yeah. 'They was made to make men happy and to obey them at all times.' "

"I'll bet he never let your grandma read that book. She must've been a tough lady."

"You ain't kiddin', man." He laughed and put the paper back in the book. "I guess I shouldn't say 'ain't' so much."

"Why not? English lords do it."

"I'm not an English lord, man." Mark flashed. "Didn't you notice? My granddaddy was a Pullman porter, and my daddy was just a dead hero."

Seth flushed. He'd been patronizing, and Mark had caught him at it. "What's that supposed to mean, 'dead hero'?" Seth asked sharply.

"Nothin'."

"Come on. What is it?" Seth took his feet off the desk.

Mark leaned forward and looked at the book he held in his hands, as though he had suddenly become interested in it. "Well, you see," he said slowly, "I was born in Korea right after the war. My father was a sergeant in the Army, and my mother was Korean. She was a schoolteacher there, I think." He looked up and asked hopefully, "Can't you tell from my cheekbones?" He touched his face delicately. "Well, anyway, she got yellow jaundice and died when I was about four. I hardly remember her. I think I remember her trying to teach me a Korean word or something."

Seth leaned forward. "Then what happened? Who took care of you?"

"I went to live with my grandparents in Virginia."

"The philosopher?"

"Yeah. He was a Pullman porter. Then when my father, he got out of the Army, he got a job in a furniture factory near the town we lived in. And one day there was a fire, and he tried to save some woman who was trapped inside. He got her out, but no one ever saw him again."

"Jesus! What did they do?"

"Oh, they gave him a big funeral. It was nice. They was nice to me and my grandparents. They gave my father a medal. I mean, the company did. They gave it to me. I was only ten, but I was real proud. And they promised to give me a college education when I grew up. They wrote my grandfather a letter that said so. But that was all jive."

"What do you mean?"

"Well, man, you ever try to get anything from a company?" he said scornfully. "Well, they send you here, and they send you there, and you talk to this one and to that one, and then they say to write a letter, and then you don't hear, so you write another letter, and you don't hear, so you call, and then they send you here, then they send you there. It's bullshit, man. I'd be too old to go to college."

"Did you get a lawyer?" Seth asked indignantly.

Mark burst out laughing. "Then the *lawyer's* kids'd go to college." He looked at Seth impishly. "Why should I send a lawyer's kids to college?"

"You've got a point there."

Suddenly there was a commotion in the outer office as though a window had blown open.

"Wake up, everybody!" a familiar voice roared. "Let's see a little more starch in that uniform, Miss Ryan! What would Florence Nightingale say?"

"Florence Nightingale would have quit nursing if she had to deal with the likes of you, Dr. Bloch."

"You're a fresh mick, Nurse Ryan. Change your ways, or I'll withdraw my offer of marriage."

"Married? To you? God forbid!" She threw her eyes heavenward. "Sure and you'd drive ten strong nursing supervisors crazy, much less this little Irish lass." She patted her 180-pound bulk demurely. When she was angry and when she joked, she became more Gaelic, even though she'd been born and raised in the Bronx.

"Boychik, I've come to take you away from all this. Pull up your socks, and let's go to Lino's for some lasagne and a little vino." He wiggled his eyebrows Groucho Marx style and, scowling, walked past Mark to the other side of the desk. "How's it going, Jones?" Without waiting for a reply, he plunked himself down on the desktop and turned to Seth.

'No way, Harv. Whit's out on a consult, he won't be back before eleven-thirty—"

"Relax, boychik. Live a little."

"Besides, Coles is the faculty on call—my luck—and he's been spooking around all night."

"Okay, have it your way." He turned to Mark. "Aren't you up late for a Taoist, Jones? Doesn't your yin and your yang get all screwed up at this hour?"

Mark gave him an insipid smile.

"Well, if you insist, boychik, I'll recommune with my muse and return for the body in exactly"—he consulted his watch—"one Freudian hour, fifty minutes." He didn't move from his perch. "You *mamzer*, you didn't even ask."

The phone rang insistently in the outer office.

"Ask what?"

"How it's going. The creative process. My art."

"I can tell how it's going. You're elated, so it must be going badly."

Mark stood up. "I guess I'll go and see how Paul's doin' on the ward." Without looking back, he waved his book in Seth's direction. "So long, Doc, and thanks for the help."

"Sure thing, Mark, anytime."

"Yeah," Mark said from the outer office.

"It's true, dear boy, that my art is low, but it is alas, my only métier—sophomoric sketches, silly songs, and medical japery—"

Mary Ryan appeared in the doorway. "Soft Focus is on the line again," she whispered, and rolled her eyes up into her head. This was the fourth call and would probably be exactly like the other three. Seth moved slowly to the phone in the outer office, and Harvey tiptoed past him like a comic thief in a musical-comedy skit.

"Hello, this is Dr. Conrad. Is there anything I can do for you, Dr. Coles?"

"Ahem, what's going on down there?"

"Everything is quiet at the moment, sir."

"Well, if you need me for anything, Ah'll be up here."

Harvey stood at the door, waving his hands and signaling in dumb show that he'd be back in forty-five minutes.

"Right, we won't hesitate, sir." Seth nodded to Harvey and waved him off.

"Who else is down there now?" Coles liked keeping tabs on people.

"I'm here alone with Mary Ryan. Dr. Shields is out on a consult. That's about it for now—unless you want a rundown on the aides—"

"No, never mind. Ah'll stop by in a while. Ah want to talk to you before you leave. Ah spoke to Dr. Ettinger this afternoon, and Ah think we have some things to discuss, don't you, Dr. Conrad?"

"I guess so, sir."

"Well, just stick around, and don't leave before Ah get to see you. Right?"

"Right." Coles clicked off.

After shuffling apathetically back into his bare office, Seth sat down at the scarred, rickety oak desk with the initials of countless residents etched into it. He was too tired to read and wondered when Whit would show up.

Leaning back in the old chair, he pulled his glasses off and massaged the bridge of his nose.

The phone rang again, and he heard Mary answer it in the distance.

"Dr. Conrad," Mary shouted urgently, "it's for you."

"Shit!" Seth muttered. "Frontline psychiatry!"

*"E*mergency on O-7 . . ." The line crackled loudly in his ear. "Hello . . ." he called into the phone, trying to maintain contact with the distant voice. Another burst of rain at the windows reminded him that even in good weather the phones didn't work. "Hello, what's up?"

The authoritative voice had identified itself as the night nursing supervisor. ". . . a call from the aide up there . . ." More static. The voice, hoarse and pressured, was unfamiliar. ". . . meet you there right aw—" Another surge of electrical activity extinguished the voice, and the line went dead.

"Hello . . . hello . . ." Seth looked at the handset, and shook it irritably, as though it were lazy or asleep. Silence. He slammed it onto its cradle and checked the time: 11:28.

"Trouble on O-7, Mary," he called out apathetically. Mary, forever tightening her ship, was deep in the treatment room, checking supplies. "I'm going up and have a look." No response. "Mary? Hear?" Seth shrugged, and moved wearily toward the elevator.

Alone in the car, he slumped dramatically against its stainless steel wall as though he had been mortally wounded, the way he used to as a child, reenacting the deaths of heroes.

He supposed he was getting silly at this hour and warned himself to think, to think about the emergency. The voice hadn't said what it was. It was tight, nervous, the voice, strange to him; even the sex of it was ambiguous. But these days it didn't matter much anyway. They all wore pants and talked like policewomen.

The elevator, imperturbable, droned upward, stupidly out of tune with the sense of emergency that had summoned it.

"Chance rewards only the prepared mind." He saw old Pasteur looking down at him. No rewards for Conrad tonight. Feckless Conrad. The old man shook his head ruefully.

When the elevator door opened, finally, he heaved himself into an upright posture, pushed his glasses back up on his nose, and told himself to look at least plausible.

Although the heavy wooden door to 0-7 hung open when he arrived, Seth had been at the hospital long enough to know that there was no regulation that couldn't—perhaps even shouldn't—be bent or broken, even the one about locked wards. "LOCKED AT ALL TIMES," it had said in caps in the poorly mimeographed set of pages issued to him on his first day at the hospital. The right half of each page, he remembered, was practically illegible where the ink hadn't come through the stencil.

Slipping quietly onto the ward, he snapped the lock shut behind him and without knowing why instantly regretted it.

There *was* something wrong.

No commotion, no violence, no activity—none of the signs of emergency. Only a peaceful silence, the sounds of a dormitory asleep, and darkness.

The ward was completely dark except for the lamp at the nursing station, which cast a harsh light on the white metal desk and empty chair. The air was steamy with an ambiguous, faintly disgusting smell—a permanent aromatic blend of disinfectant and excrement, the heritage of the asylum, from the hundreds of times over the years that patients, in their travail, had smeared feces or urinated in the corridor.

Seth bent over the open chart on the desk: no unusual nursing observations. The last note had been written by A. Valdez. Where the hell was she? He cocked his head toward the darkness that surrounded the island of light and partial knowledge where he stood. Only the sound of twenty-seven souls breathing regularly and the rain beating loudly against the ward windows and the copper flashing outside.

"Miss Valdez," he hissed softly. Nothing. "Valdez." Silence.

He stood there stupidly, as though he had forgotten how to move. What are you waiting for? Find out what's going on. That's your job.

He opened all of the desk drawers, looking for a flashlight. Finding none, he closed the bottom drawer and listened again. Again, only the breathing; the rain had let up momentarily. Where the hell was the goddamn supervisor? Maybe whatever it was was in the vestibule at the far end of the ward. He went around the desk, put his right hand in his jacket pocket, and felt to make sure his stethoscope was there—comforted by its familiar contours. What about the light? Why were the goddamn lights off? He wished he had the key that worked the wall switches. Valdez will have a goddamn lot to explain, he thought.

Come on, move.

Tentatively, slowly, he set off down the corridor, away from the oasis of light at the nursing station. As his eyes adapted to the deepening darkness, he could make out the lumpy forms lying inertly on narrow cots. There was a distant roll of thunder somewhere out in the city and a sudden increase in the intensity of the rain at the windows.

The ward was laid out in an L shape, and along its long axis, the corridor down which he was now walking, were shallow alcoves, each large enough for four cots and each with a metal bedstand which held the few possessions that patients were allowed to keep. Some twenty yards ahead the ward turned left, and along that shorter corridor were three seclusion rooms and, at the end of it, a dining alcove where patients were also allowed to watch TV.

As he moved farther and farther from the light, he found himself straining to make out anything at all. His shirt was soaked through with sweat now, and his glasses were beginning to fog. He was being stupid about this. Keep moving.

From up ahead there was a sudden sound, and his heart began to pound. A scuttling sound? A shuffling sound? A stepping sound? A closing sound? A stupid sound!

"Doc!"

He was passing the last alcove on this corridor, and from the bed closest to him he heard a voice calling softly.

"Doc!"

Coming close to the cot, he could see a slightly built young man half sitting up in bed, leaning on his elbow. His dark hair was matted with sweat, and his eyes were wide.

"Doc, I'm scared. There's a crazy guy loose. He's roamin' around here."

"Take it easy," Seth said, trying to calm himself as well. "Everything's okay. Soon as I find Valdez, we'll get you some more sleeping medicine."

"No, Doc, I mean, there's a really crazy guy around. I'm tellin' you, Doc."

"Okay, try to get some sleep. I'll check it out." Another of the countless illusions and nightmares that flitted through the nights of madmen.

"Be careful!"

Moving up the corridor more briskly, for the patient's sake, Seth made the left turn. Now not even the faint light from the nursing station reached him. He edged closer to the left wall of the corridor, the side on which the seclusion rooms were located. Only one of them was occupied, he knew, by the paranoid patient he had seen subdued the day before.

He felt his way along the wall and came to the first room. It was empty, and the door was locked as it should have been. He heard something behind him and whirled around. His glasses had fogged completely now, and he tore them off and squinted into the darkness around him. He could see no form, no movement, and the tattoo of rain beating against metal drowned out everything. Sweat was stinging his eyes. He made a quick pass with his sleeve across his face and slung his glasses back into place. The sound of the rain like the feel of his stethoscope suddenly seemed like an old friend.

Room 2 held the violent patient. He came abreast of it. His heart kicked in his chest.

The door was open! He was staring into the blackness of an empty room. He took a step into the room. Then, out of nowhere, from behind or above—as though the hand of God had struck him—came an explosive force that astonished him first and sent him sprawling onto the filthy floor of the seclusion room face first. Just as his breath was knocked out of him, he heard the door slam shut. Someone had landed on him from behind, and now he could no longer think, could only fight to breathe. He gasped, and it was the last breath he remembered taking. Crazed steel hands had closed around his throat. Determined, awe-inspiring, unconflicted hands were killing him. He heard breathing in his right ear and felt breath and lips say, "I'm gonna kill you, fag."

There was a rushing sound, a roaring sound, and then . . . nothing.

## Part Three

# DAY RESIDUE

*Chapter*

# 9

Afterward he was tied to a table and told he was fine and not to worry but they were taking him anyway to the ICU, where they could take better care of him because he needed it, because he'd had a pretty close call. What did that mean, close call? ICU? They wheeled him down a long passage with naked light bulbs over and over again and told him that it was necessary, and when he tried to sit up, a gigantic man with a black beard in a pale blue uniform with strong hands that meant business forced him down and said, "Relax, Doc, we got ya. Don't make us more trouble. You'll be okay. Relax." His head ached; his throat ached; his chest ached. He tried to swallow, but they had put a tennis ball into his throat for some reason. He supposed it was a new treatment for something. He wanted to touch the tennis ball to make sure it was all right, but his hand was too heavy or maybe they had cut the wires. He had heard of things like that. Black beard could have done it easily. He wondered where Jennie was. No, not Jennie, Elly. Where was Elly? Then he was surrounded by faces staring down at him. Some he saw through the wrong end of a telescope; some were stony and aloof like those on Mount Rushmore: Whit smiling; Coles glowering; Mark remote; Harvey worried; Silk shaking his head; Mary Ryan soothing; Ettinger gloating; Graver impassive. Then he was put into a little house and told to sleep, and every time he slept they shone lights in his eyes and asked him to recite his name and address. What seemed like days passed this way. In and out, asleep, awake, dreaming, hearing, dozing, aching.

Suddenly there was a definitive shake and a cool, tough female voice said to him, "How do you feel, Dr. Conrad? It's morning." The voice was muted and distant, but it had a definite thrust to it and so reached Seth directly. Its owner was Irene Kinsella, head nurse of the intensive care unit, a tall, big-boned woman, calm enough to command a battalion under heavy fire.

Seth was inside a tent into which poured an endless current of cold steam and oxygen to make his breathing easier. He tried to answer, but no sound came. He mouthed the word "lousy!" He knew where he was but had the impression that when he tried to think, his head hurt. He tried to sit up a little but found his neck, throat, and ribs hurt when he did. He looked at Miss Kinsella, tapped his left wrist with his right index finger, and mouthed the word "Time?"

"It's seven o'clock, Thursday. You've had a nice long sleep."

Christ, what happened to Wednesday? he thought. He tried to remember, but it was like shaking a box of jigsaw pieces.

"How would you like something cool to drink? Dr. Tesler suggested that. He'll be down soon. Maybe he'll let you out of jail." She tapped the tent.

He was in the tent, he was told by Max Tesler, the chief resident in otolaryngology, because they'd been worried that he might develop a severe laryngeal edema which would require a trache. To underline the seriousness of this possibility, Tesler picked up a large, flat package wrapped neatly in surgical green lying in readiness on the bedside table: the trache set.

Tesler was short, rosy-cheeked, irrepressibly cheerful, and probably the smartest kid in every class he'd ever been in. He told Seth, who was wide-awake now, that he was a very lucky little psychiatrist; he must have reflexively tucked his chin down when his assailant began choking him. There were no apparent breaks or tears in the cartilage of the epiglottis or trachea. Some slight laryngeal edema and spasm, but that should clear up in a day or two. He didn't know how long Seth had been unconscious, but by the time he saw him his color was almost normal. He figured he hadn't had any significant degree of cerebral anoxia. He probably hadn't lost more than ten or twenty thousand cortical neurons. Ha-ha. Seth smiled weakly. He told Seth it would be painful to swallow and hard to talk for a day or so but that he should get his voice back by then. If he didn't, he should write to him. Weak smile. Tesler ordered the tent removed and told Seth he could go home as soon as he felt like it.

The oxygen tent was eventually removed by a couple of apprentice technicians, each working against the other like a well-rehearsed vaudeville team. And when they left, Lindsay was suddenly there, at the foot of his bed, looking freshly minted and worried. Without thinking he sat up and tried to speak. Instead, he clutched at the pain in his throat. She winced and touched his shoulder with an awkward caress, as though he were made of tissue paper. He motioned for the glass of water on the bedstand and sank back with tears of pain in his eyes.

"I've come to get you out of this place. Where's your hat? Shhh!" She kissed him on the lips. "Hospitals are to die in. I'm taking you home."

When he woke again, it was four in the afternoon and he was in Lindsay's bed. She'd insisted on putting him there, and he gave only token resistance. He had been silent in the taxi as they drove northward, apparently absorbed in the minutiae of the city streets. Reflections of the blue sky in the pools of rainwater everywhere were shattered frequently by a cool breeze from the north. The sun glistened in the windows along Central Park West. The morning dog walkers were out, each one looking a little like his pet.

Before falling into a dreamless sleep, though, he had rehearsed with increasing clarity the events of Tuesday.

Now he felt stronger, and by the time he'd finished showering he heard the sounds of a piano and Harvey's booming voice in the living room.

*They measured me, they pleasured me,*
*They absolutely treasured me.*
*All for the sake of sexual science.*

*They forecasted me, contrasted me,*
*They Johnson'd and Mastered me.*
*They gave me my own sexual appliance.*

Christ! Seth shook his head. He wrapped a huge green bath towel around himself and opened the door to the sounds of laughter and music.

*They hocused me, they pocused me,*
*Exquisitely sensate-focused me—*

"Behold! He is risen!" Arms aloft, Harvey hailed him. He shifted from a Cole Porter vamp to the sonorous chords of Mahler's Resurrection Symphony.

"Last time I saw you, boychik, you looked like something from the smoked fish department at Zabar's. How the hell did you do such a stupid thing?"

Ignoring the greeting, Seth flopped down in a chair. He turned to Lindsay and asked her, half mouthing, half whispering, where his clothes were.

"I got you some fresh ones." She nodded toward Harvey.

"The others no longer inspired confidence in you, boychik, as someone who practiced modern hygiene."

"Now stop talking," Lindsay added like a schoolmarm. "You're in good hands."

"That's right. I have your kit bag right here, relax." Harvey reached for a tan canvas overnight bag behind him, unzipped it, and brought out its contents, item by item. "Something that appears, to the unaided eye, to be a pair of gray flannel Jockey shorts. How do you wash these, with a blackboard eraser? One pair of white sweat socks, including the sweat, compliments of Dr. Bloch. You were all out. One poor but honest blue shirt, left sleeve button missing. One pair of suntans, with working zipper and no cuffs— or is it working cuffs and no zipper? And from the dung heap you

call your desk, these"—he held up a packet of scientific papers—
"languishing, neglected amidst the nail parings and dandruff—prod-
ucts, no doubt, of your protean intellectual labors."

Seth, stony and unresponsive to the hypomanic chatter, reached
for the overnight bag and shuffled back to the bedroom.

The tea was warm and sweet, and he sipped it slowly, thinking
between sips. He was dressed now, except for bare feet, and telling
them—partly mouthing, partly whispering, in phrases and fragments,
telegraph style—what had happened on Tuesday night. They sat,
leaning forward, watching his lips form the phrases and following
his gestures as he was swept into the experience again. Certain
details had stayed with him: the indistinct, abrupt phone call; the
muffled voice; the open door to O-7; the absent Valdez; the patient
who tried to warn him; the wide-open seclusion room; the surprise
and force of the blow as he careened into the blackness; and the
sound, just before he lost consciousness, of the door slamming, a
sound which at the time seemed to take his breath, his will, and
his strength away.

"Okay"—he leaned accusingly toward Harvey—"now *you* tell
*me*. How did I get out of it?" He had forgotten to whisper, and
his voice, raspy and cracked, made them wince.

"Dumb luck, I suppose," Harvey said, pulling his tie open. He
began to fan himself. "For one, Dorie Walters started her rounds
about ten minutes earlier than usual. Just as she got to the PAO
to pick up the new admissions list, Valdez called to ask what the
emergency was on N-7. Somebody had called her and told her to
get over to N-7 right away. When she got there, she couldn't figure
out what was what, so she called the PAO." Warming to his
narrative, he squirmed out of his seersucker jacket and tossed it,
one sleeve inside out, on a nearby chair. "When Mary Ryan heard
that, she told Dorie Walters that you had just told her there was
an emergency on O-7. Mary and Dorie raced up to find out what
was going on. By the time they got there, Valdez was back, and
the ward was a—madhouse, if you'll permit a minor lapse of
imagination on account of illness." He felt his forehead. "Jesus, I've

got a fever." He found himself again. "The patients were shouting and pointing to the seclusion room.

"By the time I arrived, maybe thirty seconds later, Mary was galloping toward me, shouting, 'The key, the key, I don't have my key!' " He was sitting on the edge of the sofa now, acting out all of the roles, savoring each expansive gesture.

"I whipped out my key, and we covered fifty yards in five seconds. You should have seen her pounding down the home stretch—" He popped up, eager to illustrate the spectacle, but a sour look from Seth made him sink back onto the sofa. "Well, anyway, we got the door open and pulled that maniac off you. By that time there were three or four aides and Whit and Mark had arrived. Mary worked on you for ten minutes before you changed from Union blue to Confederate gray. Then Mark and Whit and I carried you downstairs. It was like Act Five of *Hamlet*." He fell back, spent, and wiped his forehead with the back of his beefy hand. "Listen, *boychik*, at this rate I wouldn't give odds on your lasting out your residency."

"Why the key?" Seth demanded. "Why did Mary need a key?"

"I told you—the seclusion room. It was locked." He stopped fanning and looked confused.

No one spoke. Only the hum of the air conditioner filled the silence. Lindsay understood. Harvey had seen it, too, but Seth, like a missile in full flight, couldn't stop. "The door was locked!" he rasped. The words hung in the air.

"That's stupid," Harvey blurted out. He shook his great, bearlike head slowly, staring at the carpet as though searching the design for clues to the puzzle. "Who? Why?" He wiped his face again; this time, without thinking, he wiped the sweat off on his shirt. "You think somebody planned this? Actually plotted this out to actually *kill* you?"

Seth was silent, stony against the resurgence of Harvey's theatrical mode.

"You mean, some crazy? The maniac on O-7?"

"You really can't conceive of 'bad,' goddammit, evil," Seth rasped, "without getting it all scrambled up in your head with sickness, can you?"

"You mean, you think that somebody tried to kill *you?*"

Seth was silent, scornful, determined. "Yes, that's what he means," Lindsay said quietly.

"What if you hadn't answered the phone, hadn't gone up? What if Whit had gone up? What if I was on duty? You really think it wouldn't have happened to one of us?"

"No, I don't think so."

"But you're not sure now."

"I'm sure. But not about everything. I can't explain everything."

"You can't explain anything. All you have is a feeling. . . ." He smiled condescendingly. "Come on, boychik, this is me, your old friend Harv. That's nutsy talk—paranoid."

"Shall I demonstrate what it felt like, old friend? Someone *did* try to kill me."

"But you believe someone was out to get *you*, Seth Conrad, not some weird phantom of a deranged mind." He was talking as though he were humoring a cranky child. "It's too farfetched." He got up and strode around the room with a random, restless energy. "What makes you so sure?"

"I don't know, but I am."

"You think that someone who knows you, someone you know did this?"

"I don't know exactly. Yes . . . maybe. I guess it depends on what you mean by 'know.' "

"You think I could have done it?"

Seth was thoughtful for a few seconds. "No, I don't think so." It was an appeal, not a disavowal.

"Who then?"

"Anyone who knew the setup in the PAO that night. Anyone who knew who was on duty and where everybody was. It could have been anyone who was there that night."

"That's just about everybody. I was there. Whit, Silk"—he searched the ceiling for names—"Ettinger, who dropped in later to view the body and make some official clucking noises."

"Coles was upstairs," Seth continued.

"Graver!" Harvey pointed a thick finger, its nail bitten down to the cuticle. "He was in the cafeteria at dinnertime. He's your man, if you ask me, boychik. He takes theoretical disagreements very seriously, and he's definitely not a good sport."

The three of them fell silent again. Standing at the window, Seth stared vacantly down at the traffic on West Eighty-first Street.

"Jesus Christ, got any morphine around here, Coop?" Harvey's large, rumpled mass lay on the sofa, one leg and one arm hanging limply to the floor, palm open, as though he had had a stroke. He grimaced dramatically and rubbed his forehead.

"It's my brain tumor. All this talk has stimulated it. Christ, I think it's replacing the whole frontal cortex. Let me know when you see my eyes bulge."

Slumped in a chair, Lindsay said in a tired voice, "Would you like an aspirin?"

"Aspirin! Are you kidding? I need a neurosurgeon." He heaved himself to his feet and made a halfhearted attempt to arrange his clothes into some kind of presentable order. "I'm going to see if I can find a cheap one. And if I can't, I'm going to find myself a kind but sexy student nurse who'll read to me when the blindness sets in."

He lurched toward the door, opened it, and, turning, looked from Seth to Lindsay and back. "I want to thank you both for a practically perfect day. I haven't had such a cheerful afternoon since my ex-wife gave me a character analysis in three short but pithy hours. We must do it again sometime," he said as he closed the door.


They left the neon of Broadway and turned east on Eighty-second Street. In the warm night several men in undershirts and straw hats sat arguing over their Friday domino game under a streetlight.

Seth's voice had improved in the Cuban-Chinese restaurant, but now, as they walked slowly toward Lindsay's apartment, fatigue crept into his posture and the hoarseness returned.

"I rescue you, nurse you, feed you wonton soup and strawberry ice cream, and what do I get? Insults. Never mind. I've lived this long without knowing. I suppose I can go on awhile longer."

"I didn't mean that you *couldn't* understand it, only that the whole thing is farfetched, even to me."

"You know, when I was young and they told me there weren't little people inside the TV set, I didn't believe them either. You'll have to take your chances."

He moved closer and slipped his arm around her shoulder. "An irresistible challenge." His voice cracked like an adolescent's.

Suddenly they were surrounded by shouts and giggles. A knot of children giddy with anxious pleasure jostled one another under the glare of the streetlight. *"Mira! Mira!"* cried a little girl, holding her hands in front of her eyes with fingers spread widely so she could see through them. Next to her, a handsome boy, his dark eyes wide with awe, jumped up and down, pointing with his left hand at two animals, as he held his crotch with his right, protecting, caressing, and constraining himself all at once.

Edging closer, they saw a dirty black-and-white bitch yelping, bearing down, and oozing a bloody discharge from her rear end; she was being mounted by a dull-eyed mongrel that had lost control of himself and was trying desperately to get his engorged penis where it belonged. Finally, with one lurching thrust, he succeeded. The bitch yelped louder, and the children danced, pointed, and gasped. None of them noticed the bulky, unkempt woman rise from the nearby stoop, sputtering angrily to herself. She shot past Seth and grabbed the handsome boy, who was still holding his crotch, and gave him a cuff that sent him sprawling. She scattered the other children with bursts of explosive Spanish and finally kicked the mongrel, which squealed and pulled out. The loving pair fled, leaving behind a bloody discharge, tears, and much food for childish thought.

They turned south on Amsterdam Avenue in silence, barely noticing the shops filled with Depression kitsch.

"When was the last time you played doctor?"

She gave him a fishy look. "Is that your idea of a proposition?"

He raised his eyebrows lasciviously. *"That* is one of its most universal derivatives."

"What is? What are you talking about? For God's sake, stop being so opaque! Between your whispering and your enigmatic sayings, you sound like a goddamn oracle."

"Take it easy. Remember what your fortune cookie said tonight, 'There are more to everything than its appearance.' "

"Well, get on with it. You have thirty seconds, then back you go where I got you!" She peered at her watch for emphasis.

"Don't you see? Enigmatic and opaque is what primal scene is all about."

"Oh, we're back to that, are we? I thought I wasn't clever enough to understand it." She turned away and started walking south again. "I think I've transcended primal scene."

"Mein dear Fräulein Coopfer, vun can never transcend ze prrimal zscene. Vun can rrrepress it, confess it, eefen exprrrress it. Integrrrate it, ja; sublimate it, perrrhaps, but trrranscend it—heh, heh, heh— neverrr."

"You're being tiresome again," she said, stifling a pretended yawn.

"Ah, now I see, Miss Coopfer, that you are in a shtate of rrresistance. You are afrrraid uf vhat I'm going to tell you."

"Your time is up, Doctor, see you next time—if there is one."

"Sex, violence, and mystery. They all go together, and *that's* what primal scene is all about."

They had come to the corner of Columbus Avenue and to the Mission Bethel, a storefront church. A sign read IGLESIAS CHRIS-TIANAS. Painted on the brick facade in bright, tropical colors was the crucifixion: tormented hollow eyes; an agony of ribs; spurting blood from bony hands and feet. Silently they gazed at the drooping form, primitive and powerful, until catcalls and obscene gestures meant for Lindsay moved them on.

"All kids play doctor sooner or later. See, it's a disguised way of dealing with their primal scene fantasies. Who could object to children playing at curing and being cured? But what the games are all about in one way or another is how babies are made, what men and women do to each other to get babies. Freud wrote a nifty little paper about it in 1908 called 'The Sexual Theories of Children.' "

He grabbed her arm and leaned toward her conspiratorially, "I suppose you're dying to know what he says; well, I'm glad you asked. Essentially he says three things: that children around the age of three or four become aware of and curious about their parents' sexual lives—"

"Old hat."

"Now, not then."

"What else?"

"That they usually develop primitive and sadistic fantasies about intercourse."

"No comment. What else?"

"That they identify with one and sometimes both parties in the scene."

They had reached Lindsay's building, where the doorman greeted them with an easy West Indian smile, par for West Side service on a warm summer evening.

"Let me tell you a story about a princess, a love story of sorts."

Lindsay had turned on one soft light, stepped out of her espadrilles, and curled up on the sofa. "Was she beautiful?"

"Very. Picture her. Dark, sensual, passionate—a French princess." As he stood in the shadows, his voice was distant, from another time. "Yet for some reason she doesn't understand, she feels discontent, desperate almost. She arrives in Vienna one day in 1925, in grandeur and great style. Immediately she goes to Nineteen Berggasse, a modest apartment house on a quiet, undistinguished street, and consults with Freud, who is almost seventy, ailing and irascible. He agrees to treat her, and after four weeks of analysis she dreams that she is lying in a small bed on the grassy slopes of a park, near a lake, and is looking intently at a married couple lying nearby in their bed. Freud tells her she must have been exposed to sexual scenes in her childhood. She becomes indignant and reacts violently to his remark"—prowling the room now, as he spoke, he picked up objects without looking, touched places without knowing why—"understandably. An analyst today would never have made such an interpretive leap so early in the treatment. But after all, Freud didn't know any better then. At that time the idea was to uncover the forgotten traumatic memories, to delve down into the patient's unconscious. Today we unpeel them layer by layer"—his hands restlessly illustrated the narrative—"like an onion, until there's nothing left but tears and bad breath.

"She was particularly indignant because her mother had died in childbirth, and she'd been raised by a wet nurse until she was three."

Pacing slowly back and forth in the center of the room, he stopped to massage his throat. "By the time the little princess was six or seven, she could write fluently and had begun to keep a diary of her everyday activities written in French.

"Now, here comes the twist." He paused for effect. "Shortly after Freud had made this very irritating interpretation, her father died, and she found among his papers a series of her own little notebooks written in *English,* which she had also learned as a child and which she'd apparently used as a sort of secret language. In those notebooks she let her imagination go and wrote wild and fantastic stories.

"When she first read them, they seemed full of crazy sadistic symbols. And of course, she had total amnesia for the wild stories even though they were in her own handwriting." His voice began to crack badly.

Following his movements and watching the excitement in his face, Lindsay suddenly raised her arms toward him.

As he sat down on the edge of the sofa where she lay, she leaned toward him and kissed his throat. He started to speak, but she put her finger up to his lips to silence him. "Shhh." She stood up. "I can see the only way to your mind is through *my* bed."

Ten minutes later Lindsay reappeared in the darkened room in a loosely tied silk robe. As he lay there inertly, peacefully, his heavy, regular breathing told her it was hopeless for now.

"Primal. Sadistic," she said, smiling to herself.

*H*e was cold and pulled the sheet over his bare shoulder and under his chin. It was no use; the air conditioner, insensitive to his autonomic nervous system, continued to pour a current of cold air over his body. He tried again, instinctively, to conserve the heat of his body, pulling the sheet tighter around himself, tried again to preserve the state of deep, dreamless, rejuvenating sleep. No use.

His senses were already telling him that he was not in his own bed: The air conditioner had a lower pitch; the room was colder, the bed softer; the pillows smelled better than his own.

Through the bathroom door, closed except for a crack, he heard the shower beating against the plastic curtains and porcelain. He hopped out of bed and over to the window. Facing down the whirlwind in his shorts, he squinted at the panel of buttons, trying to decipher the legends. Finally, guessing at the right one, he punched the air conditioner to off. Then, as though his thoughts were magic and controlled real events, the shower tap screeched, the water stopped, and he heard the shower curtain folded back.

Jumping back into the body-warm bed, he pulled the sheet up over his shoulder again. Through the crack of the door he saw the flash of her skin, her wet flank, the white of a breast. A moment later, wrapped in a towel, she pushed open the door to the bedroom and reached for a brush on the dresser. "Good morning." She smiled. Even through the blur of his myopia, brush in hand, hair dripping, she looked lithe and fresh, just as she had on that first evening.

Her eyes twisted free and changed the subject. "How's the throat?" she asked, disappearing back into the bathroom.

"Conrad is himself again," he said with as much basso as he could muster.

Lindsay raised her eyebrows and smiled at herself in the mirror. "Is he?" He could hear her brushing her hair. "How did he sleep?" she called.

"Like an innocent babe." He lay back, relaxed, talking to the ceiling, arms folded behind his head. "How about you?"

"Not so innocent. Had funny dreams about dogs and crucifixions, and French princesses. God, it was mixed up and—"

"And?" He heard a buzzing sound, like a doorbell out of control. "What's that?"

"A primal toothbrush because I get primal cavities in my primal teeth." Her words were muffled through toothpaste foam.

He lay back, not stirring a muscle, listening to the whir of the motor and thinking of her. "Where did you sleep last night?"

No answer. He heard her rinsing her mouth.

"Started out in the living room. Then came in here to see if you were all right"—more rinsing—"and never made it back. I just cuddled up."

"What did I do?" In lieu of an answer he heard a pizzicato sound as though she were plucking a dead violin string. "What did I do?" he called louder.

More plucking. "You ravaged me. It was brutal."

"Well, you asked for it."

Pluck. Pluck. Pluck.

"Christ, what are you doing?"

She poked her head through the doorway, her two hands grasping a long filament of dental floss. She was still swathed in the towel, her hair combed but wet, her face scrubbed and still bedewed with drops of water.

"This some weird dental cult you belong to?" She popped back out of sight. Pluck. Pluck. Pluck.

He lay there, unable to remember when he had last felt so completely rested and relaxed. "I thought you might be interested— I'm paralyzed."

Pluck. Pluck. "Where?" Pluck.

"Waist down. Legs definitely. I don't know about the rest."

He heard her rinse once more. "Wages of sin."

"You don't seem very concerned." Silence. "Can't you see this is serious? It's moving up! I can't move my navel at all! Hurry!"

"All right," she said, emerging from the bathroom armed with a long, serious-looking needle. "First, I think, ze reflexes ve must test—"

He grabbed her wrists as she approached and wrestled her down to him. "Who," he said forcefully, "is Leslie? And does he have a Porsche?"

Still struggling, she said between grunts, "No . . . she . . . has a . . . Plymouth. . . ."

Stirred by the strength and warmth of her body, he became aware of the irresistible scent of soap and dentifrice, and as the towel came undone, she stopped struggling.

*Chapter*

## 10

In her silk robe she looked fragile blocking Fontana's way. He filled the doorway with his benign, muscular presence.

"Afternoon, Miss Cooper. Hope I'm not disturbing anything." He smiled disingenuously. "I heard the doc had an accident, so I thought I'd check him out. He wasn't lookin' too good the last time I seen him—"

"For Christ's sake, Fontana"—Seth emerged from the living room, tucking his shirt into his suntans—"I'm off duty today," he said in a hoarse whisper. "See me on Monday."

"Gee, Doc, it's not really on business. Except you left me a message, and I just wanted to say thanks and see how you were."

Lindsay, her face still flushed, realized it was hopeless. Pulling her robe around herself, she swung the door wide, inviting Fontana in.

Nodding appreciatively, he moved into the living room and taking the room in at a glance, unwrapped a piece of chewing gum. "How ya feelin', Doc? I heard about the accident or whatever you call it. You guys live dangerously." He eased himself down onto the sofa. "Same guy we saw in the PAO, eh?"

Seth chose not to hear the question. Instead, he picked up a cup abandoned from breakfast and took a swig from the dregs of the cold liquid within.

"How'd it happen, Doc?"

"What is this, Fontana, business or pleasure?" Seth said sourly.

Fontana shrugged. "You're right, Doc, it's none of my business. Just curious. You know how it is with cops, Doc. Like you were telling me the other day." He grinned. "Sticka gum, Miss Cooper?" He shoved the pack in Lindsay's direction. "Come on now, Doc, what happened?" He said it like a patient father soothing his child's hurt feelings.

The story, when he finally retold it to Fontana, had changed. It had hardened, become cleaner, sharper at the edges. The searching was gone, and the fragmentation. Where there'd been a struggle to recollect what had been shaken out of him, there was now sureness. Where there'd been a groping for lost sights and subliminal sounds and smells and pieced-together feelings, there was now a form that made sense, a coherent narrative. Experience had become history.

And afterward Fontana was thoughtful, rubbing the dark mole on his cheek. "Who locked the door?"

"The same son of a bitch who made the call and pushed me in!"

"But why, Doc? It don't make sense." He eased himself back on the sofa, clasped his hands behind his head, and flexed his biceps. "Some kinda game? A little fun to liven things up on a dull night? Why?"

Seth glared at him. "Jennifer Light—that's why."

Fontana studied him, chewing slowly, steadily.

"Somebody tried to scare me, maybe even kill me that night because I know something about this murder!" He paused to let it sink in. "And they know that I know it. But what they don't know is that I don't know what I know."

Fontana shook his head. "That went by me too fast, Doc. Pitch it again."

"Vince, you wouldn't believe it if I told you. Even I didn't believe it until yesterday."

"Try me."

"I had a dream the night I was on duty. The night of the murder . . ."

"You dreamed about the Light girl. Yeah, I remember you told me."

"Right. Well, I dreamed about her because I saw her—or let's say I was aware of her presence—in the cafeteria just before I went on duty that night, and I'm sure she was with a man. That must have been just before the murder."

"You saw her with somebody?"

"The way you see something that doesn't register until later."

"Go on, Doc, I got ya, out of the corner of your eye . . ."

Seth told him what he could remember about the night of the murder, now passed into history, and then, without pausing, as though there were some unacknowledged, inner connection, about his encounter with Ettinger on Tuesday afternoon.

"So what's the point, Doc?" Fontana flexed his biceps again.

"The point is that, one, what happened to me the other night was no accident."

"Okay."

"And, two, it was connected in some way with Jennifer Light's murder, probably even done by the same person—"

"Whoa, hold on."

"Three, that person knows the hospital and its procedures and has a set of keys to the locked wards—in short, is a member of the staff—and four, Coles and Ettinger know more than they're telling—"

"Take it easy, Doc. Remember, you've had a hard couple a nights." He paused and looked sternly at Seth as though he were about to scold him. Slowly unwrapping another stick of gum, he parked his old wad in the paper and slipped the fresh piece into his mouth.

"You're saying that what happened the other night was no accident. I'm with you there. I don't see how someone can lock you in with a maniac by accident.

"Okay, let's say, for argument's sake, somebody meant to get you. It's a big jump from there to Jennifer Light. What's the evidence? What've you got? A look you may have taken but can't remember; a nightmare you remember but can't understand; a rumor, a whisper, and a warning. That's about it." He sat there chewing and playing with the mole on his cheek.

"My point is this, Doc. If I went to my lieutenant and said, 'Lieutenant, I got this smart young doc down at Bellevue who almost got himself wasted the other night, and he thinks that somebody on the hospital staff killed the Light kid, maybe the head of the department or someone on the faculty,' he'd say, 'Is that right, Fontana? Does he have any facts?' 'Well, sir, not exactly,' I'd have to say. 'He thought he saw something the night of the murder, but he doesn't know what, and then he had a dream, and then he found out the chairman of the department was mad at him.' "

Fontana had been looking off into the distance as he composed his hypothetical script; now he glanced at Seth to make sure he was following. "You know what he'd do if I tried to tell him what you're telling me? He'd put me on medical furlough. Look, Doc, the department has its way of doing things. It may not be the best or the fanciest, but it works for us. *You* can afford to play around with . . . subliminal whatever you call it and hunches and dreams because you don't have 'em beating down your doors—the rapists, mutilators, killers, muggers, junkies. We don't have time; we gotta keep bailing or we'll drown out there."

Arms folded across his chest, Seth stood at the window, smiling cynically.

"I understand what you mean, Doc, and for all I know, you may be right. All I'm saying is I couldn't do anything about it even if I *knew* you were. The department is like a big machine." He performed the movements of a robot. "It can't look this way or that. It grinds out a certain number of collars and convictions a year—enough to keep the commissioner and the mayor and most of the public happy—and that's it, Doc, that's it." He got up to go. "Look, Doc, I've got some other doors to knock on and a few things to check out. I'll keep it in mind—what you told me." He walked toward the door.

"Oh, by the way, Doc, thanks for the note under the door. I'll check in with this Milly McVey tomorrow or Monday." Fontana performed his gum ritual once more and walked to the door. "And Doc," he said to Seth's back, "I'm sorry you got hurt."

When the door closed, Seth knew that something was wrong. What was Fontana saying? His throat hurt, and he didn't feel like saying the words; but he knew they were wrong. *Under the door.* He'd taped the note on the door. Some childish urge made him want to run and tell Fontana. But suddenly he knew it was hopeless. "Look, Doc, the department has its way of doing things." He touched his throat. Someone else had put that note under the door. And whoever it was had read it. Read it and seen what he knew.

And he was alone once more with what he knew. And with what one other person knew he knew.

"What happened to her?"

"Who?"

"The princess."

His wrists stuck out like a scarecrow's, buttoning the top button of the borrowed yellow slicker. "Eventually she saved Freud's life." He glanced down the path behind them.

"No, I mean, about the diaries, the secret diaries—what happened?"

They'd been walking in silence for the past few minutes through the occasional drizzle and mist of Central Park. The park, at its quiet loveliest, had been deserted by its fair-weather friends and enemies alike. The trees and empty benches of the Ramble glistened with droplets, silent witnesses to their peregrinations and private thoughts.

"When she discovered them, she was stunned." Hunching his shoulders, he glanced again down the path behind them. "They were in a kind of pidgin English, and as she reread them, even she could see that the stories were symbolic representations of sexual scenes she had in some way witnessed or imagined. They had names like 'The Rabbit Without Skin,' 'The Spitting Man,' 'The Bursting Woman,' 'The Bursting Stomach.'

"When she was little"—he turned to her and buttoned the top button of her raincoat—"the princess had lived in a château outside

Paris. She was able to figure out from the stories that her nursemaid, who was really the only mother she ever knew, had been having an affair at the time with the master of the stables."

"Sorry for being hard-nosed at a time like this, but what you mean is that was her guess."

"Patience, brat." He reached up and plucked a leaf from a low-hanging branch. "I haven't finished." Then, turning again, he stood motionless, head cocked in the direction from which they'd come. "Hear something?" He pushed the glasses back up on his nose and peered down the deserted path.

"What?" There was the wail of an ambulance somewhere in the city, distant and mournful on a wet Sunday afternoon.

"I don't know. Something."

She looked around at the trees in the half mist. The Ramble was an intricate network of paths through thickets and wooded areas in the heart of the park, full of twists and turns and out of sight of the heavily trafficked areas, a bird watcher's paradise. On a day like this—gloomy, overcast, with intermittent fog and rain—it was completely deserted.

Strolling into the park at Eighty-first Street, they soon found themselves on the parapet of Belvedere Castle, a deserted weather station, looking northward through the mist over the Great Lawn. It was empty except for a figure in the half distance hidden under an umbrella, hardly more than a black raincoat and white shoes showing, and a pair of lovers of indeterminate sex in identical blue raingear, walking arm in arm along the shore of the brackish lake below. These were the only people they had seen in the last fifteen or twenty minutes since they'd crossed the little footbridge into the darkest part of the Ramble.

"Are you trying to scare me?"

Laughing, he opened his arms. "You bet I am."

She gave him a reproachful look and gave a little shudder. "Don't do that. After what happened the other night, this business is getting scary. And I'm sorry for getting you into it."

"What do you mean? You didn't get me into it. A lot of things got me into it. Fontana got me into it. Ettinger sure as hell got me into it. My dream got me into it. Christ, even Joe Burden."

He gave her a final little hug and presented her with the leaf he had plucked. "The trouble is," he added, looking back down the empty path once more, "it's gotten into me." He gave an involuntary shudder.

"Well, anyway, let me tell you how the story turned out." They started walking again, this time south and west, a direction he was sure would take them back toward more people. "The nurse had died years before, but the stable master was still alive. One day the princess went to see him, as she often had since childhood, and asked him to tell her about her childhood. When she asked about her nurse, the old man's face lit up, and he described how beautiful she was. Then, mustering all her courage, she asked him bluntly whether he had been Lucie's lover—Lucie, the nurse. He turned pale and began to protest, but she kept pushing. 'I'm not accusing you,' she said, 'but you've got to tell me the truth. You must.'"

Seth whirled around, suddenly, this time grabbing Lindsay's arm.

"What is it?" Lindsay hissed, frightened. "Seth! What?"

They could see nothing but a light swirl of mist and hear nothing but the sound of the light rain as it fell on the trees around them.

"I don't know. I heard footsteps behind us. I don't know what's the matter with me. Got the jumps today."

Looking back again, and then forward, he shook himself and raised the hood on his slicker. It was raining harder now, heightening their sense of urgency and their indecision about which way to go.

He grabbed Lindsay's hand and jerked her into a briskly paced trot. The rain came still faster, running down their faces now.

"I hear it, too. Footsteps," she gasped as they fled down one turn after another. Every turn seemed to take them into a more densely wooded place, every path narrowing and pulling them farther into secret places they didn't want to be.

They sloshed over a wooden footbridge, along a parapet with an iron railing, and down along a rocky shoreline. They could see barely ten yards across the deserted lake; the rain was coming in sheets now. Breathless and lost, he could feel himself flushing and sweating despite the blinding torrent. The din was deafening. He tore his glasses off and squinted in every direction. He could neither see nor hear anything that would give him a clue to where safety lay. His heart was pounding now. Safety from what? He didn't know. He knew only that he was lost and frightened and that he had to get away.

They were rooted to the spot, the rain pouring off them, unable to choose a course. Then Lindsay grabbed his hand and lurched for a path that led away from the lake and wound its way upward through the dense foliage and the deluge that made them flinch.

Suddenly emerging through the Naturalist's Gate onto Central Park West, they saw the powerful and friendly forces of the American Museum of Natural History led by Theodore Roosevelt and his two Indian scouts. They raced north and up the broad steps to the porch of the museum, where, from behind the huge, protective figure of Teddy Roosevelt astride his horse, they felt safe from any evil, visible or not.

Gasping for breath, they hugged each other, laughing at the melodrama of their adventure and escape. They unpeeled their raingear, wrung themselves out, and stood for several minutes, shivering and surveying the downpour and the park across the street, no longer sinister.

"Look"—Lindsay glanced at her watch—"there's half an hour left." She pulled him toward the museum entrance. "It's dry in there—and safe." She shuddered.

Some atavistic impulse, some small but enduring cautionary signal made him glance just once more over his shoulder as he entered the building. Through the heavy rain he could see, walking slowly northward from the Naturalist's Gate, a man hidden by an umbrella, so that only his black raincoat and black-and-white shoes were visible. The image registered and disappeared as Lindsay whisked him inside.

She led him up empty staircases and, like Natty Bumppo, with stealth, through the Eastern Woodlands and Plains Indians.

"So there she was, confronting the old man face-to-face, demanding the truth. He was miserable but finally confessed that the princess had seen them—him and Lucie—make love many times until she was two or three. Old Freud had been right after all. He'd timed his interpretation poorly, but his clinical hunch paid off."

They were passing through Reptiles and Amphibians, Lindsay taking the lead, Seth lagging behind as he lectured. "I suppose," she said, stopping at a display of lizards, "all this is supposed to mean something, Professor."

He looked at her over the rims of his glasses, sensitive to the strength of his own pedantic impulses. A hurt look came into his imperfect eyes. "You're bored."

"No, excited. I sense a climax coming," she said as she stared at the creatures in the glass case.

He shrugged and pushed the glasses up on his nose. "It means that all kids think about how babies get made. Some of them observe, some only imagine, but whatever the mixture, they get it wrong. And they get it wrong in a very predictable way. They all get the idea that it's a cruel and violent act—"

"God, they're stupid-looking, aren't they?"

"Some kids have more sadistic fantasies than others. Why? Because some kids live in families that stimulate more aggression and more sexual excitement than other families." He paused. "Cooper, you're not listening. Listen."

She looked at him with a patronizing smile, turned, and hurried down the high-ceilinged room toward another glacial epoch, Seth bringing up the rear.

"Listen, this is the best part. The more sadistic these fantasies are, the more trouble with the opposite sex later in life. Even in normal sex there has to be some aggression. No aggression, no excitement; no excitement, no pleasure." She turned back to him. "Ha! I knew that would get your attention. But in normal sex it's *played* out, not acted out. There's a little playful sadism in every act of love. We hurt a little when we love." They had entered the great gloomy Hall of African Mammals.

"You sound like a bad French movie," she said with a snort. "And I suppose next you'll be telling me that there's a little love in every murder."

"Maybe a little sexual excitement in every murder would be closer to the truth." His voice echoed in the deserted hall. "Anyway, if your primal scene fantasies are too sadistic—"

"My primal scene fantasies are incredibly sadistic." She pressed her damp, slender body against his. "You wouldn't believe how sadistic they are. I find tusks and fangs terribly exciting."

Alone, in the Akeley Hall of African Mammals, amid huge elephants, great maned lions, sensuous leopards, they were aware only of their own excitement as they stood, limbs entwined, surrounded by the magnificent beasts.

Pulling free, suddenly, Seth glared up at the gallery that curved above them around the perimeter of the hall. "Someone up there," he whispered. In the dim light he'd seen only a blurred movement. Perhaps not even that.

"So? It's a museum," she said. "Public, see? Bored. You're bored with me—already. That's it."

"On the contrary, it was interesting, really. Only I'm jumpy today, I guess."

"Doctor's naughty fantasies," she chided.

"I suppose. Come on, let's get out of here—enough fang and claw." He pulled her toward the Tribes of Africa in the next exhibition room.

It had gotten into him. Something had gotten into him. He'd been looking for something out there. In the trees, in the mist, in the rain, in the room they stood in now, surrounded by war clubs, spears, circumcision knives, ritual masks—the tribal culture of Africa. His eyes searched restlessly for something, for some revelatory symbol with the power to transmute what haunted him into something he could see, make sense of.

Out of the array of magical objects around him, he floated momentarily toward a ritual tribal mask, made of black leather and roughly triangular in shape. Moving to it like a sleepwalker to an inner vision, he studied its powerful abstract features: its staring white eyes and fierce, grinning mouth; the bands of white dots across the forehead, repeated in swirling patterns over the cheeks and chin. He bent forward, studying the mask, taking in its details as though he were trying to memorize them or remember another mask. He read, without thought, the legend beneath. "The Lele . . . use magic, witchcraft and sorcery as a defense against neighbors. . . ."

Unharnessing his glasses, he wiped them on his shirt and squinted again at the mask. "The dream," he mumbled, "the face in the dream . . . the marks . . . the face . . . of course—black and white! The shoes! Of course . . ." His voice rising in volume and excitement, he began to move. Suddenly he tore away from Lindsay, and running toward the exit, he called over his shoulder, "Out front! Meet me out front!"

In a few seconds he had pushed through the heavy doors and stood peering up and down Central Park West. Suddenly he spotted what he was looking for and raced north toward the umbrella and black-and-white shoes ahead. Breathless, he caught up and passed in front of the tall figure, blocking its way. Drenched, water pouring down his face, he stood with his old blue work shirt stuck to his chest and faced the ashen old man with white hair and steel-rimmed glasses—a perfect stranger.


"For Christ's sake, you sure have a lousy temper!" He was still breathing hard from his race up Central Park West.

"So they say. Now, if you'll be kind enough to step aside, I'll be heading home, and you can buzz off in any direction you like." She tried again to move around him.

"Wait a minute!" He grabbed her arm. "Let me explain!"

She pushed past him and marched down the broad steps of the museum into the rain. He followed her the two short blocks to her apartment, and they shared the elevator in silence. Once inside, she busied herself with the raingear, stepping around him like a vacuum cleaner someone had forgotten to put away.

He handed her the slicker she'd lent him. She took it, tight-lipped, without looking at him.

"Hey"—he trapped her hand before she could withdraw it—"give me a chance. Let me explain."

"I won't be taken for granted, Seth." She pulled her hand free. "I'm not one of Harvey's nursing students. If you want me, you're not going to leave me standing alone somewhere, while you go into orbit on some paranoid mission. I don't like being frightened. My life is not a comic strip."

"You're right. Absolutely. It was asinine." Her lower lip began to tremble, and brimming, her blue eyes became more brilliant. "I'm sorry I frightened you." He coaxed her toward him, and she let herself be comforted.


"*I* don't know," he said slowly, stifling a yawn, "the mask, I suppose." They lay in the darkness, only half aware of the rhythm of their bodies and the flashes of irrelevant sound from the city below, like distant lightning. "It ticked the whole thing off. Pow"— he flicked his fingers into the darkness as though he were conjuring— "just like that there they were—the shoes. Incredible," he said without conviction, "the way the mind works."

"The body, too." She ran her finger across his chest. " 'Old-fashioned'—you said 'old-fashioned.' What was old-fashioned about them?"

"I don't know." The question seemed severe in the darkness, unnecessarily sharp for the setting. Her body was smooth and comfortable, warm under the sheet. The rain beat gently at the windowpane. "Just old-fashioned. Black-and-white, the kind they wore in the twenties and thirties maybe. I can't move my fingers."

"Don't start that again."

"No, it's your head. It's on my brachial plexus."

"Sorry. Is that some part I should know?" Lying comfortably in the crook of his arm, she didn't bother to move.

"You know, wing tips, swirls all over the toe." His arm squirmed free. "There, I can hear again." He closed his eyes and scowled up at the dark ceiling. "Scott Fitzgerald, the Riviera, white flannels. That's what I saw that night in the cafeteria—those shoes. Hey! Cut it out, I'm trying to concentrate—you're breathing on my nipple."

"I thought men liked that."

"Where'd you get that idea"—he put his hand over his breast as though he were about to pledge allegiance, "some Red Cross sex manual?"

She pulled his hand away. "Who did you expect to find under that umbrella?"

"I don't know. I didn't think. I just ran like hell after those shoes."

"But think about it now. It must have taken you a minute or two to catch up to that old man. What—who was on your mind?"

"I tell you, I wasn't thinking, I was running. I guess I can't think and run at the same time. I never realized that until now." He poked her. "Don't go blabbing that around."

"You must have had some idea who you'd find."

"Graver," he said quietly. "Jonathan Graver."

She sat up, naked to the waist. "Why?"

"Cooper, why are you hounding me this way? You're insatiable!" He pulled her on top of him.

"Why?" she whispered.

"I don't know . . . First of all, he was close to Jennie Light. Second, you yourself said he was hiding something when you talked to him. Third, he's a bastard." He thought of Milly McVey, bruised and moaning on the stairs that afternoon. "And . . . he's a big man—strong. In my mind whoever did it is a powerfully built man, with big hands." He stared up at the ceiling. "Christ, I frightened the wits out of that poor old man. You'd better nail me into my coffin tonight."

Lindsay squirmed free and sat up. She reached for the phone and dialed a number. "God, I'd like to get to Milly before Fontana does. It'd make all the difference."

"Maybe, maybe not. Phyl Rowan is right. Milly's quirky. She may not talk at all. I told you Milly's a strange woman—angry, and grieving all the time. 'Tragic,' Harvey says, but then you know Harvey—the king of tragedy. Her husband committed suicide."

"Still the machine." She slammed the phone back onto its cradle. "Damn!" She sank back onto Seth's chest. "What were you saying about 'tragic'?"

"Nothing."

Her finger absentmindedly inscribed a *G* on his pectoralis muscle. "I don't think Graver's capable of something like that."

"That's because you didn't see him that afternoon." Seth raised himself on one elbow. "The bastard hit that poor woman, socked her, just like that. Pow. Listen, I know something now I didn't know before: Anyone is capable of practically anything." He fell back on the pillow.

"You?" She kissed his nipple.

"How can I take your question seriously? Do it again!"

"No. I am serious," she said languidly. "Could *you* kill?"

"I never really knew until . . . *that* happened." He jerked his head southward in the direction of the hospital. "Now I know I could kill the bastard—actually kill."

"Really?" She roused herself slightly and turned over. "Would you really kill him? There he is. How would you like him? In chains? Sitting in the electric chair? On the loose, with a club in his hand? How do you see him—defiant, menacing, enraged, contrite, pleading? How do you want to do it—pull the trigger, push the button? Smash him over the head, stab him?"

"Cooper, did your father ever tell you that you were a difficult child?"

"Yes, he did. But he also told me that was why he loved me."

"Lindsay, *I* will not love you if you are difficult. Now stop destroying my illusions."

"Okay, you're a killer at heart."

"No, not at heart. But I could kill under the right circumstances, I know now."

"You mean, if you were scared enough. So could a lot of people. But could you kill out of jealousy or envy, or could you push the button in cold-blooded revenge?"

"I don't know, but I do know that if I could kill under the right circumstances, then Graver could because I know he's more of a bastard than I am."

"Now you're shattering *my* illusions. Well, you're enough of a bastard to suit me—"

The phone rang. In the darkness the sound was like a shower of angry sparks, startling them, and scattering their fugitive thoughts.

"Milly!" Seth lunged for the phone.

It was Milly. Grim as usual, quietly suffering her return, as she'd suffered her holiday. Yes, it was okay. Not great but okay. Slept a lot. Nothing better to do. What was up? Why had he left so many messages? "Is Coles on your case again? Listen, Seth, make it short, I'm bushed. What's up?"

"Milly, have you been in touch with Phyl Rowan yet?"

"No. Why?" The edge of suspicion flicked into her voice.

"Then . . . Jennie Light . . . you haven't heard?" How do
you say it. How do you say, "Your friend is dead"? He'd never
learned how during all those months after the accident. Each time
the same awkward pauses, the same shrugs, the same self-conscious
taking off and putting on his glasses and in the end blurting it out
and running away. Now he didn't have to blurt it out. She did.

"She's dead, isn't she?"

"Murdered."

"I knew it! I knew it would happen. Jesus! Jesus!" Her voice
was husky, and then he couldn't tell whether she was laughing or
crying.

"Milly, I have to talk to you," he said. "We can help each
other."

"Jonathan. What about Jonathan? Is he all right? I was afraid
of this. She was so mixed up. God, I can't believe it. I warned her
before I left." There was bitterness now. "I threatened to kick her
out when she brought home that disgusting little monster. I guess
she was trying to get my goat. Well, she got it. God. God."

"Milly, the police will be trying to get hold of you—a cop
named Fontana—"

"They'll want to see her stuff . . . God, I knew it. I just knew
it . . . her diary . . . I'm going to burn it before they get their
paws on it. Nobody's going to see that. That was hers—"

"For God's sake, Milly, don't burn anything. Promise me you
won't touch anything. I'll be there in fifteen minutes. We'll talk
about it when I get there." Seth heard a harsh buzz over the phone.

"For Christ's sake," she said, "who the hell is that? God . . .
she had to do it," she said angrily, and hung up.


"*H*e must have seen me that night in the cafeteria. He didn't know
at that moment that he was going to kill her." It was almost ten
o'clock as they turned onto Fifth Avenue and drove swiftly southward. The steady rain throughout the evening had driven the
pedestrians and window-shoppers indoors, and the Sunday night traffic

was light. "So he wasn't on guard, and he didn't pay any attention to whether I noticed him or not."

As they sped eastward through the rain-soaked city, Lindsay was keyed up, excited, Seth sensed, by the prospect of talking to Milly McVey and seeing Jennie Light's diary.

"He still doesn't know that I only know his shoes. And he doesn't know what I'm waiting for."

Seth cornered sharply onto Forty-eighth, across Madison, then down Park Avenue. Lindsay's knuckles whitened around the safety grip, and her right leg stiffened as she braked in tandem with him. "Find F. Scott and those shoes, and you've got your killer. Say, this little car handles very nicely."

"Oh?"

He sped up over the ramp that loops its way around the body of Grand Central like a belt. "Drifts a little on the turns, but in city driving that's not too bad."

"I'm really relieved. I was worried about that."

"Yeah"—he nodded—"nice little car. Peppy, too." He gunned the engine once or twice, and the car leaped ahead.

"She had a kid. That was before she came to Bellevue. She once mentioned it. A little girl—she died."

They entered the tunnel at Park Avenue and Fortieth Street. It was open and empty, and Seth pushed the pedal down to the floor. The silver car surged forward—fifty-five, sixty, seventy. Lindsay's knuckles whitened again, and her legs tensed. "For Pete's sake, take it easy, it's not paid off yet."

He gave her a reassuring smile as they came out of the tunnel at Thirty-third Street. "That's what she's like—you'll see. She's a hard-luck lady." He slowed the car in front of a grim gray tenement on Thirtieth Street off Third. "There it is." Even before the car had come to a full stop, Lindsay snapped the door open and darted out.

"Hey, hold on—"

"Never mind." She slammed the door hard. "I'll get out while I'm still in one piece. See you upstairs." Pulling her raincoat over her head, she ran up the steps of the building and into the front hallway.

He peered after her, then shrugged. She did have a lousy temper. It was Sunday night and still summer—a moment in the rhythm of civilized life when all parking places disappear off the face of the earth. It took him a full ten minutes of cruising up and down the side streets like a kestrel looking for its prey before he spotted an opportunity. He spied it halfway down Thirtieth Street—a dark green Jaguar burning rubber as it sped away—and blessed the driver, whoever he was.

The building in which Milly McVey lived was wedged between a unisex haircutting establishment and a dreary little grocery store that catered to the handful of Pakistanis in the neighborhood; both were dark and silent. In the slow rain a large black-and-white cat stared from behind the window of the grocery, a mute witness to the secret sights and sounds of the neighborhood. Seth swept up the low flight of steps to a tiny entrance hall.

In the dim light he saw that there were ten apartments in the building, one front and one rear on each of the five floors. Each mailbox had two or three names marked on it. McVey and Light—recently added—rear, shared the fifth floor with Mukerji-Singh, front.

He pushed the button under the mailbox and waited—until he realized that there was no ring-back mechanism and that the main door was open. He pushed it cautiously and peered down a narrow hallway lit by a fluorescent tube that flickered between life and death. Stale food odors left from Sunday dinner made the long passage seem crowded. The white-tiled floor, although cracked in several places, was clean, and the old-fashioned walls made of embossed sheet iron were freshly painted. He passed a door on his right painted the color of rare roast beef, which led to the front apartment, and peered down to the end of the hall to the door that led to the rear apartment. On the left between these two doors a flight of stairs led steeply upward and doubled back on itself on its journey to the second-floor hall.

He climbed slowly toward the top of the building, pausing on each floor for no reason that he knew, listening for the sound of human voices whenever he paused. The weak light of the fluorescent tube did not even reach the full length of the hallway, which left the doorways of each apartment cast in flickering shadow. Loud sounds of television melodrama poured out of the fourth-floor rear and contrasted with the dim blue silence of the fifth-floor hallway.

By the time he reached there, his heart was pounding and he was breathing rapidly. Was it only the exertion? He was hardly aware of the tension in his throat as he turned left toward the rear apartment. He took a deep breath and, brushing aside his caution, walked purposefully toward the reddish brown door.

He didn't see until he was within arm's length that the door was open a few inches and that the apartment within was in semidarkness. He pushed the door and called out, "Hello?" No reply. Pushing into the darkened room a little farther, suddenly he saw the body sprawled just inside the door. He took in the graceful curve of the arm, the spreading fan of hair before he realized. It was Lindsay.

Chapter

## 11

"The day after tomorrow. Thursday morning. Definitely." He kissed the back of her neck, just below the bandage. "You smell like an OR." She stared out the window without smiling.

"Why? Why not today? I want to go home. I hate this place." She whirled around to face him. Her face contracted in pain. "God!" She held her head in both hands as if it were a helmet she wanted to pull off. Swaying for a moment, she pitched forward.

"Hey!" Seth caught her and held her. "That's why, brat. Steinmetz said you'd have rubber legs. And a headache for a couple of days." She touched the bandage behind her right ear and winced. A pain tear slid out of the corner of her eye. "Big Irv knows. Why do you think they call him Big Irv?" He rocked her in his arms and wiped the tear.

"What else did Big Irv tell Big Seth?"

"Did his thing, I suppose, half sermon, half circus—"

"Tell me something! Hold me!" She pulled the shapeless white hospital robe tightly around herself.

"He said"—he hunched his shoulders and made a sour face the way Steinmetz had—" 'Kid's got a good brain. Tough.' " He spoke in blunt New York tones and pointed to imaginary CAT scan images with an imaginary dead black cigar. "That's what he said." She seemed thin and small in his arms. "Did you know Big Irv wears his cowboy boots in the OR?"

"Big Irv" Steinmetz stood five feet four in his Nocoma boots: a restless, disagreeable man with rounded shoulders and a little potbelly. The "Big" was not a mockery but a reflection of the fear and admiration that the neurosurgical house staff felt for its chief. The gutsiest, sharpest brain surgeon in North America, they claimed and spoke with awe of his operating room concentration and technical brilliance.

"Ya see, Doctor, some brains stink," Steinmetz had said, glaring at the view box, cigar clenched between his teeth. "Ya just look at 'em, and they bruise." He ran his finger from image to image, tracing the interesting anatomical details. "Not this one. Tough little lady, your friend. Got guts. She'll be okay."

The CAT scan showed that no blood had leaked into Lindsay's brain. The worst had not happened. Her cerebral blood vessels had not been breached. There was no pool of bloody fluid slowly forming between her brain and its tough fibrous covering, no increase of pressure inside her head to insupportable levels.

"Ya see, what makes a good brain, Doctor . . ." He had cocked his head toward the array of pictures. Seth could have been any doctor; they were all the same to Steinmetz—names, faces; he never bothered. They were all the same. All there to be taught, to be told what he knew and no one else knew because no one else had been where he had been and done what he had done. All doctors were "Doctor," all nurses "doll," all patients "guy"—"How ya doin' today, guy?"—or "little lady." He never knew their names and couldn't tell one face from another. But what he did know was anatomy. "It's all in the vasculature, Doctor, connective tissue and vasculature. If you don't have good vessels, arteries—the little guys— then it doesn't matter how many gray cells ya got. This little lady's got the goods. Look here." He stood on tiptoe and pointed to a delicate curve in one of the films and traced its course. "What the hell difference does it make how many neurons ya got if you don't have good vessels to supply 'em? Couple hundred thousand cells one way or the other—doesn't make a damn bit of difference." His voice was gravelly, and he snorted whenever he could, by way of explanation.

"They don't take time anymore, Doctor. That's the trouble. It takes time to be gentle, to *care* about tissues. I tell ya—listen to this, Doctor, and remember it—you can piss into a surgical wound and it won't get infected if you don't injure the tissues, if you handle 'em gently—understand?" He snorted, and without waiting for a reply, he shoved the dead cigar back into his mouth and waddled away.

"Spiky little lady, your friend," he said over his shoulder. "She'll be okay—if you handle her gently."


"Spiky, he said, and you had terrific little arteries. 'Little guys,'" he called them."

"I don't feel tough. God, if my dad knew about this, he'd come down and have me back in Springfield faster than a hawk can snatch a chicken. I'd be covering weddings and funerals for the rest of my life. . . . Seth, I'm scared. What if he tries again?" Burrowing her head into his shoulder, she shuddered.

"Hey," he said too loudly, and tightened his embrace. "You're here now. Safe, with me. With people to look after you: my friends on the house staff; the nurses; Big Irv. Don't forget him. He's one tough hombre."

He glimpsed her exposed neck and the pulse that beat there seemed to be advertising her isolation and vulnerability. He covered it with his hand.

"He said you'd be okay . . . as long as I handled your tissues . . . gently . . . and checked your pulse." He kissed the pulse in her neck. "Just to make sure it was still working right." He kissed it again and pulled the green drapes that surrounded the bed, creating for a moment the sense of a fortress within a fortress—a child's illusion of safety in blindness.

"Did you know there are pulses all over the human body?" He eased her onto the bed.

She mustered a smile.

"The first thing we do after taking the Hippocratic oath"—he leaned over her with a certain professional keenness—"is learn all the throbbing places of the body. Clinical Throbbing 103. Some are easy, trite even . . ." He took her wrist pulse, this time glancing at his watch. "Rapid. You're very excitable, Miss Cooper. Some, on the other hand, or rather, foot"—he felt for the exact spot on the dorsal surface of her foot—"are surprising, and I might add, a little—shall we say?—downscale." He wiggled her big toe. "Some are in places that are open only on certain holidays, while others are . . ." He felt her heart and the breast over it. "Please, Miss Cooper, don't be alarmed. Your throbs are safe with me. Shhhh"—he raised a finger to his lips—"I must auscultate." Laying his head on her breast, he sighed and closed his eyes.

Beguiled for the moment by her body and its vulnerability, he didn't hear the rustle of drapes at the foot of the bed. He let the steady sound of her heart and the regular rhythm of her respiration surround them and comfort them as he had taken comfort in the green curtains that surrounded them.

"Seth . . ." Her heart surged.

Bolting upright, Seth could make out through the blur of his vision a form moving outside the curtained fortress. Instantly he was grabbing at the billowing green wall.

"Goddammit! Who's that?" he shouted, clawing for an opening and getting tangled.

Suddenly the drapes parted. "Hey, what's all the fuss?"

"Fontana! Goddammit! What the hell is this—"

Stopped dead in his tracks, Fontana flushed and stopped chewing.

"Why the hell are you skulking around?"

"Hey! Take it easy."

Ears burning, "Ever hear of knocking?" he blurted out.

"The door was open, hotshot. I didn't want to wake no one. I come to see Miss Cooper." He nodded in Lindsay's direction. "I didn't hear nothing." He looked uncomfortable in a polyester cord suit, white shirt, and dark blue tie, as though he'd come to a funeral. "Sorry, Miss Cooper, if I disturbed you." He glared at Seth. Lindsay pulled her robe around herself, and Fontana flushed again. He transferred the thick manila envelope from under his right arm to his left.

"How're you doin'?"

"Fine." She smiled a pallid smile. "Really, feeling much better."

"You wasn't in such good shape last time I saw ya. Oh"—he smiled—"almost forgot." He slipped a small box of candy out of his jacket pocket and put it on the bed next to Lindsay. "Lorraine. She thought you might . . . like it. Imported. Italy." He looked down at his manila envelope.

"Vince, that was sweet of you." She fumbled for the opening in the cellophane. "Lorraine—tell her thanks, will you?"

Arms across his chest, Seth lounged at the window, in stony detachment. In the silence the cellophane crackled loudly as the two men watched Lindsay struggle with the box.

Fontana cleared his throat softly. "You know . . . Miss Cooper, Murphy—Lieutenant Murphy—my boss, he assigned four more guys to this thing. I thought you'd want to know."

"So what?" Seth demanded.

"What d'ya mean, 'So what?' You know how many cases got five guys on 'em in this precinct? He made a zero with his thick thumb and forefinger. "Zilch, zip! Look"—he appealed to Lindsay—"the more guys, more legs. More legs, more legwork." He grinned at the inescapable conclusion of his logic as though he were Leibniz and had just demonstrated the existence of monads.

"Who does the brainwork?" Seth asked icily.

Fontana's chewing slowed. "The taxpayers get what they can afford." He smiled coolly. "Same as your department, hotshot." He nodded toward Bellevue across the street. "Hey, c'mon, Doc, lay off. You got no beef with me. So what're ya tryin' to make a monkey outta me? Besides, like I said, I come to talk to Miss Cooper." Abruptly he turned away.

"Hmmm, delicious—nougat." Lindsay held the box out to Seth. "Try some."

Scowling, Seth thrust his hands into his pockets as though the candy were contaminated and turned to stare out at the traffic heading north and south on the East River Drive. The midafternoon shadows were lengthening, and the hospital itself cast a huge dark blue patch across the drive almost to the brink of the river.

What *was* his beef? He didn't really know. "Take care of her," Steinmetz had enjoined. He hadn't taken care. He hadn't done enough. For any of them. The midafternoon sun glistened on the river as it had on the Great Salt Pond that day, that wonderful day, irrecoverable now.

"Look, Miss Cooper, I know this isn't such a hot time for you—to start asking you a lot of questions, I mean, but . . . well, you know." The prism of chocolate he held looked tiny between his thumb and forefinger, like an aspirin. And he didn't seem to know what to do with it.

Laying aside the box of chocolates, Lindsay hunched her shoulders up to do her duty like the good soldier that she was. "I told you all I could yesterday." She touched the bandage behind her right ear.

"I know, Miss Cooper, but"—not knowing what else to do with the chocolate, he popped it into his mouth—"I thought maybe if we went over it again, you might think of something—anything"—he swallowed the sweet with a gulp—"some little thing." He held his chocolate-smeared fingers up stiffly as he pleaded, as though they were injured. "Look, I know you didn't see the mother, but maybe, just maybe, you noticed something. You know what I mean?"

"Maybe I did see him. Maybe I even had a chat with him." She reached him some Kleenex from her table. "The point is I just don't know."

Taking the tissues, he absentmindedly licked his fingers clean and then wiped them. "What about his hands? What about gloves? Was he wearing gloves?" He leaned forward insistently.

"She told you, Fontana. She doesn't know." Turning back to them, Seth pushed his glasses back up on his nose. "She has a retrograde amnesia. She can't remember. Anything after she got upstairs—gone, vanished, lost." He whisked her memories away with his hand.

"I remember climbing the stairs"—she looked grim and shook her head—"but that's all. Sorry."

Thwarted, Fontana sprawled backward in his chair. They watched him as he fingered the mole on his cheek. "He wore gloves. The son of a bitch wore gloves. He must have. He wrecked the place, but there isn't a single print on the stuff. It's like he went crazy." He reached for the manila envelope and extracted a sheaf of eight-by-ten glossy photographs.

"There was one print," he said softly, almost as an afterthought, "one lousy fingerprint. On the coffee table. Guess whose." He began rearranging the photos, turning them this way and that like a fussy old maid.

Grim, preoccupied with the river again, Seth pretended not to hear.

"Give up," Lindsay said with a weary smile.

"Graver." Fontana tapped the pack of photographs smartly on the arm of the chair like a magician ready to do tricks with his deck of cards. "Dr. L. Jonathan Graver. How does that grab ya, Doc?"

"It doesn't, Fontana." He didn't bother turning. "He was having an affair with her."

"Maybe with both of them," Lindsay added with a shrug.

"Everyone knew about it, so why shouldn't his fingerprints be there?"

"Yeah, I figured." He touched his mole as though it were the secret source of his powers. "The boys from the lab said it was an old print anyway. Look," he said suddenly, flipping through the photos, "I'd like ya to take a look at these. Shots the boys took that night." He handed them to her with an apologetic shrug. "Not pretty. Sorry." Swinging around suddenly, he said: "Hey, Doc, loosen up. Join the human race. Take a look. You were there."

Seth moved grudgingly to Lindsay's side, and they looked at the harshly lit photos in fascinated silence.

"God! What kind of human being did this?" Lindsay said quietly. The apartment and Milly McVey's body, viewed from every imaginable angle and in every agonizing detail, looked as though some supernatural force, some great punishing hand had swept over them, twisting, crushing, and breaking what it could find. Each scene seemed to confirm anew the presence of a destructive intelligence at work. Not some impersonal force like an earthquake, or whirlwind, or explosion, but some perversely selective vengeful spirit.

"Christ!" Seth's features contracted as though he had been suddenly punched. He studied Milly's bruised and swollen face, grotesque in death. "What a mess!" He shook his head. "He really messed her up, didn't he?"

"Makes ya wonder, huh, Doc?"

What? What does it make you wonder, Fontana? What? Seth wanted to ask. What goes on in that poor muscle-bound brain of yours? What do you make of all this? How do you figure it? How will you ever put it together? How will you ever protect us? Keep it from happening again? To her? To me? What?

"Yeah." He handed the photo back to Fontana.

"Now here's a beauty." Fontana held out a close-up of a monstrous reptilian head. Every detail of its scaly hide and warty skin stood out in relief. Frozen in time, its stupid goggle eye seemed to call out from the Jurassic Period.

"This little fella scared the lasagne out of me that night. I opened the bathroom door, switched on the light, and—wham— there we were, eyeball to eyeball. He was just sittin' there in the washbowl near the tap. Just sittin' and staring at me. Jeez, I thought it was plastic for a minute. Then all of a sudden it began to move. Give you three guesses which one of us backed off. . . ."

"It's an iguana," Seth said softly, staring at the animal as though it were someone he knew. ". . . disgusting little monster . . ." Milly's words that night sprang to mind.

"Lady at the museum says people actually keep these things as pets. Would ya believe that? All they need is a little water and some plants to nibble on." He fingered his mole. "I wonder whose pet—the nurse or the kid."

"Jennie Light," Seth said quietly, handing the photo back. Fontana studied him for a moment quizzically. His eyes demanded an explanation.

"Just a hunch," Seth added with a shrug.

"Yeah." Fontana flipped mechanically through the photographs. "You're good on hunches, Doc." He flashed a chewy, mirthless smile at Seth. "See these?" He handed each of them a different view of the chaos and wreckage of Milly's apartment.

"Look"—Fontana pointed to the photo Lindsay was holding, "here's where the body was found—these marks. I don't know whether you can tell from the picture, but . . . well, there's something peculiar—you know what I mean?"

Lindsay looked up, hopeful, rooting for him; Seth remembered him at the precinct that night, index fingers poised over the typewriter keyboard, besieged by the twenty-six letters of the alphabet, and felt a wave of pity again.

Uncomprehending, they waited as he slowly unwrapped another stick of gum. "Well, the place was a wreck, but I mean, really . . . you were there, Doc, you know what I'm sayin'. But if you just stood there in the middle of it, like this, the way I'm standin' now"—he gestured with his huge hands as though he were a conjurer, re-creating the scene for himself—"you get the idea that . . . he wasn't just breakin' . . . he was lookin' "—he made another little pass—"he was searchin' for something."

"The diary!" They both said it at once.

"Of course!" Seth smacked his forehead. "*That's* why she was murdered! The diary. The diary. Jennie Light's diary was still alive, pointing a finger, still there. That's what he wanted. Maybe it's there now." He was bubbling now, overflowing, enjoying Fontana's incomprehension. "She knew, Milly knew what was in the diary, so when he showed up, she knew he was it, the murderer—"

"What, Doc? What? What're we lookin' for? What diary?"

"Look, Fontana, Milly told me that night that Jennie Light kept a diary. She wanted to destroy it."

"Why?" Fontana asked innocently.

"How the hell should I know?" Seth snapped. "Personal reasons, I suppose. Don't you see? She must have told *him* about it too, Jennie Light. And it must have been someone—a relationship—no one knew about."

Fontana looked unhappy. "*Everything* that broad did was secret. I still don't know who her friends were, who knew her—except maybe the nurse—"

"Irrelevant. The point is, Fontana," Seth said with unnecessary emphasis, like a parent talking to a child, "What happened to the diary? Did he get it? Did she destroy it? Did she hide it? What?" Seth moved to the window and looked out at Queens across the river. The massive, windowless warehouses along the eastern bank glowed, ageless, in the late-afternoon sun like granite cliffs. He watched a great gray bird—a kestrel, he thought—soaring high over the river, mostly flecked with gold now. Alone it circled, under the deepening blue sky, hovering there, a revenant, a silent accuser from the past.

"Lonely spirit . . ." he remembered. It was true he hadn't taken care of them. He had failed them, all of them, in one way or another: Lindsay, his father, Mrs. Scola, Milly, Elly—Elly more than any of them. He watched the great gray bird as it hung motionless for a moment over the river before it swerved westward into the sun. "What about her stuff?" he asked without turning.

"Usual junk. Some records—you know, that punk rock crap; lotta mean-lookin' guys on the covers. Believe it or not, some old kids' books." He searched the green floor tiles for more of "her stuff," as though it were laid out before him. "Oh, yeah, a pack of letters—old letters—go back ten years, maybe. I can't make too much sense out of 'em. Clothes—you know, the usual, nothing special." Then, talking to Seth's back, he raised his voice. "Definitely no diary in her room. Combed it clean."

"Mind if I take a look at those things?" Lindsay asked, and ran her fingers through her hair, a habit Seth had noticed she had when asking favors.

Fontana shrugged. "Be my guest. Stuff is at the precinct." He leafed abstractedly through the photos. "You know, I don't think we worked the rest of the apartment like we should've. Trouble was we didn't know what we were lookin' for—ya know what I mean?" But no one was listening.


Hunched over his fifth and final case report of the day, Seth could see at a glance that it was not his best. It was late in the afternoon, and his sentences had become simple, almost primitive—syntactical shards. His handwriting had become more and more disheveled, and his thoughts ragged. He paused and searched the grain of the scarred table over which he was bent for a detail from an interview he had finished half an hour before.

His tiny office on N-6 had, at one time, been a seclusion room. Since then only the padding had been removed from its walls, and two rickety chairs and an old table—the words "Department of Correction" branded on it—had been added. The suicide window, only seven or eight inches wide and covered with a heavy-gauge wire mesh, was open and allowed a warm slab of light into the cubicle. A drop of sweat rolled down his temple as he stared through the dirty mesh screen at the yellow end-of-summer light. With little sleep, his ability to concentrate had begun to show signs of slippage. For two nights he'd stood vigil over Lindsay, the first, hovering impotently in the ICU, getting in the way, making a pest of himself, until he knew for sure she was in the clear; the second, just being there for her during the fitful, panicky night.

Through the open door a sound—half sob, half moan—drifted in from the ward beyond. He was dead tired, and for a moment he wasn't sure whether it was real and not one of the spectral sounds that had been recirculating on the ward like its stale air for the last forty years. It was the same sound, he thought, that had leaked from Milly McVey along with her life the other night. In her agony he had heard her moan amid the debris that had been her life before lapsing into her final coma. He stared at the scrawl on the paper in front of him and shook himself. Then he pushed forward against the pull of entropy, bent over the table, and began to write again.

As he raced headlong, almost blindly through the final sentences of the report, he heard the cough behind him, the unmistakable light cough. He bent lower over the page and began to sign his name slowly, elaborately, with exquisite care and attention to detail, even including his middle name this time—Bowen. Behind him Coles cleared his fragile throat, and Seth could feel the dreadful eye boring into his back. He stiffened and closed his eyes in a childish attempt to wish Coles away. He could feel him standing there, a soft pink hand at his lips, poised lightly on his toes like a shy girl ready to strike and run. Seth's fingers whitened around his pen as he waited for the inevitable.

"Ahem, Dr. Conrad . . ."

Seth twisted around in his chair and looked surprised. "Oh, hi."
He mustered a collegial smile. Creep. "Sorry, guess I got caught up
in this." He nodded at the papers on the table. "Fascinating case."

"Right, Ah could see that, Dr. Conrad." A drawl still curled
around his open vowels in rare moments of self-confidence, a linguistic
talisman. "Conscientious, very conscientious." His dead eye fixed
Seth cruelly, as the live one slid timidly away.

Seth smiled stupidly again at the sightless eye and nodded. Creep,
bastard.

"Ah wonder, Dr. Conrad, if Ah could tear you away from your
. . . duties. This matter puzzles me." He held a patient chart,
metal-clad, and tapped it with the exposure meter that hung always
from around his pink, hairless neck by a black ribbon. "You and
Ah seem to have"—he grinned—"misunderstood each other. Right?"
He backed away on his toes, like a courtier in the royal presence.
Seth half expected him to bow. "Soon! Right?"


*"T*here, that's better," Coles said, shutting out the buzz of psychotic
confusion that radiated from the ward. The door to his office was
heavy, specially soundproofed, creating a silence that was unnatural
within the jumble of the room. Once safely inside, he seemed to
relax. His step was heavier, falling on the flat of the foot now rather
than the toe; his gait became rolling, more powerful; relaxing the
tight, fixed smile, his lips became fuller, epicene. Gathering the skirt
of his white coat about him, like a fussy spinster, he sat down
behind his desk. Leaning forward, he shoved the pile of photography
catalogs and gadgets to one side and tossed the metal chart into
the clearing with a clatter. "There," he said comfortably, "nice and
quiet here. We can reason together, as the Scripture says." He
smiled. His eyes were hooded now from the light above him by his
shaggy red brows, and for the moment it was as though he were
completely sightless, a doughy creature attuned to his lightless world
by touch and sound.

Seth smiled blandly. Creep. "Yes, been . . . a hectic day." He
let his gaze slide past Coles to one of the large photographs scattered

about the walls. In marked contrast to the gloomy chaos of the room with its muddle of obsolete photo equipment—tripods, reels, cameras—the photos were hard-edged, needle-sharp close-ups, tight and well organized. Most were tropical flowers, shameless in the uninhibited display of their sexual organs, and reptiles, grotesque, epochal misfits, like Coles himself.

"Like it? The picture? You were smiling."

"Oh, yeah. Yes. Very unusual. What is it? Orchid?"

"Maybe. Ah wouldn't know. Ah'm not partial to flowers." He reached for an old 35 mm camera from the pile of hardware next to him. "Panatomic-X—verrrry slow"—he drew the word out proudly as though the film and he had some special bond—"and this fella"— he held up the camera—"did all these." He nodded at the photos on the wall, the only personal touches in the room. "Focal plane shutter." Click, he snapped the shutter. "Nice sound." Click. He touched it fondly. "Nobody uses 'em anymore. No one even knows about 'em." Then, as though he'd said too much, he glanced up and folded his thick, powerful hands in front of him. "Know anything about cameras, Dr. Conrad?" he asked, making a smile and tilting backward in his swivel chair.

Christ, get on with it! He knew what Coles wanted. "Afraid not," he said making a point of looking at his watch. "Guess I'm the Instamatic type." He watched the color rise in Coles's neck and the smile slowly disappear.

What was he doing? he asked himself as he breathed furiously on his glasses. Two weeks' work down the toilet. Fifteen minutes, and he'd be home free. Why screw it up now? He squinted as he wiped the lenses of his glasses meticulously and prayed for self-restraint. Through the blur of the gloomy office he sensed Coles's withdrawal.

Looking down at the little camera in front of him, Coles's eyes became even more hooded. He fondled it and made the friendly click again. "Yes, right," he said quietly. Blowing softly onto the camera, he removed an invisible speck of dust. "Dr. Ettinger said you had . . . more important things on your mind. He also thought you were . . . spreading yourself a little thin, Dr. Conrad." He spoke to the camera, as though Seth were somehow imprisoned inside.

"Did he mention that to you?" Without waiting for a reply, he leaned back in his chair and peered through the viewfinder of the camera at the metal-covered chart on his desk.

" 'Seek not out the things that are too hard for thee, neither search the things that are above thy strength.' " Turning the lens back and forth, he focused it with exquisite care. "The Bible, Dr. Conrad. Ecclesiasticus. People don't read it much around here. Has good psychology, though, and good advice." Lowering the camera, he grinned so that the gap between his front teeth showed. "Now," he said, leaning forward over the metal chart, "what the hell is this all about?" He tapped the chart with the edge of the camera. "Ah thought we agreed that Mrs. Scola would be put on the roster for a course of shock treatments, Dr. Conrad." He cleared his throat. "Mrs. Scola is a sixty-year-old woman who presents a classical picture of involutional melancholia. Ah know how you young people feel about shock treatment, but it is still the treatment of choice for involutional depression. Besides, Dr. Conrad"—he leaned back in his swivel chair and brought the 35 mm camera to eye level again, this time focusing on some object over Seth's shoulder—"the effect of ECT is one of the most spectacular treatments in modern medicine. Try it. You'll see." Coles slowly shifted the camera until finally it held Seth's image in the viewfinder. Seth squirmed. Creep, bastard! Again he searched for the strength to resist the impulse to reach across the desk and yank the camera out of Coles's strong, stubby fingers.

"So, Dr. Conrad, stop fahtin' around—excuse my bluntness— and give Mrs. Scola her ECT. Just push the button." Click. He snapped Seth's picture, lowered the camera, and half smiled, half leered at his little joke. "See, it's not hard."

The air conditioner droned on, accompanied by an occasional click as Coles fussed with the camera mechanism. What do you want, big shot? he asked himself, making an effort to look troubled and thoughtful: to save Helen Scola from another fifteen years as a zombie or to rub Coles's nose in it? He struggled silently and prayed for guile.

"But *is* she a classical involutional?" he asked suddenly, striving for the naive, puzzled tone in his voice. Pay attention, he told himself. Concentrate! "After all, didn't her first depression begin fifteen years ago? I believe that was it. You have the chart there, sir. She was about forty-five. Isn't that a little early for involutional?" He lowered his voice on the last question, apologizing, almost.

Coles frowned. "That so?" He put the camera to one side and began to flip through the hospital chart. "Done a lot of work on this case. How come?" He didn't wait for a reply or look up but continued to riffle through the voluminous record, pausing here and there.

Seth waited, accused, he thought, of interest, thoroughness. A pulse of rage shot through him. Creep, bastard! He bent forward and recrossed his legs. Hold it! Concentrate! Don't screw it up now! He watched as Coles pursed his lips and whistled soundlessly, like a dry wind in an arid land. He decided to play his losing trick.

"Sorry she's been here for so long, Dr. Coles. I know you like to get patients out quickly."

Coles looked up. "It's not fair to patients to keep them longer, Dr. Conrad. This isn't a long-term facility. Over four weeks!" he said righteously.

Pious bullshit! Creep, bastard, hypocrite! Quick turnover, keep the merchandise moving. In and out fast, and no worries about spoilage; no complications; let the next guy worry about treatment. "You're absolutely right, sir." He nodded in self-reproach.

Coles's face flushed, and his eyes receded into their dark little caves as he bent over the chart. And with the clarity that exhaustion sometimes brings, Seth knew that he had gone too far.

Tilting backward in his chair so that his living eye, half closed, was visible, Coles swiveled from side to side for a few long moments. "Dr. Conrad, Ah know you don't like me. Fortunately for me, you don't have to. All you have to do is what Ah tell you to do. And Ah'm sure you won't mind that too much. Ah like having you on the ward; you're a smart fella, and you do good work; but if you hadn't crapped around and had put her on ECT right away, she would have been out by now. Now, why did you take this patient off the ECT roster?"

Urgently glancing around the room, as though searching for some means of escape, Seth finally took a deep breath and turned to face Coles. "Well, first of all, she had ECT fifteen years ago, when her depression first started, and it didn't help. Second of all, clinically she doesn't present a typical involutional picture. She's depressed, yes, but there's no ideational content that's consonant with her mood."

"What's your point? What do you mean?" Click. He was fidgeting with the camera again.

"Look, ordinarily patients are depressed *about* something. They're afraid of getting poor or losing their job, or they're full of self-reproaches. They feel they've been bad mothers or bad wives. You know what I mean. This woman has nothing of that. She complains of being tired and not having any pep or interest in the ordinary things in her life. It's as though her whole vegetative nervous system were being depleted."

Coles bounced back in his chair comfortably and smiled. "You know, Dr. Conrad, that not every syndrome has to be absolutely typical. She could be an involutional depressive and still benefit from ECT. How do you know it didn't help the first time?"

"I have all the records. That's what's taken so long. There was something peculiar about her history, so I got in touch with all the doctors who've been treating her over the past fifteen years. There were seven of them. And it's been a disaster!"

It was too late now. His resolution and restraint were gone. He had worked hard digging up and documenting all of the details of the case, and he'd been able to put together the final pieces just that afternoon. But now he wanted only to shove it to Coles, regardless of the consequences, and he couldn't stop.

"Get to the point, Dr. Conrad, if there is one." The soft red color that had climbed into Coles's face looked purple under the fluorescent light. Glaring at Seth across the desk, his good eye narrowed, his false eye stared blankly.

"There is." He took another deep breath. "She's been misdiagnosed and mistreated for fifteen years. She's been passed around among seven upstate doctors who are at best ignorant and misguided and at worst incompetent. And if we shock her and send her home on the wrong medication, we'll be repeating the same mistakes that the others made."

Leaning back, almost languidly, Coles unconsciously began rubbing his cheek with the smooth, metallic surface of the small camera. "Well, Dr. Conrad, what do *you* think is wrong with Mrs. Scola?" he asked with a grim smile.

"Look"—Seth stood up without thinking, excited—"I've been able to document the entire course of her depression, and it correlates almost completely with the onset and treatment of her high blood pressure."

"High blood pressure doesn't cause depression."

"It can if you're sensitive to rauwolfia derivatives and get treated with them," he said with undisguised contempt.

Christ, this was stupid! What was he doing? His crazy hero bit again. His whole life. "Paper hero," Cal and Elly used to taunt him. Forever rescuing mangy dogs, lost cats, and later, in college, lost, dippy girls, actresses mostly. At seven he'd freed Cal's white parrot from its cage, and at eight his father's mice from their laboratory prison—"the last of this foolishness," his father had told him with an impressive display of thunder and lightning. Animals were to study, not to rescue. Apostasy. Conrads examined experience, prepared their minds, and discovered the secrets of nature. They didn't rescue; they weren't heroes.

The scene of the previous night's savage assault flashed into his mind. The bright red blood oozing and trickling down the back of Lindsay's neck, under her ear, matting her soft hair, and making a sticky, interesting Rorschach design on her white blouse. He felt a painful sensation at the back of his own head and a sick feeling in his stomach. Paper hero. All that he knew at that moment was that he hankered for some kind of confrontation. He wanted to close with someone, some paper villain maybe, in the only way he knew: with words, with evidence—the way a Conrad would. He smiled to himself.

"She had her first depression in February of 1959. She went to some local jerkwater psychiatrist, and he gave her shock treatments that didn't work. What he didn't know, because he didn't take a careful enough medical history, was that she had begun treatment for her hypertension and had just started taking a drug called Hydrotens, which contains reserpine." He looked up at the ceiling to check his memory. "She stayed depressed for the next year, while her friend the psychiatrist tried her on Darnate, a mood elevator which is absolutely contraindicated in patients with hypertension. Brilliant!" In one small part of his brain he knew that his dogs of war had slipped their leashes and that he was on some crazy, suicidal mission.

Now, quite composed, Coles sat back watching the pyrotechnical display as Seth went on through the vicissitudes of Mrs. Scola's mental states and mistreatments doctor by doctor, year by year; occasionally he glanced down and riffled through the hospital record before him to check some point.

"In '63 her internist finally took her off Hydrotens and put her on a new antihypertensive, one without reserpine in it, and what do you think happened? Right. Her depression lifted, and she lived normally, holding down a good job as a secretary until '66, when she had the misfortune to move to a better neighborhood and changed to a new doctor. Represton contains reserpine, and within a week she's depressed again."

Back and forth across the office he paced as he spoke, prudence having left him completely. He was hardly aware of Coles's presence now. He was aware only of what he wanted to say and of wanting to say it freely.

"I don't know where she found these jokers"—he whirled around and glared at Coles accusingly—"but they really did a job on her. All the time they were giving her medication for blood pressure with reserpine in it, they were trying to get rid of her depression with different combinations of tranquilizers. Until finally she was not only depressed but agitated, irritable, and having orgasms all day long. Iatrogenic! It was all iatrogenic.

"Now Mrs. Scola wasn't exactly looking for romance at this time in her life—past sixty and a widow for ten years. All she wanted was to be free of her depression, to have some peace and be a good grandma. So she complained to her GP about her constant sexual feelings." He paused and smiled grimly. "Now comes the moment that'll live forever in the annals of medicine. He sends her to his buddy the local gynecology ace, and what do you think he does. Jesus, this really deserves the Nobel Prize for schmuckiness.

He removes her clitoris and anterior labia to cure the problem. Christ Almighty, I couldn't believe it." He turned on Coles again. "Thank God she wasn't complaining of headaches.

"It's all there"—he pointed—"in the chart. You asked me what I thought was wrong with her, Dr. Coles." He bent over the desk and spoke to Coles's good eye—only a slit now—the one that had followed his every movement with cool precision the whole time, as though his life depended on it. "Well, in my opinion, what's wrong with her is that she's been treated for the last fifteen years by seven of the stupidest, most incompetent fuck-ups I've ever heard of. And if you ask me, we'll be doing the same thing by giving her ECT. But then again," he added, pausing for breath, "it's not really my decision. It's yours."

Still holding the miniature camera, Coles sat motionless and silent, a purplish hue rising in his cheeks again. Finally, dropping his gaze, he fidgeted with the camera for a moment. "Yes, Dr. Conrad, you've made yourself perfectly clear. Ah see how you feel." He paused, glanced up at Seth, and returned to inspect the camera. "And you are right. It is my decision. You needn't worry about Mrs. Scola anymore. Ah'll handle it." He put the camera down and placed the metal-covered chart in his desk drawer. Looking up once more, he smiled politely. "Thank you, Dr. Conrad, Ah think we understand each other." His final, frigid look dismissed Seth.

Spent, breathing hard, legs still trembling with excitement, he stood facing Coles in disbelief—dazed, like a bull, before it falls. No, he refused to move. It had come out wrong, all wrong. Coles had somehow won. He had been right. He'd held all of the cards, knew all the facts. He'd been right, incontestably right. Yet Coles had defeated him. He wanted to do it over, make it come out different, better. "Paper hero." The words rang in his burning ears as he finally turned away.


"Never mind! Screw Coles! Forget about him, boychik!" Harvey poured the last of the wine into his glass and shook the dregs into Seth's. "He'll die in miserable obscurity." He waved the spirit of Coles away as though it were a fly. It was already ten o'clock, and Harvey's speech was as thick, almost, as the vile red house wine that Lino served with suspicious fanfare. "But you"—he tore off a piece of bread and pointed to Seth with it—"you're a genius, boychik. You have discovered the secret of life!" He dabbed at the spaghetti sauce in his plate and shoved the soaked bread into his mouth. "Forget about the philosophers' stone! Forget about the Fountain of Youth! Forget about all that base metal shit! You say she was having constant orgasms?" He raised his arms in gratitude to the gods above. "Do you know how much time I spent in medical school looking for that formula, boychik? Now, start again, slowly." He fumbled awkwardly for a sheet of paper and a pen. "What were the drugs? Shoot! Boychik, boychik, we'll make a fortune." Eyes wide, he'd come alive for the first time that night.

Throughout dinner the conversation had drifted morbidly between apathetic reassurances about Lindsay and routine consolation over Mrs. Scola. But now he chewed and swallowed with gusto and bent forward over the table, pen poised.

"What do you mean, 'we'?" Seth said sourly. "Whose discovery is this anyway?" He poked dully at his cold eggplant.

"Chance rewards only the prepared *pupik*." Harvey made an obscene gesture with his fist.

"You're disgusting," Seth said apathetically.

"Yes"—Harvey lurched forward—"but creative. Virgins will pray for you. Shy men will toast you. Nuns will bless you." He made the sign of the cross over Seth. "The Catholic market alone—we'll make millions." He raised his glass in celebration.

"Conrad—the name will be immortal!" With a wave of his hand he put Seth's name in lights above them. "My friend, my boychik, you'll be up there with all the big boys now: Darwin, Pasteur, Dr. Ruth . . . where the hell is that *mamzer* Lino?" He twisted around violently in his chair like a bull in captivity.

Smiling, Lino appeared out of nowhere. "Can I get you somethin' else, Dottore Bloch?" Handsome in the white jacket he'd worn as a waiter on the Via Veneto, Lino now took entrepreneurial pride in his ability to remember the name of each young doctor on the hospital staff and intuitively treated each with the princely respect he or she yearned for.

"How's the wife, Lino?" Harvey asked with a leer.

*"Benissimo,"*

"Kids?" Harvey winked.

*"Molto bene, grazie,"* he said with a gracious bow.

"Oh, and Lino"—he picked up the empty wine bottle and turned it upside down—*"encore vino!"*

Lino smiled knowingly and nodded. *"Si,* Dottore Bloch, at once."

Harvey looked after the departing Lino. "Lying bastard. He's not even married." He looked to Seth for justice. "Dja hear me, boychik?" he demanded, blinking stupidly. "Sly little bastard, lives with his *mama mia* around the corner. I see him in the supermarket all the time." He snorted.

Half listening, through the haze of noise and bad wine, to Harvey's nonsense, Seth shrugged and made a meaningless sound of involvement.

The waiter arrived with the new wine and served it, being careful to wait for Harvey's approval.

"Christ, she looked awful today."

"Who?"

"Lindsay," Seth snapped, tossing his napkin onto the table.

"I didn't know we were talking about Lindsay," Harvey said with a sulky shrug.

"Jesus, that fucking son of a bitch almost killed her. I still can't believe it."

"You're right, it was damn close," Harvey said into his wine. He picked at a bit of cork in his glass. "But you said she was okay."

"I said she had a concussion, and that's not okay. It's just lucky," he said indignantly. "That's why Steinmetz did the CAT scan. He was worried about how long she was out."

"How long?"

"Half hour, at least, maybe longer."

"Long time." Harvey looked worried. "She *was* lucky, Seth." With his wild hair, rumpled bulk, and bushy beard, when he wasn't joking, he seemed only comically sad. "Listen, boychik"—he grabbed Seth's arm urgently—"don't be a schmuck. Cut this crap out already. Enough. There's a real, determined killer around here." He spoke loudly, emphatically, as though talking to a foreigner. He was neither comic nor sad now. One or two of the remaining diners turned to stare at him. He shook Seth's arm, and their eyes met. "He knows who you are and where you are." The thickness in his speech had disappeared, and he'd lowered his voice to a harsh whisper. "He's dangerous, he's clever, but most of all, he's *very highly motivated.*" He underlined the three words with his forefinger. "And you're trying to be some kind of a stupid-ass hero. I know you. You're acting like an adolescent asshole for her, Lindsay. You'll get yourself and her killed. For chrissake, you never got over your late show complex. It's for real, Seth; it's for real." He yanked a filthy tabloid up from the bench beside him and pointed to the headline, NURSE STRANGLED.

He grabbed Seth's arm again in a moist, beefy grip. "Look at what your kid games have accomplished so far. You're lucky you're alive, and she's lucky her brain isn't a Waldorf salad." He stopped suddenly, sighed, and fell back, spent.

Seth saw her again as she'd been the other night in the ICU, hooked up to bleeping monitors, ashen and scrawny and helpless like a drowned child—like Elly that day. The neurosurgeon doing the L.P. was botching it; the X-ray technician doing the skull film and yanking her head around like a bowling ball; the ICU nurses checking her blood pressure every few minutes and yelling at her to wake up. Jesus.

"Do you know what you're doing, boychik?" Harvey asked, his eyelids heavy, his speech thick again. "Drop it, cool it, forget it. Take Coop to the movies. Study. Write up your cases. Do anything. Only stay out of this crazy business."

Lino ciaoed them out with plenty of charm and an invitation to come back soon. "Kiss the bambinos," Harvey called over his shoulder with a foolish grin. "Phony bastard," he mumbled, once through the door.

There had been a sharp drop in the temperature, and Seth took a deep breath. The overcast sky that had made the afternoon gloomy and leaden had fragmented, and small, puffy clouds scudded across a clear night blue sky.

They walked in silence, the two of them, Seth stumbling now and then and weaving. Remote now, his body seemed part of yesterday's panic and fatigue. His feet, as they touched the pavement, were numb and distant. But his mind, he thought, his mind was brilliant and clear like the city stars above. He smiled stupidly to them, a secret salutation. There were only a handful visible: the toughest, the brightest—survivors. The city overwhelmed the others, drowned them, killed them—like Jennie Light and now Milly. But he had survived, would survive. The thick red wine had made him numb, easy, had made him a survivor. He felt buoyant, devoid of personal history, no longer earthbound.

Lurching against Harvey, he poked him. "Don't worry, Harv, everything'll be okay. Lindsay's okay. She's okay."

Hands clasped behind his back, huge head sunk between his shoulders, Harvey glared and mumbled to the sidewalk, "Goddammit, I said what's his name's been looking for you. Your muscle-bound friend the cop. Montana—whatever the hell his name is—was looking for you today—"

"He'll find me," Seth said quietly. "He'll find me." He smiled again at the bright, hardy stars above and gave them a slow, comradely wink. And when he does, I'll be ready for him, he thought. There was an inevitability in all this now. He was pulled by it, tied to it, inhabited. It was in his head all the time, and he couldn't shake it out, didn't want to. He studied it—murder, murderers, victims—as he knew, somehow, he was being studied. He had to meet him once more, this time face-to-face and on his own terms.

In the elevator they rode in silence, Seth slumped against the cab wall, head back, eyes closed, unable to think anymore.

Harvey fumbled with the lock. "Bad news . . . she was bad news. You didn't know her. . . ." He shoved Seth inside. "Wanna hear something, boychik?" In answer Seth flung himself on the living-room sofa, his arm shielding his eyes from the light.

"Everybody—everybody wanted her . . . listen to this. . . ."

Seth heard himself think: Later. Tomorrow. But his mouth wouldn't work. He heard the flick of a switch, a hiss of tape. His brain was turning.

"She was bad news before, and she's bad news now. . . ."
Harvey's words receded into the kitchen, lost in the crashing chords
of Brahms's Second Piano Concerto.

"Serkin!" Harvey shouted from the kitchen.

"He knew what she was all about. . . ." Harvey's words
returned and along with them the clink of glasses. "She was there
. . . that day. Listen to this, they don't make 'em like this anymore
. . . drove back to the city together. . . ." He stood intoning over
Seth like a rabbi over a corpse. "In his neat little XK40 . . . with
the tan glove leather upholstery. Here, want some wine, boychik?
. . . You got to admit it. He's got style. Silk really has style. . . .
Hey, boychik, wake up," Harvey shouted over the music. "You're
missing a great performance. . . ."

*Part Four*

# DREAMWORK

*Chapter*

# 12

Bad weather always cheers a hospital, comforting those confined by duty or disease with the illusion that they're not missing anything.

The next days, the late days of September, brought with them harbinger clouds, heavy and gray, flying low over the dingy red-brick buildings. For days, then, the wind and rain roiled the river and tore the yellowing leaves from the few trees that lined the East River Drive; it kept the medical students longer than usual at their work in the hospital's grim laboratories and made the nurses in their flaring blue capes huddle together in pairs as they crossed the street to their endless round of duties; it beat and beat at the countless windows and heavy green copper roof of the hospital.

Bellevue, like some great ocean of travail, had an infinite capacity to absorb the suffering that rained down upon it. Its business each day was pain, poverty, obscenity, and death, and it had no time for pity. Otherwise, who would do what had to be done? One pain more or less, one death more or less. . . . Milly McVey's funeral was over in twenty-three minutes by Seth's watch.

A handful of people attended the gloomy service in the nonde-nominational hospital chapel the city provided. The Catholic chaplain, a flabby, cheerless young Irishman with watery blue eyes, presided. He had never met Milly McVey and had only that morning met her father and brother. They had come to claim the body from the medical examiner and take it back to Wilkes-Barre, "where she belonged." Standing in front of the closed wooden coffin—painfully simple—the priest intoned the obligatory words with an apathy that came from shepherding a constantly dying flock.

Phyl Rowan was among the solemn group that formed around the father and brother after the service, offering awkward words of consolation. Her face set in a grim mask, she ignored Seth's sympathetic nod, turning coolly away; reproachful, almost, Seth thought.

When he got to them, Seth found that he had nothing to say to the father and brother and only shook their hands. The brother, tight-lipped, had a brown, weather-beaten face and had gotten a new haircut for the occasion. Seth could feel the tough, strong grip of a man who had worked all his life out of doors. And the old man, whose pink neck seemed shrunken inside a starched collar several sizes too big for him, looked dazed and mumbled to no one in particular, "I never could see it—never—why she liked it here."

Late for the four o'clock appointment, he slammed out of his room and came face-to-face with the two of them.

"Seth, old man!"

"Gangway, I'm in a hurry!" The two of them blocking his way made an imposing barrier. Of late, like Rosencrantz and Guildenstern, they had become oddly inseparable. And today they seemed to have transcended separation altogether, as though they had both passed through the looking glass and come out on the other side transposed. Whit, barefoot, was in the white Oriental pajama suit, and Mark, in the fencer's tunic and breeches, flashed an excited grin.

"Look at him, Marcus, young Parsifal, flushed with the secret pleasure of bloodlust. Off to kill another swan?"

"How ya doin', Doc? How's it goin'?"

They were in high spirits, the two of them, and breathing hard with a fine sheen of sweat on their faces, they were like a pair of twitchy thoroughbreds.

Standing before them, unable to pass, he was confronted again, momentarily, with the evidence of his own frailty. Where his shoulders were narrow and drooped, theirs seemed wide and square; where their eyes sparkled with clarity and confidence, his, through their filthy lenses, were blurred and circumspect; where his muscles felt stringy and loose, like raveled yarn, theirs seemed vibrant and tonic, like highly tuned kettledrums.

"Fun and games another time, Whit. Sorry." Slouching defiantly, he sliced his way between them with a journal he was holding. "Late for Burden," he added, and took off at a brisk pace.

"I said how's it goin'?" Mark shouted after him. "Come on, Doc, give you a few pointers."

"You haven't got what I need, Jonesie," Seth called back over his shoulder.

"You don't know everything, Doc!"

Like a knife between his shoulder blades, it felt. The tone, it was the tone more than anything—rasping, serrated. It stopped him and turned him around completely. He stood there, studying Mark.

"Say, you really mean it, don't you?"

"He's arguably quite right about that, old man. You don't." Whit blinked a quick smile into life.

"You know perspicacious ain't the only thing that counts, Doc."

"Maybe you're right." He took a few conciliatory steps back toward Mark. "Maybe it's time I learned something from someone else. Okay, let's make it Saturday."

Mark smiled tightly. "Nah, forget it, Doc. You guys got enough to do."

"No, you're right." Seth pushed his glasses back up on his nose. "I need something different." Mark gave him a fishy look. "Saturday," Seth said emphatically. "Definitely," he added even more emphatically. "What's it going to be? Tae kan do?" He shrugged. "Who knows? Maybe it'll come in handy someday."


"Yes, of course! I remember," Burden said, suddenly swiveling around in his chair to face Seth. "I saw her that day standing outside the library. Must have been last"—absentmindedly he flipped the pages of a journal on his desk as though they were cards in his memory—"June or July." Burden had been cranky, for some reason,

that afternoon. At first he'd turned laconic and then inattentive, and
it was pure accident that Seth had mentioned the iguana at all.

"Stunning sight! Absolutely!" It had caught Burden's attention
all right, and now he had come alive again. "And I don't stun
easily." A gust of rain slashing in from the northeast beat at the
window, blurring the Queens landscape across the river. Seth removed
his white jacket and started to roll up his sleeves, still damp from
his crossing to the medical school.

"Creepy little monsters, aren't they?" he said.

"It's that immobility, that incredible dead quality. Creates a kind
of cognitive dissonance. They look real"—Burden held his hands
motionless in front of him, re-creating the creature out of thin air—
"and artificial at the same time. And then there was the"—he
thought for a moment—"the aesthetic dissonance." He leaned forward. "Here was this striking young woman, elegant, voluptuous,
with an iguana—this repulsive, monstrous creature—on her shoulder,
as though it were a part of herself." He turned away and looked
out over the wet, gray city. "So that was Jennifer Light." He was
silent for a moment or two. "Strange . . ."

"You'd never noticed her?" Seth asked disingenuously.

"I wouldn't say that." Burden smoked long, slender cheroots
that came in a tin. Lighting one, he studied its terminal glow. "One
couldn't help it—noticing her, I mean," he said, and turned his
attention to the storm outside. "Like not noticing a woman on
fire." He paused. "She was *that* beautiful."

"What did it mean, then, the iguana?"

Not expecting an answer at all, he didn't know why he'd asked
and was surprised when Burden turned to him. The shrewd eyes
studied him for a moment, searching for motives in the play of his
fingers and the shuffling of his feet. Finally, the older man shrugged
wearily. "How would I know? You people still think analysts are
mind readers." He gave Seth a crooked little smile. "Look, Dr.
Conrad, to know *accurately*"—he underlined the word with his
index finger—"fully the meaning of an act requires some introspective
process like psychoanalysis. If you want to play speculative games,
that's something else"—he pointed his cigar at Seth—"as long as

you don't take them too seriously. Of course, the iguana had some specific unconscious meaning to Jennifer Light."

Reaching across the desk, he switched on the lamp. The room had begun to darken, and the gray clouds outside had turned blue and swollen as though the wild wind had bruised them. "And *wearing* it that day in the hospital had a meaning. God knows it had meaning enough to those of us who saw her. Maybe she wanted—unconsciously, of course—to attract us"—he shrugged and with a wave of his hand erased himself from the picture—"whoever— 'us' is just a symbolic representation of some specter from her past— or repel us, or tease us, or maybe scare us with that awful thing."

A burst of rain exploded at the window and ran down the pane in a hundred fitful rivulets. Burden drew ruminatively on his cigar and peered out at the windswept river. "You know, sometimes people come, consciously or unconsciously, to love or value some defective part of themselves, some ugliness, some deformity, some badness . . . and they want others . . . people to love that part . . . even especially, I mean . . ." He paused and peered into the deepening dusk as though he were trying to find someone. "Oh, who knows?" He stood up suddenly, as though he wanted to be rid of something, and flicked some ashes from his cigar into the wastebasket.

*You* know! The thought shot through Seth's head without warning, like a gust from the gale outside, unexpected and irresistible. He knew then that somehow Burden had become hooked into the circuit, the way *he* was maybe, that Burden was an inescapable part of it now.

"The point is this, Dr. Conrad." Burden exhaled a heavy blue cloud. "*Whatever* that creature meant to her is forever lost. Gone. Gone with the last moment of her consciousness."

Despite his disavowals, it seemed to him that Burden, like some modern necromancer, could know the heart of Jennifer Light, could touch it there in the grave. He knew that through Burden he had a powerful connection with the past now, that he would someday have a chance to know her again.

". . . the last moment of her consciousness." The words hung in the blue air above him. What had she been thinking that last

moment when the life ebbed out of her . . . when she knew? He
saw her again, Elly, struggling in the black waters of Vineyard
Sound, slipping beneath the surface for the last time. Her last
thought . . .

In silent communion they sat, looking out over the rain-soaked
city, the two men, both in shirt sleeves, divided by a generation of
time and experience and momentarily lost in their respective lives.
The lamplight, proof against the gusty wind and leaden sky, fell
with impartiality on the younger doctor's solid brown forearms and
the older one's hands, on which the discolorations of age had begun
to appear.

Looking down over the city, he envied Burden his view, and
his knowledge, and his experience. When did it come, that sense of
mastery, that view? How long did it take? Could Burden bear to
know what he knew without passing it on to someone? To him?
Knowing what he knew now, would Burden do it over, do what
*he* was just starting out to do?

They sat silently for several moments longer before parting, the
younger doctor and the older one, each needing the other and both
needing their miseries and mysteries.

"Remember, Dr. Conrad, don't take these speculations too seriously."


"Don't bother dressing on my account," he shouted into the empty
refrigerator.

"Don't bother undressing on my account," she called back from
the bedroom. "What's it going to be tonight?"

Straightening up, he shrugged. "Can't blame a healthy young
doctor for trying." He reached in and plucked out a shabby head
of lettuce. "Same as last night, tuna salad," he called. Since her
discharge from the hospital Seth had been feeding her scrambled
eggs, hospital gossip, psychological theory, takeout Chinese food,
and tuna fish in various forms. "I'm on a roll with the tuna salad.
I've got to go with it tonight." He snapped his tie off and rolled
his sleeves up energetically. "I think I'm on to something really big
in tuna."

"What do you think *he'd* make out of all that stuff? Burden?" Lindsay, in jeans and gray T-shirt, drifted into the tight little kitchen. Her hair was tied back tightly as though she were trying to punish it.

"Christ! Sit down before you fall down!" Her first day back at work, she'd overdone it and had to leave early, feeling dizzy and exhausted. "Who does your color these days? Dracula? Here, hold this." He handed her the lettuce and dragged a chair to where she was standing. "Sit down. You look terrible for a living person." He tried to wrangle her into the chair.

She pulled away. "Oh, stop fussing. I'm fine. I'm okay. I hate being fussed over." She had lost weight, and there were drooping lines at the corners of her mouth.

"Jesus, it's been a pleasure examining you, but I'm sure as hell glad I don't have to treat you." He shrugged. "Suit yourself."

She sat down in the chair and touched the patch behind her right ear that had now only an adhesive plaster the size of a half-dollar. "I guess I did get carried away today. It was those letters from Dot. I read until I couldn't see straight. And God, it was hot in there! They've sealed the place up completely." Her voice drooped. "I think that's what did it."

"He let you see all of it—Fontana?" he asked doubtfully.

"I think so." She bent forward over the lettuce as though it were a crystal ball. "Funny collection of stuff. I think he actually wanted me to see those letters—I mean, especially. Feedback, he wanted, I suppose. . . . What are you looking for?"

Head thrust forward and squinting intensely, Seth was rummaging through the refrigerator again. "Mayonnaise. No diary, huh?"

"Not yet." She paused and studied Seth, growing more frantic in his search. "They were going over every inch of the bedroom today. If it's there, I suppose they'll find it." She punched apathetically at the lettuce head. "You know Fontana, everything by the book. Very thorough. No lead too small, no stone unturned—there it is, bottom shelf."

"Yeah, I've heard that sermon already: 'Try every door.'" He slammed the refrigerator and assumed one of Fontana's stances, characteristically pugnacious. " 'If we get him, Doc, we'll get him by outwalking him, not outsmarting him.' Bullshit!"

"Oh, Fontana's okay. He tries—"

"Knocking on doors is for salesmen, and maybe 'okay' isn't enough. Maybe with a highly motivated killer"—he pointed a chopping knife at her—"who's sharp and who knows his way around, 'okay' just isn't enough."

"God, you're smug!" She threw the lettuce at him. "You know, you don't know everything!"

"Jesus, you're the second person who's said that to me today. If I didn't know better, I'd start believing it." He tossed the lettuce back to her and began squeezing some lemon juice into a bowl. "This Saturday—guess what?"

"You're working in the PAO," she snapped, "and I don't like guessing games."

"I mean besides that. *Karate!*" He made one or two foolish chopping movements in the air. "Jonesie's going to teach me to make my points with—shall we say?—compelling logic." He made one final pass, this time on the body of a celery stalk lying on the chopping board. "Thus"—he struck the hapless vegetable, which jumped, out of control, onto the floor—"I, er, refute you!"

Raising his hands, he stared at them dramatically. "Today these hands"—he sniffed his fingers—"reeking of lemon juice and compassion; Saturday, licensed to kill!"

Throughout his little entertainment Lindsay remained blank, her eyes distant and clouded. "Not what I expected, her stuff. She's about four different people. God knows who's the real one." She tore a lettuce leaf from the head and studied it as though it held the key to Jennie Light's secret life. "Dozens of books. None of them look as if they'd been read except *The Story of O*. Clothes, not much but good, expensive. All beautiful and just a little sexy."

"Onion?"

She ignored the question.

"A couple of introductory textbooks on chemistry and biology. Dipped into here and there, something to do with the work she was doing for Graver maybe. Some stuff on cinematography. The *Confessions* of Rousseau—just the first fifteen or twenty pages, the spanking part. Did you know that Rousseau liked to be spanked by his women?"

"Well, so much for the Romantic movement. About the onion . . ."

"No onion! There is none!" she said with unnecessary vehemence. "I'll tell you one thing about her. She wasn't just plain old vanilla. Quite a collection of soft porn, mostly SM. Funny thing about all those books. She'd torn the covers off or hidden the titles with tape. The nonsexy ones, too. All of them."

"How can I make tuna salad without onion? It's like trying to make scrambled eggs without scramble."

"Damn it, you're not listening. Your eyes have that glazed look."

"What about my ears? Do they have a glazed look?"

"Your irrepressible spirit is beginning to pall."

"What's with you?"

"In case you hadn't noticed, I'm trying to be serious. I've got to talk to that girl, the cousin. Dot. Those letters. There's a story in them, but all allusive and implied. You said you had her address."

"Somewhere." He was searching noisily through one of the utensil drawers.

"And the mirror. There was no mirror. Have you ever known a woman who didn't have a mirror in her room?" Without thinking she tore several more leaves into pieces and let them fall, one by one, onto the countertop. "What would *he* make of all this?"

"Who?"

"Your guru—what's his name? Could I talk to him?"

"Burden? Are you kidding?" Her eyes were cool blue, unsmiling. He could see she was not. "He hardly even talks to me. I'm lucky if I get three sentences a week out of him."

"But he'd know. He would, wouldn't he?" She put the lettuce down and stood up. "He'd be able to put it together."

"Of course. Why do you think he reads in the dark? To hone his perceptions to razor sharpness." He was opening the tuna can now, addressing it as he wound the handle. "Why do you think he sleeps on a narrow analytic couch at night? Never to be out of contact with the unconscious for a moment. That CAT scan the other day was able to read your brain"—he pointed the can opener at her—"but Burden can read your soul. Just walk into a room, and he knows what you're thinking. Forget it, there isn't a chance. Besides, you have me. Sweet pickles?"

"There's a sequence of letters. The summer she was sixteen she was an au pair girl at the beach. The letters from Dot suggest she developed a crush on some older man. She teases Dot, won't tell her his name, only the usual adolescent gush: He's gorgeous; he's a brilliant doctor." Aiming her words at Seth's back as he bent over the chopping board, she talked rapidly, in a rush, like someone trying not to know something. "Dot gets mad at her, feels betrayed—jealous, obviously. Then a few weeks pass, and Jennie must have said something in one of her letters about missing a period. The end of September that letter was dated, which means that she must have missed her period early in September, which means . . ."

"Well?" The silence made him turn.

"Damn it, why did you let me . . . go up there alone, that night? Goddammit, why?"

Without waiting for an answer she marched out of the kitchen.

"Hey," he said, looking after her, and removed his spectacles. The quiet blur of the room did not diminish the hard edge of his knowledge. He knew she was right.

"*C*'mon, Doc, don't be bashful, it's on me. When did she tell you all this?"

"I'm not bashful, Fontana. I just don't want any coffee. Last night. For chrissake, let's get on with it; I'm already behind schedule." He writhed restlessly at the table. "Jesus, I don't know why I'm doing this."

The breakfast rush over, only a faint blue cloud of bacon smoke hung over the hospital coffee shop. The Friday midmorning lull had provided a table some distance from the twenty-four-hour polyglot hum of the place. Occasionally the chatter of a happy Chinese family celebrating the safe arrival of a new baby reached them.

"Take it easy, Doc, just tryin' to make sure, get it all straight." He flipped open his little black leather book and placed it conspicuously on the table in front of him. "How ya doin', hon?" He smiled up at the pretty dark-eyed waitress who had appeared suddenly. "I'll have a cuppa coffee, black. What'll you have, Doc? You from Italy, hon?"

"Hoboken. This one check or two? There's a seventy-five-cent minimum."

"Nothing, thanks," Seth mumbled.

"One check, hon. Bring my friend a cuppa coffee, too. Where ya folks from? *Siciliano?*"

"Why? You wanna marry me?" she said flatly, scribbling a quick mark on her pad. "I got a boyfriend already, God help me." Her eyes smiled cynically. "One is plenty. Take a jelly doughnut; they're fresh. Otherwise you won't have enough. I hate to see them get away with gettin' and not givin'." She tossed her head in the direction of the cashier. "They get enough outta me." She made a final note. "I'll bring you the jelly doughnut. Two coffees and one jelly doughnut," she said decisively, and, turning, strode with an easy insolence toward the kitchen.

Fontana smiled at her backside and shrugged. "Okay, Doc, now tell me what you got."

"She called me late yesterday afternoon. I was on the ward, finishing up. She asked me to come down. Something important, she said, and hung up."

"She didn't say what it was about?"

"It was late when I got there, maybe six o'clock. Just about everybody had cleared out by then. She was still working." Leaning back, he paused and stared past the Chinese family. "I could hear her halfway down the hall."

Lemmon's outer office had been empty, making the clatter of Phyl Rowan's typewriter sound solitary and distant, like a train whistle in the country darkness. She sat tall, straight, and gaunt in the room, which was quite dark now, except for the circle of light illuminating the keyboard and her flying fingers.

Ignoring Seth, she'd gone on typing, looking straight ahead at the copy she was working on until she'd finished the page in a staccato burst. She looked up at him then, over her half glasses, and motioned for him to sit down in the chair next to the desk.

For several quiet moments she sat scowling at him, reluctant to talk. Finally, as though released from a struggle, she blurted out, "Damn it, do you mind if I call you Seth? I don't think I can say this to a stranger."

He'd nodded and given her an encouraging smile, which she ignored. She had clearly made up her own mind and didn't need encouragement.

"I don't know why I called you." She sighed. "Maybe because you were at the funeral—the only one. The only doctor, I mean." She continued. "I told you this was a nasty business, and I warned you to keep clear of it. But I guess you have to do what you do just like I have to do what I do. I've been around too long to give much of a damn about what happens in this place. And I wouldn't give a spoonful of cow spit for that girl. But Milly McVey was different." She looked away, into the dark corner of the room, as though Milly were standing there, returned from her Pennsylvania grave. "I don't know why she took her in, but I didn't interfere. And I probably shouldn't interfere now, but I have to do this for her. Even though I don't know what good it'll do."

Seth had never had any sense of Phyl Rowan except as western leather tanned and toughened with eastern cynicism. He could see now that there were soft places in her she was afraid of, and foolishly he wanted to say something to ease her but realized in time that words were less important, held less power for her than for him.

She shifted restlessly in her chair. "I like to think of myself as a decent person, somebody who can be trusted. But there's something that I know that has to be told. And I'm not going to tell it to anybody but you, and I'm going to tell it to you only once, and then I'm going to forget about it. I don't know why, but I think that you'll use what I have to tell you in a decent way. If you decide to tell it to anybody else—the police—that's your business. I'll be quit of it. Do you understand?"

He was silent.

"All I know is I have to get it off my chest. It probably won't sound like much to you, and it probably doesn't mean a damn thing. But knowing it bothers me, and nobody else knowing it bothers me even more. It's about Ettinger."

"She stopped then," Seth told Fontana, "and looked off again into the shadows. The office was practically dark by then." He lifted his coffee mug without thinking and took a sip. "In fact, she never looked at me again during the whole thing.

"It happened about a week or two before the murder, Jennie Light's murder. Birdie Smart, Ettinger's secretary, called Phyl and asked her to cover while she was away on vacation the next week, and since Lemmon was away, she agreed." He stopped suddenly and stared into his cup, as though he had come to the edge of a precipice. "Christ," he muttered. Shrewdly Fontana remained silent, only clearing his throat. With the sound Seth seemed to find his place in the narrative.

"Anyway, that first morning she got in early just to give herself time to get the hang of the place. It must have been around seven-thirty. She said the door to Ettinger's office was closed when she got there. She knew—Birdie had told her—that the couch he has there is a convertible and he sometimes sleeps there overnight." He pushed his glasses back up on his nose and peered through the smear at Fontana. "A poorly kept departmental secret. She's a chronic alcoholic, Ettinger's wife, and they don't live together.

"Anyway, she was poking around, finding where Birdie kept things, when suddenly the door to Ettinger's office opens, and who comes out half dressed but Jennie Light. She saw Phyl and closed the door fast. Phyl went about her business, trying to act like nothing happened, and about fifteen minutes later the old man steps out all smiles and gives her a big welcome and tells her that he forgot Birdie would be on vacation that week, and he had had some work to finish over the weekend, and would she mind running down and getting him some coffee?" By the time she got back up Jennie Light was gone, and she never saw her again up there. Ettinger said no more about it, and she forgot the whole thing until what happened to Milly."

"Jelly doughnut? Not bad." Fontana had cut the bloated pastry in half, and still chewing, he shoved the plate in Seth's direction. "So that's it?"

Like a goaltender, Seth intercepted the plate and bounced it back toward Fontana. "What do you mean, 'So that's it?' "

Fontana flipped his notebook closed. "I mean, guess who came to see me yesterday?"

"Come on, Fontana, I don't have time to play games. Ettinger?"

"He told me the whole story, Doc." Fanning the little leather notebook in front of Seth's face, Fontana smiled wickedly.

"He told you everything? That he was having sex with her? That he was screwing her in the chairman's office?"

"He said"—he slapped the little notebook back on the table and flipped it open again—"quote, that she was a charming young women who assisted him on several projects, and because they worked late some nights, he took her out three or four times, unquote."

"Come on! You're kidding! You think it was all microbe hunters stuff? That's bullshit, naive bullshit!"

Fontana flushed. "Listen, smartass, I've been in homicide for six years, maybe five, six hundred cases, but this one takes the cake. You think it's so easy, big shot?" He slammed his book closed and into his pocket. "You think I just get out the ol' rubber hose and lay it on the old man? Push on this top professor." He leaned forward and lowered his voice. " 'You're a fucking old lech and a liar!' " Glowering, vessels standing out in his bullneck, he sat back. "Listen, Doc, I'm good at my job, but they're all bad guys I talk to. Mean kids that grow up into mean men. I know how to talk to them." He leaned forward again, quieter, more confident. "These guys I know how to probe. You talk tough to 'em, you push on 'em; eventually you wear 'em down." He poked the table righteously with his forefinger. "You know why I can do it with those guys? 'Cause I know in ninety-nine cases out of a hundred they're guilty or their friends are guilty." He was silent now and looked away. "I can't push on anybody around here. They're respectable men. There isn't one of them that's a real suspect."

"You know, you guys give me a laugh," Seth said, leaning forward. "You'd be jumping all over the place doing a war dance if she'd been raped, but all of a sudden you big, tough guys get all goose bumps and shy when it comes to her private sex life."

"What difference does it make? This wasn't a sex crime. So what the hell do I care who slept with her two weeks before the murder? That's her business."

"Christ, Fontana, maybe they're connected—her murder and her sex life."

"Maybe, Doc, maybe. But I'm trying to tell you that in this case it doesn't matter."

"What the hell do you mean, it doesn't matter? Of course, it matters!" Seth turned away in disgust.

"In this case. I mean Ettinger. He has an alibi. He was with Coles all evening, and they both can prove it—maybe not airtight but good enough. That's why it doesn't matter. Forget Ettinger. He may have slept with her or screwed her or sniffed her underpants. I don't care as long as it didn't have anything to do with who killed her."

"That be all?" The pretty waitress with the brazen eyes had reappeared without warning. "You a cop?"

"Yeah," Fontana said glumly. Seth rose to go.

"My girl friend's brother's a cop. I can tell 'em every time." She stood, legs apart, tray dug into her abdomen, reckoning the bill. "Conceited. Big talk, small results." She slapped the check on the table. "Pay the cashier," she said, and swung over to the happy Chinese.

"Listen, Doc, what about Silk?" Fontana fished a piece of paper out of his shirt pocket, damp with his moral exertions. "This Paul Silk, what's his story?" He laid the paper on the table in front of him. Seth could make out only that it was in Silk's handwriting, famous for its fussiness and brown ink. "He wants to see me. Seems he's got something to say now, too."

"Maybe that he drove her home that night, from Fire Island." He shrugged. "Thanks for the coffee."

Fontana grabbed his arm and pulled him back down into his seat. "Doc, you're holdin' out on me. How'd you know that?"

"Christ, Fontana"—he yanked his arm away—"cut it out! This isn't Russia, you know. I don't know." He got up again and, proof against further interference, shoved both hands into his pockets.

Fontana studied him for a moment. "You know, Doc, sometimes I worry about you." He smiled. "You keep too much"—he tapped the side of his head—"inside. You get all fucked up when you keep too much inside. Isn't that what that joker Freud said? Loosen up. It's good."

The pieces began to fall into place on Saturday—even as Seth, standing like a plucked chicken, asked himself why once again. What am I *doing* here? He shivered in the warmth and gloom of the hospital gymnasium. He had asked himself the same question as he donned, probably for the last time, he thought, the baggy old tennis shorts that were now two sizes too large. This is stupid. Dumb.

"C'mon, Doc, ain't got much time," Mark called, emerging barefoot from the equipment closet.

"Be right there." He slipped his tired tennis shoes on over a mixed pair of socks, one blue, one brown. He tried humming.

"Isn't it written somewhere that if the feet are not in the right shoes, a karateka's heart cannot be pure? You don't want my heart to be impure, do you?" Humming tunelessly again, he tied the shredded laces that would go only to the second eye of each shoe. "So, this is the way the examined life ends," he said, and stood up.

Without pockets, without a scholarly journal to hang on to, his hands suddenly seemed supernumerary, redundant, like a pair of gauche friends arriving unannounced. He pulled his glasses back up on his nose with unnecessary force and wrapped his arms around himself.

"Roundhouse kick." Mark made a sudden great leap and pirouetted with the force of a dervish, sending his heel whooshing past Seth's face.

"Hey! Take it easy!"

The maneuver had been effortless. In his tight jeans and naked to the waist the smooth flow of power from one limb to another was visible and voluptuous. There was no redundancy there, no gaucherie. "Listen, Doc, you sure you want to do this thing? I don't really mind." He shrugged, and his eyes slid away, fretful. "You don't have to, you know. I got plenty to do."

□  □  □

$A$s usual he'd muddled it, his good intentions. With his characteristic finesse he'd transformed his triple reverse antisnobbism into acrid feelings and rue. He'd made the date with Mark for his lunch break and then forgotten it. By the time Mark had caught up with him he'd already left the PAO and was halfway out of the building.

He'd remembered, of course, instantly. "Yes, of course, Mark. God, is it that time already?" He looked at his watch dramatically. "Jesus, it's after twelve. I thought I'd—I was just going to . . . Hang Loy"—he fumbled in his pockets for a nonexistent laundry ticket—"shirts"—he tugged at his shirt as proof—"out of them." He shrugged. "Thought I'd get into an Oriental mood." He gave Mark a silly grin. "Oh, the hell with it. Get 'em later. Let's go!" He gave Mark a hearty clap on the back. "Lay on, Macduff!"

"Hey, Doc, you don't have to bullshit me," Mark had said. And then the fretful look had come into his eyes. "We can do it some other time. I got other things . . ."

$N$ow that quiet, crushed look again.

"Come on now, cut it out. Jesus, I've got a real case on my hands. How many times do I have to tell you I *want* to learn karate, tae kwan do, whatever? I'm *dying* to learn it. I've been wanting to learn it *all my life*. I can't wait to start pushing someone around. Now let's see that roundhouse trick again."

Mustering the wisp of a smile, Mark performed the maneuver once more, this time with even more precision and éclat. This time, also, holding himself more tightly, Seth stood his ground.

Landing lightly, Mark stood with his hands on his hips. "Shit, that's good, Doc. Ya see, it's all control." He grinned, "I'll teach ya the right block for that kick."

"Great!" Seth burst out enthusiastically, and as though the session were over, he ducked into the equipment closet for a towel. "Hey, Mark," he called, wiping first the palms of his hands and then his glasses. "That night, the night Jennie Light was killed. Did Silk drive her home from the Island? I heard that." Squinting, he thrust his head forward like an eager puppy. "Was she there?"

With a huge and forceful sound like the bark of a seal Mark

lunged at him. There was no time to react, and Seth stood dumbly
with his spectacles in one hand and towel in the other. The first
two knuckles of Mark's bony right fist had ended their powerful
thrust half an inch from the bridge of his nose.

"Now, if I was lettin' it all out, you'd be blind with pain an'
wouldn't have no nose left." He grinned and waggled his knuckles
in front of Seth's face. "Now, you get the point? Four things, man
strength, speed"—his hand whooshed through the air again—"concentration, an' knowin' where to hit." He tapped gently on the
bridge of Seth's nose. "That's what it boils down to." Stepping
back, Seth reinstalled his glasses and wiped the palms of his hands
again. "And all you got to do is practice three hours a day for five
or six years an' you'll be okay—win any argument, Doc." He
reached down suddenly and plucked Seth's spectacles and towel
away. "Hey, man, you won't need these."

"Hey, I can't see without those. C'mon—"

"You like to see too much, Doc." Mark made a nest of the
towel off to the side and gently laid the glasses within. "Ya got
to sense things"—he crouched, catlike, and began to sway sensuously—"feel movement, the wind on your skin, the smell of a
body. . . ."

"Oh, yeah? It may interest you to know, Mark, old man, that
we'd still be swinging from the banana trees if it weren't for binocular
vision, sharp-focusing eyes"—he squinted in Mark's direction—"op-
posable thumbs"—he opened and closed his fingers as though they
were jaws—"erect posture, and a reasoning brain." Without thinking
he straightened from his usually sloppy stance. "And now you want
me to give all that up—twenty million years of evolution—and go
back to crouching and reflexes like a goddamn spinal preparation."

"Shit, Doc, you guys kill me. Words, words, words." Sinking
down on one knee, he smiled weakly, "That's all you guys do.
Talk, talk, talk. Jabber, jabber. You and that Bloch and Paul and
even Whit . . ." He threw his arms up in surrender.

"You never answered my question about Paul. Was Jennie Light
with him that night?" Seth asked, reaching for his glasses.

"Hey, c'mon, Doc, Paul's my friend. Besides, he don't tell me
things."

"Thought you and Silk—"

"Look, I don't know what Paul done with her. Like I said, he don't tell me things—I mean, a lotta things. All I know is she wouldn't listen to him. He tried. He tried to tell her, you know, what was good for her." He stood up, unfolding like a jackknife, and reached a long arm into the equipment closet. Pulling out a white towel, he snapped it open. "You know, the way he tells me. Only I listen." All of a sudden his eyes were begging. "Shit, man, when Paul cares about someone, he goes all the way for you, like he done for me . . . well, you know what I mean." He wiped the fine sheen of sweat from the back of his neck. "Hey, lookee here . . ." he said with sudden brightness, and ducked into the equipment closet again. "C'm'ere."

Standing inertly like an extinguished candle, with his arms folded across his chest, Seth peered warily through glasses already beginning to mist again.

"C'mon, remember what I said the other day," Mark said, almost pleading now. He was striding toward Seth with one of Whit's sabers. "Here, catch!" He tossed the saber, handle first. Reached for too late, the sword clattered to the floor. Halfheartedly Seth picked it up and hefted it. The tip was now safely wadded in a lump of surgical tape.

"Okay, ready? Come on, hold it up! Higher! That's it. Now, lookee, there's only one way to get someone with somethin' this long. You got to get past it with a foot sweep against the sword arm. That breaks the arm"—he acted this out slowly, demonstrating how his right foot would come around and under the sword, pushing Seth's arm out of the way—" then, once ya get inside, real close, a right knife-hand attack to the collarbone." With a grand swoop the edge of his right hand was at Seth's left clavicle, tapping it gently. "See?"

"What if you can't get past the sword?" Seth stepped back and waggled the saber with clumsy energy.

"No problem with a beginner," Mark said with a complacent smile. "Come on, try it!"

"Not a beginner," Seth said ruefully, and made two dramatic slashes through the air. "Failed. There's a difference, old man. See,

'Failed' is tragic. 'Beginner' is comic—a laugh. I fenced. I'm a failed fencer"—he saluted Mark—"and soon to be a failed karateka."

"Okay"—Mark shrugged condescendingly—" 'failed.' Talk, talk, talk. Come on! Let's see some action!" Like a rubber band released, he snapped into a classic cat stance and began to circle menacingly.

Backing off, Seth assumed his failed fencer's position, readier to defend and parry than attack. "Now, take it easy. Remember I'm not Whit." He pushed his glasses up on his nose and peered through the smear as Mark coiled and wove his way around him. Suddenly he feinted to the left and as Seth moved to parry the blow, with invisible swiftness Mark's foot, heel first, flashed up and slammed into his arm. The saber flew into the air, and before it crashed to the hardwood floor, the edge of Mark's right hand was at his throat.

"Okay, okay! I believe you!"

"See, easy with a—" He grinned and shrugged. "With you. But it's different with a guy like Whit." He snatched his towel from where he'd dropped it and dabbed at his face. "He's fast, real fast— and sharp. It's a matter of who's faster and sharper. I don't know," he added wistfully, "maybe someday we'll see."

"Listen, Mark, in the meantime, you can kill somebody with this stuff, right?"

"You bet your ass you can."

"Listen, maybe this isn't such a good idea. Maybe we should start with the philosophy of it. That's probably a very important part of it, right? I think I'd like that. As a matter of fact, I know I would."

Unmindful, Mark only smiled and barked like a seal once again.


He was incredulous when he heard the news. Incredulous even later when he read the suicide note, and unaccountably oppressed besides.

"What do you mean, 'over'? What are you talking about?" Lindsay's call had come in to the PAO on Saturday afternoon just as he was briefing Avi and Fiona for the night shift.

Her voice was tinny and excited over the phone. "I'm telling you, his body was found in the courtyard of his building. I saw it! They just took it away. He did it last night, Fontana says. Jumped from the eighth floor. Just no question about it—he left a note. Can you get down here? Prince Street, Sixty-Seven Prince. Eighth floor." She hung up without waiting for an answer.

Slamming the phone down, he became aware again of the ache in his wrist, a bone-and-tissue reminder of his foolish sword games with Mark. What Harvey would have called his "failed phallic exhibitionism—can't you do anything right, boychik?"

"Shit!" Rubbing his wrist, he realized that he'd found Lindsay's certitude, her excitement, euphoria even, irritating. He'd wanted to shake her, quiet her, slow her down.

Now, in the midst of a chaotic scene which was just beginning to wind down, again he wanted to shake her. They'd been standing by the window from which Silk had gone to his death. The body had been removed from the courtyard below, where it had been discovered that morning by a building janitor making his rounds. Now its final earthly position was memorialized only by a white chalk outline. Viewed from eight stories up, it reminded Seth of Jennie Light spread-eagled on the dusty subbasement floor. Finally full circle?

"It's over here," she said in what Seth took to be her official army tone. Stepping easily between the four or five busy lab technicians, she strode through the huge studio-loft apartment. "Say, what's with you anyway?" she said over her shoulder at Seth, trailing behind. "I'm sorry if this wasn't on your agenda for today."

"Just another small personal humiliation," he said, rubbing his wrist again. "Nothing you'd understand."

"Licensed to kill yet?" she asked, waggling her hands at him without turning around. "There, read it yourself." She pointed to a large desk of glass and stainless steel. "Listen, I've got to get this stuff into the hopper. I want to make the first edition." She tossed her steno pad into her bag and zipped it shut. "I've got to run," she added without moving. She watched as he bent over the desk.

The notepaper was still there, popping up out of the typewriter, calling attention to itself as Silk would have wanted: "i killed jennifer light. she was blackmailing me. she was a bitch. she deserved it. i know what jail is like for a gay. i would rather die."

He straightened up. "So he finished tap-tap-tapping this and bye-bye, out the window?" He waved his hand airily in that direction.

"That's not what I said," Lindsay snapped, color rising in her cheeks. "I said he probably sent Fontana that note because he wanted to confess. He did send Fontana a note—you can't deny *that*. Then he realized, as he says there"—she pointed to the typewriter—"that life in prison would be worse than death for him."

"So he jumped out of his window? Is that it?" Seth said with a look of quiet scorn.

"You don't like that scenario? You've got a better one, I suppose."

"Probably." He punched his glasses back up on his nose and turned away.

Flooding in through a northern skylight, the late-afternoon light gave a bluish caste to the stark white walls of the huge room. They were set off by bold stabs of color—deep blue, orange, yellow— that divided one living area from another. The studio in which they stood skirmishing took up about half the space. In it were several worktables, easels, cabinets, and open shelves for paints and brushes. One of the easels held a full-length study, almost finished, of a nude youth, slender, arms akimbo, with pale, luxurious hair falling over insolent eyes. Silk had had a gift for draftsmanship, and as Seth bent forward to study the skin highlights and musculature, Lindsay yanked him around to face her again.

"Goddammit, you're disappointed!"

"Hey, cut it out!" The violence of her maneuver had dislodged one of the earpieces of his glasses, and now they hung limply under his chin. "That your idea of reasoned discourse?"

"You're disappointed, aren't you? That's it, isn't it?" Her voice rose triumphantly.

"Of witty discussion? Jesus, I've had enough bullying for one day." Adjusting his spectacles, he turned away to examine a stack of paintings on a worktable nearby.

"You wanted it to turn out different, and you're sore because it didn't."

"Don't be ridiculous," he said without looking up. From the stack of paintings he pulled a stretcher from which the picture had been cut away, leaving only a rim of bare canvas.

"Graver!" She exploded at the back of his head.

Fontana, halfway across the huge loft space, looked up, acknowledging her accusation with a puzzled frown. With vigorous, sweeping movements he'd been directing the lab crew in what photos he wanted made. Beyond them a cheerless, round-shouldered young woman from the *SoHo Expressionist* pursued her dogged interrogation of a bored, paunchy detective. While she did most of the talking, he tilted his head back and blew smoke rings at the ceiling.

"You want it to be Graver, don't you?" Lindsay challenged him. The round-shouldered reporter turned to stare at them.

"Hey, pipe down," Seth said, making dampening movements with his hands. "It's nobody else's business what I think. If you're interested in what I think, ask me, I'll tell you. But don't put your silly ideas into my head." He turned away and again picked up the painting that had been mutilated.

She leaned forward in hot pursuit. "I know you, I know what you're thinking. You have this crazy vendetta going against Graver." She pushed her hair behind her right ear. "For God's sake, this isn't cowboys and Indians, black and white. So things don't turn out the way you want—"

"How ya doin', Doc?" Fontana approached, looking worried. "I told ya not to worry. Sooner or later we get lucky. You just got to hang in there. Right, Miss Cooper?" He winked at her and pulled a stick of gum out of his powder blue slacks.

"I'm afraid Dr. Conrad doesn't like the idea that Silk confessed and committed suicide, Vince." Lindsay pushed her hair behind her ear again.

"Oh, yeah, that's tough." He grinned. "The doc's got a lot of funny ideas. Don't make 'em right." He shoved the gum into his mouth.

"Look, I've got to go." Straightening up, Lindsay hoisted her bag onto her shoulder. "This is a great story, and I've got a lot of work to do before I file it." She turned to go.

"Lindsay . . ."

"Look, you know where I'll be. When you get over your . . . whatever, call me." She strode off toward the elevator.

"Write nice, Miss Cooper," Fontana called after her. "Give us a break." With a shrug he turned to Seth. "Tough lady."

Ignoring Fontana's remark, Seth surveyed the huge loft with renewed interest.

"Some pad, huh, Doc? Almost makes me want to be a bachelor again. What d'ya think?" He indicated a large yellow and red Abstract Expressionist canvas hanging over a handsome black leather sofa.

Silk's reputation for elegance had not been exaggerated. The large loft area had been reworked into a well-orchestrated masculine living machine. A cool, ruthless intelligence had replaced most of the fussy architectural irrelevancies with the best geometric planes and surfaces money could buy.

"When did it happened?"

"They called it in around nine-thirty." He pulled a soiled envelope out of his back pocket, checked its contents, and slid it back. "The ME says time of death was somewhere between midnight and three, probably closer to midnight. So let's say between midnight and one. Ya see, he threw a little party first. C'mere." Shepherding Seth past the technicians, he brought them to the kitchen-dining area and a green marble table set for two.

"Nice, huh? Champagne." He picked up the bottle and read the label. "Dom Pérignon. Brut." He faltered on the name, insincerely, Seth thought. "Good?" he asked, holding up the bottle.

"The best," Seth said with a little smile.

"Let's see, then oysters, a nice thick steak, two bottles of red wine"—he leaned over and studied the label—"Château Latour, 1961, probably a good year, huh, Doc?" This time he didn't wait for Seth's answer. "Cheese, cognac, cigars. Not bad, huh? This guy really knew how to live."

"He didn't die too well."

Fontana was unmoved. "You don't live like this on a city salary. This guy must have had some big practice."

"He didn't practice at all," Seth said absentmindedly. "He had money. Came from a rich family, lawyers in Philadelphia."

"Yeah? Well, anyway, him and his friend drank a lot. By the time his guest left, he knew what he was going to tell me today. He thought about it some more and typed the letter here at this desk." Fontana walked over to the desk where the typewriter was poised, ready for use. "Then, along around one o'clock, he launched himself out the window. Nothing more curvy than that, Doc. Shit, will ya look at this?" He spied a smudge of chalk dust on his slacks and attacked it vigorously, as though it were alive. "All there in black and white."

For a moment Seth stood looking back and forth from the dining table, now a grisly still life, to the poised typewriter. "Pretty neat." Pausing, he smiled a shallow smile. "All fits together. No loose ends. How'd you do it?"

"Cut the crap, Doc, no more games. I'm tired. I wanna wrap this thing up. You don't like it, tell me. Only don't crap around." He flexed his shoulders and cracked all ten of his knuckles as though preparing for combat. "Tell me what you don't like. Go ahead."

"It doesn't work! It doesn't hang together. He writes you a note, says he wants to see you, says it's important, and then does this. It doesn't make sense. He takes the trouble to make this elaborate dinner, with champagne, great wine, brandy, cigars, and then heaves himself out the window. Also inconsistent."

"Condemned man ate a hearty breakfast—" Fontana shrugged and nodded at the dining table. "Dinner—you know what I mean. He knew what he was gonna do, so he puts on this little show with a friend and—" Suddenly at a loss for words, he turned sour. "Besides, you know people ain't so consistent—"

"But his character," Seth broke in, "it doesn't fit. Look, he was a cool, restrained, careful type. Look at this room, those pictures, every one of them neat, precise, extremely detailed. He's not impulsive. He wasn't the kind of person to go into a rage or a panic. He thought things through."

"Listen, I've heard of plenty of killers who're quiet and peaceful all their lives; then, pow"—his hands exploded, palms upward—"they blow a fuse and kill a dozen people all of a sudden. I don't know too much about psychology, Doc, but believe me there's no such thing as 'not the type.' Everyone's the type."

"Jesus, anyone could have written that note. There's no evidence that Silk typed it. Why didn't he write it by hand? Why didn't he sign it? It's typed all wrong. There aren't even any capital letters."

"Okay, maybe anybody could have typed that note. Maybe he was too drunk to write it. Maybe he ain't a good typist. I don't know." He slammed his wad of gum into a wastebasket.

"What if it didn't happen the way you said, Fontana? What if it happened this way? What if he knew who the real murderer was? What if it was even a friend or colleague? What if he invited him to dinner and this person appreciated fine wine and good food . . . had even modeled for him?" Seth pointed to the mutilated painting in the studio. "What if *that's* what he wanted to tell you today: who the real murderer was? What if he was trying to get the murderer to give himself up? Then what if the murderer got mad and rough?" He leaned toward Fontana. "It wouldn't take much to subdue a drunken man like Silk. The only way to make it look like suicide then"—he pushed the empty air in front of him—"is to shove him out the window. Then the killer *has to* type the note. Christ, Silk was a very sharp guy—savvy. He knew there were a dozen better ways of committing suicide than jumping out the window. He knew ten different kinds of surefire poisons. Painless. Reliable."

Half listening, Fontana had been going through his chewing gum ritual. He turned suddenly to the only technician left, hurriedly packing up his gear. "Did you dust the typewriter?"

"Vince, I never got a print worth a shit from a keyboard."

"Never mind, dust it anyway, and lemme know what you find." He turned back to Seth. "Well, Doc, it's a nice theory. But that's all it is. A theory. Show me some evidence." He held his hand out like a beggar. "I've got two humongous murders on my hands and an ugly captain on my back, telling me I have to get some results or I can forget about my promotion. I've got a confession right here, clear and simple, in black and white, and you're trying to feed me bullshit theories. Forget it, Doc. This wraps it up for me. You're a nice guy, a little weird if you ask me, but I like ya. But, Jesus, I've got four other homicides on my desk since this one started, and I don't have time to fart around with a lot of bullshit theories."

"Fontana, do you want to wrap the case up, or do you want to find the killer?"

"Doc, you're gettin' to be a royal pain in the ass." The veins in his neck stood out. "There's nothing here that tells me I don't have the whole thing wrapped up." He turned away.

"The diary—what about the diary?" He reached out to touch Fontana, to hold him there a moment longer. Lindsay had been right. He couldn't let it end this way.

Fontana spun around, still angry. "There ain't no diary! And I'll tell ya something else, Doc." He stabbed an accusing finger at Seth. "Maybe there never was one. All I had was your word. Your cockamamie theory, maybe. We fine-tooth-combed every goddamn closet, bookcase, drawer. Every fucking piece of paper in the McVey apartment. Two days. Three men. Nothing. Zilch."

"The whole apartment, did you do the *whole* apartment?" He was reaching out again, stretching, desperately holding on like a child refusing to let his parents go off for the evening.

"Yeah—no. I don't know, and I don't care." He took a deep breath. "What difference does it make? It's wrapped up. Forget it, Doc. Go back to your dream stuff." He started to move off.

Turning suddenly, he pulled the soiled envelope out of his back pocket and slid a gold cigarette lighter onto the marble table. "Got any theories about this, Doc? Ever see it? Found it right there by the brandy."

Seth didn't have to push the glasses back up on his nose to make out the initials engraved on its side: WS III.

"The guest, huh?"

## Chapter

# 13

"Jesus, Whit, if I had any time to spare, I'd get some REM sleep myself." He was shouting and shaking his head for good measure, to be understood over the lunchtime noise and clamor of the PAO.

Monday mornings were always busy in the PAO, and this one was no exception. There were the usual weekend chickens coming home to roost: the bleary-eyed alkies, run aground and begging for some fluids and sedatives to keep afloat; the hung-over depressives after unsuccessful ODs and gastric lavages; the eloped schizophrenics hoping to be transported back to some upstate hospital. And always the endless flow of new casualties, begging for and protesting help at the same time: mute catatonics; violent paranoids; fragile anorexics; freaky adolescents out of their minds on angel dust; decrepit old men and women who had lost forever the names of their children.

Monday mornings were also for institutional musical chairs, the day that all city agencies decided to clear their dockets, rosters, wards, cells, and beds. From prisons, courtrooms, bureaus, institutes, hospitals, and shelters for the destitute, they came that morning, like a mighty river of loose associations and monstrous fancies on the rampage.

Standing in the midst of this surging flood, he stared into the teeth of one of Whit's most disarming smiles. Why should he? In recent days a silence had grown between them. Lindsay maybe; some secret grief in him perhaps—who knew? Why should he pull Whit's chestnuts out of the fire now?

"Chance of a lifetime, old man, really," Whit said in confidential tones, bending toward him. He looked tanned and more relaxed than Seth had seen him in weeks, like a man released from some invisible bondage, Seth thought. "Wouldn't take more than seven or eight hours a week. Techniques would be a snap for you, old man. And of course, we'd publish it with Paul's name on it." He searched Whit's impassive blue eyes—"a heart of stone and water from the Skagerrak" in his veins.

Milling around them, the Monday cohort of uniformed men and women filled the PAO with color and the acrid odor of pent-up energy: regular cops, caps off, jackets open, looking out of place; officers from the Department of Correction, older, bored, and flabby; dykey policewomen; ambulance attendants in white; nurse's aides in blue; nursing students in stripes.

Swirling through this ferment like a powerful kitchen appliance, homogenizing problems wherever she went, Lisa Stone, in a tight-fitting black turtleneck under her white coat, remained, as always, the voluptuous professional.

"Take arms against this sea of troubles, Seth, darling, or buzz off. You're in the way."

Seth watched her for a moment. As she reached past him for a chart, the aroma from her lustrous hair brushed his face. "You're magnificent! Marry me!" he whispered to her.

"Husbands bore me, darling." She kissed the air in front of him. "If you're naughty, you can be my lover." She whirred off to give the admitting nurse another order, calling over her shoulder, "And don't forget Friday!"

"Friday. How could I forget?"

"You don't have to make up your mind right away, old man," Whit said, blinking a faint smile into existence. "Look, meet me later, and I'll give you all the precious details."

"No way . . ."

"Five-thirty, Lino's. Think about it, old man."

"Forget it!"

He watched as Whit Shields, unruffled, princely, flowed away like a silken ribbon through the crowd, making a soft but decisive impact on whomever he touched.

Bending over the admissions book, Seth ran his finger absent-mindedly down the list of admissions, looking for those who had been sent to his ward. Confident bastard. Why? Why the hell should he?

"We've got twelve cases already. Volumes of data—a Campari, Lino, please. On the rocks."

"*Si,* Dottore Shields."

"I'll just have a cup of coffee, Lino."

Lino bowed himself away. The restaurant was nearly empty. The dinner rush hadn't started yet, and there were only a couple of Lino's cronies at the bar."

"How's Patrick?"

"Who?"

"Patrick."

"Oh, yes. Patrick. Well, I think she's found a better home. Someone who appreciates her . . . assets more than I was able to."

"What *were* her assets?"

Whit inhaled deeply from his ivory holder. "Well, you must admit, old man, she had very good bones." He flicked his ashes into the Asti Spumante ashtray. "Not very big on mentation, though. She'd get up in the morning, yawn, and that would be it for intellectual activity for the day." He smiled at his own cleverness. "Not at all like Lindsay. And how *is* the intrepid Lindsay?"

"Good, back to normal, I'd say. Fresher, even."

"Let me know when you get tired of her, will you?"

He was serious, Seth knew, despite his sculptured little laugh. There it was again, that tiny, grating sound, that gnawing he felt when he was with Whit, like a secret rodent working away behind the walls somewhere.

"Cheers."

Seth nodded, and over the rim of his cup he studied the smooth, tanned face, devoid, he noticed now for the first time, of the common landmarks of feeling. Missing were those avenues and pathways worn into a face that tell the heart. Suddenly he was desperate to get behind that tombstone of a face with its polished surface and meaningless features. Behind those clear, blue, impervious eyes. One feeling, one recognizable emotion. Out in the open.

"Look, we'll need fifteen, maybe twenty more cases at most. We're doing temporal and occipital leads—both hemispheres—during REM and non-REM sleep—"

"Why, Whit? Why the hell are you doing all this?"

"It would be irresponsible not to finish it." He checked the ice in his glass and swirled it around. "A betrayal of Paul not to publish. I told you, his name would appear as senior author."

"Come on, Whit, you know what I mean."

"Ah, yes, I see." He blinked owlishly and studied the ash growing at the end of his cigarette. "Confession softens the brain, you know, old man."

"It's just that I like to know who my collaborators are. After all, an unexamined collaboration isn't worth having, is it? Besides, Golden Boy, it's about time, don't you think?"

Hanging stubbornly between them, the reproach seemed to drive Whit even farther into some distant landscape. It was as if he were suddenly at the wrong end of a telescope.

"What the hell are you doing here? You don't belong in a psych residency." Trying to reach him, to bring him back, Seth had raised his voice and stirred interest among Lino's friends at the bar. Quieting, he leaned toward Whit. "Christ, you're a prince, a goddamn scientific prince. This stuff"—he nodded in the direction of the hospital—"is for guys with soft brains and bad eyes. Why, for chrissake, why?"

"Aunt Gretchen, a very stately old girl"—he toasted himself—"her favorite—would say it was because of Blair." He sipped the Campari, inhaled, and watched Seth through the smoke. "Blair is the Shields boy who doesn't exist. He's the one we don't talk about." He checked his ashes again, carefully. "I'm not the youngest. I'm only the youngest if you don't count Blair. So it depends on who you ask. Dad says I'm the youngest because for him Blair is dead, maybe never even existed. Mother's different, though. I think Blair was her favorite." He studied Seth for several moments, like a surgeon deciding to operate. "Blair is two years younger than I am, and he lives in an institution for retarded people. A very quiet and now very well-endowed place in northwest Wisconsin." Whit looked west, past Seth, toward Wisconsin. "Aunt Gretchen would say that after Blair's accident I got interested in how the brain works. But I really don't remember that far back. And I doubt that she does either." He stubbed out his cigarette emphatically, as though what remained of it offended him.

Aware suddenly of his tiny, thoughtless act of violence, he stopped and looked quizzically at Seth. "Funny. I was speaking the unspeakable—about Blair, I mean—on Friday. Telling Paul." He shook his head. "I still can't believe it. He was very sweet, really, and very misunderstood." He looked to Seth for confirmation.

Seth shrugged noncommittally and sipped his coffee.

"A cunning little man—in the good sense, I mean." He fidgeted with his ivory holder, finally inserting another cigarette. "Hard to believe," he repeated, and shook his head again. "Stunned, absolutely, when I heard about it this morning. From your chum, Fontana."

"He's not my chum any more than he is yours."

"Sorry." He shrugged innocently. "No offense, old man. Afraid I disappointed, though. He heard a very dull weekend saga. The eye-closing spectacle of what goes on within the Shields family compound." He held up his right hand and clenched it once or twice. "Stiff from all the bridge and croquet." He smiled and blinked. "A little filial piety every now and then never hurts." Inserting his ivory holder between clenched teeth at something less than its usual brazen angle, he puffed the cigarette into life. "He was wrong, you know"—he waved the match out—"about the lighter." He smiled hopefully. "I know you won't believe this, old man, but I haven't seen that lighter in over two weeks. I thought I'd lost it." He tossed a book of matches onto the table.

"But you *were* there Friday night? You *did* have dinner with him? You were . . . the last one to see him."

"I was there Friday night." Whit blinked. "I had dinner with him." His gaze had slipped past Seth now. He was looking vacantly down the corridor of some other place. "He made us a superb dinner. A great claret." He smiled sadly. "He was in a marvelous mood—at his bitchy best."

"Then he wasn't depressed. Suicidal."

"No more than I am. But then"—he shrugged apologetically—"who knows? Like Richard Cory. . . . 'we thought that he was everything/To make us wish that we were in his place.' " He smiled one of his more golden smiles—a rare commodity in recent weeks.

"Listen, Seth"—leaning back suddenly, he slouched against the booth wall like a wounded toy soldier—"this is probably a bad idea. These things usually are." He looked up from his glass. "But I wanted to explain something, so at least *you* would understand." He touched the matchbook on the table and studied its bold promise of success to those who learned accounting. "Some of this will come out anyway, I'm afraid, because of the lighter, and when it does, it will come out twisted, and bent, and misunderstood. And"—he flicked his ashes again, this time until the glowing end was visible—"I suppose, O guileless one, I want you more than the others to understand."

He was silent for a few moments now, staring at the watery Campari, which he held in place with both hands as though it were a bird that might fly away.

"You remember when I first arrived, I was a week or so late."

"Sure, the storm. The hurricane. You got caught in it."

"White lie, old man. I'd been in a hurricane, all right"—he looked up, asking for understanding—"but that was the summer before." He looked away again. "The problem was that I was asked to resign from NIMH suddenly, the week before, without any notice." He paused and looked at Seth, who had been watching him over the rim of his glasses. "I'm not being very coherent, am I? Sorry about that."

"Forget it. Take your time." Seth leaned back.

Whit smiled gratefully. "Look," he said, leaning toward Seth. He lowered his voice. "A woman . . . tried to commit suicide in my apartment." He lapsed into silence again and stared into the pale pink liquid in his glass. "She was very, very young, immature,

I mean, and very romantic, and *very* histrionic. Spanish family. And she misunderstood. Just absolutely misunderstood the whole thing. It's ironic in a way. I was with her only as a favor in the first place. Because of her father."

"I don't get it." Seth squinted quizzically.

"Her father was Ruiz-Capalbos. The man I was doing my research with."

"Christ! And she went"—he made a diving gesture with his hand—"out your window!"

"What the hell are you talking about?" Whit shot upright, eyes blazing. "She OD'd on aspirin and Dramamine. She was fine the next morning." He stabbed out his cigarette once again and shoved the holder into his pocket. "Damn it, I knew this wouldn't work. I don't know where the hell you got this moronic window business, but forget it."

He stood up. Lino and his cronies were staring at him now. The red and green neon sign outside the restaurant blinked on and off, making him seem furious one moment, frightened the next.

"In fact, forget the whole thing. Sorry I took up your time, old man. I'll know better next time." He threw a five-dollar bill on the table and stalked out.

Seth sat for a long while, playing with the bill and the rest of the pieces in the puzzle. Whit had forgotten about the unfinished research, but somehow he wasn't surprised. He knew that had never been the point at all.


Dull. He knew it would be stupefying as soon as little old Morris Waxman wheezed the name, "this terrible thing over the weekend. Paul, I mean, so shocking . . ."

He had had enough of Paul Silk for one weekend and almost enough of Lindsay. And now this. Trapped. It was Tuesday, and as he looked around the lunch table, he knew he should have been pleased—honored even. In fact, his face said he was. He knew he was smiling to these distinguished men—Burden, Waxman, Homburg, Tom Freeman—but behind his unsmiling eyes he felt a thick wad of cotton and behind that a distant depressing throb.

This was to be their—what had Lindsay called it?—their "truce lunch." She'd sounded perfectly reasonable on the phone. "Look, let's just sit down and talk quietly. Untie all the knots. I'll bring sandwiches; you bring the terrace." That had been last night, and now came Burden. Out of nowhere he had just jammed his foot in the elevator door as it was closing.

Out of breath, and with his jacket collar turned up against the drizzle, he looked halfway between a shrewd underworld figure and a worried poet. He had acknowledged Seth with one of his cool nods. "Going to lunch?" he asked, eyeing Lindsay.

"No . . . yes .   I mean, no, not exactly—"

"I hope you're less confused about your other appetites, Conrad." He pulled off his wrinkled linen jacket, wet from the rain, and slung it over his shoulder.

Seth held up the brown paper bag Lindsay had brought. "We were going to picnic on the terrace."

"Nice idea. Too bad. The weather, I mean."

The elevator droned and whined its painful way up, and in the momentary silence it happened. All knowledge of Lindsay's name— her family name—vanished without a trace from his functioning brain.

Knowing he should introduce them, Lindsay and Burden, he began suddenly to sweat. He blinked at the floor indicator above the door, desperately searching for a name. "Hatchback" kept coming to mind, blocking out other contenders. The indicator light said three. He pursed his lips, and a dry little whistle came out. Hunchback, backpack, crunchpack, oh, shit.

Suddenly, raising the brown paper bag again, eyes wild with mirthless good humor, he announced loudly, "A little cold lobster, huh?" and grinned with manic intensity. Crackpot, cough drop, cowpox.

"The leftover tuna salad," Lindsay answered with a look that suggested a diagnosis of severe derangement.

The indicator told him they were only at the fourth floor. Corn Belt, O Jesus, cornstarch . . .

"Would you like to join us for lunch, Dr. Conrad? You and Miss?"

"I'm afraid—" Cowpen, Cowper . . .

Lindsay advanced a step or two and thrust her hand out, "Lindsay—"

"—Cooper! Cooper!" Seth shouted.

"I believe you, Dr. Conrad, really." And turning to Lindsay, he added, "Burden, Joe Burden."

"We'd like that very much, Dr. Burden. Seth's told me so much about you."

Afterward, when he heard about it, Harvey only added to the dissonance. "Mental masturbation, boychik. A mutual mental jerkoff. The great gods unzipped their codpieces and got their intellectual rocks off. Four old menopausal cockers drooling over Coop's beautiful, melony boobs. Listen, boychik, don't look at me that way. Shiksas have good boobs. They don't droop. That's what they're known for."

"Jesus, Harv."

"Listen, don't argue with me, I'm a student of boobs—the comparative religion of boobs." He swirled the cheap cognac in his juice glass and made a face when he sniffed it. "Whew! Where'd ya buy this stuff, the Exxon station?" He swallowed what was in the glass in one gulp and poured himself some more. "Why do you think rich Jewish men take shiksas as fetishistic objects?"

"I want to talk to you—seriously, I mean. It's important."

"What's more important than the study of boobs? Scholarship, boychik, scholarship." He drank to scholarship.

"We're not talking about boobs, for chrissake—"

"Oh, yeah, what was it that Maxie Homburg couldn't take his big, greedy eyes off, I'll bet? That old blowhard."

It was true. Homburg couldn't take his eyes off Lindsay—when he wasn't blustering and guffawing, that is.

"I think that's a lot of crap. Forgive me, Miss Cooper, not what you say, what they say. They're jerks, those guys. They just want to close the books on the matter."

Homburg had just finished giving his order to Marge and was sitting back, his thumb tucked into his belt, his ample belly protruding. Pulling his heavy black briar pipe from between his thick lips, he leaned toward Lindsay over the snowy tablecloth. "When you've been around as long as I have, Miss Cooper, you learn that most cops are just guys with high school diplomas and guns." He had a habit of winking when he thought he was shocking—to ease the pain of his revelations. Now, through yellowed teeth, he grinned at Lindsay and winked. "Furthermore, what is laughingly known as the criminal justice system is not there to discover criminals or dispense justice. It's there to put bread on the tables of the bureaucrats. Am I right, Thomas? You're the sociologist, not me." Reaching across the table, he clapped the huge black man on the arm and roared with laughter. Several people across the half-empty dining room turned to stare and smiled at his familiar blast.

To his detractors in the medical school Homburg was the world's loudest and therefore best-known forensic pathologist. "When things get rough, cops want to stay alive and get their pensions, the DA wants to get reelected, and the judge wants to clear the docket and get to the country for the weekend. It's not a matter of corruption, Miss Cooper, but—shall we say?—enlightened self-interest." He sat like a praying mantis, poised with his soup spoon halfway between his plate and his thick lips.

Lindsay had remained silent except for a demure glance at Burden, but the faint color in her cheeks said it all. She was loving every moment—all five pairs of eyes. Christ, he thought afterward, maybe Harvey was right.

"You've got trouble, boychik, real trouble. She likes mind fucking. I know. Selma was like that. Some asshole would come along and say two or three consecutive sentences with words like 'algorithm' or 'nothingness' or 'iconography,' as in 'The algorithm for love results in the transformation from nothingness to iconography through the inflection of feeling as metaphor.' And she'd come in her pants, just like that." He shook his head mournfully. "Boychik, boychik, sounds bad. She really went for all that bullshit—Waxman, and ol' Uncle Tom Freeman? See my paper on 'The Erotization of Bullshit,' based on three years of marriage to Selma. She was insatiable, boychik. Beware! All night long she wanted penetrating insights and climactic formulations. And wordplay." He raised his eyebrows Groucho style. "She forced me to perform all kinds of unspeakable acts." He turned his head in mock shame. "Lingua franca. Reductio. Banal intercourse—with three, sometimes four of her intellectual asshole buddies." He waved four fingers in front of Seth's nose. "Be brilliant! Be allusive! Be subtle, articulate, witty. Talk. Talk. Talk. Bitch! Watch your step, boychik. Beware the word nympho," he said with an admonitory shake of his dead cigar. "So Burden was good today, huh? Bastard!"

"He gave me a headache. They all gave me a headache."

"The best. The greatest mind fucker of them all. Bastard!"

"She loved it. The whole goddamn show. *She* gave me a headache. Supposed to be a nice, cozy lunch. The two of us, goddammit."

"Did the earth move for her, boychik?"

"You give me a headache."


"Listen, Miss Cooper, when you've been around cops and robbers awhile and testified in court as many times as I have, you get a sense about these things. You develop an idea of who's capable of murder and who isn't—damn it!" He twisted around in his chair and brushed the back of his famous silvery mane. "Damn it, Jonathan, why the hell are you buzzing around like a goddamn tsetse fly? Sit down, will you?" He pointed with his soup spoon to an empty place across the table.

"A charming welcome, Max, as usual."

Acknowledging Graver with a sour glance, Homburg turned back to Lindsay. "Now, I didn't know Paul Silk well enough to be a close friend of his, but I do know that he was not capable of cold-blooded murder." The beefy medical examiner sat back in his chair, satisfied with himself and his melodramatic verdict.

Graver, coiling into a chair, leaned toward Seth confidentially. "I see you've made it into the big time, Conrad."

"Both of us, I guess," Seth said. What the hell, he thought. He hoped Lindsay had heard.

"Max, my friend"—the deep, reasonable voice of Tom Freeman rolled across the table—"if you had made that statement in open court, they would have made chopped liver out of you." The black man smiled fondly behind thick lenses. "Essentially your argument boils down to two points: one, that you're a wise old goat, and two, that you think you're a keen judge of human nature." Freeman talked in outlines. Born four or five hundred years too late, he was one of those jesuitical men who had thought life through early, had card-indexed it, had footnoted it, and could argue either side of any argument in his card file. "Now that's not a very compelling argument, even though I would kill anybody who said you weren't a wise old goat. I am afraid, however," he added almost sadly, "I do not hold with your view of human nature—namely, that some people are capable of murder and some people are not." Patient, articulate, he was an inexhaustible panelist and the darling of giant foundations, which fought to support his studies of urban violence.

"When I was a member of the national commission, we wrote a thirteen-volume report. At least five of those volumes presented powerful evidence of the importance of social and cultural factors in the expression of violence—"

"And the other eight probably presented contradictory evidence." Homburg chuckled.

"No, not exactly, Max."

"You see, Miss Cooper, this young fella here"—Homburg poked in Freeman's direction with his spoon—"knows more about the theory of violence and less about its practice than anybody around." He sat back, satisfied momentarily.

Freeman went on quietly. "None of your biology," he said, nodding at Graver, "and none of your psychology"—nodding at Burden—"can account for the fact that most crimes of violence are committed by poor young men from urban slums. Max, if you had grown up in Harlem in a culture where violent behavior was socially rewarded, you might not have turned out to be the eminent and lovable professor of forensic pathology that you are."

"Tom, Tom." Writhing in his seat, Homburg pulled his pipe out of his white coat. "What do you know about Harlem? You were born wearing a cap and gown. You've lived all your life on a college campus. I *was* born in Harlem, One Hundred and Fifteenth Street, a tenement, I'll show you the house. Nineteen hundred and thirteen. It was a slum then; it's a slum now. The only difference:

They collect the garbage more often now. My father was a cutter in a dress factory on Rivington Street. I had an older brother and three sisters. My brother is a radiologist, and he's even louder and more opinionated than I am, but none of us ever killed anybody or robbed anybody. Pass the bread," he commanded.

"Talk about violence." He tore a slice of pale, flaccid rye bread in half. "Every day was violence. We fought our way to school, we fought in school, and we fought our way home. It wasn't blacks and Puerto Ricans then; it was Irish and Italians. What do you say, Morris, my friend? Are you going to back me up?"

Morris Waxman's blue eyes watered as he wheezed his fragile reply. "I came from a better neighborhood, Max; we only had to fight in school."

Freeman had taken off his thick glasses as he listened to Homburg's operatic memoir. Absentmindedly he began to wipe the lenses as he squinted out at the blur and hum of the dining room, now a cheerful refuge against the steady gray drizzle outside.

"You know, Max, your own personal experience notwithstanding," Freeman went on imperturbably, "you cannot fly in the face of facts. We know you are uniquely impervious to social pressure, Max." He smiled. "Even at this table among the unique, you are unique. It would be ill advised, therefore, to try to generalize too much from the lessons of your life. You cannot dismiss facts that you don't like—facts which say in one way or another that violent behavior is learned and can be unlearned." He put down his knife and fork as though he wanted nothing to distract him.

"The fact is that the threat of violence is the ultimate social instrument for protecting society from its enemies. So we glorify those agents that have the sanction to use that force. Star warriors, policemen—we mythologize them in our mass media. Is it any surprise, then, that by the time youngsters reach adolescence, violence and the use of force mean masculinity and machismo to them?"

As Seth sat there, his attention—divided among the dull throb behind his eyes, Graver's sour glances, and Freeman's lecture—drifted back in time. Pretending to listen, he stared past Freeman at the rain as it fell on the sooty terrace and thought of Lindsay. Since Saturday she'd been playing games. Saturday cold war. Sunday love and peace. Monday war again over nothing. Less than nothing: Lisa Stone's silly party. Now this stupid ploy. What the hell was going on with her? He glanced over. He noticed for the first time a hard-etched line at the corner of her near-perfect mouth. She was gazing at Freeman raptly while Max Homburg gazed with equal rapture at the outline of her near-perfect breasts under her blue button-down shirt.

"In certain social contexts the resort to violence in response to chronic frustration does not represent individual pathological behavior but, in fact, is the normal—shall we say, modal response. And is indeed adaptive. And if you lived in those parts of the city, Max, you had damned well better learn the uses of force."

Smiling broadly now, Freeman looked about for challenges and, finding none, picked up his knife and fork again.

"Thomas." Waxman raised a frail, almost translucent hand, as though asking permission to speak. "Thomas, I'll bet you didn't know I was in the Public Health Service before I came to psychiatry— tropical medicine," he wheezed.

"His crazy explorer phase." Homburg burst in. "That's where we parted company." He leaned toward Lindsay with a broad yellow grin. "He went to South America, and I went to the South Bronx." Indeed, they were inseparable. They had grown up in the same neighborhood, gone to the same city college, the same medical school. They lived in the same New Jersey suburb, where their rosebushes touched, and, with their wives, had played bridge together every Friday night for the past thirty years.

"Several things bother me about what you say, Thomas," Waxman said gently. "One of them is this idea of what's normal. You know," he said, turning to Lindsay, "in certain South American Indian tribes there is a facially disfiguring spirochetal disease called yaws. Virtually all of the members of these tribes suffer from the disease. Occasionally it happens that one or two members of a tribe seem to be naturally immune to it. But the tribes—and this is the interesting part—consider the healthy and immune members abnormal." Pausing, he took two or three breaths and touched his bow tie as though to make sure it was still crisply tied. "They actually

restrict their activities, forbid them the right to marry, and treat
them like pariahs.

"From your point of view, Thomas, *society* defines what's sick
or healthy, what's normal or abnormal. It's true that in these
subcultures of violence, violence may be highly prevalent, just as in
these Indian tribes, yaws is prevalent, but is it really normal or
healthy? I think sometimes one has to take a longer view. What
do you think, Joe? Would you agree?" Waxman took a sip of water,
exhausted by his effort.

Lindsay was smiling at Waxman now, one of her charmed smiles
that made Seth think of chlorophyll and sunlight. What interest
could this tiny, wheezing man have for her? he wondered. Was she
charmed by his frailty? God knows if it was frailty she wanted
. . . Was it his infirmity that touched her? How would a thundering,
throbbing sick headache rate for some friendly interest and consolation? He removed his glasses and, with his eyes closed, dramatically
massaged the bridge of his nose.

"Yes, Joe." Graver smiled slyly. "Haven't you kept us in suspense
long enough? Isn't it time we heard the last word?"

"Well, Jonathan, I don't know about big ideas like society and
violence. I'm not even sure I have an opinion about Paul. About
murder, though, I do know something, I think. But I doubt it'll be
the last word." He looked past Graver. "Not with Hans around."

Hans Lucas circled the table and took the one remaining seat,
on Burden's right. "Good morning, my friends, or rather good
afternoon. *Bon appétit.* I hope I am not interrupting anything." He
gave them a Swiss smile, urbane and measured. Lucas spoke in
Oxonian English, accented with German.

"You may not be interested, Hans," Freeman said dryly. "We
were just about to hear what an analyst has to say about murder."

Although Lucas was usually three or four ideas ahead of anybody
around, he had a disarming way of working his eyebrows so that
he always looked amazed at what was said. Now, looking amazed,
he opened his white linen napkin, shook it out as though seeking
a truce, and let it fall into his lap, "Ah, yes, the religious point of
view." Then, looking past Burden to Lindsay, "But you must tell
me who our lovely young guest is. Forgive my colleagues. I am

Hans Lucas," he said, half nodding, half bowing. His chestnut hair fell in a lock over his forehead, giving him a boyish appearance.

"But that's exactly what seems so naive to me, Jonathan," Burden was saying. "It was an open secret. I knew it. You knew it. Morris. Tom. We didn't talk about it, but we all knew it. And God knows, Paul was quite discreet about it. He did his work quietly and well. There was never even the faintest suggestion of any compromising behavior with the boys on the ward. So what was the fear of blackmail, even if this young woman had let a cat out of the bag? I find it hard to believe that Paul would be threatened by that."

"But what if the blackmail that she was threatening wasn't that?" Graver leaned forward, his voice tight. "What if it referred to something you *don't* know about?" He looked at Burden and after a moment smiled a little smile. "After all, Joe, we can't know everything. What if it refers to something that you can't even conceive of in connection with Paul Silk? Something that might have compromised him or even wrecked his professional life—"

"Like what?" Seth asked quietly, looking alert for the first time.

"Still asking the wrong questions, Conrad," Graver said with a contemptuous smile, and turned back to Burden. "What then? Do you think he could have murdered her under those circumstances?"

The triumph in Graver's voice commanded the attention of everyone at the table. They watched in silence for several moments as Burden scratched a design in the tablecloth with his fork. "No." He looked up. "I don't think so. There I would have to trust my intuition about Paul. And what I know about the murdering kind."

"Meaning what?" Lucas asked, looking amazed again.

"Meaning, first of all, that we're dealing with more than just a crime of passion. I don't mean to rule out passion from the original murder. But there's been another murder and, if my intuition is correct, now a third murder."

"You mean Silk," Seth said.

"I mean Silk. Because if you don't accept Jonathan's hypothesis that Silk had reason to kill the Light woman, then he had no reason to commit suicide."

Burden turned suddenly to Waxman. "For God's sake, Morris,

you know more about these things than all of us put together. What kind of murderer are we looking for?"

Waxman cleared his throat and said with a frail smile, "Do you want the five-hundred-dollar lecture or the deluxe version?"

"Oh, God, not the deluxe version, Moe, we don't have the time or the money," Homburg said, with a burst of belly laughter. Turning to the others, he said, "You know, he once testified so long the judge took it off the prisoner's sentence. The short one, Moe, please."

Waxman sipped his water again and looked down at the crisp white tablecloth as though reading a text. "Well, there's the dissociative type, usually an ordinary person under some great psychological strain, sometimes intoxicated as well, who commits a homicidal act in an altered state of consciousness. He doesn't know what he's doing at the moment and usually can't remember having done it afterward. The crucial thing, though, is that he never tries to conceal it. He's cooperative with the authorities, remorseful, even a decent, law-abiding person in other respects." Pausing, he touched his tie once more, as though for breath. "Obviously we're not dealing with that kind of murder in this case."

Slowly, almost breath by breath, he continued, his pale blue eyes watering from the exertion. Without realizing it, the others—even Graver—bent imperceptibly forward, to hear the words almost as pale and transparent as Waxman's labored breath as he described the psychotic murderer, usually a chronically ill, isolated, tormented individual whose behavior is ruled by delusions and demons of all sorts. He hears voices that tell him to murder and destroy. Confused and contradictory, he gives fantastic reasons for why he has to kill but feels justified in these delusions. This kind of killer, he went on, usually leaves many, many clues, a trail a mile long, and isn't as interested in concealing his crimes as he is in being allowed to continue them to mollify his tormenting demons.

"Does our murderer fall into this class?" he went on. "My guess is no. This kind of killer can function minimally in society, but in order to do so, he has to keep to himself. So he might live alone and work at some kind of marginal job where he had little contact with other people. I don't believe anybody around here, anybody connected with our staff could be that crazy without our being able to detect it." He smiled. "A little crazy maybe, but not that crazy. And it's clear that whoever the killer is, he knows us." His voice grew stronger, almost urgent. "He knows our staff: He knew this young woman; he knew Milly McVey; he knew Paul Silk. So it seems unlikely to me that such an individual would be able both to enact his psychotic behavior and to dissemble his psychosis among us. Then there is a third type—the psychopathic murderer, who kills and feels justified in killing—who kills and conceals."

Waxman faltered and took a deep breath. Burden put his hand on the old man's forearm as though to signal a time-out.

"And the most important thing about the criminal psychopath," Burden said, "is that he can pass as a perfectly stable and even attractive personality. He can be quite superficially charming and pleasant to be with. It's the alternation of these normal phases with his criminal outbursts that distinguishes him from the neurotic and the psychotic individual. The criminal psychopath walks on the razor's edge between reality and unreality."

"From the dynamic point of view, Joe, that is correct," Waxman said, obviously now ready to continue, "but it's this other characteristic—his friendly, plausible, smooth manner—that makes him so deceptive . . . and dangerous. He's quite intelligent and manipulative with people, cleverly so, and often they don't mind it because he does it in such an attractive way.

"Now, what makes him incorrigible as a criminal"—Waxman raised one of his tiny hands for emphasis—"is that he justifies all of his psychopathic behavior and blames others or society for it with clever rationalizations; therefore, he can never learn through punishment because he always feels that punishment is unjustified." Breathing hard, Waxman again reached for his water.

Seth wondered whether he would live to finish the five-hundred-dollar version.

"Let me add just one more point, Morris," Burden said. The old man nodded with relief and sat back, spent. "The criminal psychopath is almost always touchy about his masculinity. He thinks of himself as a superstud and takes pride in exploiting women sexually.

He might even have homosexual contacts as long as he is the sadistic or masculine partner. He can then go on fancying himself a stud."

Freeman, who had been listening through half-closed eyes, looked up now. "You mean all we have to do is find some ruthless, unprincipled liar who's incapable of any kind of decent relationship and is extremely clever at concealing all this." He smiled wryly. "That's very helpful, Joe."

"I never said this kind of knowledge is a substitute for detective work. I was really addressing myself to the question that Jonathan raised—namely, did I think that Paul Silk was capable of a psychopathic homicide? And based on what I know of him, my answer has to be no." He paused as he folded his napkin. "In my opinion, the killer is still at large."

"Well said, Joe, well said," Max Homburg burst out. "I couldn't have said it better myself."

"That is certainly true, Max. I am amazed that you realize it," Lucas added.

"No, Tom, we are not all murderers." Tossing his napkin on the table in front of him, Burden leaned in Freeman's direction. "We are not all guilty. Society is not the criminal. And if you melted all the plastic guns and took all the cops-and-robbers programs off the air and outlawed war, you'd still have murder and violence. As long as human beings have human nature, as long as there are two or more people alive on earth, as long as there are differences between people, there will be love and hate and jealousy and envy. *That's* what murder is all about.

"Society is the *tool* of the criminal. The criminal uses society as a stage to enact his inner conflicts. Society merely lends itself to that enactment. The criminal *must* play out his role, and he *will* play out his role no matter what the setting is. And he'll find someone to play it out with. He'll find accomplices, he'll find victims, he'll find judges, and eventually he'll find himself an executioner. He has a need to repeat his past compulsively to make what went wrong come out right. But instead, it always comes out wrong until ultimately he destroys himself."

"So, Joe, you do agree with me that the criminal has no choice, that he is a victim," Freeman said.

"Yes, it's true. He *is* a victim. He *is* a prisoner. He *is* trapped— but not by society. He is a victim of his past; he is trapped by the forces inside his own head. He is a prisoner of his inner conflicts. And you can't set him free by changing society, by giving him more love, more food, more money. He can never get enough food or money or love to resolve his inner conflicts. That's what he *says* he wants. That's even what he *thinks* he wants. 'Give me money, and I won't steal. Give me things, and I won't be envious. Give me love, and I won't be jealous.' That's not what he wants. He doesn't know it, but what he wants, society *can't* give him. The kind of food, the kind of love he yearns for are the food and love of infantile fantasies, fantasies which couldn't be gratified then and can't be gratified now."

"As usual, Joe, you are being magnificently obscure," Lucas said. "Less poetry, if you please, and more data. Be specific!"

"Look here, Hans, a criminal psychopath is constantly having to reassure himself of three things: that he is a man, that he is not helpless, and that he is not guilty. And he does so in ways that turn him into a monster."

Retreating under the heavy barrage of Burden's words, Seth studied Lindsay's imperfect features again and was not surprised to see what he took to be a trancelike state as she listened to Burden.

Burden seemed to have reached some kind of peroration. Wrestling his mind back into place, Seth told himself to pay attention. He was missing Burden's drift, and the throb behind his eyes seemed to blur the words, like faces in a mob coming at him.

"He develops fantasies that tell him in one way or another that he is a superman, that he is omnipotent, that he is powerful, that he is fearless, that he is a sexual superstar, that he is completely self-sufficient. These fantasies are enjoyed in childhood, as fantasies, but as he grows into adolescence and adulthood, they are put into action. He begins to act the part.

"There's the picture of your macho delinquent, Tom. What drives him is not TV, but intense paranoid anxiety. In addition to these fantastic scenarios he writes for himself in which he is powerful and fearless, he is constantly warding off unconscious self-reproaches that he is vicious, greedy, and hostile. So throughout his childhood, adolescence, and adulthood he has to tell himself, '*I* am not bad; *I* am not vicious. *They* are bad; *they* are vicious. *They* are out to get *me*. I've got to beat them to the punch. If I don't screw them, they'll screw me.' "

As Seth tried to make his mind contain the outpouring of Burden's words, he felt an uncanny restlessness. Its center seemed to be at the back of his neck and to radiate from that point. He put his hand back there as though he expected to find some lesion.

"But it's his unconscious need for punishment that finally makes the criminal behavior possible. Eventually the punishment will come through his act of murder, in which he can condense his vengeance and his self-punishment; that is his ultimate masochistic attempt to overcome his feelings of helplessness. The murder is his act of suicide. It is the Roman running on his sword, the ultimate bravado, the ultimate reassurance."

Now he *knew* that someone was watching him, staring at his back. He turned.

"Look here, you must understand that the murderer is under tremendous tension, always waiting for the other shoe to drop; in fact, he is always trying to make it drop. To find some peace."

Their eyes met across the dining room, and Harvey, caught in a moment of uncharacteristic gravity, waved a hand in friendly greeting. Seth smiled back, and, as he turned away, a locked door fell open, and unexpected thoughts and unwanted memories pushed themselves into consciousness.

*Part Five*

# WISH FULFILLMENT

# Chapter

# 14

"Listen," he said, grasping her arm, "we've got to talk."

Resisting his lead, Lindsay stood flat-footed. "What did he say?"

A gust of river wind ruffled their hair in unison, creating a chill choreography as they stood outside the hospital, locked in a momentary impasse.

"Who?" Seth asked, releasing her.

"Him," she said with a capital *H,* "the great one, Burden."

"Someplace quiet . . ." He shivered and dug his hands deep into his trouser pockets. "Look," he said, glancing at his watch, "we've got about an hour." The crisp evening air of early October made them start moving again, briskly, up First Avenue toward the United Nations. "I want to tell you about this before we meet Harvey."

"Why? What difference does it make?" She paced him easily, stride for stride.

The question puzzled him, as though she'd spoken some alien dialect. He understood the words, but the meaning seemed to drift away.

What difference *did* it make whether Harvey heard about the diary? He left the question unanswered and wished it hadn't been asked.

□ □ □

"**W**hy did he change his mind?" The half-filled, quietly lit room which looked out over the East River was at the top of Beekman Place. Its chrome identity, COCKTAIL LOUNGE, over the entrance was out of another time. From where they sat they could see the lights across the Queensboro Bridge and the cable car as it made its transit between Roosevelt Island and Manhattan.

"The report came back yesterday. No fingerprints at all. The keyboard was clean. Wiped clean." He shrugged. "So he sent 'em back to Milly's apartment to finish looking for it."

Mindlessly Seth once again rolled several sheets of hospital stationery into a scroll.

"They found it in the bathroom with the iguana, believe it or not. On a shelf over the bathtub, with the goddamn lizard sitting on it. The whole time."

"So that's where she'd hid it." Lindsay shuddered. "That repulsive little beast—all this time. And you actually saw it?"

"This afternoon." He had missed lunch entirely that day— Thursday. As he sat hunched over the diary in Fontana's tiny office, the gripping of his stomach had given way to heavy preoccupied breathing, a racing heart, and, finally, grim, dry lips and a sour taste. "Saw it, read it, and for you"—he tossed the scroll across the table—"took notes."

"He obviously trusts you more than I do. But, then, he doesn't know you as well as I do."

She unrolled the sheets and looked them over, carefully scanning both sides, getting their depth and dimension.

Seth studied her in the pink light of the Art Deco lamp, studied the planes and angles of her face for several moments. No, she didn't have such good bones. Not sculptured, too preppy.

"Burden liked you. He said you had grain. 'Rare, these days, in young people.' I think I'm quoting him accurately."

"What does that mean, grain?"

"You can ask him yourself, if you'd like."

"He *agreed?*"

"On two conditions."

"I knew it. What's the catch?"

"First, no attributions. Take whatever you want from what he says, use it however you want to, but his name doesn't appear. Agreed?"

"Agreed. What's the other condition?"

"He suggests that you read"—he pulled a packet of folded papers out of his inner pocket and handed it to her—"this."

She opened the packet and read the first few sentences: "It is surprising how often people who seek analytic treatment for hysteria or an obsessional neurosis confess to having indulged in the fantasy: 'a child is being beaten.' . . . The fantasy has feelings of pleasure attached to it, and on their account the patient has reproduced it on innumerable occasions in the past or may even still be doing so. . . ." The paper bore the title " 'A Child Is Being Beaten'— A Contribution to the Study of the Origin of Sexual Perversions." Puzzled, she looked up.

"Freud's paper on masochism." He'd been studying her face again as she read and had decided that he liked her preppy, imperfect bones after all. "Not the final word," he said, "but the first and maybe the best. He thought it might be helpful. Background."

She shook her head. "I have a feeling I'm getting in over my head." She flipped through the dozen or so pages, stopping occasionally to test the water.

The red plastic stirrer Seth had been playing with snapped, and Lindsay looked up.

"Want to know who the doctor was? Her adolescent crush? The wonderful guy who made her pregnant?"

"I know." She looked down again at the Freud paper. "I saw 'little Dot' today. She told me the whole story."

"Half the story. The other half is in the diary. What did she say?"

Lindsay looked up. "That summer in East Hampton when she worked as an au pair, she used to have Mondays off." Laying the paper aside, she leaned forward over the highly polished wooden table.

"One day in the middle of August she spent the day in the city, and he invited her to have dinner with him. Of course, they spent the night together." She paused and sipped the last of her wine. "God, she's a sad creature. Little Dot, I mean." She shook her head. "She got back late the next morning, made up some excuse, and the whole thing was forgotten until she missed her period in September. She panicked, and then the rape episode with the boys. He never even knew about it."

"According to the diary, not until last April. That's when she told him"—a note of righteousness crept into his tone—"what she'd never told him before. All those years. That he screwed her, just like he screws everybody, made her pregnant, and then forgot about her.

"Naturally"—he looked at her over his glasses, which had slipped down the bridge of his nose again—"he denied it, and that's when she got mad." He paused and looked out as though the story were written in the lights of the city. "Then it's hard to know exactly what happened. The writing gets fragmented and careless in that section; it's only a spiral notebook, about so big." He made a rectangle with his hands, about the size of a paperback book. "The script was so tiny I don't think she ever meant it to be read—even by her.

"Well, anyway, it's hard to know whether she was teasing him or threatening him—you know, to tell her parents, or maybe his wife, about the affair and the pregnancy."

Draining his empty glass again, Seth remembered this time to hail the waiter. He had slid down in his chair, like a restless child, so that his legs stuck out from under the table.

"Compassionate, mature, he grabs her and slugs her." He struggled upright again. "Just like what happened with Milly McVey that time. Bastard!" He picked up a fragment of the plastic stirrer and threw it down again so that it skidded across the polished wooden surface. "He just walks over people. You heard the way he talked to Burden the other day." He lowered his voice. "Prick!"

Lindsay looked southward, past the UN. "What was the word that night at Whit's? 'Guileless'?" She turned back to Seth. "You don't think . . . she was asking for it?" she asked coolly.

Without waiting for an answer, she reached for her bag. "What time are we supposed to meet him? Ha:vey?"

Looking away, he dismissed Lindsay's question and stared glumly at the next table, where a Japanese in a houndstooth check jacket with deep side vents was paying court to a statuesque Scandinavian airline hostess.

When the waiter arrived, he ordered two more. White wine for Lindsay, dry sherry—"Fino"—for himself.

"He's been pissing and moaning all week"—Seth lounged in his chair again—"and tonight I suppose we'll hear the dress rehearsal blues."

He tilted his head back and looked apathetically at the ceiling. There was a faded blue mural, with powerful bare-breasted women in a pseudomythological scene. He pushed the glasses back on his nose and tried for a moment to figure out the myth.

"Nobody knows their lines, blah, blah, blah; nobody shows up, blah, blah, blah; nobody cares, blah, blah, blah. He alone is carrying this monumental burden. Single-handed." Seth threw his head from side to side as he recounted each complaint. "He should have quit while he was ahead. He'll be a laughingstock at the dinner tomorrow night. Why didn't I stop him? If I'd been a real friend, I'd have chloroformed him, blah, blah, blah, blah, blah."

Harvey's chickens had come home to roost, as he was fond of reminding everyone who would listen, and he was about to lay the biggest goddamn egg of his short but brilliant career. The next day was October 2, Founders Day, the day of the show. The program called for academic festivities and honors all day, followed by assorted cocktail parties, and in the evening a chairman's dinner at nine-thirty, preceded by Harvey's doomed production.

The waiter arrived with the wine, and to celebrate the event, Seth sat up straight in his chair. He noted that the fino was served in a martini glass and wondered whether Whit would have sent it back. He pretended not to notice.

"I've been saving the best for last," he said sourly. "Up to now simple, unmitigated brutality. Now," he said, toasting her, "we plunge into the umbilicus of the human spirit."

"Do I look okay?" She touched her hair. "Never know who you'll meet in places like that."

Without bothering to smile, Seth snapped her picture with his fingers.

"Coles?"

"Coles. She began to do some work for him early in the year. He needed somebody to wind reels and splice film." He paused momentarily and looked out over the river again.

"After a month or two," he resumed, "she became his 'photographic assistant,' setting up the lighting and then photographing his interviews." Little by little—he supposed at first she invited it, and then she didn't have to invite it, he offered it—Coles began to give her advice and then finally offered to treat her in payment for her work. "He'd see her once or twice a week. This was the doctor she wouldn't tell Cousin Dot about."

According to the diary, he went on, the "therapy" became more intimate.

"You mean he slept with her?"

"No, not as simple as that." Seth glanced at the houndstooth-checked Japanese at the next table. He was busy caressing the blonde's forearm and making her smile with businessman's jokes.

"The diary said that the 'therapy' was in the evening. And sometimes Coles took her out to dinner afterward. There would be physical contact. At first only fatherly embraces—to console her. Then they became more sexual. Still, only embraces. But that wasn't enough. She wanted more. And here's where it gets kinkier."

The sky was quite dark now and clear, and he was no longer talking to Lindsay but to the headlights speeding homeward on the East River Drive, to the red and blue neon sign across the river that proclaimed PEARLWICK HAMPERS to an indifferent city. He spoke to the BMT train as it rattled across the Williamsburg Bridge, carrying dozing pattern makers from the garment district home to their evening meals.

"He began to photograph *her*. Still photographs. He told her he was writing a book on sex and needed illustrations and asked if she wanted to help. At first it was sexual anatomy, then sexual techniques. He never touched her. The diary is clear about that.

"Then in July, this past July, he took her to Mexico with him—he's got some kind of villa in the hills outside Cuernavaca—and that's where he began to do movies of her." He shook his head. "Christ, she must have been irresistible!

"He had her act out sexual scenarios with Mexican men while he watched and filmed." He turned back to Lindsay. "Bastard told her he was making some kind of medical film." He made quotes around the word "medical" with his fingers.

He had lowered his voice and now looked over at the Japanese. He was whispering something to the blonde, who looked flushed and beautiful.

"Maybe she actually believed it. I don't know." He shrugged. "It's hard to tell. I suppose she wanted to."

He lapsed into silence for a few moments and sipped his fino. "That's where the iguana comes from." He looked back at Lindsay. "She actually smuggled it in from Mexico on the way home."

It was almost over by then, he continued. When they got back from Mexico, Coles had cooled off, and she broke off with him. "That was around the time she had the last blowup with her mother and moved in with Milly."

The blonde at the next table gave a husky laugh and said something Swedish and sensual.

Seth swirled the remains of his sherry and studied the patterns of golden liquid.

"I'll go over this tonight," Lindsay said, and held up the monograph and notes Seth had given her. She glanced at her watch. "It's late." She reached for her bag.

"That's all?" Seth punched his glasses back up on his nose and leaned forward across the table. "That's all you have to say? 'It's late?' "

"Harvey—what about—"

"Screw Harvey! Why aren't you outraged?"

Lindsay folded the papers slowly and found a neat berth for them in her tan canvas shoulder bag. "Maybe I don't outrage easily." She put the bag down and folded her hands on the table in front of her. "Or maybe your outrage is enough for both of us." Without flinching or turning away, she tapped her watch. "Don't you think we've kept him waiting long enough?"

"You mean deceit, exploitation, and betrayal aren't enough to excite even a tiny gasp of surprise?"

"I mean maybe she was not deceived, exploited, or betrayed."

Seth shoved his glass off to the side of the table. "You think this unethical creep, this one-eyed pervert didn't use her?"

The lovers at the next table looked at them and smiled.

"God—" Lindsay bit off the rest of the impulse with clenched teeth. "Whenever you talk about her, you get woolly-headed, misty-eyed, and sound like an adoring four-year-old. What's the matter with you? Her whole life," she said with a sweeping gesture, "was seduction." She turned away and spoke to the river, as though she were afraid she'd go too far. "Why are you so naive?"

"Christ, why are you like stainless steel? Where the hell is your compassion? I thought you wanted to find out the truth about her."

She wheeled back toward Seth, her eyes glistening. "That's not compassion; it's sentimentality. And it's not the truth. You're trying to reconstruct her—to make her into someone else."

Seth wanted to tell her, at that moment, about her imperfect bones.

There was only the whine of the high-speed elevator as it descended into Beekman Place. Their ears popped.

"The only decent one in the whole mess was Silk," Seth said dully, as though he knew that no one was listening. "He tried to warn her and get her into real treatment." He kicked at some ashes on the elevator floor. "I suppose she just couldn't hear it."

The whir of the elevator machinery embraced them again. The car slowed suddenly, and their legs wanted to fold up as the door rattled open.

His face lit up when he saw them.

"Lino," he shouted. "Lino!" He made an expansive gesture with a breadstick as though he were conducting Beethoven. "Water for everyone!"

"Oh, God," Seth muttered. Worse than he thought.

Harvey had grabbed him that morning. "Have dinner with me, boychik!" His usual blend of sweaty charm and arm-twisting neediness. "Your treat. How's that for generosity? You can work off your existential guilt."

"Not tonight, Harv," Seth had told him. "Lindsay tonight."

"The *girlchik,* too," Harvey had said, staring into the hall mirror. "How the hell is she? C'mon, we'll have a mass suicide together."

"Not tonight."

"What d'ya mean, not tonight?" Harvey had leaned toward the mirror and pulled his left lower eyelid down. "Your buddy is dying of terminal jitters. How can you say no? Christ, look at this! Not even bloodshot! No sleep for five nights and not even bloodshot! Christ, I've got some kind of chronic anemia!" He stuck his tongue out at himself and studied it for a moment. "I was only kidding, boychik. My treat. I'll throw in the *girlchik,* too. Bloch's last rites. Come on, just nod your head if you can read my lips. . . ."

Now Harvey raised his glass of Chianti and drained it as they took their places opposite him in the Leatherette booth. "Boychik! Coop! My friends! The penultimate scene." He grabbed a hand from each of them and squeezed it warmly. "The peroration, and tomorrow the curtain falls." He released them and poured himself some wine out of the straw-covered bottle. "A comfort, in my final agony. My best friends." He drank another toast to them. A steampipe banged overhead.

"Listen, I hear Him knocking at my door. The butt end of my young days," Harvey declaimed.

Seth picked up the menu and began to study it.

Harvey leaned across the table. "Do you realize what it's like back there, boychik?" He nodded in the direction of the hospital. "I could get a better performance out of the catatonics on O-7. They're like idiot children. Three rehearsals—three"—he shook three fingers at Lindsay—"and each one lousier than the last."

He bit off half a breadstick and railed at them between crunches and swallows.

"Five sketches, five musical numbers—note the balance," he said, using his hands as though they each held a fragile crystal, "the structural symmetry, and each a gem." He made his fingers sparkle. "Coop," he appealed, "this is no piece of schlock. It's satire."

Seth reached across the table and poured Lindsay and himself a glass of wine.

"Brilliant. Savage. Brechtian. And these clowns, these fuck-ups"—he held his head in his hands and shook it slowly from side to side as though he were in excruciating pain—"are killing it."

Seth hailed the waiter.

Harvey had managed, through a combination of threats, promises, crude charm, and implacable nagging, to enlist the entire resident staff, a number of attractive and large-breasted nursing students, and even some of the younger members of the faculty in the production.

"Make that two." Lindsay had finally settled on eggplant par-magiana. Seth handed the menu back to the waiter.

"And in case anyone cares, I am planning to OD on a double order of baked ziti." He turned to the waiter. "Be sure and tell Mario it's for Dr. Bloch. And, *signor*"—he poured the last few drops into his glass and handed the bottle to the waiter—*"vino.*

"They don't know their lines. They don't know their cues. They can't sing. They can't even talk. Shields acts as though he were trying out for Mount Rushmore, but at least he shows up. The others don't even show up, and when they show up, they don't care." He beat his breast. "I care!"

He railed on through antipasto. "I care! That's my curse. Why did you let me, boychik? Tonight Brecht, tomorrow Dr. Floppo."

The euphoric, self-pitying frenzy slowed during pasta, and mellower themes emerged. "Behind those chronically red eyes there's a really, really deep depression. But between the red eyes and the depression, there's a great comic talent." He was talking about "Pammy Price, my little starlet—you'll see." He tore off another piece of bread and mopped his sauce. "Golden Boy? Harmless. He stands there, tall, neat, beaming smile." He flashed his teeth between swallows. "Every once in a while he says something mordant and blinks." He gulped some Chianti. "It's like having an intelligent lighthouse on stage."

Finally, swollen with ziti, soaked with Chianti, his excitement spent, Harvey slumped against the wall of the booth, exhausted. He blinked at Lindsay. "How ya doing, sleuth? How's the head?" He tapped the back of his head and smiled stupidly. "Coming tomorrow? Good. Don't miss the last act."

There was nothing Burden said to Lindsay that afternoon that didn't irritate him. And that, he supposed afterward, was the beginning of the end.

Later he reproached himself. He should have known it would have that effect on him. After all, why the hell had he been examining life all these years? But the truth is that he didn't even know it was happening until it was too late.

"I'd like to help you, Miss Cooper, really, but"—he had said it mournfully, as though he really meant it, but then, after a moment's reflection, shook his head emphatically—"you want magic. Conrad, you know what I'm talking about—"

He nodded to Burden as though he'd understood. This world-class psychoanalytic guru was playing games. Cat and mouse. Shit! He watched Lindsay's jaw tighten.

"Look here," Burden said, swiveling away from his river view. As usual, he had studied the traffic on the river, north and south, as he listened to Lindsay's proposal. "You say all you want me to do is tell you about this Jennie Light—her psychology, what made her tick. You say you have a few scraps of information about her—"

"I didn't say that." She pushed her hair behind her right ear with nervous intensity. "We've got a lot of information about her."

Bastard! He could see the color rising in her cheeks. And she'd been edgy enough before.

Her hands had been cold on their way over from the psychiatric hospital. Colder than the crisp air that made the late-afternoon sounds of the city hard-edged and sharp. As they walked toward Ten North and Burden's office, Seth squeezed the icy hand.

"God, I think I'm nervous." She'd grabbed at her abdomen. "Why am I nervous? I've interviewed senators, Nobel Prizewinners, kidnappers; I've been mugged, assaulted, practically murdered—"

"Your unconscious fantasies are showing."

"What's that supposed to mean?" she snapped.

"Just a joke, Hatchback, poorly timed, maybe, but only a joke. Come on, it's right down the hall—"

She stopped suddenly and faced him. "Just a minute. I'd like to get one or two things straight." Readjusting her shoulder bag and pushing her hair out of the way, she signaled battle. "First of all, your humor has a dreary medical quality that makes you unpopular with the laity. Secondly, although it's true I wanted this interview with Burden, I do not welcome the idea of consorting with some of your other colleagues at this famous cocktail party. I don't like cocktails, and I don't like some of your colleagues. Understood? We leave early, Founders Day or no Founders Day—okay?" She brushed at her hair again, making the question rhetorical.

Turning energetically, she marched toward Ten North. A moment later, as they passed a stairwell, he grabbed her arm and shoved her into it.

"Hey! Stop it! Leave me"—she twisted away from him—"alone!"

"Christ, what's with you, Hatchback? You're acting like a goddamn virgin on her wedding night. It's only a goddamn interview."

"Quit calling me that—Hatchback. Why do you keep calling me that?"

"I dunno," he lied. " 'Cause you're revved up all the time, maybe. Christ, relax. Burden isn't God."

"I didn't think he was," she said, still glaring at him.

"Then why are you acting this way?"

"I don't know," she said ruefully.

Wrapping his arms around her embattled body, he kissed her carotid pulse. "Hey, I'm here. I'm with you." The muscles in her shoulders relented a little. "I love you. You got a good brain—doesn't bruise easy. And I like your preppy bones and your—"

"What do you mean, 'preppy bones'?"

"I like imperfection, I guess. The point is, I'm here. Your paper hero. Now. Later. Cocktail party. Chairman's dinner. The works."

*S*he had told Burden straight out, prairie style, what she was after. Seth watched the color subside in her cheeks and the electric dance of her fingers settle into the graceful gestures that animated her thoughts. He watched her pulse slow and her breathing quiet. Harvey was right: She did have terrific breasts. He studied them. Euclidean, he had thought, definitely, in their definition and congruence. And assertive. The honest, midwestern, stand-up-and-be-counted kind. He thought of her in bed. And charmingly, hopelessly asymmetrical. The right one an erogenous genius; the left a feckless ne'er-do-well.

The squeaking of Burden's swivel chair, his restless squirming, and the deepening gloom in his eyes should have tipped him off.


"*S*craps." Burden brushed them aside with a contemptuous wave. "What you don't have is the introspective evidence of her own mind—her own thoughts and feelings."

"Diary entries—what about that?" Seth demanded. Bastard. What was he getting at?

Ignoring Seth, Burden stood up. "It takes me weeks, months, even years sometimes to piece together the pathological fantasies that control the lives of people. Rivers"—he opened his arms as though he were conducting an orchestra—"oceans of data are generated in an analysis. And you want me to figure out the mind of a girl who's dead. *That's* fantasy. Illusion." He looked at her as though she had wounded him mortally. "TV stuff—Joyce Cousins, or whatever her name is." He dismissed her, whatever her name was, with a wave of his hand.


"*W*e are all patients," he had told them on more than one occasion, "more or less. Sick from illusions. That's what it means to be a patient. Having a case of illusions. And we love them—our illusions. We cling to them like drowning men to matchwood."

In unguarded moments, often at the end of a long conference, he talked like that. Weary and distracted, he was like a man in the grip of an old illness, racked by some momentary spiritual agony.

"The hateful, thankless, illimitable task of analysis is to disillusion. To wrest, little by little, from those that cherish them their personal myths and to extinguish them." He would catch himself at moments like this and smile as though he had been amusing himself at their expense, as though it were not his personal mission in life to free the world from magic and fantasy, as though he had no illusions at all, not even that one.

"And illusions are dangerous, Miss Cooper, because they seduce and betray, comfort and destroy."

And now Burden, stalker of dreams, was on one of his missionary rampages.

"No," he said, waving a wooden match at her until it flickered and went out, "it's a no-win situation. If I go beyond the few scraps of data you throw me—diaries included, Conrad—if I speculate, I'll sound like a character out of a Viennese comic opera, false beard and all. Wild analysis—and you'd have every right to snicker and forget it. No!" He exhaled a cloud of blue cigar smoke for emphasis.

"Then don't go beyond the facts. Don't speculate," Seth urged. He could see the color rising again in Lindsay's cheeks.

"Worse. I'd end up telling you what any hairdresser could tell you. Banal. Trivial. You'd say, 'So what?'—and you'd be right again. You see, damned if I do, and damned if I don't."

Moving to the edge of her chair, Lindsay hoisted her bag onto her shoulder. "I'm sorry," she said, her eyes bright with anger. "When Seth told me you'd agreed to talk to me, I thought, well, I thought that's what it would be—just talk. A friendly talk. And I'd learn something about Jennie Light, some little bit about her. But—well, you make it sound like"—she paused, searching for the right word—"forever. Apocalyptic." She stood up. "I guess I misunderstood."

In silence they confronted each other. Lindsay, flushed, standing at attention, the army brat, waiting, it seemed, to be dismissed. And Burden, head in a cloud of blue tobacco smoke, his shrewd eyes taking her measure.

"Apocalyptic . . ." he murmured. "Maybe . . ."

Then, suddenly, he took a deep breath and shrugged. "Okay, Miss Cooper." He waved her back to her seat. "We'll try it your way—a friendly talk." He smiled. "Nothing apocalyptic. Choice, that word," he said, inspecting his cheroot. "I didn't want you to be disappointed, disillusioned."

"That's a risk we'll both have to take, I suppose," she said stiffly.

"Sit down. You, too, Conrad. I'll probably live to regret this," he murmured with a shake of his head. "Now tell me everything you can about her." He looked at them both. "Everything. Even what seems like the most trivial and insignificant detail." He swiveled away, toward the window and the river traffic below.

It was one of those brilliant, crystal days of early October that turn the city into a flashing jewel. It had already provided the opportunity for much self-congratulatory chatter that morning at the Founders Day ceremony. Now, as the late-afternoon sun ignited bursts of golden light in the windows of Brooklyn and Queens, Burden listened.

He listened as the life of Jennifer Light came tumbling out in disconnected pieces, the way Fontana had poured out the contents of her handbag in front of Seth that night. Anecdotes, diary excerpts, gossip, opinions, history—ancient and modern—friends, lovers, enemies: every shred of her life, every scrap they had been able to collect.

Burden listened. His head inclined, supported by two fingers at the temple, he listened, doing what he had been teaching them all these weeks: how to listen to the unknown, to see the latent images that flutter to life in sleep, to know the ghostly affections of the heart.

Staring out at the glistening river, he betrayed no strong emotion, perhaps only a slight weariness around the eyes. Occasionally, in a cloud of smoke, he would exhale a question or ask to hear again a quotation from the diary or for information about some particular detail.

When they had finished, Burden was silent, as though he had succumbed to the story. The shadows had eaten their way eastward, across the river, nibbling away at time. This man who slept dreamless nights and lived disillusioned days—what was he thinking, this mournful, grim-lipped man? Was it what he had said once before? "Men get what they want most—what they deserve in a sense. We're all in the grip of our biochemistry, Dr. Conrad"—he had made a tight fist with his left hand—"and our unconscious"—he'd made another fist—"and between the two it's surprising that we poor bastards do as well as we do."

Motionless, he sat, reading the river and the shadows and Jennifer Light's sad history as it receded before him. His cigar had grown cold in his hand, but not before it had cast a pale blue pall in the room.

"Miss Cooper," Burden said, slowly turning away from the window. He stared at her for a moment, silent, as though he'd forgotten what he wanted to say. "If this young woman had died crossing First Avenue one afternoon, the victim, let's say, of a reckless driver, would you be here? Would you be trying to write about her, understand her, 'solve her mysteries'?" With the last phrase he turned to Seth so that the question embraced them both.

"I don't know. I suppose not." She clicked her pen shut and laid it down on her pad.

"No, I don't think so either. One of the things that fascinate us, that you want to know, that your readers want to know is the answer to the question, Was her death meaningful or trivial?"

"Trivial? How could any death be trivial?" With a surge of restless energy she brushed her hair behind her right ear.

"You see, already you're annoyed with me, and we haven't even come to the bad part. No, of course, every death is important to the victim and his family. But an accidental death is trivial in the sense that we can't generalize from it." He shrugged. "There's nothing to learn from it.

"But if her death was motivated, caused by something other than chance, if she wittingly or unwittingly had a hand in her own end, then we want to"—he clenched his fist urgently—"*have* to know how and why. The solution of the mystery has to tell us not only the murderer's motivation but also the victim's motivation. If she is just a random target, someone who accidentally gets in the way of an escaping bank robber, then, except for her family, she's highly forgettable by the rest of us." He let his dead cigar drop into the ashtray on his desk. "But if she somehow participates in her own death, then she's as interesting as the murderer because she shares some of the guilt for the crime."

"Not very nice—is it—what you're saying? That victims and innocents aren't psychologically interesting."

"*Innocent* victims. Innocence is boring. Yes, that's right. And you're right, it's not very nice." He smiled. "But you didn't come to me expecting to hear nice things."

"I suppose not." She smiled back.

Seth watched as Burden lit another cigar. He noticed, suddenly, that Burden's hands looked effeminate. Strong but effeminate, like the hands of a female musician. Definitely effeminate.

"Look, there's a certain amount of spectral guilt in everyone. Me, you, your readers." Burden waved the match out. "It's left over from our earliest years and goes on haunting us until we die. It also makes us sensitive to and fascinated by other people's guilt-ridden behavior. There's a part of all of us that identifies with the criminal when we read a murder mystery—"

"Not normally."

"Well, perhaps not you, Dr. Conrad. You're obviously made of tougher stuff. But the rest of us"—he gestured to Lindsay and himself—"are weaker vessels."

Pompous bastard. Suddenly he found Burden's smugness intolerable. Despite his burning ears, he gave Burden a tight little sporting smile.

"When we dream, you see, the dreamer is everyone in his dream. The author is everyone in his creation. And the reader must be everyone in his re-creation in order to enjoy himself fully—the detective, the murderer, and the victim. Which brings us back to Jennifer Light."

"Was it meaningful—her death, I mean?" Lindsay snapped her pen open.

"Yes, I think so. I do."

"No accident—she was not an innocent victim?" She scribbled several lines rapidly.

"What was accidental, I think, were the time, the place, and the *particular* murderer. The rest was foreshadowed by what you've told me about her. Fated, if you will."

"But what else is there, and if *they* are accidental—"

"There was her spectral fantasy. It was that unconscious scenario that compelled her death and in that particularly brutal way. Perhaps it could have been a knife, but it had to be direct, physical, and violent. She was a dreamer awake, as intensely interested in her dream as you and I are when we're asleep. She was living out her unconscious fantasy, and so was the murderer, living out an unconscious fantasy. They, the murderer and the victim, were like two somnambulist dancers, wheeling and turning in their respective orbits, each dancing to an inner choreography. But Jennifer's dance was the more dangerous one, and it had to take her into the path of other dancers until one of them danced hers with her."

"This . . . unconscious fantasy or scenario, whatever—you make it sound so . . . well, mysterious."

Ignoring her mocking smile, Burden stared eastward again, as though the answer lay somewhere in the vast darkness over the distant ocean. "What comes through is like an underdeveloped photograph. A kind of ghostly presentiment, visible yet still too faint. What you've told me about her suggests certain themes—patterns I've heard before."

Queens and the far shore of the river were in shadow now. The golden reflections of the late-afternoon sun glanced off the bridge towers and, in the darkening office, illuminated Lindsay's face as she followed the threads of Burden's dynamic tapestry.

"Our minds are like palimpsests—'mystic writing pads.' As children we form highly emotional primitive fantasies. Like first drafts of a story, they're erased, but they leave telltale traces. Later the story is rewritten in more sophisticated ways. In their final versions these unconscious fantasies shape our characters. They tell us whom to love and hate and how. They decide what excites and repels us, and they create our dreams.

"Jennifer Light was caught between impossible desire and implacable reproach." He bent forward in Lindsay's direction. "Look here, what was this suicidal choreography she was dancing out? It contained three themes, all related and interwoven." He meshed his fingers together for emphasis. "One was a femme fatale fantasy, another was a primal scene fantasy, and the third was a beating fantasy."

Sifting through the evidence they had presented him, he selected detail after detail, holding each one up to them, turning it over, asking for meaning, proposing motivation, extrapolating, combining it with another apparently meaningless detail in a way which made them both resonate. Like a spider, spinning and wheeling, he wove. He wove theory, fact, experience, personal history, myth, and literature until a design began to emerge.

"When she was fifteen, according to her cousin—isn't that right?—she managed to get her father so furious—the person she felt loved her more than anyone else in the world—she got him so mad that even *he* beat her up. In her bedroom, you said, when she was half undressed."

He reminded them of her library, with its well-thumbed passages of torture scenes, Nazi concentration camps, her fascination with the idea that Rousseau had lived out his whole life dominated by a masochistic fantasy, of that other excerpt from her diary. "What was it? Read it again, Conrad."

Watching the passage downstream of the body of an animal— a dead dog, it looked to him from the distance—Seth was taken by surprise and had to reshuffle his notes hurriedly.

" 'I have to be terrified—convinced that my life is on the line— rape isn't terrible enough—' " He read in a flat voice, objective, as though he were reading the terms of a contract. " '. . . the silhouette of a man standing over me—imminent danger—I'd kill for that buildup, that turn-on. I want pain—fury—force! Maybe when he's on me with a knife at my belly—to be cut and have visible wounds to show—people to feel sorry for me. God, I want to be cruel and manipulating and cold. I'm afraid that's how I really am. . . .' "

Aware of the hollowness of his voice as he read, he wondered what was wrong with him. There was tightness in his chest, and he cleared his throat to make it go away. But it didn't, and the realization only made him more restless. He recrossed his legs and tried to concentrate on what Burden was saying, but nothing came through. He thought again of the dead dog floating down the end-of-summer river with the rest of the garbage of the city, unseen and uncelebrated except by him this very moment. More of the unsung wreckage of summer. He had never actually seen his sister's body when it was found, only heard it described by the state police when it finally floated onto Cuttyhunk Island, across the sound. They had told his parents they were lucky because the tide was right.

He felt like walking now—fast. Running. Running out of Burden's office and down the hall and out of the building. He recrossed his legs again and tried to find the dog, but it had disappeared, swept out of sight by the current, he thought, into the bay and from there alone into the vastness of the night ocean.

Studying the weary features of Burden's face, Seth became deaf to what he was saying as he leaned toward Lindsay, talking exclusively, it seemed, to her.

"You see, when Freud observed beating fantasies in his female patients, he noticed they were formed in several stages. The earliest was characterized by the image 'a child is being beaten.' It soon became clear that the beater was the little girl's father and the victim was the little girl's rival, very often her brother. So, now, the complete form of the little girl's first fantasy is: 'My father is beating my rival because he loves only me.'

"The second version occurs because she feels guilty about her sadistic wish and changes the fantasy to 'I am being beaten by my father.' " He paused and looked hard at her as though he were trying to reckon her thoughts.

"Now the crucial connection, Miss Cooper, the key link between the first stage of the fantasy"—he held up one of his strong womanly hands—"the punishment of the rival—and the second stage"—he held up the other—"the sexualized beating—is a primal scene fantasy. Without this connection between sex and violence—or, rather, this infantile view of sex as violent and brutal—it is unlikely that Jennifer Light would have died in the way she did.

"Maybe you can see now, Conrad," he said, turning in the half darkness to Seth, "why I say that murder, suicide, madness are all corruptions of love." Seth smiled blankly in deaf acknowledgment.

"This is what your readers want to know, Miss Cooper. This is what you should tell them—if you dare." He tilted backward in his chair and gave her one of his Mona Lisa smiles.

"They have the same unconscious primitive curiosity that Jennifer Light had as a little girl. Everybody wants to know what goes on in the parental bedroom. That's *the* mystery of life. There are really only two important mysteries—what happens when we get conceived and what happens when we die—and primal scene fantasies condense both those mysteries. That's why we're all so fascinated by detective stories.

"A murder mystery is a reenactment of a primal scene." He held up his cigar. "With one crucial difference: no guilt or anxiety for the reader." He studied her as he exhaled a long, slow ribbon of smoke. "Your readers, Miss Cooper, can allow themselves to satisfy their unbridled curiosity because they identify with you as the 'detective,' allowed to investigate and intrude without guilt or anxiety."

The office was almost completely in shadow now, and through the crystal evening sky Seth could see the planes taking off and landing at La Guardia. Unaccountably it seemed to him that Burden had won and that he had somehow lost. Lost something—or forgotten something. He was not sure.

"Well, Conrad." Burden had swung away from them again, as though he had suddenly grown tired of the present, like some old people before they die. Caught and held by the clarity of the dusky light, he let the shadowy silence grow. When, finally, he spoke again, it seemed as if he spoke to the river and its currents as they flowed into the ocean. "Are you satisfied? You wanted to know . . . about her. Well, now you do." He turned, and although his face was deep in shadow, Seth fancied that Burden could read his disconsolate thoughts.

"You've had a good shot at this, Conrad. I think it's finished for now." He stood up and threw the end of his cigar into the ashtray. "Let's see what you can do with a live patient."

That was it. She was just another patient now—Jennie Light. Burden had somehow taken *her* away, taken her mystery away. And she didn't need a hero anymore, not even a paper one—only a psychiatrist.

☐ ☐ ☐

"*O*ne last thing." He touched Lindsay's arm. They were standing in the open doorway, Seth smiling grimly, Lindsay expressing bewildered gratitude. "This is a wild idea, I know, but . . ." He shrugged apologetically. "Jennie Light was about two and a half when her brother was born. Tell me, did Mrs. Light have a cesarian section?"

"How did you know that?" Lindsay's eyes narrowed.

"Just a guess," Burden replied with false modesty, smiling as he shut the door behind them.


"*E*nough what?" Seth shouted from the bathroom. Both taps were on full blast, and a wisp of steam drifted out of the crack in the door like some restless spirit in search of deliverance.

"Material, stuff, copy—for the piece." Lindsay stared at herself in the mirror that hung crookedly over Seth's dresser. "Burden was good—helpful, I mean. I can use what he said." She raised her voice. "Some of it, I—"

"What? Some of what? What time is it?"

"Never mind," she shouted. "What a mess," she added, surveying the gloom-ridden room through the mirror. The sound of rushing water from the bathroom suddenly ceased. "Don't you ever make the bed?"

"Make the bed?" She heard the sound of a razor scraping at the sensitive underside of his jaw. "Nurses make beds. If I wanted to make beds, I'd've gone to nursing school." Scrape, scrape. "Christ, nurses don't even make beds anymore. . . . What time?"

"Six-fifteen"—the water roared back to life—"but don't hurry," she said to her image in the mirror. Squinting suddenly, she looked hard at herself, assessing her appearance as though she were an enemy. Plain, she thought, midwestern drab. And flashing a bright smile made it only worse, like something out of an L. L. Bean catalog.

Pushing up the corners of her eyes, she tried an alluring Oriental look. With a sense of growing desperation she pulled open the top two buttons of her white cotton blouse, exaggerating the cleavage.

Glancing sidewise at her profile, she studied herself intently, shook her head, and gave up.

"Almost finished," Seth called over the water. "Be with you in a minute. You won't recognize me—fortunately."

"Don't rush. Not on my account," she said softly, her fingers playing over the chaos of the dresser top. "This thing's like a snake pit," she called.

Surveying the mess—a wild accumulation of laundry, monographs, drug samples, keys, soiled ties, unopened mail—with a certain clinical fascination, she gave it a tentative poke. "God, what's underneath there? I swear, there are things moving down there," she called again.

"Socks mating, probably. Watch it, they get very . . . well, violent when they're . . . you know. How'd you like all that primal scene bullshit?" He turned the water up, releasing another wraithlike puff of steam.

Pushing aside an empty can of stain remover, she picked up a notebook and began leafing absentmindedly through its formula-ridden pages. "I liked it, I guess," she said, flipping to the last written page in the notebook. "Made sense in some peculiar way." The page was dated the day before yesterday, Wednesday, September 30, and she recited the topic for that day in a mocking baritone, "Phenothiazine Derivatives." Running down the page, her eye paused momentarily at each heading: "Indications," "Contraindications," "Dosage," "Side Reactions," "Mechanism of Action."

"Very impressive," she called out, her fingers catching at a thread of paper trapped in the spiral spine of the notebook.

"You haven't even seen me yet."

Tossing the notebook back onto the dresser, she studied the saw-toothed shred of paper she held, and letting it fall, she watched it flutter onto the chaotic dresser top. Leaning forward, she checked the cover of the notebook again. "Did anyone count the pages?"

"What? Louder! Didn't hear." He turned the water down.

"Never mind," she said with a shrug. "When you get out," she called. She picked up the fragment of paper once more, looked at it with interest, and placed it in her handbag. "What are you doing in there, plastic surgery?"

"Be right out. Just one more patch. Sorry, dull blade," he called with forced good humor. Since their meeting with Burden he had been aggressively cheery.

Staring apathetically at her unbuttoned blouse once more, she noticed for the first time a snapshot stuck in the lower left-hand corner of the mirror, hidden behind a massive neurology textbook.

Exhuming it, like an archaeological artifact, from its surrounding chaos, she held the photograph in both hands, close to her face, and moved automatically toward the bedside lamp. Shoving it under the light, she sat down on the edge of the bed and studied it.

It was old and had been around, like a battered suitcase. There were several folds, and one corner was missing. It was a snapshot of Seth and his sister, taken one summer at the seashore. Seth, in shorts and a T-shirt—he couldn't have been more than ten or eleven—looked up at his sister in scrawny boyish admiration. She, a full head taller, had thrown a patronizing arm over his shoulder. She was already womanly and voluptuous, and her dark, irritable eyes suggested a knowledge of her own beauty. In a denim miniskirt and white peasant blouse, she looked as though she'd been roped into the scene.

"I haven't looked at that in years." He reached down and took it from her. "I mean, really looked."

Absorbed, she hadn't heard the cascade of water subside and the bare footfalls behind her. Now, looking up at him, she searched momentarily for the adoring little boy. She studied him, shirtless, solitary, puzzled, caught in the act of wiping soap from his neck and smelling innocently of lime.

"Was it that summer?"

" 'Lonely spirit . . .' " he murmured. " 'Lonely spirit . . .' " he repeated, looking up at the ceiling and closing his eyes. "Christ, I can't remember her epitaph." He pulled his glasses back on as if he expected them to help him recapture what he had lost.

"No, it happened the next year. This one"—he held up the snapshot—"was our last good one together. She was fourteen." He stared into the scene. "It's funny." He stopped and searched Lindsay's face. "I never found out . . . whether she ever liked me." He smiled a quirky smile. "I guess it doesn't matter, does it?"

Rousing himself, he stuck the photo, with obvious care, back
into the corner of the mirror where Lindsay had discovered it. He
stood for a moment or two, looking past it, then turned and finished
dressing.

On the way to Lisa Stone's apartment, Seth remained low-keyed,
staring out the window as Lindsay drove up Third Avenue.

"She was beautiful," Lindsay said, breaking the silence finally.
"Did they ever find out—what happened, I mean?"

He shook his head, "The boy she was with was too scared to
tell the truth. Maybe she had some beer or pot—God knows what.
He said they had an argument and she went off by herself." He
shook his head again and looked straight ahead, up Third Avenue.
"No one knew what happened after that. Whether she fell, how
she hit her head . . ." He shrugged. "Anyway, the Coast Guard
found the body washed ashore on Cuttyhunk the next day. It's
funny"—he turned away again—"about the epitaph—'Lonely spirit'—
my not remembering. It's because I always hated it. I didn't want
to remember her that way, 'Lonely.' "

Turning north onto Park from Fifty-seventh Street, Seth watched
a doorman in a snappy uniform hail a taxicab for a couple in evening
clothes. "I suppose Katie was right."

"Katie?"

"Katie, she wrote the epitaph—my grandmother." He smiled.
"Not very grandmotherly, she was. She was the *original* army brat.
Tough, stubborn, but she loved Elly. Elly was her favorite. I mean,
she loved me, but Elly was her special favorite. When no one could
talk to her, she could. That's where she's buried—Katie's Hill.
That's what we called it because that's where Katie wanted to be
buried—on the farm, next to Martin. They're there now—the three
of them. Martin, my grandfather"—he made a grave with his hands
over his left knee. "Katie and Elly. She wanted to be between the
people she loved the best. She died only a couple of years ago—no,
longer. Four." He was speaking to the window now, to Park
Avenue, to the double-parked diplomatic limousines, to pedestrians
hurrying to dinner parties in the crisp light blue air of dusk.

"The pasture slopes up behind the house to this hill. You can
see the house from the top. Katie always said she'd be able to keep

an eye on things after she was gone. And it faces south so it always gets the sun; she liked that, too. And Elly used to sit up there a lot, next to Martin's grave." He paused, remembering her sitting there in early summer, after school was out and before they went away. She'd never let him come up there with her.

"Anyway, that day—the day she was buried—we all were standing on Katie's Hill for the service. It was one of those hot, lazy Indian summer days, and I wasn't really listening—I guess I didn't want to—and I saw this beautiful golden eagle soaring overhead—*Aquila chrysaëtos.*" He paused and savored the name.

"I don't know, maybe it was a hallucination or some kind of illusion; golden eagles are pretty rare in northern Illinois. I've never seen one since. Anyway, that's what it was, I thought, and then I had the idea that it was Elly up there. Trying to tell me it was her. But I wasn't sure, so I said to myself, If it soars to the left and then comes back and circles over us, I'll know it's her. And that's what it did." He turned to her. "I forgot all about that until I saw her again in the picture. As soon as I saw her, I remembered that eagle—*Aquila chrysaëtos.*" He smiled. "What do you think? Pretty nutty, huh?"

They had reached their destination on upper Park Avenue, an impressive imitation of a Florentine palazzo where Lisa Stone held court.

"I think we're late."

# Chapter

## 15

Lisa Stone was born to rule. Perhaps not to govern, but to rule. And her parties were incontestable demonstrations of that vanishing gift.

The first conquest and most loyal subject of the daughter and only child of I. J. Breslau, a doting multimillionaire father, was I. J. himself. Smiling, he looked down on his daughter's guests with coarse, satisfied lips, from a portrait above the fireplace.

"I.J." Seth nodded up at the portrait. "That's what she calls him. He would've gladly bought her a place in medical school. Christ, he could have bought her the whole medical school." Huddling together, they talked in low tones, like aliens in an alien land. "But she's brilliant, she didn't need it. Jesus"—he pushed the glasses back up on his nose—"she's creamed the top off three departments. Look, see that chap there," he said over the rim of his glass. He directed Lindsay's gaze across the high-ceilinged room toward the library, where, through the doorway, they could see Lisa bending over Joe Burden as though he were some delicious morsel. "The bald, jolly-looking fellow next to Burden, the one who looks like Bacchus? In a couple of years Nobel Prize for sure. The immunoprophylaxis of malaria." He shook his head. "She's incredible." He gave her a tiny salute with his gin and tonic.

"I think I need some wine," Lindsay said with a reptilian blink.

Almost before she could finish uttering the words, Alain, the poet-bartender, had reappeared with another glass for her. Alain, a white-jacketed gaunt young man with sad, intelligent eyes and a European haircut, had welcomed them when they arrived. Seth studied him as he worked his way through the hum and clink of unbroken social pleasure and sensed the secret pride that enabled him to serve the others with such serene humility. He pegged Alain as a Ph.D. candidate in something like comparative literature and wondered whether his services included bedding Lisa down after the party, bilingually, of course.

"Some dump, huh?" Seth said with a wry smile, embarrassed by the secret sense of well-being and excitement he felt in sharing, even momentarily, unambiguous wealth. It was indeed the way Myra Karp had described it—"unconflicted bourgeois." Like I.J. himself, the place was copious, overflowing. Wherever one looked, or stood, or touched, or sat there was voluptuous brown, soft russet, velvet, and velour.

Circulating slowly through the spacious rooms, one pouring into another, they watched Lisa, also voluptuous, whisper concise instructions to maids in black and swirl among her army of guests, marshaling their admiration and allegiance like a great monarch before a battle.

Seth was on his second drink—make it stiff, he had told Alain— and perhaps that was it. Or maybe it was the aroma of sage and dill filling the room or the endless supply of hors d'oeuvres pouring out of the kitchen and carried by generous and attentive messengers to every corner of the kingdom. Perhaps it was the tinkly charm of Gershwin and Jerome Kern played sedately in a distant corner of the living room. Whatever the reasons, his oppressive fatigue and heaviness had disappeared and left him light-headed and amiably forgetful. "Then she told I.J.," he said. "As though the guy were a nifty little sports car—"

"That she wanted young Dr. Stone in her Christmas stocking— just like that," Lindsay said, snapping her fingers. "I wish I had a daddy like that."

"Why not? He was brilliant; he was her cardiology instructor; he was comely enough."

Near the buffet, with its formidable array of chafing dishes, they passed Tom Freeman spellbinding a small group from the immunology lab, this time on Herstedvester, the Danish institution for incorrigible criminals. Lindsay greeted him with a smile, but between his myopia and his lecture he seemed not to recognize her.

"Anyway," Seth went on, "she told Daddy, and he called his personal physician, who happened by the merest coincidence to be the chairman of the Department of Medicine. The net result was a new cardiology lab for the department, a promotion for young Dr. Stone, and wedding bells for Lisa." He clinked glasses with Lindsay and raised his. "To love."

"So where is the comely Dr. Stone? I'd like to meet someone who's brilliant and knows how to mend broken hearts."

"Ah, where indeed?" He hailed a passing hors d'oeuvres tray and studied the situation carefully for a moment or two before settling on a pastry stuffed with crab. "I'm glad you noticed." He popped the tiny aromatic ball into his mouth. "Gone. Poof." He held up his open hand like a magician. "Went off to Washington last year. NIH. Terrific job running their cardiology lab. Soooo . . ."

"So poor Lisa had to choose between going with comely Dr. Stone and staying near doting Papa?"

"So it would appear." He shrugged. "Easy come, easy go. Can't say that about us, eh, Hatchback?" He poked her in the chest.

"And this"—Lindsay looked about her, catching the eye of the piano player—"was her little consolation prize. Ah, the sacrifices of the rich." The piano player, a handsome, dissolute man with a black tie and a hacking cough, gave her a wink and a cynical smile.

As though to celebrate Lisa's good fortune, Seth stooped again, like some scrawny bird of prey, to snare from a passing chafing dish a Swedish meatball soaking in a bubbling dill sauce.

"Boychik," Harvey boomed, "how can I take you anywhere? You're not supposed to shovel it in." He pushed Seth aside. "Dainty. See, like this." Balancing the savory sphere with his little finger extended, like an elephantine ballet dancer, he wolfed it in one gulp and washed it down with a swallow of wine. "There, boychik, like that." He bent forward and kissed Lindsay on the cheek. "How ya doin', Coop? How ya like?" he asked, looking about. "The house that Sure-Lax built. 'No worry, no strain, no pushing, no pain.'" Grinning, he told how I. J. Breslau, a Brooklyn pharmacist, had parlayed the quiet passions and ignominious suffering of constipated men into a fortune. A man with restless dreams and a shrewd eye for his customers' daily torments, he mixed up a palatable concoction of mint and phenolphthalein and coined the slogan that silenced the nagging conscience of a worried nation: "Let Sure-Lax do your duty."

"The old bastard." He nodded to I.J., grinning over the fireplace. "Made millions. Really hit the jackpot in the war." Known to a generation of GIs as green lightning, it eased the way for millions of shy boys who had never used a twelve-seater before.

"The moral of the story, boychik, is never underestimate the economic power of a good crap." He smiled through half-closed eyes and toasted the portrait of I.J. "Watch his eyes move. The fat old *mamzer* is picking out Lisa's next husband."

Lurching forward suddenly, he grabbed Seth's arm. "Boychik, you're coming tonight, right? You and Coop?" He looked around. "Where the hell is she?" He shrugged. "You. You're coming, right?" That pained hound dog look had come into his eyes. "It's a disaster. Curtains for your old buddy." He raised his empty glass with unsteady dignity. *"La commedia è finita."* He grabbed at his crotch all of a sudden. "Excuse me, I have some business of a personal nature to transact."

*H*e found Lindsay alone in the wood-paneled library. Closing the door for privacy, he flopped down on the couch with a groan of deep satisfaction. "Not bad"—he kicked off one of his shoes—a scuffed, deformed loafer—and ensconced himself in the plush softness of the couch—"not bad at all, the life of the mind." He picked up a luxurious art book from the coffee table next to him.

"Did you ever count the pages?" Lindsay asked from behind a desk topped in green leather.

He began flipping through the book, *French Romanticism— Delacroix to Corot.*

"Seth," she said, absentmindedly fingering a book lying on the desk, "those pages—did you by any chance happen to count them?"

"What pages?" he said without looking up. "Funny . . . no such thing." He was studying a Delacroix drawing.

"The diary." She held up a red leather address book with the word "Diary" embossed in gold on its cover and pointed to the word as though he were stupid. "Her diary. Jennie Light's. You said it was a notebook."

"Yes," he said, eyes still glued to the book. "Interesting."

"A spiral notebook, right? That's what you said." She tossed the red leather book back on the desk. "Did you count the pages?"

"Count the pages? Why would I count the pages?" he said, still studying the drawing. "I was reading it. I'm a reader, not a counter." He looked up. "Do I look like a counter? Counters have more fingers than I do. See this?" he said, rising from the couch. He thrust the book toward her. The drawing showed a powerful lion rearing up on its hind legs and locked in a violent embrace with a tigress. "Impossible. Lion—Africa. Tiger—India." He pointed to the picture. "No way! Get it? Primal scene symbolism, *mein* dear." He held the book closer. "How'd you like all that primal scene crap?"

"Never mind that." She shoved the book aside. "Seth, listen. Every notebook has a standard number of pages—fifty, a hundred, whatever. The number is marked on the cover." She began pacing back and forth. "What if Milly McVey wasn't able to hide the diary and the murderer did find it and was mentioned in it?" She fished around in her bag. "And instead of destroying the whole notebook, he tore out the pages that referred only to him"—she held up the shred of paper she had rescued—"and then rehid the book to—"

The door burst open, momentarily trapping Lindsay behind it.

"*Cher!* Lover! Why are you hiding in here?" Lisa flung herself at him, and like a startled infant's, his arms closed around her.

A luscious cloud of green perfume embraced him, and he felt

her soft, large breasts and warm skin. For the moment he was paralyzed, as though he had been injected with a dose of curare.

"Well . . . hello . . ." Lindsay's words were cool and steely, like the rasp of a saber unsheathed. "Glad to see your knee is so much better."

Turning, Lisa smiled one of her famous nonsmiles. "What a nice surprise," she said, allowing her arm to rest casually on Seth's shoulder, as though they were chums. "Miss, ah, what was it? I'm so terrible with names." He felt her playing with the hair at the back of his neck—another dose of curare, robbing him of his will and giving him goose bumps instead.

In a soft silk dress, open to the sternum, she was all sensuous movement and burnished gold flashing in her hair.

With mouth agape and one shoe off, Seth stood like a dazed bull at the end of the corrida.

"Yes, indeed, I remember," Lindsay said emphatically—almost rudely, it seemed to Seth. It roused him.

"Ah, Cooper," he blurted out. "Lisa, this is . . . I'd like you to meet Lindsay Cooper."

"Oh, we've met. I'm sure Dr. Stone remembers, *n'est-ce pas?*"

Seth looked at the two women. Lindsay seemed suddenly angular, plain, belligerent.

"Oh, yes. Yes, I do remember. You were the quiet one in the back seat on our way to that poor girl's funeral. Well, anyway, it *is* a nice surprise to see you again so soon. Seth's so full of surprises these days. Aren't you?" she said, kissing him on the cheek. "And thanks again for your bed the other night. Saved my life." She moved to the door. "I'm yours forever. Call me if *you* ever need something. You, too, Miss Cooper," she added without looking back, and closed the door behind her.

"What did she mean, 'thanks for your bed'?" She didn't wait for his explanation that he wasn't in it at the time. "What did she mean she was surprised? Didn't you bother telling her about me?" Vigorously she pushed her hair behind her ear. With each question she took a step in his direction, as though she were going to hit him, the color rising in her face with each advance. "How could you let her crawl all over you like that in public, in front of me,

as if you were in a"—she groped for words—"a massage parlor?
How could you? How could you stand there and let that . . .
bitch . . ."

She stopped suddenly, her throat constricting. He saw her eyes
brim and reached out. "Hey." He took a step toward her.

"Leave me alone." She pushed him away and slammed out of
the room.

Some of the guests were already saying good-bye as he shuffled
aimlessly in search of comforting and another drink. Alain was
nowhere to be seen, and the maids in black hovered like furies over
the dying buffet table, unresponsive for the moment to the needs of
disconsolate guests. Hoping that it might lead to the butler's pantry
and relief, he wandered off down a long passage. Almost at once
he was cheered by a familiar voice. Unmistakably Harvey's, he
thought at first, and placed it as coming from one of the rooms at
the end of the corridor. He was in the bedroom wing of the apartment,
and for a moment or two the booming voice was drowned by the
copious flush of a nearby toilet.

Arriving at the half-open door, he stopped, suddenly uncertain.
"He knows . . . there's no question about it." The words were
tight and strained, even urgent. The boom was gone altogether, and
the voice was no longer drunk or stupefied. Hovering motionless in
the hallway, Seth could make Harvey out through the crack in the
door, as he paced restlessly to the limits of the telephone cord.

"Because I overheard him say it, goddammit. Listen, you still
have a key, haven't you? . . . Okay, it's in an envelope in my top
drawer. Go and get it, just to be on the safe side, and I'll see you
in twenty minutes." He slammed the phone down.

Seth met him in the doorway. "Harv, I want to talk to you.
It's important." He stretched his arm across to the other doorpost,
barring Harvey's way.

"Sure, boychik, later," he said with a tense smile. I've got to
get down there now and whip my little troupe into shape." He
glanced at his watch and tried to get past Seth. "Forty-five minutes
to curtain time," he said with a tense smile. "Come on, Seth, lemme
go. I'm late. I'll talk to you later."

"Now!"

"Later!"

Red with rage, he grabbed the arm barring his way. With one forceful yank he pulled it aside and strode off down the hall in the direction of the front door.

"Albert Schweitzer! Reverence for life! Bullshit!" Seth shouted after him."

Massaging his arm, he slouched against the wall and remembered a freezing winter morning when Harvey smashed through the door of a bus with his fist after the driver had refused to open it. And that horrendous moment on the stairs in Swift Hall when he tore a paper he had written into bits and flung it in the face of a professor he hated.

"Goddamn ape," he muttered, and decided once again to find his friend Alain.

Bereft and overtaken again by his earlier lassitude, he reentered the living room. Alain was nowhere in sight. Standing unsteadily in the center of the room, he drained the dregs of his glass to dramatize his plight. Still no Alain. Looking dully about, he cursed the indifference of the world.

The music had stopped, and the tide of guests had begun to ebb rapidly now. Behind him he could hear Lisa staging larger-than-life farewells to departing friends, and he thought again of Lindsay. He had probably lost her for good this time.

He spotted her then, across the room, lost in smiling conversation with Joe Burden. God, she was a glutton for punishment, he thought, and slouched listlessly in their direction. Ensconced in the curve of the now-silent piano, they stood in inadvertent intimacy, Burden bent forward, gently touching her arm as though sharing a confidence. Lecherous bastard.

"Hi!" he called, and toasted them heartily with his empty glass.

Nodding, coolly, Seth thought, Burden drew deeply on his cigar. "Just adding a few footnotes to this afternoon." He turned back to Lindsay. "In some sense then the reader must identify with the criminal in a murder mystery."

Christ, more. No end. Thank God. Alain had sailed past, white coat flying. Hailing him, Seth tipped his glass upside down and, with a look of quiet supplication, handed it to him. Alain accepted it noncommittally, almost coldly, and disappeared.

With a vigorous movement signaling intense resolve, he shoved his glasses back up on his nose and tried to focus again on Burden's words.

"The basic difference between detective stories and what we call literature with a capital *L*"—he wrote the letter large with his cigar—"is the degree to which this identification is acknowledged by both the reader and the detective. In a murder mystery like *Oedipus Rex* the detective finally discovers that he himself is the criminal.

He wondered whether Alain would remember or had disappeared from his life forever. Studying Lisa across the room, vast now that it was almost empty, he watched her good-byes to Wertzman, the immunologist. Holding his face in her two hands and laughing, she kissed him on both bearded cheeks. In turn, he embraced her in a great bear hug. Where was Alain? He looked around again and for no reason remembered that he had never said a proper good-bye to Mrs. Scola. Like Alain, he supposed, she, too, had disappeared forever from his life without a proper good-bye. He thought of Elly again— the snapshot—and reckoned that she would have been a beautiful woman now, past thirty. . . .

"But the truth of literature"—Burden made the capital *L* again— "is disturbing, and we don't read *Oedipus Rex* for everyday pleasure. In detective fiction the emphasis is shifted from psychological truth to the game of puzzle solving. The writer connives with the reader and the detective to deny any guilt in themselves, and together they find a scapegoat to bear the burden of guilt."

. . . but in the time warp of his mind she'd always be fifteen, as frozen in time as if she'd been encased in a magical crystal and set free to float forever in outer space. He thought again of the golden eagle and tried once more to recall the epitaph that Katie had written for her. . . .

"That's the pleasure of detective stories: They do the opposite of what psychoanalysis does. They bury guilty feelings."

Now that the show was over, what Seth wanted was confrontation—a chance to set things right again. Closure. That was what he wanted more than anything else that night. But he didn't know it then—before he had it.

What he thought he wanted, as he watched Lindsay through half-closed eyes, was escape, respite, relief from threadbare memories and foolish discontents. Fuzzy thoughts—dulled first by gin and now by sangria, official beverage of the chairman's dinner—made a distinction where there was none, between closure and escape, between taking arms and freedom from torment. A natural mistake for one educated to examine rather than fight.

But it was past eleven, and he had given up trying to be intelligent for the evening—or so Lindsay had told him. That was just before she had accepted Burden's invitation. "May I have the honor, Miss Cooper? As a Freudian, the waltz is the only dance I am permitted."

Ha-ha.

He supposed, as he watched her across the candlelit hospital dining room, that he had no one to blame but himself. He had been silent and preoccupied—she would have said sullen—on the ride back downtown from the party and had been exiled to the back seat so that Burden could sit up front. Her idea, naturally.

Sprawling at the table, now empty—he had just bidden a drunken farewell to Myra Karp and her chubby accountant husband—he welcomed the chance for release. He wanted to be embraced by the noise and flashing colored lights. He wanted oblivion and to sip some more of the warm sickly sweet sangria that he knew was giving him a headache. He was tired of thinking; maybe that's what was giving him the headache. He wanted only to watch and listen and feel his headache grow.

"How ya doin', Doc?" Fontana, looking as though he were about to explode out of the tan suit and natty necktie that imprisoned him, loomed above.

"Fontana, I thought you'd never get here." He smiled stupidly, never quite certain whether his little ironies registered with Fontana. "Never mind. Sometimes I wonder about you, Fontana."

"That's okay, Doc. I wonder about you, too. Ya look like you lost your last friend." He grinned.

"I probably have." Harvey had not yet appeared in the dining room from his earlier comedic triumph. They had missed half of his performance, arriving just in time for a glimpse of Whit singing off key in his adorable white flannels, straw boater, and malacca cane.

"She dances nice," Fontana said, nodding at Lindsay and Burden gliding by. He shoved a chair under himself, straddling it back to front.

"Won't you join us, Fontana?" Seth opened his arms expansively.

"Nice girl, Miss Cooper. She's like Lorraine. You gotta meet her someday, Doc."

"Yeah," Seth said, studying Lindsay. She was smiling as she swayed to Freudian cadences, enjoying herself in the effeminate hands of this wiry little man who talked half the time like a scientist and the other half like a necromancer.

"She's in Philly this weekend. Family. Comes from Philly. You'll get a kick outta Lo."

"Yeah." Seth sipped the warm sangria and stared into the flashing lights, hoping again for early oblivion. Amplified and throbbing, the Viennese waltzes sounded kinky and comic played on electric guitars, bass, and drums by a medical student combo.

"How come you're not out there, Doc? Want some gum?" He shoved a stick in Seth's direction. "I ain't big on dancing either. Never had much time for it. Lo's good, though."

Seth rubbed his left temple. "Headache," he explained with a pained smile.

"That lousy wine." Fontana nodded at the glass in Seth's hand. "Jesus, my little old grandmother made better."

Across the dining room they heard shouts and a ruffle of applause, followed by an overamplified fanfare from the student combo. Harvey had entered, jacket thrown proudly over one shoulder, the other arm raised in triumph, the conquistador.

"Funny guy," Fontana said, watching him strut through the dining room, spreading the germs of his hypomania wherever he went. "He really write all that stuff?" He craned his neck, smiling, as he tracked Harvey's movements. Behind him, bobbing in his turbulent wake, was Pam Price, still dressed in her costume—a white lab coat and fake horn-rimmed glasses—and carrying a bunch of half-dead chrysanthemums. Harvey had arranged to have them delivered to himself as he took his final modest bows. Now he was tossing them one by one to those around the room whom he hated or loved the most—it was hard to tell. Face streaming sweat, eyes glistening, he was like a man in the grip of a high fever. He tossed a flower to Whit Shields. Whit caught it, gave him a hearty wave with his straw hat, and tucked the flower behind the ear of Fiona Drummond, sitting next to him.

"Funny guy," Fontana repeated.

"Very funny." Seth rubbed the bruised place on his arm where Harvey had grabbed it.

"Shields was good, too. D'ya see him? Kind of went over my head, but he was cute—you know what I mean? The soft-shoe routine and the little mustache—cute."

"Deep Thought" the sketch was called, and in an elegant pencil-line mustache and monocle, Whit had poked irreverently at the great Heinz Blauhardt, esoteric founder of self psychology. Even Jonathan Graver smiled.

"Yeah, cute," Seth echoed, but the words were swallowed up instantly by a pulse of music with a disco beat. Someone had sped up the strobe lights now, and the older members of the faculty, taking the hint, returned to their tables to observe with mixed emotions the dances of the young.

Smiling for no reason, Seth watched as Burden and Lindsay strolled to the buffet table and an urn containing thick, vile coffee. His head was throbbing now, pushed by the thunderous rhythm which he could feel coming up from the floor through the soles of his feet into his chest. His suffering was almost complete, he thought, and took another sip of the heavy, sweetish wine.

"Hey, Doc. Looks like you got a good buddy over there." Fontana motioned with his head to a table off to Seth's right where Benson Coles sat Buddha-like. "He's been starin' at ya. Maybe he likes ya. Ya know what I mean?" He winked.

Through the smoke and flashing strobe lights, Coles's face was theatrical—a comic opera villain who had strayed offstage. Which eye, he tried to think. All of a sudden Coles raised his hand and, turning his fingers into an invisible camera, snapped Seth's picture again. He grinned then and turned away.

From somewhere deep within, a pulse of shame and rage surged through him. At last, some long-hidden current of latent energy began to percolate. "Jesus Christ, Fontana, when are you going to do something about that"—he leaned toward the policeman—"creep?" He sat up straight and pushed his glasses up on his nose. "Why the fuck is he still walking around loose? He's a menace. He's a pervert. He's a creep. Christ, you read the diary."

"Pervert."

"You mean he's not a menace?"

"I didn't say that." Fontana spit his gum into the gum wrapper. "Relax, Doc, we're checkin' it."

"You sure take your goddamn time."

"I told you, Doc, we do what we do." He smiled. "We got our ways, same as you."

"But you read the diary. You saw what he did with her, how he used her."

"So he was a freak. So he was a scumbag. That don't mean he punched her head in."

"Jesus, he had the best motive of anyone."

"Hey, Doc, lighten up. I'm here on my own time tonight, not the department's. I'm off. Lorraine's in Philly, and I'm here for the hell of it. So lay off. Besides"—he got up and turned his chair around so he faced Seth squarely—"what the fuck do you know about workin' a case? There's things you gotta do—in the right way, the right order. Boom. Boom. Boom." He made a series of chopping movements with his hand in Seth's direction. "It's not like ya get a whim or something, you know. Like you wake up in the middle of the night with a brilliant idea. There aren't any hotshots on the force. No hotshots! Boom. Boom. Boom." He made the movements again.

His lust for closure had returned. "For chrissake, did you ever take the trouble to count the goddamn pages in her diary?" All of a sudden he had become unzipped, and an urge for action had overwhelmed all other feelings. The headache, the noise, the lights, everything began to work in the opposite direction, as though a magnetic field had suddenly been reversed. He wanted action; he wanted closure. And if it couldn't be with Coles, then it would be with Fontana.

"Why, hotshot?"

"Never mind," Seth said scornfully. "Drop it." With a tight smile he turned away.

"Hey, Doc, you shoulda been a cop"—Fontana stood up—"you got no imagination. That's the one thing we know how to do good—count. Two pages missing, hotshot. The killer's either a very dumb bastard or a very smart bastard. You tell me which, hotshot." He adjusted his jacket with dignity and buttoned it. "Join the force, Doc. Only lighten up a little bit first."


"**N**ow, goddammit, talk!" The steady breeze off the river made the air bracing and helped him focus.

"Did you see it, boychik? It was beautiful, gorgeous." Still sweating with excitement, Harvey tore his jacket off and slung it over the terrace railing. "Fiona was gorgeous, Pammy was gorgeous, even Shields was gorgeous—had that nice warm, plastic quality. I tell you, boychik, it was great. Better than Chicago, and *that* was great. Admit it, boychik." He poked Seth in the chest. "Admit it." He took a deep, triumphant breath of the cooling night air.

"Cut it out." Seth stepped back defensively. "Jesus, get serious."

"What for, Seth, baby? Laugh and the world laughs with you." With a broad grin he leaned back, spreading his arms Christ-like against the bronze railing that bordered the terrace. "Why'd you drag me out here? I thought maybe you wanted to share your old buddy's last night of glory. A touching moment of intimacy, right, boychik?"

Seth had pried him loose from Pam Price at the buffet table— a low-budget spread of cold cuts and tacky salads prepared by the hospital dietitians—and bulldozed him out the French doors and onto the brick terrace without explanation, almost wordlessly.

"Wait till Sadie hears. She'll love it. Vindicated! My comic genius!" He reached into his jacket for a celebratory cigar. "God, that Vibes number was good. She was terrific, wasn't she—Pammy, I mean?" He bit the tip of the cigar off—a Monte Cristo, his best—and spat it over the parapet onto the light midnight traffic of First Avenue. "I really should expand that Vibes number, maybe add some music."

"It was disgusting. 'Gratuitously slimy and chauvinistic' Lisa called it." He quoted the words slowly, with obvious relish, articulating each one precisely, as much to test the doubtful state of his reflexes as to drive home his point.

"Bullshit! It was brilliant." Harvey puffed his cigar into a fierce glow. "Hey, boychik, why are you giving me all this grief? This is your old buddy. Here, have a Monte Cristo. Celebrate your old buddy's glory." He pushed a long brown cigar at him. "After all, I couldn't have done it without your unflagging encouragement and support. Right, old buddy?" He grinned fiercely.

"You know goddamn well why." He pushed the cigar aside, and turned away, back toward the music and noise coming from the dining room. In the darkness a bus ground its way slowly, like a fat old woman, northward up First Avenue.

"For Christ's sake, boychik, what do you want from me?"

"I want you to cut out this stupid charade." He turned unsteadily to face Harvey again. "You owe me some goddamn answers."

"Bullshit," Harvey snapped. "I don't owe you answers. I don't even owe Sadie any answers, and she's my mother." He turned northward, as though he were suddenly interested in Canada, and took a furious puff on his Monte Cristo. "Jesus, you are one helluva royal pain in the ass." He turned back, facing Seth squarely now. "It's still this murder bullshit, isn't it? Talk about charades, you're the goddamn comic on this team. When are *you* going to stop this crap?" He smashed the bronze railing with the flat of his hand. "There's nothing I have to or want to tell you."

"You see, you're doing it now." Seth smiled a patronizing smile. "You've been acting like a goddamn nut case for the past month— how about that for openers?"

"I don't know what the fuck you're talking about."

"Okay, genius, I'll make myself irresistibly clear. You lied to

me on Labor Day. Why? You said you were going to spend the
night out on the Island. You didn't. You slept at the apartment
while I took your midnight shift—the night Jennie Light was
murdered. And then you lied to me again—the next morning at the
hospital. *Buddy!*

"Two." He raised his fingers in a victory sign. "You told me
that Jennie Light came home from Fire Island with Silk. How did
you know unless you were there yourself?

"Three. You know goddamned well Lindsay has been breaking
her ass trying to do this story, but every time I've asked you about
Jennie Light you've stonewalled it. Why?

"Four. I'll skip the subtler forms of your madness and mention
only the black moods and rages, the veiled threats and Cassandra-
like warnings to me to stay out of this thing—or else." He leaned
forward, almost losing his balance. "Or else what?

"Five." He thrust his five fingers toward Harvey like a policeman
stopping traffic. "Not three hours ago"—he looked at his watch—
"four. Not four hours ago I heard you conspiring with someone—
you remember, when you used your comic genius so persuasively."
He rubbed the bruise on his arm again. "It was about an envelope.
Hidden somewhere. Where was it?" He put his finger to his head
and pretended to think. "Oh, yes. Your top drawer, wasn't it? and
X, your . . . accomplice. You know, the other buddy. The one
you keep in reserve in case you run out of buddies, which you are
doing at a very rapid rate. So X was supposed to get this little
critter, the envelope, 'Just to be on the safe side.' I think your exact
words." He poked his glasses up on his nose. "Now what the fuck
was that all about? What was in the goddamn envelope?"

He took a deep breath of cool air and waited for the fog in his
head to clear, but it didn't. He worked at keeping his words crisp.
"Now I ask you, buddy, in the face of all that, who but a first-
class naive schmuck like me would've waited this long?

"This is my last night with this. I'm finished with it, and I
want an explanation! Either we're friends or we're not. And if we're
not, I want to know now. Fontana's in there"—he nodded toward
the French doors—"and I can tell him what's on my mind."

Harvey turned away and blew a great cloud of smoke at the

survivor stars—at one in particular, it seemed. Then, throwing his jacket over his shoulders, grandly, like an artiste, he walked slowly, thoughtfully, to the north end of the terrace, his shoes making a gritty sound as they ground the soot into the surface of the brick. The terrace swept around two sides of the building in an L. The long, north-south leg, running seven stories above First Avenue, could be seen easily from the dining room, except at the north end, where it turned east. That leg of the terrace, which ran about ten yards toward the river above Thirtieth Street, was narrower and blind to the dining room.

Standing in the angle of the L, Harvey leaned over the railing and flicked a disk of white ash from the glowing end of his cigar. He watched it as it fell to the deserted, dimly lit side street below, transformed in its descent into a fine powder by the river wind.

Still leaning against the rail, he half turned to Seth. "C'm'ere," he said quietly. Even though his face was in shadows, Seth knew he was smiling. "C'm'ere, boychik." The red glow of Harvey's cigar waved him on, signaling stop and go at the same time.

His footsteps made the same unpleasant gritty sound, and as the disco music receded behind him, he heard an eighteen-wheeler shift into low gear on its way north up First Avenue and into the New England night, headed for sleeping Hartford or Providence or Boston or Woods Hole.

"Seth," Harvey said with that old undergraduate warmth that had disappeared recently, and threw a comradely arm around him. Taking in a deep draft of the night, he glanced up at the stars for a moment. Then, with a smile, he exhaled and bent forward over the parapet, his inertia carrying Seth with him. Together they stood watching the light traffic below and the buildings of the medical school across the street. Silent, thoughtful, Harvey seemed to be studying each lighted window for signs of life.

Smiling then, he gave Seth a little hug and leaned toward him as though he were going to kiss him on the cheek.

"Boychik, believe me you're definitely not a first-class schmuck." He stood up, and a puff of blue smoke came out of his mouth. "You're lucky if you make third-class. Ever since this whole thing started, you've been walking around with your head up your colon. Sigmoid we should call you. You turn facts into shit!

"Let's start with that last little item." He walked restlessly down the terrace a few paces. "The 'conspiracy.'" He pointed at Seth with the Monte Cristo. "What the fuck was that paranoid comic strip mind of yours thinking? What were you doing sneaking around like that, eavesdropping on decent, law-abiding people? You're like some fucking glandular case. You never grew up." He turned and walked away, exasperated, then turned again. "I happened to be talking to Pammy Price, who happens to be the only person who's given me any real help or encouragement on this show, *buddy*. And maybe I was talking urgently. So what? I'm an urgent person. That's what makes me lovable.

"Furthermore, if you were able to transcend your incredible narcissism and grandiosity for one tiny moment, you might realize that we were not talking about you, alas, but our poor wooden friend with the chiseled features. Pamela, being conscientious—perhaps to a fault—was worried that Golden Boy didn't know the new addition to his number. And I told her that—quote—just in case—close quote—there was a copy of it in an envelope in my top drawer. Got all that, sleuth, or do you want me to go over it again?" He walked to the edge of the terrace again and looked down.

A bus pulled up to the hospital bus stop, and he watched a fat old black lady in a nurse's uniform board it. She was coming off the four-to-twelve shift and she heaved herself onto the bus platform with difficulty, bone tired. He could see her through the big front window of the bus, picking carefully through her change for the fare.

"You're right, *boychik*," he said, still watching the old black lady make the exact fare, "I did lie to you that day. I *was* in town the night of Labor Day. I spent the night with Pammy at the apartment. I'd just started seeing her." He glanced at Seth with a scowl. "As you fucking midwestern prudes would put it, and since she's shy, she asked me to keep it quiet. I happen to like Pam Price, red eyes, allergies, and all." He glared at Seth. "I didn't tell you about it because it was none of your fucking business.

"And you're right, I did stop off at Silk's place that day, on my way back from Montauk. I spent the day, and we all left his place together that evening. She went with them, and I came on alone. Paul was okay, you know." Turning away, he leaned on the heavy bronze railing and clasped his hands in front of him as though he were about to pray.

"You know, Seth, there are some women who are so beautiful that everything else just seems to fade away. It's their skin, maybe. There's something special about it. And their eyes, violet, maybe, and clear—I don't know." He paused and studied his hands. "I never knew a woman like that, I don't think I ever really saw a woman like that, until I met Jennie Light. She was like that. There was something about her that—well, just went beyond ordinary good looks. She just stopped you dead.

"When I first met her, she made me feel like a kid, a stupid, bumbling kid. She also liked me, or at least I thought she did. I guess I was funny and made her laugh, maybe I made her a little less self-conscious, I don't know.

"That was last year. You were still getting it together in Chicago. Anyway, I thought she liked me, I mean, really liked me. Or maybe I was deluding myself—I do that, don't I, boychik? Who knows? Anyway, last summer that's all I could think about. She was on my mind all the time, and I suppose I was kidding myself that something would come of it."

He paused and looked past Seth, who had moved next to him at the railing. A breeze from the river fluttered the skirt of his jacket, and he took another huge gulp of air. He let it out slowly, almost reverently, and looked down again at his hands. His cigar had grown quite cold, robbed of its life by reminiscence and regret. "Something. I don't remember now what it was. To sleep with her? Yeah, I suppose so; who wouldn't? Marry her? Yeah, I suppose so; I guess I would've done anything she wanted.

"You probably wouldn't understand this, boychik; it's different with you. Selma and I were in the middle of the divorce, and I was feeling like a reject anyway, kind of like Quasimodo without the bells.

"But the point is, she didn't want me. She didn't want anything."

He looked up at the survivor stars for some measure of corroboration. "Yeah, she did want something. If she wanted anything, it was to disappoint. To be loved and to disappoint."

"Look, I'm sorry . . . for butting in—" Seth put his hand on Harvey's shoulder.

"Oh, for Christ's sake!" Harvey yanked himself away. "Don't sentimentalize it. I was stupid and crazy. And she was wacko, out of her mind. A space cadet. She didn't know what the hell she wanted except to have men sniffing around her like a pack of dogs. She was screwing around—Graver mostly—but there were other guys, too," he added bitterly.

"She didn't deserve what she got, but I felt like doing it to her myself plenty of times. She was a goddamn ice maiden, a beautiful, supremely beautiful ice maiden.

"I'm sorry she died that way, but I'm not surprised." He said the last coolly, like a surgeon after a hopeless operation. For a few moments they watched in abstracted silence as a helicopter made its transit across the night sky from one great airport to another. "I liked her anyway." He gave a great, sad sigh. "I suppose you get to like anyone who laughs at your jokes."

He noticed his dead cigar and shrugged.

"As for you, you third-rate schmuck, I tried to warn you off her." He fumbled for some matches. "I don't know. Everybody who ever tried to help her got hurt. I tried; Milly McVey tried; Silk tried. People broke their hearts trying to help her. It never worked. Forget about her, she's someone else's story, not yours. You're all mixed up.

"Here, boychik, have a cigar." He pushed a long dark Monte Cristo at Seth like a consolation prize. "Let's forget all this shit."

The match flared and danced for a moment or two as they puffed away. Then, caught by a gust of river wind, it flickered and was gone. "Remember, boychik," Harvey said quietly, holding up the spent match. *"'La commedia è finita.'"*

*B*ack in the dining room their ways parted. "Remember—*finita!"* He waved his big cigar and turned in search of his delicate red-eyed sweetheart.

Maybe for him, Seth thought. He drew deeply on the cigar. It was acrid and harsh in his mouth, and he hated it; but without knowing why, he drew deeply again and instantly felt giddy. He wanted to rouse himself, scourge himself maybe. It couldn't be over. That's exactly what he didn't want. How could it be? Was he just supposed to forget Milly McVey's broken face, or the blood he couldn't keep from coming out of Lindsay's head and spreading over her honey-colored hair, or the rasping threat in his ear before he blacked out, or Jennie Light lying there in the dust, looking surprised and small? They were stuck forever in his craw, these sights and sounds. How was he supposed to vomit them out of his life and go on as usual? How was he supposed to pretend that he wasn't choking on these fishbone memories?

No, it wasn't over. He drew again on the vile cigar. Not yet.

He spotted Lindsay finally. Squinting through the haze of music and half darkness, he saw her across the dining room alone at their table, looking abandoned. Lost in thought, she sat with her chin in her hand. In the distance she seemed vaguely sad. He knew that look and loved it. Suddenly he wanted to take her home, pull the shades down, and spend the rest of the weekend in bed with her.

Closure. Resolution. Release. In the fuzziness of his brain he knew that was what he needed. Some kind of primal scene, he thought, and smiled at his own little joke. He headed for Lindsay to tell her more of what he knew about the subject. The unexamined primal scene was, after all, not worth having. Listing slightly to the left, he made his unsteady way toward her.

Suddenly he was yanked around as though he'd been caught in a machine. "Hey! For chrissake! Watch it with that thing."

"Old man!" Whit Shields blinked at him amiably. "A sight for sore eyes." Whit, sprawling languidly across three chairs, had hooked him around the forearm with the handle of his malacca cane and was reeling him in.

"Yours or mine, Golden Boy?" Taking a step or two in Whit's direction, he uncoupled himself and, frowning, pushed the cane back at Whit. He had never seen the humor in physical jokes.

"Yours, old man, yours. Mine are healthy and clear. Come join the players in our little comedy." He put his straw boater on Fiona's head with a little tap on the crown and set it at a rakish angle. She had done yeoman service, as she was fond of putting it—many times—at the piano during the musical numbers. She wasn't good, but she was plucky and loud, like a kindergarten teacher. At the moment she was leaning against Whit, giggling to herself.

"Sethy," she said with difficulty, slurring the name. "Where've you *been?*" As though he'd somehow missed an appointment with her. "I want to *dance* with you." She pouted for a moment and then gave him a silly grin.

"Not tonight, hon. I don't think either of us'd make it. Where's old Avi? I understand he was a dancer before he took the cloth." He smiled sympathetically.

"Join us, old man," Whit called over the noise and music. "Plenty of champers—compliments of Aunt Gretchen. Marcus!" he called across the table. The music had increased in pitch and tempo, and someone had turned the strobe lights up so that they all were characters in a silent movie or a nightmare now. "The booze, if you please." Mark reached into an aluminum bedpan packed with ice and pulled a dripping champagne bottle from it.

Receiving the champagne, Whit waved it under Seth's nose. "For us clowns really, but you'll qualify, old man. Marcus! Glass, if you please."

Mark picked up a half-empty tumbler, sloshed the remains into the bedpan, and handed it across the table.

"Lovely, lovely booze," Fiona burbled, and took the glass that Whit had poured. "Cheers!" she shouted to Seth, and began singing "I Could Have Danced All Night" through the crescendo of rock music that filled the room.

"How about it, old man? Plenty more." He waved the bottle again and grinned. "Blanc de blanc. Not bad." In the near darkness and din, dressed from another life, peering through his monocle and twitching his pencil-line mustache, he was no longer golden, no longer princely, only alien and melodramatic.

"Sorry, Golden Boy. Can't keep a friend waiting, even for blanc de blanc."

"Of course, the lovely Lindsay. Listen, old man." He hooked Seth's arm with the cane again, and drew him closer. "The other night, at Lino's, silly business. Sorry. Forget it, will you? Stupid, really."

"Forgotten."

"Bygones?" Whit held out his hand and blinked innocently.

But there was no answer. Seth remained motionless, as though suddenly trapped in a negative force field—a lapse he knew even then he'd regret.

"Bygones?" Whit repeated, louder, assuming that the music had drowned his earlier plea. His hand remained extended, and as he smiled, his little mustache twitched again.

Seth's body had known before his mind—registering the whole time he'd been standing there—and finally it made him sick to his stomach. And though it all happened within the compass of three heartbeats, for him it seemed an interminable delirium of time: three hours; three years; three lifetimes. Then the nausea came. It welled up from the latent spaces within him, where fear and excitement waited for moments like this. Again he felt the disco beat pulsing up through the soles of his feet into his chest.

"You all right, old man?" Whit asked with an insincere smile— par for Whit.

"There was a young man with aphasia/Whose name was Conrad, I'll wagia . . ." Fiona burbled, and waved the straw boater.

"Fine." He touched his abdomen. "Nothing like a little nausea to make one regret." Oh, Christ, I'm falling apart, he thought. He grabbed Whit's hand and pumped it vigorously.

"You don't like them, old man." He pointed to his shoes with the malacca cane and pretended to look crushed. "But they're family treasures, old man." He waggled the ancient black-and-white wing tips at Seth.

"The shoes? Oh, yeah. Pretty nifty, Golden Boy. It's this cigar— Harvey's." He made a sour face and tossed the vile brown body into an ashtray on the table. "Look, I've got to go."

"Ah, yes, the adorable Lindsay. She's too good for the likes of you, old man."

"Not to worry, Golden Boy—bygones."

"Tell her I adore her," he called after Seth.

On rubber legs he made his way across the dining room, threading his way between tables, reminding himself to smile and greet where necessary. Once or twice he felt light-headed and had to steady himself on a table edge. Finally, he flopped into a chair next to Lindsay and loosened his collar. "Jesus!"

"My God, you look awful. Where've you been? You all right?"

Leaning toward her, he put a finger to her lips. "Shhh, just listen for once." The music slowed and softened. Thank God, he thought. His headache had returned and brought friends, and he was having trouble keeping track of his thoughts. He rubbed his forehead. "I saw them," he said quietly. "Shhh, just listen," he repeated. "The shoes. Scott Fitzgerald. Exactly the way I remembered. Black and white, wing tips, perforations—everything. Exactly. Only it's not Fitzgerald; it's Whit. They're his."

"What do you mean?" she said almost angrily.

He rubbed his head again. Somebody had turned the strobe lights down to a walk and signaled the orchestra to start on another incongruous round of Viennese waltzes.

Without looking up, he continued. "I know it sounds crazy. But I'm sure about the shoes. It's them, that night in the cafeteria, my dream. No, don't turn around! I think he knows already."

"You can't mean—"

"That's the point. I don't know, goddammit. Let me think." He pulled his tie off, as though that had somehow been keeping him stupid, and stuffed it into his coat pocket.

"He could be, why not? He was there that night. On duty before I came on." He shook his head. "But does it make any sense? It's got to make some sense. Christ, the world isn't crazy. People are crazy. But the craziness has to make sense." That was his father talking, he knew. His father was there, standing over his shoulder, and maybe old tight-assed Pasteur, demanding some rational cause, some working hypothesis, and he had none.

His heart was pounding now, and he watched, detached, the tremor in his own hand as it fidgeted with a forgotten teaspoon. He tried again to focus his attention. Think! Think, goddammit! Maybe he hadn't seen the shoes that night but somewhere else on some other occasion when Whit had worn them, an occasion he'd somehow forgotten. Maybe all this was more of his penchant for melodrama, overheated imagination, dream bullshit—paper hero stuff. He slumped backward suddenly and seemed to fade like a tired child.

Lindsay studied him a moment, then kissed him. "Hey. You calm down." She kissed him again. "Hear?"

His heart slowed, and with fresh resolve he began to polish his glasses with the fat end of the tie from his pocket, as though clean lenses were the key to clear thinking. Again he tried to parse out the complex grammar of fact and fancy.

"Ah, the fair Lindsay." Whit loomed out of the darkness over them like the prow of a ship. "I've come to rescue you from this nauseous man, my dear. You deserve better." He smiled one of his glass smiles—brittle and transparent—and watched her eyes.

Oh, Christ, what an idiot! What a stupid fool he was. Seth dug the teaspoon into the palm of his hand until it hurt. Of course, he shouldn't have told her. She couldn't help it, glancing at the shoes. And of course, Whit had seen it, the merest flicker of her eyes, and had known. Now it was just a matter of cat and mouse. He was grinning broadly.

"You like?" he was asking her, lifting his creamy white flannel trousers over the shoe tops for her to savor them. "They're rather witty, I think, don't you?" He looked down at them. "Belonged to the Robber Baron himself. Made for him by the great René Bougie, cobbler to the kings of Europe." He looked up and smiled one of his famous old irresistible smiles, and he was the Golden Boy again. "Your feet were nowhere in those good old days if they were not in Bougie's shoes, Lindsay, my dear. Nowhere.

"Now"—he reached down suddenly and took Lindsay's hands in his—"I'll show you how they dance, the shoes of René Bougie." With one powerfully persuasive movement, he coaxed her to her feet. "This depressing man"—he blinked good-naturedly at Seth—"with his foolish preoccupations has bored you long enough."

With one hand leading her and one pressing at the small of her back, he swept her toward the empty terrace to the music of disarming chatter and amusing promises. When they reached the door to the terrace, Lindsay turned, and her eyes said, This time, take care of me. *Please.* She waved and he nodded.

Leaning forward, he peered onto the darkened terrace and satisfied himself that as long as Whit did not take her to the north end— the blind end—he could monitor their movements well enough from where he was.

Whit danced almost as well as he fenced, with mastery and grace, and Seth acknowledged sourly that they made an extraordinarily handsome couple. As they turned and wheeled in the half dark, the possibility that Whit could be anything but what he was— a Golden Boy—seemed to recede into the darkness of the sleeping city beyond the terrace. For a moment he forgot the shoes and the three murders and watched them with unqualified pleasure.

Suddenly he was on guard again as they edged northward. She had no way of knowing, he thought, that she would be out of his sight at the end of the terrace.

Twisting around, he scanned the room for Fontana and spotted him finally at the buffet table drinking coffee with Tom Freeman. His back was to Seth. He checked the terrace again. They had drifted south again and were in full view.

Settling back, he thought of Fontana. What could he tell him? What was there to tell? "More dream bullshit, Doc," he'd say with a patronizing smile. "Shoes? C'mon, Doc, you gotta be kidding."

Was there one single unambiguous fact to start with? One really credible piece of evidence he could shove into Fontana's meaty face and say, "Here, you big dumb ox, look at this and tell me no!"

Riffling through the ragged, disordered card file of his brain, he stopped at various entries and discarded them one by one. He tried to remember what Burden had said that day at lunch. Did it fit, what he'd said about the criminal psychopath? ". . . he can pass as a perfectly stable and even attractive personality . . . charming and pleasant to be with." Whit to a T.

They were drifting north again, it seemed to him, as he watched Whit spin out clever anecdotes. Lindsay was frightened. He could tell from the stiff way she held her body and the distance she put between herself and Whit.

For no reason his anxiety suddenly intensified. The diagnosis, he thought, Christ, what if it wasn't criminal psychopath? What if it was something else—some kind of latent psychosis? A psychopath wouldn't do anything he couldn't get away with. And there was no way now in front of a hundred people. But what if he *was* psychotic and didn't, couldn't care? What if he just had to do what his inner voices told him? Idiot! He dug the spoon into his hand again.

Suddenly his view was cut off by a pair of tight-fitting jeans.

"Man, I been lookin' for you all day."

"Yeah? Hey, move it, Jonesie." He peered around Mark to keep visual contact with the terrace. They had stopped, and Whit was pointing heavenward. The great helmsman, with his "heart of stone and water from the Skagerrak" in his veins had found a captive audience for his navigational exploits. She was actually smiling— plucky lady.

"Hey, listen, Doc, I gotta talk to you."

"Not now, Jonesie. I'm busy."

"It's important." Mark leaned toward him from the other side of the table.

"What is it, more words?" he asked without looking up. "Save it till Monday."

"I've *got* to talk to you."

"Jesus!" He glared at Mark. "Okay, talk!"

"I—I can't. Listen, Doc, I'm scared. I got somethin'. It's about him." He glanced over his shoulder at the terrace and looked worried. "Whit. He's a brother, man, but this is somethin' different. I don't even wanna touch it. You *gotta* come and see it."

"For chrissake, Mark, what the fuck are you talking about?" He had stopped watching Lindsay.

"I found 'em today, this afternoon, upstairs in the gym—in the closet."

"What, goddammit, what?" He had grabbed Mark's arm and was shaking him.

"I—I don't know. Pieces of paper, pages, I guess. They fell outta Whit's book. I dropped it by accident, and they fell out. I guess he forgot the book; it was wrapped in an old towel. I don't know."

What was it Whit had called him ". . . Teller of tales . . . at least half of them true." Christ, which half now.

"Listen to me, Mark." Seth peered through the dim light at him, trying to read between the lines of his face and feelings. The words had said fear, but the eyes were darkened, hooded. "Describe the pages. What did they look like?" He glanced out to the terrace. Whit was taking them northward again, this time dancing a slow fox-trot. Lindsay looked relaxed, almost as though she were enjoying herself, as though he had cast one of his golden spells and made her forget. "Think," he commanded Mark. "What did they look like?" Suddenly Mark was no longer an interruption, a distraction, but the central focus, the holder of the keys to the mystery.

He shrugged. "I don't know, just pages. Like out of a notebook. Tore out—ya know what I mean? About yea big." He made a rectangle with his fingers about the size of a steno pad.

"What was on the pages?"

"Writin'."

"What color?"

"Man, I don't know. Green, I think. It was personal stuff, you know. A lotta crazy stuff about him." He nodded in the direction of the terrace. "Whit . . ."

"Shit, the diary." Until that moment, he realized, he hadn't *really* believed in his own theory. Hadn't really believed in the possibility that *his* colleague, *his* friend could have actually hurt, inflicted pain and mutilation with his own hands. He sank back in his chair. That's how stupid and naive he'd been. "Go and get the pages, Mark."

"No way. I ain't touchin' those pages. It's that crazy girl, ain't it, the murdered kid? No way, man. Leave me out of it."

"Shit!"

On the terrace they had stopped again to talk, just barely in view. A match lit up Whit's face as he inhaled from his ivory holder, and before it was extinguished, Seth knew what had to be done.

Whit wasn't psychotic. He was playing out a masterful game of concealment, and for the time being, as long he and Lindsay remained apart, no harm could come to either of them. Then he remembered that look, her unspoken plea, and his unspoken promise— and all the people he hadn't taken care of.

What if he was wrong?

His mind was all over the place now, and there didn't seem to be any time left. In two minutes he could be back with the pages. In two minutes he'd be shoving them in front of Fontana. "Here, you big dumb ox. Look!"

"Let's go," he said.

## Chapter

# 16

"Come on, let's go. Move." He squinted at his watch in the dim
light of the deserted corridor. Almost two minutes had elapsed since
they'd slipped away from the party below. Mark, fumbling inter-
minably with the lock on the gymnasium door, at last had it open,
and Seth shot past him into the cavernous darkness.

Suddenly even the dead, crepuscular light from the corridor was
gone as the heavy door slammed shut. Unable to see anything at
all now in the windowless dark, he pulled up, breathing heavily,
hands on hips. "Come on, come on. Where'd you say it was?" He
peered off to the right in the direction of the equipment closet. The
lock snapped shut on the heavy door and vibrated in the vault of
his memory. "Christ, what's with you? Stop screwing around with
the door and turn on the goddamn lights."

There was no response, only the darkness swallowing up the
echo of his commands. He heard his own heavy breathing and cocked
his head to listen for some movement. "The lights. Turn on the
goddamn lights."

Silence.

His throat constricted suddenly, for no reason, and he had to
cough.

Walking slowly, almost casually, he found the door handle and
tried it. Locked. "Is this some kind of stupid joke?"

Rattling the door again, he suddenly felt the blood rising in his face. At this hour he knew there was nobody on the eighth floor, and no one was likely to be there until morning.

"Mark, if this is a gag, it's not funny." He spoke reasonably, in measured tones, as one would to a wayward child. "If you've got something to show me, let's see it and get back downstairs."

"It's no gag, Doc." Mark's voice was behind him, and he wheeled around. "It's for real." The tone had changed. It was all wrong, no longer appealing, no longer pleading. "It was the shoes," he said softly. "I knew you must've caught somethin' that night, but I didn't know what."

"I don't know what the fuck you're talking about." His heart was pounding now.

"Man, you practically had a shit hemorrhage when you saw those shoes tonight. Then I knew."

"What shoes? What the hell are you talking about?"

"Don't bullshit me, man. You know. *I* was wearing 'em that night. You see, like Whit says, they're shoes fit for a king. You feel like someone for a change. I like it—Whit's stuff. And he lets me, like this jacket"—there was a faint blur of movement, and the safari jacket he'd been wearing landed at Seth's feet—"and this tie"—he heard the tie snapped off; stream of sweat poured down from under Seth's arms—"and this shirt"—there was a rustle of cloth—"and his gold lighter." Seth heard a shoe drop and then another shoe. His head was pounding now, throbbing.

"See, man, you're on my turf now." From somewhere off in the whirling darkness the voice teased him. "My world, Dr. Seth, and I'm watchin' you, so you be real nice now." The voice came from somewhere up above him on the running track.

Backing away, he searched the blackness, but with no cues from the surroundings he was like someone in a sensory deprivation experiment. Disoriented, he tried to listen for movement, but the sounds he was making—the throbbing in his head, the labored breathing—were too loud.

"There ain't no place to hide, Doc." The voice came from yet another direction. "I know every piece of wood in this place. Every squeak. There ain't no place for ya."

"Jesus, Mark, what do you want?" He was shouting, and worse, he heard *himself* pleading.

"What do I want, Dr. Seth? I want you." The voice, cool, taunting, was closing in on him. "Then I don't have to worry no more. With you gone, there ain't no connection between me an' her."

Backing away from the oncoming voice, he blurted out, "I'm not the only one." His mind was all over the place now, and suddenly he couldn't think. Only Lindsay knew. Sweat was pouring down his chest and back now, and tearing his jacket off, he was able finally to wrench his mind away from her. "Fontana! He knows!"

"You're jiving me, man," the voice said with a smile. "I don't like white doctor shit. And I don't like you, Dr. Seth." The voice was on top of him now.

In clumsy desperation he lurched backward and slipped on the polished floor. Falling to one knee, he missed the full impact of a powerful kick, catching it instead just above the left ear—a glancing blow. It sent him sprawling, and he fell heavily on his right elbow and face. A stab of pain shot up and down his right arm. He groaned, and for a moment his right hand didn't work at all.

Scrambling to his feet, he began to run, wildly, in any direction, sliding, slipping, falling, his arms windmilling like a blind man's, until he found, finally, the cold safety of the tile wall and slumped against it.

"Animal, you fucking wild animal!" he roared at the blackness, to no one, and knew instantly he'd made a mistake. Shut up, he told himself, and move. Quickly he pulled off his shoes and socks and began to pad along the perimeter of the gym, hugging the wall closely.

"Sure I'm an animal. I'm a black baboon. I'm a gorilla. I'm an ape. You ain't the first, Dr. Seth." This time the voice came from across the gym and to his right. He reversed his field and began to move to the left, inching his way. "I know where you are, Dr. Seth. I can hear your lily-white heart beatin' away over there."

"Then why don't you kill me? What are you waiting for?"

"I'm just havin' a little fun. Can't blame me for havin' a little fun." His voice was grinning. "I'm gonna piss on you first. Like they pissed on me. Then I'm gonna break you up piece by piece till you're all in parts like a slimy white chicken in the supermarket. Then I'm goin' to stuff what's left in that air vent over there." Now the voice had ascended and was again on the running track above and off to the left. Seth backtracked and began to move in the opposite direction again. He felt the warm, salty taste of blood in his mouth. He must have gashed the inside of his cheek. He explored the swollen laceration with his tongue.

"They won't find ya till you stink up the place, and by then, man, I'll be a million miles from here. Africa. Korea maybe. I got friends. I got brothers all over, man. You better believe it. When you got a black belt, you got brothers everywhere."

Silently, holding his breath, he slid away from the voice. Keep talking, he thought, keep talking. He shook his right hand to wake it up. Three fingers were numb and felt weak. Nerve damage, he knew. Ulnar nerve—when he fell on his elbow.

For the first time in his life he wanted a weapon. Anything. "We must reason together," his father would say when the dinner conversation turned to issues of war and peace, force and persuasion.

His belt. He unhitched it quickly and hefted the heavy brass buckle. Maybe, he thought. He grasped the tail end of it as tightly as he could with his two working fingers and readied himself. His shirt was soaked with sweat now, and he pulled it over his head and let it fall into a soggy heap. How to stay alive. Let us reason together, Mark, old man. He tried again to make the numb fingers work.

"You was lucky back there, Dr. Seth. But no more. See, I gotta teach *you* somethin' before I go. I owe ya. You helped me; I gonna help you. You gotta learn about darkness, Dr. Seth. I can teach you about that. I know that real well. A real professor. A professor of darkness." Seth knew he was grinning again, and then he was quiet.

Keep talking, Seth commanded silently. As long as Mark talked, he knew where he was. Time. He needed a little time. To think, to calm down. To find a way. To live a little longer. Goddammit, keep talking.

Where was Lindsay? Whit? He was sure no one had seen him leave with Mark, but Lindsay would know that he was still in the building. They'd start looking for him soon, downstairs, in the PAO maybe. But it was only a matter of time. They'd have to come up here. Keep moving. Ten minutes, twenty—how long? Move. Back to the wall he moved, sideways, stifling his labored breathing.

Then Mark was on top of him again. "Here I am, Doc!" He felt an explosive and crushing blow to his right side. The pain shot up through his neck and right shoulder, and he fell in a heap, gasping and clutching himself. He wanted to moan, but there was no breath left in his body. His mouth gaped and worked, but no breath came. He was crawling, scrambling across the floor now without knowing how or why, like a headless chicken. Breathe, he commanded. Nothing. Hours passed, and he began to panic. Finally, overpowering his nervous system, he took one heaving gasp, and another pain shot up into his neck and shoulder. His ribs were broken, he knew. God knows how many.

Eyes streaming with pain and bending over to protect his ribs, he hoisted himself to his feet and found the wall again. He slumped against it and heard himself moan. Shut up, he thought, but couldn't. As though silence made any difference. Mark had let him get away.

"Hey, man, that's it. You learnin' what it's like." The voice, taunting again, was far off now, biding its time.

He didn't know what to do now and shuddered, and suddenly he couldn't stop his teeth from chattering. Christ, he was falling apart—what was left of him. He moved apathetically now, listing to one side like an old man. He tried to stop the chattering; but the pain in his chest was making him sick to his stomach again, and he thought he might vomit. Maybe he'd punctured a lung. He felt light-headed and had to stop and hold on to something. He was breathing hard and holding on to the doorknob as hard as he could to stave off the nausea. It puzzled him, the doorknob, in some distant theoretical part of his mind. He couldn't think where the doorway led. It didn't matter, he thought, and shivered again. He wished he hadn't thrown his shirt away. He wondered whether he had a fever. It led to a place he knew—if only he could think. But a new wave of nausea overtook him, and he had to breathe again and hold on tightly. The knob turned then, without his willing it, almost without his knowledge. The door opened a few inches, and the friendly smell of sporting goods and freshly laundered towels reached him.

"Was you ever spooked, Dr. Seth? Scared outta your fuckin' mind till you pissed in yo' bed?" He wasn't listening. Hugging his ribs tightly, he reached into the corner of the closet where Whit kept the saber bag. "Waitin' for the old guy to come in and bash yo' motherfuckin' head in like he done to the dog—"

It was gone. His fingers scrambled desperately. Not there. Taking care to move slowly, he raised himself, and with a silent moan he let himself fall back against the cold, unforgiving tile wall.

"—or cut your motherfuckin' evil heart out like he told you he would. They ever do that to you, Dr. Seth?"

Massaging the bridge of his nose as he had since childhood in moments of stress or distraction—a gesture of secret consolation— he realized for the first time that his glasses were gone. The first attack, he thought. In the dark, it didn't matter much, did it? Christ, try again. It's got to be there. Do it. The tiles felt pleasantly cool against his back. *Do it.* He lowered himself, cautiously, slowly, pampering his right side, and this time reached into the opposite corner of the closet. He touched canvas and then steel.

Inch by inch, his heart pounding thunderously, like a thief he withdrew the saber.

"They ever kick your ass an' lock you in a closet for lookin' or askin' somethin'? That's jail, man—the dark. Spend enough time in jail, and ya learn to see in the dark. Like you doin' now."

Breathing hard, concentrating, he worked the ball of surgical tape—the guard Whit had put there—off the tip and felt the point. He hefted it with his good hand and ran his thumb lightly along the cutting edge. He liked the feel of it, the weight of a weapon he had scorned and barely knew.

Stupid, he thought. Right hand practically useless, ribs broken, and Mark's whole life, his whole being, action, kicks and blows, the way his was words and ideas. Let us reason together.

Where were they now, Lindsay, Whit, Fontana? Had they reached the sixth floor? He pictured them tearing through each ward, frantic, out of breath, racing up stairs and down darkened corridors, calling him.

"Time for another lesson, Dr. Seth." The voice was at the far end of the gym. Leaning forward, he strained to hear the sounds of movement. Nothing. Which direction this time? What if they hadn't even noticed he was gone. How long had he been there? Two minutes? Ten? Twenty? His thoughts were racing now, a blur of movement, like looking into the windows of a train going the other way.

Left, he decided. Move left. He pictured them on the terrace still, Whit pointing out constellations and making her laugh. Perhaps he'd brought out the champagne and a couple of glasses. His teeth chattered again, and he hefted the sword to quiet them. He thought apathetically of hurting Mark with it. Stop dreaming, he told himself. Pay attention. He listened again and heard a sound—off to his left, he thought. Reverse. Right. Go right. His head felt very light now, and his mouth and lips were bone dry. Fever, probably.

"No way out, man." The voice was off to the left, stalking him. It seemed soothing now, persuasive, almost loving. He was right: There was no way out.

They're not coming for you. No one is coming. Wake up! Think! Do something. Some goddamn thing. You wanted closure—this is it. He shivered again and clamped his jaw together to control the racket his teeth were making. More time, he told himself, a little more, to think it through. To prepare. He thought of his father's old lab and wished he were back there again. "Knowledge is safety, Sethy. It's your friend . . . sometimes your only friend." Think, goddammit, think.

He began to scramble for some strategy, primitive, fragmented. The fever was making his mind work faster, more clearly, he thought. Or maybe it was the false power in the sword he held that infused him with false energy and false hope.

Buy time. Talk, for chrissake. You know how to talk. Maybe you're blind, and you've got shit for muscles, but you've got a goddamn brain. "Knowledge is safety." You know some goddamn thing about psychology—his psychology. That day at lunch, what Burden had said, and little Waxman, about criminal psychopaths.

What was it? What? Why hadn't he listened better? Shit, what was it? "Chance rewards only the prepared mind." Think, goddammit. Talk. Talk! Say something!

"Mark! Mark, can you hear me?"

"I hear you, Doc." The voice was closer now, much closer and honeyed. "But my name ain't Mark. Never was 'cept for Paul. He liked it. One of his old studs."

"What's your name then?" Buy time. He edged away from the voice. Think, goddammit, concentrate.

"My name? Don't matter much now, does it, Doc?"

"Bullshit! I've got a right to know a few things before . . ." He didn't bother finishing it and edged farther away. "Comic heroes don't die," someone had told him once, "they figure things out." Shit! Figure!

"Rights? Oh, yeah, I forgot. You guys know a lot about rights. How come you know all about rights an' I know all about darkness? Shee-it, man, I make the rights aroun' here. In the College of Darkness the professor makes the rights. An' I'll tell you what rights you got, smartass Dr. Seth. You got the right to shit in your pants before you die. *That's* your right."

In the silence he could hear Mark's heavy breathing across the gym and willed him to speak again. His own thoughts, he realized, came more easily then.

"You wanna know things? Okay, Dr. Seth." He was being sweet again. "But that's more'n you'd give me, smartass. What you wanna know—my name?

"When I was a kid, my big brother called me Shitface till he got stabbed. Then he never called me nothin'. When I got to be a young blood, they called me Smoky. But my mama, she called me Willie. She liked guys who liked Willie Mays. So that's what they called me. Lotta guys fuck your mama, Dr. Seth? Or didn't you know about things like that? Bet you didn't learn about pussy till you got to college. In Badassville, where I come from, you don't start out in kindergarten, man; you start out in medical school. Man, when I was seven, I was a pussy doctor already—a gyn-ee-cologist."

"Why'd you do it, Willie? Why'd you kill her?" Keep him talking.

"I didn't kill her. I just hit her. Then she just decided to die." His voice was grinning again. "You askin' a lot of questions for a dyin' man. She deserved it—bitch! She was a cold, frozen-hearted white bitch. She deserved it," he repeated, with fury. Seth could hear his heavy breathing again.

"What was that word, succubus? She got inside me, an' I couldn't get inside her."

All those times she was stringing him along. At Paul's place on the island she let him kiss her one day, even said she liked him. "Shee-it!" His voice had changed gradually. He was no longer talking to anyone but to the darkness.

Keep him talking, whatever you do. Keep the initiative. Off-balance. Keep him off-balance. Rattle him; force errors, even small errors. Any edge. Mark had already lost contact with him, he knew, settling and resettling the old scores of his life through Jennie Light.

Christ! What had he said—Burden—that day? Remember!

They had come home from the Island together that evening, and it was hot, so they walked around the Village. "All the time fuckin' me over, jivin' me. Askin' me how tall I was, tellin' me how good-lookin' I was." He was brooding now, deeply, over some ancient loss.

On the way home they stopped at the cafeteria for a cup of coffee. He saw Seth in the cafeteria that night, but shee-it, he didn't pay him much mind 'cause nothin' happened till later.

He knew that bitch Milly McVey was away, so he told her he'd show her what it was like to sleep with a real buck. She started to walk away, so he went after her. She laughed at him and told him he was a stupid child. So then it happened.

He fell silent, still brooding, Seth knew.

Oh, Christ, that was it. His mind was working finally. That's what Burden had said made them tick, made them crack. Steadying himself on the saber, he tried to recapture the exact words, the ideas.

"So that's my story to a dyin' man." He was smiling again,

being coy. "Where are you, Dr. Seth? Where you-all hidin'? I think it's comin' time for me to find you again."

"Willie, that true about your father? What you told me about the medal?" More time. Stretch it out. He knew now what to do, that he had one small chance to force the error.

"Father?" He laughed. "Dr. Seth, you tryin' to psychoanalyze me? You tryin' to give me your white doctor shit? I think I give you enough time. More'n you'd give me. Now I've got to be on my way."

Now!

Suddenly the darkness echoed with the sound of clattering steel.

"Why, you smartass dude. Got that knife outta the closet." The voice was no longer mocking. "Well, now I gotta be a little careful, don't I?"

"You sure do." Seth scooped the saber up from where he'd let it fall. "Let's see what you can do against somebody you can't bully." Now he could force him to do the predictable. Mark had already rehearsed him in his dance of mutilation: Break the right arm—the sword-holding arm—with a roundhouse kick, then come in on the left with a crushing blow to the neck and collarbone.

"You're a big shot against girls and gays. Let's see what you can do with me. Ever fight anybody who had an even chance?"

He hefted the sword in his good hand—the left one. That would be his even chance, and when Mark came roaring in for the kill on the left . . .

"You're an asshole, Willie. A stupid asshole. You think being a man is hitting women and sticking your cock in a hole. Any gorilla can do that. Are you a faggot, Willie?"

"You motherfuckin' superior white bastard. I'll show you who's queer."

Standing ready, arms spread, feet solidly planted, he heard Mark pounding down on him. "Come on, come on, you stupid faggot." He wanted Mark to home in cleanly and accurately.

He was ready for the kick, but when it came, he had underestimated the pain. He heard the radius snap, and the pain shot up his right arm and across his chest. Concentrate! He swallowed the pain that shrieked in his head. Mark was on him. Now! With all his strength he thrust forward and felt the blade drive through the layers of muscle, through the coelomic cavity and out the back.

Falling backward through space and darkness in the confusion of his fever and agony, he heard other sounds—sounds of rebuke and absolution—and rescue, he thought. Then there was only the explosion of pain in his chest and head as he hit the floor.

The harsh fluorescent light overhead hurt his eyes, and he closed them again. The back of his head throbbed, and he knew that sometime in the night someone had taken a picture of it. Hold still, don't move, Dr. Conrad. Good, you can move now. Only he didn't want to. He only wanted them to leave him alone and let him finish the work of his dream. Then he dozed, and a few weeks later someone shouted cheerfully at him that the skull films were clear and they were taking him to the OR to reduce that radial fracture. Didn't look too bad, they said, but he wouldn't be pitching for a while. Chuckle. He tried to signal some acknowledgment with his eyes but succeeded only in closing them. And then he didn't know how to open them again. They let him go back to his frantic hallucinatory labors then and repeat the hopeless mistakes he'd made the last time he dozed.

When he opened his eyes again, he heard a blur of distant voices murmuring the medical facts of someone else's life. Ventricular fibrillation. Code four. Posterior wall. He was in a little room made of green cloth that flapped when someone went by, and he noticed that one of the fluorescent tubes above him had gone out. He had the idea that that happened whenever someone died in the ICU and wondered why no one had ever noticed that before.

When he moved his left arm and found it tethered to an IV tube, he shrugged mentally and let his arm fall back onto the bed. The label on the IV bottle said "Saline." A liter of tears, he thought, and turned away. How many tears to a liter? A conversion they never taught him in medical school. He wanted to get back to his dream. There was unfinished business there, tugging at him.

He watched the saline drip slowly into his body, proof he didn't need that it hadn't all been a delirious fantasy. He knew Mark had been real and wondered whether he had killed him. Another drop began to grow in the tube and hung in the balance. He watched it and willed it to fall. It didn't matter. They were all dead to him now: Milly, Paul Silk, Mark, Jennie Light. He'd kept his appointments after all, paid his debts, and they were out of his system. He tried to remember what Jennifer Light had looked like in the photo he'd studied so carefully that day, but nothing came. He was tired, terribly tired suddenly. He thought of Elly's picture stuck in the mirror, protected behind a barrier of unread journals and forgotten books, trapped in the time warp of his mind, forever fifteen. "Lonely spirit . . ." Another drop began to form in the IV tube and, growing heavier, seemed to catch a bit of the light.

He remembered the way the water caught the light on the Great Edgartown Pond one day that summer. One of those blue crystal days of late summer with a fresh northwest breeze. The pond was full of herons and Canadian geese resting on their journey southward. She liked him that day, it seemed, and they went out together in the sailing dinghy, and she let him take the tiller and tack back and forth across the sparkling pond and taught him how to come up safely on a lee shore. That was the time she'd spent the whole day with him, telling him things as they watched the breakers pile onto the empty golden beach, teaching him things, helping him do things he'd never done. Maybe it was the best day of his life.

And maybe there'd been other times like that before she died— times he'd forgotten since that wet, chilly day they found her body. And for the first time since then—for the first time since he'd stood beside her grave on Katie's Hill in the noon glare—he missed her, missed her terribly. And for the first time knew—with that knowledge that is akin to deep physical exhaustion—that he would never, never be with her again. Never, never hear her stories, see her quirky smile, know her teasing and her grudging embrace, never, after all, know for sure she loved him.

When the drop fell, his eyelids, heavy with the unfinished business and improprieties of his inner life, closed once more.

□  □  □

". . . no, he was never in Korea, Miss Cooper. Never even in the service. All that was crap. He'll be okay . . . right lung . . . chest surgery—"

His attention fluttered to life again and reached out involuntarily for pieces of conversation floating beyond the green walls.

"—real name? Willie Preston Jones."

He heard Lindsay and halfheartedly tried to grasp what she was saying. But her voice was lost in the desperate argument with death taking place a few beds away.

"Christ, I can't get a pressure reading at all."

"Put the goddamn leads on! *Schnell! Schnell!*"

Cardiac, he thought, and touched his own chest. It was bound tightly with tape and bandage, making it difficult to breathe. The fingers of his injured hand tingled and were working better now.

". . . don't know," Fontana was saying. "Maybe we'll never know. That's the way it is with real mysteries. Sticka gum?" He could see Fontana shoving his big hand at her. "There ain't no whole truth—know what I mean? Only a lot of mixed-up little lies."

A chair moved suddenly, harshly, it seemed to Seth. "Need a lift home, Miss Cooper? I can have one of the boys drop you off."

"No, thanks, Vince. I'll stick around awhile longer. Maybe he'll wake up soon."

She spoke slowly. Tired, Seth thought, and alone now. But he was not ready for her yet. Not yet. He closed his eyes again. There they were, the familiar beckoning images, his revenants. He turned his head to the right to see them better. He needed more time. Just a little more time.

When he half woke again, there was only the reassuring hum of the fluorescent lights and the irregular pulse of the dying man's cardiac monitor. They were letting him die in peace, finally, having discovered their own limitations, their own place in nature.

Maybe he would die tonight, he thought. It was strange to be on such intimate terms with the final music of a man's heart and not know the man. He heard a page turn at the far end of the intensive care unit, and a voice whispered that it was almost five o'clock. He knew that even Lindsay was gone now, in troubled sleep somewhere. He listened to the unsteady music of his neighbor's heart again and thought that it would be morning soon. Even now the sun was rising over the Great Edgartown Pond, making a brilliant golden path in the dark waters.

Suddenly he could hear no longer the beating of the heart, only the beating of powerful wings as he flew high above the ocean on the edge of time, racing westward with the sun, between life and death, between darkness and day. Below him he saw the islands shimmer into the light, and Vineyard Sound, where the rushing tides had taken Elly from him. There was only a soaring silence, only the beating of great wings and the whooshing of wind and, below, the knife-edge of day undoing the darkness.

Now he was on Katie's Hill again in the brilliant sunshine. It was greener than he remembered, and gentler as it sloped down to the white farmhouse. He was young again, a boy, as he was when she died: scrawny, tanned, his steel-rimmed spectacles smeared and falling down the bridge of his nose.

High overhead, the eagle—*Aquila chrysaëtos*—raced westward, wings flashing, in pursuit of the sun.

"Elly, Elly, don't go!" he shouted, almost angrily. "Not without saying good-bye . . ."

Wheeling suddenly, reluctantly—as she had in life where it came to him—the great bird swooped low, made one forgiving circle over Katie's Hill and soared away into the sun.

He woke to the image of her grave, weathered and softened somehow with time, and through the tears he could barely make out the lettering:

> *Lonely spirit,*
> *All is past.*
> *All forgiven,*
> *Home at last.*

Only the old man, fitfully dying nearby, heard his sobs and wondered.